DECISION BY DARK

The facts are the facts, Walter thought. This is my city.

I have the home-field advantage, and the crowd, and I'll take Manhattan—the Bronx and Staten Island too, if necessary—and if all I have to do is ditch a desperate cop, two FBI agents, some hired thugs, and a couple of professional killers and deliver the goods to the enemies of my country at nine o'clock, then that's all I have to do.

And if the strength-sapping question arises in my doubt-ridden psyche—How can you do what you have to do tonight?—well, the answer is inherent in the question, isn't it, my boy . . . ?

A WINTER SPY

A WINTER SPY

MacDonald Lloyd

A SIGNET BOOK

SIGNET
Published by the Penguin Group
Penguin Books USA Inc., 375 Hudson Street,
New York, New York 10014, U.S.A.
Penguin Books Ltd, 27 Wrights Lane,
London W8 5TZ, England
Penguin Books Australia Ltd,
Ringwood, Victoria, Australia
Penguin Books Canada Ltd, 10 Alcorn Avenue,
Toronto, Ontario, Canada M4V 3B2
Penguin Books (N.Z.) Ltd, 182–190 Wairau Road,
Auckland 10, New Zealand

Penguin Books Ltd, Registered Offices:
Harmondsworth, Middlesex, England

First published by Signet, an imprint of Dutton Signet,
a division of Penguin Books USA Inc.

First Printing, April, 1997
10 9 8 7 6 5 4 3 2 1

   REGISTERED TRADEMARK—MARCA REGISTRADA

Printed in the United States of America

PUBLISHER'S NOTE
This is a work of fiction. Names, characters, places and incidents either are the
product of the author's imagination or are used fictitiously, and any resemblance to
actual persons, living or dead, events, or locales is entirely coincidental.

ACKNOWLEDGMENTS

The author wishes to thank Bill McEneaney
for his many hours of sharing his
encyclopedic knowledge of the jazz world of 1958.

Dear Old Stockholm

Walter Withers wasn't unhappy at CIA. He just missed New York.

Or, as he'd put it to Morrison, his soon to be ex-colleague at ScandAmerican Import/Export, "It's not that I love the Company less, but that I love Manhattan more."

Walter didn't believe for a second that Morrison would catch the Shakespearean reference or appreciate the symmetry, but the fun of a well-spoken sentence was not, after all, in the reaction but in the speaking.

But Morrison, as Walter knew from their three years of working together, did not really like fun. The earth's gravity seemed to pull Morrison's already long face a little lower every week. Morrison, it seemed to Walter, had absorbed the Swedish winter darkness into his very soul. To be sure, Morrison chased the long-legged Scandinavian women with as much vigor as any of them did, but his pursuits had a kind of perpetual pessimism about them.

Not that Morrison failed to attract partners to his bed. In fact, the sheets barely had time to cool. No, the problem was that even while escorting his date up the stairs to his second-floor hovel on the transparent pretext of listening to his collection of American jazz albums, he was already busily worrying. In his bleak fantasies the young lady was already leaving in a pre-dawn taxi, or sitting in the waiting room of her obstetrician, *or*—imagined horrors of imagined horrors—debriefing his sexual technique to her Soviet case officer, in Morrison's mind's eye a greasy, toad-like fat man who chained-smoked cheap, stinking Soviet cigarettes as he smirked at the sad tales of Morrison's sexual ineptitude.

This last vivid image had become something of a self-fulfilling prophecy.

"It's better than batting averages," Walter had observed when Morrison confessed his dilemma one drunken evening.

"What do you mean?"

"Well," Walter began as he searched for words, "some men—or so I'm told—think about batting averages when they're trying to delay the . . . inevitable. Your . . . de-accelerant . . . is an imaginary KGB operative, that's all."

"That's *all?*" Morrison croaked. He laid his head on the table, closed his eyes, and moaned softly. "And it's not a 'de-accelerant.' It's a complete deflator."

"In that case," Walter said, "you simply worry too much."

Morrison opened one eye, trained it on Walter, and said accusingly, "It's what we do to them, isn't it?"

Walter recognized this as the rhetorical question it was. Walter, in fact, was famous in the greater northern European allied intelligence community for doing it to them. Sometimes it seemed that Walter "Whoremaster" Withers had procured beautiful bed partners for just about every Eastern European consular official, weak-kneed fellow traveler, and out-and-out Soviet spy in Scandinavia. Walter ran a stable of sincere Swedes, imaginative Danes, and ardent Norwegians who took their Warsaw Pack lovers through Olympian sexual gymnastics for pleasure, money, and Walter's microphones.

In the wonderfully uninhibited Sweden of 1958, Walter Withers had a sexual library that would have turned Kinsey emerald green. Walter was too much a gentleman to fall to the blandishments, urgings, and bribes of his colleagues to borrow a reel or two for a spicy evening at home, or to sneak a girlfriend into the offices for a quick dirty listen, or even to have a boys-only smoker in the back room with Walter's audio collection in place of the stripper. And Walter himself had heard far too many of the damn things to find them even remotely erotic.

No, for Walter it was all business, a dirty business at that, and he didn't have the heart to tell his salacious co-workers that the best business was not in beautiful girls but in beautiful boys. There was, after all, little blackmail value in confronting a middle-aged Slav with tapes of his sexual adventures with a gorgeous young blonde. Marital infidelity didn't shame them, and the replaying of their vocal excesses only whetted their appetites for more of the same. But to present them with evidence of a homosexual union, that was something else again.

That was pay dirt.

However, sexual blackmail was a mere pretext. Walter thought of it as only the overture to the symphony of recruitment in which he himself was the conductor, concert master, and first-chair clarinet. Blackmail was the excuse that the marks needed to persuade themselves to be turned, but Walter knew that what they were really buying was style.

His style.

Walter had inherited some of his style from his stockbroker father, one of the few who hadn't leveraged himself up to his chin and so was only hurt and not mortally wounded when the Crash hit. Walter's father had taught him how to dress—a few good, expensive basics with a dash of color—when and how to pick up a tab, and how to work very hard at a job without seeming to do so.

Some of Walter's style was a gift, coming to him by osmosis from prep school days at Loomis and undergraduate nights at Yale. Many of those nights had been spent in the city learning about mixed drinks, pure champagne, and the complicated women who sang torch songs at Le Ruban Bleu and Spivey's Roof.

And the rest of his style Walter had deliberately acquired from the silky black-and-white images that flickered in the dark quiet of the movie houses. Walter brought to these cinematic tutorials a calm self-perception, knowing that he was never going to be Bogart or Cagney or Wayne. Walter knew he was more the Leslie Howard, Fred Astaire, Charles Boyer type. He was Cary Grant without the accent or the looks, although Walter Withers was a good-looking kid, with his button nose, apple cheeks, and his sandy hair combed straight back.

No, Walter Withers was not a tough guy. Walter Withers killed with charm. He kept a trappist silence about his romantic conquests, never bragged about poker triumphs, and jumped the tennis net only after *losing* a match.

Everyone in New Haven loved Walter—even though he had rejected Skull and Crossbones as a bit too clichéd for him—and it wasn't long after he was graduated with a degree in history—after an uneventful, stateside stint in the navy during the war—that a professor took him to lunch and said that he knew of a company that could use a man like Walter Withers.

So Walter joined CIA and eventually became the Great Scandinavian Pimp and Deadly Recruiter, putting his style on the line for God and country. It was the rare mark who could ring up a no-sale on Walter's style. For Walter seemed to be saying—although he never actually *said* it, of course—in his every graceful move and action, that his style was the Western style, his lifestyle the lifestyle of the great capitalist democracies. He was saying to the marks from the gray, concrete countries something to the effect of "all this can be yours." From the cut of his jacket to the break of his trousers, from the way he whipped out his Dunhill cigarette case to the way he lit two cigs from one match, from the way his eyes silently brought the waiter around to the way the tab disappeared into his hand—all effortless, all understated, all somehow self-deprecatory—Walter Withers made people want to be around him.

The marks couldn't resist him. They never had a chance, did these poor bastards with their tiny walk-up flats they shared with mama, guys who had to stand in line for two hours at home to buy a piece of inferior meat, women whose socialist workers' paradise could never provide them with even a whiff of the latest cosmetics what Walter would shyly bring out of his pocket and offer as if it were something the dry cleaners had left.

But he never made them feel inferior, did Walter. Instead he made them feel as if they were all fellow players in the great game of living well, and of course it was only a small step from that game to the next one, when Walter would pass them on to the unsmiling boys who wanted to know about grain production, or budget figures, or who was sitting next to whom at the big meetings.

Walter never asked his marks any of these questions. He flattered them, seduced them, pampered them, listened to their problems, bought them drinks and meals, arranged for discreet beds and bed mates, loaned them cash, and held their hands. He truly liked his marks, not that affection stopped him from sitting down with one who was getting too stroppy and saying something like, "Now look, chum, you really do need to get back in line, or *our* unsmiling boys will drop a word to *your* unsmiling boys, and . . ." Walter would trail off, allowing the mark to picture himself kneeling on the floor of some bureaucratic basement waiting for a bullet in the back of the head.

But then Walter would light a cigarette and put it in the mark's quivering hand, or freshen his drink, and then conjure up some bit of fun for that evening. During which time Walter would seize a moment to look soulfully into the mark's eyes and ask, "Do you trust me?" and the answer was invariably "Yes," and they would be pals again.

Walter was pals with everyone. Women loved him because he took them to fun places, bought them good meals, listened to them, and never tried to get them into bed unless they had clearly signaled that he should. In those cases he left before breakfast, always sent a note and flowers, and otherwise never indicated by word, glance, or expression that he had as much as kissed them at the door. Men liked him because he was a regular guy. He could talk politics, sports, and writing, played a decent game of tennis, a sharp game of poker, and always paid his share of the bills.

Most of the professionals in the northern European intelligence business liked Walter, even the Brits, who didn't like anybody, including and especially each other. The only spooks who didn't warm to Walter's charms were the good people of the Swedish home ministry who, always chary of the neighboring Soviet bear, thought that Walter Withers was perhaps a little too good at his job. In fact, they were about five minutes from deporting him when he developed a sudden, powerful yearning for the joys of New York.

The story around the corridors went that the Old One himself had asked Walter what new posting he'd like now that the Swedes were throwing him out. Rumor had it that they'd sat in the dank Hamburg rathskeller the Old One preferred for his rare European visits and personally discussed it. This was a great honor, for the assistant director rarely left his office to talk to an actual agent.

Several theories as to how the Old One had gotten his nickname abounded among the Company's junior ranks. The one that held the most currency was that it came from his years of sitting in his windowless office, poring over files on his obsessive search for an alleged Soviet mole.

Walter Withers himself claimed pride of authorship on the assistant's moniker, when some colleague at a cocktail party had observed that the assistant director had been fighting communism since before Marx and another said he was as old as Adam. "Older," Walter had countered. "I have it on good authority that he ran the serpent that 'turned' Eve. The A.D. is the Old One himself."

Rumor had it—and Morrison had heard the rumor from a solid source—that when the Old One brought up the topic of Walter's next posting, it came as something of a shock when Walter smiled and answered, "As a matter of fact, sir, I think I'd just like to turn in my locker key at this point and give the private sector a whirl."

Reliable witnesses claim that the Old One turned a little more pale, but Company types who heard this story said that it wasn't possible—the assistant director being bloodless and therefore already deathly white. Instead, he ignored Walter's answer and intoned, "I think it's safe to say that Europe is off limits to you for a while, but I can offer you—after a suitable hiatus—a very interesting Asian posting."

Walter wouldn't say one way or the other, but Morrison heard that Walter looked into the sepulchral pallor of the man who knew—literally—where all the bodies were buried and said, "That's a tempting offer, sir, but I really want to get back to New York."

"The Company doesn't do business in New York," the Old One snapped, asking Walter to accept the obvious lie that CIA didn't traipse its dirty feet onto the pristine soil that contained, among other things, the happy hunting ground known as the United Nations.

"Exactly," Walter answered. He pulled his Dunhill from his jacket pocket and offered the A.D. a cigarette, even though he was perfectly aware that the Old One didn't smoke. When the old man shook his head, Walter took a cigarette out and tapped it on the table. Then he bent over the cheap cut-glass candle bowl and drew in the flame.

"You would leave the Company, young man?" the Old One asked.

"It's not that I love the Company less, but that I love Manhattan more," Walter answered.

"Julius Caesar," the Old One said, "Brutus explaining why he stabbed Caesar in the back."

And that was end to the discussion, so the story went, and the line had worked so well on the Old One that Walter trotted it out again for Morrison.

"Bullshit," said Morrison.

"God's truth," Walter pledged, holding up his right hand as if he were taking an oath.

Morrison twisted his jaw into a crooked grimace that was his face's best recollection of a smile. "Walter, how can you leave me in this cold and desolate place?"

"I'm sure you'll find some consolation," Walter answered.

"The finding isn't the problem," Morrison moaned. "It's the consolation."

A nice touch, Walter thought, that delicate echo of *consolation* with *consummation*. Nicely done, Morrison. Didn't think you had it in you.

Walter said, "The world is not one big honey trap, you know."

Morrison looked at him with disbelieving eyes.

"The world, Walter," he said, "is nothing but one big honey trap."

Walter shrugged, flipped open his cigarette case, and offered one to Morrison. He lit Morrison's cigarette and then his own.

Morrison stared at him.

Walter raised his eyebrows.

"New York, my butt," Morrison finally said.

"New York, *my* butt," Walter answered.

"Won't you miss the Swedish women?"

Walter sat on the corner of Morrison's desk and said, "When I was a child in Greenwich, every year sometime shortly after Thanksgiving my mother would get my sister and me all dressed up and bundle us aboard the train. We would get off in Grand Central Station, which at the time I thought was the center of the known universe, and unless it was very cold we would walk uptown to Rockefeller Center to see the Christmas tree. It was so pretty, Michael—the dark green of the pine needles set off against Mr. Rockefeller's gray buildings . . . the lights sparkling . . . all the decorations . . . Christmas music would be playing from some unseen loudspeakers, and the Salvation Army troops would be ringing bells, and after a suitable time standing in the crowd gazing up at the tree, we would make our way out to Fifth Avenue to start our Christmas shopping. And one thing I especially recall, to answer the question that you asked some time ago, was that even then I thought that the loveliest women in the world walked there. Even as a boy I recognized their style, their sense of fashion, their confidence, their grace, and I was just in awe."

"So now that you're a big boy, you're going back to realize your dirty childhood fantasies?" Morrison asked.

"It was all of a piece, you see," Walter said. "Grand Central Station, and Rockefeller Center, and the Christmas tree and Fifth Avenue, and, yes, I suppose the lovely women."

"Well, good luck, Walter," Morrison said as he stood up to shake Walter's hand.

"And good luck to you, Michael," Walter answered.

An hour later Walter got off a bus on Skeppsholmen, one of the three islands in the center of Stockholm, walked along the water to an old two-story house, climbed the stairs to the second floor, and knocked on the door.

Anne Blanchard opened the door, smiled broadly, and kissed him on the mouth. Then she brushed the snow off the collar of his black wool overcoat, took him by the hand, and led him inside the flat.

"Darling, you must be frozen," she said. "Did you walk?"

He shook his head. "I took the bus from Central, got off, and strolled along the water. A valedictory stroll."

"I'll put some water on for tea," she said. "Unless you'd rather have coffee. I think there's still some coffee here."

"If the intent is to warm me up," Walter answered, "I'd rather have another kiss."

She slid into his arms and kissed him for a long time. Then she broke away and put the kettle on the stove. Walter took off his coat and hat, hung them on the coat rack, and sat on the small sofa to watch her.

Anne Blanchard was a tiny woman, five foot one in her stocking feet, and the columnists who wrote about night-clubs usually called her "petite," which she liked, or "pixie-ish," which annoyed her. Her blond hair was cut short and curled into waves. Her eyes were gray, the color of the Atlantic just before a storm, as Walter had once observed.

On this particular late afternoon in March she was dressed all in black—a black blouse over a long black skirt, and black ballet slippers. She had on her oversize tortoise-shell glasses, without which she was virtually blind, and her trademark blood red lipstick.

Walter loved her to distraction.

He could tell from the heat of the cushion and imprint of the pillow that she had been lying on the sofa reading. The book, Sean McGuire's *The Highway by Night*, lay splayed on the combination lamp stand and side table. The apartment was a studio, what realtors were just learning to call an efficiency. Its spare furniture was bleached pine with inexpensive cushions. The flooring was broad planking, waxed to a high shine. A cheap rectangular rug and a few pillows had been thrown down to give it some warmth.

A floor-to-ceiling bookcase filled the opposite wall, its shelves lined with oversize photographic books, African sculptures, dozens of paperbacks, and an expensive high-fidelity system that included a turntable and reel-to-reel tape recorder. An upright piano—Anne could never be without a piano—was set in front of the bookcase.

A large picture window occupied most of another wall. Outside, the sky over the Maaleren's black water was softening into faint pastels. The snow falling on the cobblestone street glimmered from the streetlights in stark relief.

Anne was renting the apartment from a young Swedish pianist on tour in Germany. She always tried to rent apartments when she had a sufficiently long engagement in any city because she wanted a piano and hated hotels. It usually wasn't too hard to do in the close-knit circle of American jazz musicians who worked mostly in Europe because there weren't enough jobs in the States.

Anne had explained to him that most of the American expatriates were Negroes—like the trio who usually backed her up—who preferred Europe because of the racial attitude, or rather the lack of it. Paris had become their European base, with Stockholm a close second because the Swedes were just crazy for jazz.

Walter flipped through *The Highway by Night* and asked, "How is this?"

"*Won*derful," she enthused. "He's reinventing prose in a way that hasn't been done since James Joyce wrote *Ulysses*."

Walter wished that Joyce hadn't troubled himself to reinvent prose in the first place. He preferred James Jones to James Joyce anyway, but refrained from saying so. Anne already thought he was too "establishment."

"Are you all packed?" she asked.

"Packed and ready. How about you?"

She poured the hot water into a teapot, swished it around, and said, "Almost packed, not quite ready. Never quite ready to leave Europe."

Although they had met in Stockholm—at one of Morrison's famous Fourth of July parties—they had carried on their affair all over Europe. She had lived in Paris in the early years of her career, singing in small clubs and returning to New York only to record that first album that had brought a small measure of celebrity.

She and Walter had met shortly after that. He had escorted her from Morrison's party to the club where she was singing, stayed for four sets, and fell in love with her. After that he'd traveled to meet her as often as "business allowed," staying for a night in Hamburg, or a weekend in Copenhagen, or that wonderful August on the Côte d'Azur when he took a vacation and she sang in the hotels. It wasn't as easy for him to get to Paris very often, so they were both happy when the three-month gig in Stockholm came along.

But now it was time for her to go back to New York to make the second album and play the big rooms.

She poured two cups of steaming tea, set them down on the coffee table, and sat on the sofa beside him.

"Marry me?" he asked for perhaps the hundredth time.

She shook her head.

"We'll be living in the same city at the same time for a change," he reminded her.

They had been together for almost two years, never more than three months in the same place.

"You know I'll have to go on the road again after the album is released. Probably another stint over here. What would my sweet husband do then?"

"Wait for you."

"It's too much to ask."

"You didn't. I offered."

"I can't accept."

He kept it light, in that tone he always used with serious matters, as if he were discussing whether to have dinner before or after the theater.

"Wouldn't you enjoy a real home for a change?" he asked.

"I have a real home."

She had an apartment off Washington Square that she was renting out to a young poet from Wyoming.

"I'm never there," she added, "but it's my home, and yes, I would enjoy being home for a change."

"Then marry me and give it up," he said. "I can support us nicely."

" 'Let me take you away from all this?' " she mimicked.

"Something on that order," he said.

"And give up singing?"

"Professionally."

"I love you," Anne answered. "I do, very much, you know that."

Walter nodded. "But?"

"But singing is what I do."

"I know."

She sipped her tea, set the cup down again, and said, "Besides, you wouldn't love me if I didn't sing."

"What a terrible thing to say!"

"What a *true* thing to say." She got up and pulled the drapes closed. "Much as I love you, I won't marry you, honey. Not just yet."

She stepped over to the hi-fi and turned on the tape system.

"Arthur is thinking about using a couple of live cuts on the new album," she said, "and there's something I've always wanted to do."

"What's that?"

She smiled mischievously. She stood looking at him as if making up her mind.

"What?" Walter laughed.

She looked at him seriously, as if deciding whether to take a chance.

"Seduce you while I'm singing," she said.

"Darling," Walter said, "you're always seducing me when you're singing."

The sound of a piano filled the small flat.

She shook her head. "But that's in a nightclub, and there are things I can't do in a nightclub."

"Such as?"

"Such as . . ."

She took off her glasses and set them on the bookshelf. Her voice, high and crystalline, started on the tape.

"I'll take Manhattan,
The Bronx and Staten Island, too . . ."

"You planned this," Walter accused. The tape had been precisely cued up.

She nodded her head as she danced small steps to the music and unbuttoned the top button of her blouse.

"It's such fun going through
The zoo . . ."

She shucked off her blouse, then her black lace brassiere. Her breasts were large for such a small woman. Her nipples, Walter thought, the color of a spring twilight.

"It's very fancy
On Old Delancey Street, you know . . ."

He'd once described her voice as a pure silver blade slicing through liquid gold, and it was like that now as his throat got dry watching her and listening to her. She sang softly and delicately, every note pitch perfect, every syllable precisely phrased.

"The subway charms are so . . .
When balmy breezes blow . . .
To and fro . . ."

She kicked off her slippers, and slid her skirt and panties down her legs to the carpet, and the nudity now between her legs brought to his mind again the image of liquid gold.

"When I sing a love song," she said, looking him in the eye, "I think about you being inside me."

"Well, we have that in common," he said tightly as he started to stand up.

But she pushed him back on the sofa, then reached down and unzipped his trousers.

"And tell me what street
Compares with Mott Street in July . . ."

She moved slowly on him, holding herself up as her voice held a long note, then letting herself slide down as the note settled into a warm chord.

"Sweet pushcarts slowly
Gliding by . . ."

He held her tightly against him, and she dropped her face into his neck.

"*The great big city's a wondrous toy*
Made for a girl and a boy . . ."

"You feel so good," she murmured.

"You."

"*Je t'aime,*" she murmured.

He answered, "*Je t'aime aussi.*"

He did love her, more than anything.

CHAPTER ONE

Christmas Time
in the City

Wednesday, December 24, 1958

They ushered in Christmas Eve in a carriage in Central Park.

It was Walter's idea, as were most of the wildly romantic, sentimental notions that overtook their affair from time to time, and he was a little drunk when the notion struck him. So was Anne as they careened arms-over-shoulders along Fifty-fifth Street on a freezing Manhattan night.

Walter had stopped suddenly in the street, pulled her in to his chest, kissed her red nose, and said, "Let's go for a carriage ride in the park."

"You're a romantic."

"Let's."

"It's freezing!" she protested.

"We'll canoodle to stay warm."

"*Canoodle?!*"

"It's a word," he said solemnly.

"It's a lovely word," she agreed. Then she broke away from him and ran down the street toward Fifth Avenue and Central Park. She shouted back at him, "Come on! If you're planning to canoodle me, I want to know you have stamina!"

"I'll show you stamina!" he hollered as he chased after her.

"Promises, promises!"

Her laughter sliced through the cold air.

She stretched her arms out akimbo as she ran and hollered, "I love New Yoooorrkk! I love Walter Witherrrrs! I love New Yooorrkk!"

There had been nothing not to love since their return from Stockholm, Walter thought.

She had kept her place in the Village, and he had taken a small apartment in Murray Hill. They led separate lives together, she sometimes spending the night at his place or he at hers. Some nights they spent apart.

But most nights they spent together in the company of the city. He often spent the earlier part of the evening dining out, at The Palm or Dempseys or L'Amerique, then perhaps caught a movie on Broadway, then wandered over to whatever club Anne was performing in to catch her last set.

She'd been busy since coming back, recording over in Jersey during the days, doing two or three sets a night for the expense-account crowd at the mainstream clubs in Midtown, then more often than not heading down to the Village or over to "Downstairs at the Upstairs" to sing her recherché jazz pieces for the hip crowd. The club owners loved her because she showed up on time and sober and delivered what the audience wanted to hear.

She'd be more exhilarated than tired after her shows, so she and Walter would usually linger at one of the Village jazz spots—The Five Spot or The Vanguard or The Blue Note—to catch some after-hours jamming and a few drinks, or meander along the string of downtown coffee houses for earnest conversation and cigarettes with Anne's left-wing pals.

On a rare night they would just go home, put some

music on the hi-fi, have a late home-cooked meal or Chinese takeout, and snuggle in bed.

But not this night. She'd had the evening off from a gig at the Blue Angel, and they'd gone out to paint the town. Dinner at "21," then to Broadway for the opening night of Comden and Green's *A Party*, then dancing, then a round of holiday drinks at half the joints in Midtown. They'd hit The Living Room to listen to Bobby Short, then up to Bickford's, then over to Goldie's New York to hear Goldie and Sanders play their back-to-back pianos. (Goldie's was a magical spot for Walter because he had been there on the night that Gene Kelly and Fred Astaire did an impromptu duet at their table.)

Then they hopped a cab down to the Duane Hotel on Thirty-seventh and Madison, where a foul-mouthed young comedian named Lenny Bruce annoyed Walter but made Anne howl. To make it up to him Anne agreed to a quiet round at Billy Reed's Little Club on Fifty-fifth and Sixth. Then it was a short trot over to The Baq Room, so called because it was in back of a quite decent Irish pub unpretentiously named The Midtown Bar. Walter would have been perfectly happy to test out the ameliorating effects of a some single-malt whisky in the front room, but agreed to accompany Anne to the "baq," where Janice Mars held forth on her baby grand for the pleasure of the Actors' Studio crowd. Then they made their unsteady way over to Third Avenue and sat in the black-and-white checkered cocktail bar of the Blue Angel, where they could still drink and hear Tom Lehrer—who annoyed Anne and made Walter laugh—hold forth in the main room.

Jacoby, the rail-thin French co-owner, stopped by the table to say hello to Anne and bought them a round, and they drank some more and then somehow they found themselves marching down the street unsuccessfully trying to remember the words to "The Internationale" and settling for "La Marseillaise" instead. Anne had been just belting out, "Avant, les citoyens!" when Walter suggested they take a carriage ride.

He caught up with her after half a block. She was doubled over, gasping for air, on the sidewalk of Fifth Avenue when he reached her and did the same.

"Stamina," he huffed.

"I'll show you stamina," she gasped.

They were laughing and hugging when a white limousine pulled up. The back passenger window rolled down, and a middled-aged woman stuck her head out and asked in a Continental accent as thick as was diverse, "Darlings! Are you all right?"

"Terrific!" Walter laughed.

It was the Contessa, the rich and much beloved matron of jazz musicians in New York. They both knew her well from every club in New York and half the clubs in Europe. The Contessa would ride around late at night, or if she was otherwise engaged just send her chauffeur Theo, looking for drunk or stoned musicians who needed a ride or even a place to stay. It had become an expression in the jazz demi-monde: an artist who'd hit bottom was said to be "riding with the Contessa."

She kept a suite at the Stanhope Hotel and often brought her wards home to stay with her, never laying a hand on them except perhaps to steady their heads as she ladled them soup or cradle them through the DT's and the heroin shakes. Walter had heard her sadly tell, on a rare occasion when she was in her cups, how Charlie Parker had died in her suite—collapsed while listening to Tommy Dorsey do "Just Friends"—because the hotel doctor wouldn't make a house call for a "nigger."

"We were just going for a carriage ride," Anne explained.

"My dears, I think you forgot the horses!" the Contessa said. "And the carriage!"

"I knew there was something," Anne said.

"Hop in, I'll give you a ride to the park."

"Not on your life," Walter said. "We have our pride!"

"And we're idiots," Anne added.

"And we're idiots," Walter echoed.

The Contessa blew them a kiss, the limousine pulled away, and Walter and Anne marched—singing all the way—up Fifth to Grand Army Plaza, where Walter hailed a driver bundled in blankets in the front of a carriage.

"Once around the park, my good man!" Walter said. "And may I say, I have always wanted to say that."

"And may I say," the driver warbled in a thick Irish brogue, "that I think you've had a sip of the stuff."

"More than a sip," said Walter as he helped Anne into the backseat of the carriage. The driver handed them a blanket.

"I've promised to canoodle with her," Walter said.

"Take the blanket," the driver advised.

Walter snugged the blanket around them, then slipped his arm underneath to pull Anne close.

The driver clicked his tongue, and the horse started out in a slow clip-clop that was muted by the falling snow. The park at night was a study in black and silver. The trees glistened with ice and sparkled in the moonlight.

"You *are* a romantic," she said. "Kiss me, you fool."

He kissed her almost chastely on the lips and said, "It's Christmas Eve."

"Oh, and I suppose you want to open your presents?" she teased. "Forget it, boy, it's too damn cold. A girl could freeze to death surrendering her virtue on a night like this. Much as I otherwise relish love alfresco."

"I was just thinking about the glories of the season," Walter said innocently.

"Oh, you were."

"Yes, I was."

She inched closer.

"And tell me," she whispered, "am I included among the glories of the season?"

"You are the gloriest."

"I do love you."

"As do I you," he said. "Or something like that."

"Let the canoodling commence."

They kissed and canoodled, and the driver sang a soft Gaelic song to himself but really for them. And if there was anyplace else in the world that Walter would rather have seen in the morning of Christmas Eve, he couldn't imagine where it might be.

After their carriage ride they took a taxi to his place and fell into bed.

Anne shook Walter awake.

"Darling?" she said. "I think you were having a bad dream."

Groggy as he was, he instantly thought, not *a* bad dream, *the* bad dream. The *same* bad dream.

"Did I say anything?" he asked.

"No." She looked puzzled. And sleepy. And lovely.

"It's early," Walter said. It was 5:43, two minutes before the alarm was set to go off. "Go back to sleep."

"Are you all right?"

"Now that you've chased the bogeyman away?" he asked. "I'm fine."

She kissed him softly on the lips, rolled over, and burrowed under the blankets. Anne Blanchard loved to sleep.

Walter hated sleeping. Part of it was that his natural energy fought against it. Mostly it was because he feared the dream. It was never exactly the same dream, of course, but its salient details had their same horrifying sameness: It was always nighttime, and his marks—*his* marks—clung to a big rock like the survivors of a shipwreck. Then the waves came. Swelling from the ocean into massive, inexorable walls of water, and one at a time—always one at a time—swept his marks into the sea. And himself? In his dream he lay on the edge of the seaside cliff, stretching his hands out, trying to reach his marks, trying to pull them up, trying to save them. Sometimes he even managed to touch their cold hands before they slipped away. One after the other after the other. Inevitable as the waves rising from the sea. One after the other after the other.

It didn't, he mused as he staggered into his morning shower, take a Sigmund Freud to analyze the dream; nor would hours on any couch make it go away.

No, Walter thought as he stood under the spray of near scalding water, his marks were doubtless dead. Dead or worse than dead, suffering in some cell. Put there by the "alleged" mole.

The Great Scandinavian Pimp and Deadly Recruiter, indeed, he thought. Stress on the *deadly*. I seduced them and recruited them but could not protect them. And they vanished one after the other after the other until even the Old One had had enough.

And were I not my father's son, he thought as he stepped out into the chilly apartment, I might have been carted to some cell myself, to be interrogated and squeezed until the Old One was satisfied that I was not the mole myself.

The Old One had told him as much, in fact, in the actual version of the Hamburg conversation, so different from the proffered cover story.

"If you weren't Sam Wither's son," the Old One had said. "I'd almost suspect you. Your father was a fine man."

"He was."

"And a great friend to me," said the Old One. "I miss him."

"So do I."

"This can't go on, young Withers," the Old One had murmured. "Half your marks are gone, and the other half are impossibly compromised. So are you."

Walter had wanted to argue, make a case for staying in Stockholm and finding the mole. But there was no good case to be made. The mole could be anywhere, could be anyone. And Walter was finished in Stockholm. He could be of use only to the other side, in fact, as sort of a negative security test. All he could do was to recruit their unreliables, who in turn would be exposed, so Walter had to go and to try to build some sort of life in the dull job the Company had found for him. And so far it hadn't been bad, save for the dreams. He was in New York, he was in love, and a man with his past might simply have to live with bad dreams.

He showered, shaved, and got ready to go to the office. He wasn't due at Forbes and Forbes until the civilized hour of nine, but nevertheless made it his habit to be there by seven.

"When you're the new guy," his father had told him some years ago, "you need about two additional hours a day at first to get a grasp of the job. If you stay late, you appear to be either struggling or currying favor. The best thing to do is to come in early. You get your work done,

and as far as anyone else knows, you just got there a few minutes ahead of them."

So it had become Walter's ritual, in the eight months he had worked at Forbes and Forbes, to use the hours between seven and nine to catch up on his paperwork. Besides, he had the Howard file on his mind.

"Paperwork is my life," he explained to Anne as he got out of the shower that morning to see her staring at him, the blankets tucked up to her nose.

"Ick," Anne answered.

"Not really," Walter answered, taking a white, button-down cotton broadcloth shirt from the silent butler. "There is, as your beatnik buddies might say, a 'Zen' to paperwork."

"There's a Zen to sleeping," she said, and pulled the blanket back over her head.

He put on his standard black socks and a pair of wool gabardine, pleatless trousers and said, "You work nights."

And play until morning, he thought.

He chose a red-and-green striped Christmas tie from the rack, knotted it, then took the cedar shoe trees from his pair of black wing tips, sat on the edge of the bed, and used a shoe horn to get the shoes on. He got up and brushed the shoulders of a gray wool, three-button jacket and climbed into it.

"The organization man," she said, peeping again over the blanket. "The Man in the Gray Flannel Suit."

"And proud of it." He leaned over to kiss her, then said, "See you tonight."

"See you," she mumbled.

He knew she'd be asleep again in seconds.

He put on his black wool Chesterfield overcoat, red scarf, and gray, narrow-brimmed fedora and walked out of his second floor apartment onto Thirty-sixth Street. He bought a truncated version of the *New York Times*—the deliverymen were on strike—and because it was cold and he was tired, he hailed a taxi on Second Avenue for the quick ride up to One Rockefeller Center. He flipped through the two-page paper on the way and was glad to see that Brooks Atkinson had given *A Party* a rave on the basis of "style, taste, standards, and manners," all of which slipping Old World virtues Walter heartily approved.

Me, my late father, and the dinosaurs, Walter thought as the cab pulled up to Rockefeller Center.

Even the Christmas tree looks cold and sleepy, he thought as he paid the driver and stepped out onto Rockefeller Plaza and walked up to his building.

"You're in early, Mr. Withers," the doorman said. He was an older, red-faced Irishman who'd said this every working day since Walter had started work at Forbes and Forbes. In fact, Walter saw a number of Mallons every day, as the elder of the clan had managed over the years to bring his three strapping sons on to the job, the lobby crew therefore known as "Mallon and the Mallonettes." He handed Walter a steaming cardboard cup of coffee and an apricot Danish wrapped in a paper napkin.

"Or out late, Mr. Mallon," Walt answered ritually. He handed Mallon a Christmas card. "Compliments of the season."

Mallon peeked at the ten-dollar bill inside the card and said, "And to you, Mr. Withers. Big plans tomorrow?"

"Just a quick pop up to Greenwich to see the family. And yourself?"

"The grandkids."

"Yes, well, Christmas is for children," Walter answered. "Have they been in to see the tree?"

"Every year since they was little. They grow up so fast," Mallon said. "You got kids?"

"None that I'm aware of, Mr. Mallon."

They shared a laugh over the old joke, and then Mallon leaned forward and confided, "Me and the crew are going to have a little 'eggnog' throughout the day, you know what I mean. Stop down if you get a chance and have a cup." He winked conspiratorially.

"Well, I'll do that," Walter answered. "Thank you very much."

He couldn't see the Christmas tree from his office at Forbes and Forbes. Not that this troubled him. As the new guy he was lucky to have his own office at all, even if it was a sliver of space with a window that faced east onto Fifth instead of south onto Rockefeller Plaza. The building across Fifth blocked most of his view, although by opening the window and craning his neck he could see the top of St. Patrick's Cathedral and two of the front doors at Saks, thereby providing, as Walter observed to Forbes Jr., "a view of both God and mammon."

But while sitting at his desk, his view, if he swiveled around to gaze out the window, was dominated by the office building across the way—a huge gray stone building with columns and files of rectangular windows. Walter had developed a waving relationship with several of the office workers on the sixteenth floor of the neighboring building, especially with a harried-looking executive in the window Walter designated as 16-C, third from the left as you looked out the window. The man in 16-C often stood in the window with a cardboard cup of what was probably coffee in his hand, and Walter was tempted to buy him a real mug and have it delivered as a Christmas present. Walter had so far resisted the temptation, however, concerned that 16-C might misinterpret the gesture.

He was also reluctant to disturb a man's office rituals, which he knew were often as important to a person's work as a pen, a desk, or an adding machine.

Walter poured his own coffee—cream with two sugars—into a real mug, and quickly consumed it and the Danish as he stared out the window. Then he settled in to work.

First up was the Daily Expense Report, a matter of great importance and unending anguish to Mr. Tracy, inevitably known as "Dickless" Tracy, the office gnome who vainly struggled to keep track of the investigators' cash expenditures. Private investigators, even those who worked for big outfits like Forbes and Forbes, were notoriously sloppy about recording expenses, and the office joke was that the weekly expense reports went directly from Tracy's desk to the Pulitzer prize committee for fiction.

"Receipts," Tracy had said to Walter his first day on the job. "I want receipts. You want reimbursement, get receipts."

Tracy loved Walter. His expense reports were things of beauty—neat, accurate, and punctiliously documented.

"Not like that bastard Dietz," Tracy hissed to Walter one day. Walter had listened very seriously, even though he already knew that Bill Dietz from the Matrimonial Department had tried to actually *kill* Dickless by turning in a receipt for $3,428 for a brand-new Lincoln Continental and putting it down as "Transportation."

Above all, Walter gave Tracy receipts. Tracy didn't know that Walter also gave everyone else receipts. He had an amazing collection of blank receipts from cab companies, restaurants, toll booths, parking lots, railroads, and all the other services that the guys were likely to use in the course of their work. Any investigator who had left a slip in a jacket pocket, or otherwise misplaced it, or had just neglected to get one in the first place, was welcome to take one from the library in the bottom right drawer of Walter's desk. Walter had only one penalty for a colleague who used this service to turn in a false expense, and that was permanent banishment from the Withers Collection.

"Banishment?" Jack Griffin—Insurance Fraud—had asked when Walter confronted him in the men's room with a New Haven Railroad expense that could not possibly have been legit. "For how long?"

"Life," Walter had answered.

"Geez, Walt, life?!" Griffin had moaned. His rabbity little face bent into a frown as he tore off a sheet of toilet paper and asked, "That's a little severe, don't you think?"

Walter didn't bother to remind him that less than a year ago there had been no receipt library from which to be expelled, but simply said, "Life, commuted to thirty days with good behavior."

Echoes of his father's voice: Don't hold other people to the same standards to which I hold you or to which you hold yourself. That's a high bar to jump, son, and most people don't have the legs.

So on this particular morning Walter took yesterday's receipts from their designated compartment in his wallet and laid them out beside the expense report. There were only three, he having spent most of the day before at his desk, and he had already written on the back of each one the date, time, and what it was for. Now he entered the case number in the left-hand column of the report, followed by the date, amount, and purpose. Then he stapled the receipts, in order, to the back of the report, and paper-clipped that report to the week's two previous dailies. The collected dailies went to Tracy every Friday.

Next up was the Activity Log, the hour-by-hour record of how the investigator spent his time and the single most important document at Forbes and Forbes, which billed its clients by the hour. The Activity Log was also the spider web in which fraudulent expenses became inextricably enmeshed. Expenses, of course, had to be reconciled with activity; an investigator could not claim an expense for, say, a motel room in Yonkers at the same time that he was on a surveillance in Brooklyn.

Walter was amazed at how many investigators, especially those whose whole jobs involved revealing inconsistencies in other people's documents, could not reconcile their expense reports with their activity logs. Jack Griffin was hopeless at it, and he was justly famous for having uncovered the "Miracle on 35th Street," a medical report on a car-accident victim named Alice Guggenheiser that cited not only whiplash but testicular bruising.

"This lying quack was doing so many inflated reports he just forgot which one was which," Griffin had told a rapt audience in the coffee room.

But even Griffin couldn't reconcile his own documents.

Walter had no trouble. For one thing, he was honest. For another, he kept on his person a small spiral notebook in which he jotted down each activity as it occurred. Then it was a simple matter of entering the case number onto the Activity Log and filling the rest in. A simple thing if you kept up with it, an ordeal if you tried to play catch-up, as most of the investigators did.

Walter finished the Activity Log, allowed himself a minute to gaze out the window and brood on his hangover, then took two sheets of clean white paper, slipped a carbon between them, rolled them into his Underwood, and started to write his investigation reports.

Walter worked in the Personnel Security Department—

not to be confused, as often was the case, however—with the Personal Security Department. Walter's job in the Personnel Security Department was to do background checks on new employees for Forbes and Forbes corporate clients.

"Personnel security," Forbes Jr. had said to Walter in his official welcome-on-board chat, "is the very lifeblood of our agency. That and Insurance Fraud, of course. Together, these corporate clients compose eighty-six percent of our income."

Forbes and Forbes was a personnel security factory, Walter discovered, taking in people's personal histories, processing them, and then spitting them out again with one of three labels: a green flag for "cleared," a yellow flag for "questionable," and a red flag for "alarm."

"It should be a black flag," Dietz had said to Walter, "because that poor sucker is dead."

Walter also learned that the agency had a piecework arrangement with most of its corporate clients, who paid Forbes and Forbes by the applicant, not by the hour. So it was important to "profitability," Forbes Jr.'s favorite word, that the machine run quickly and smoothly.

"Here's how it works," Forbes Jr. said between jaws clenched around his pipe. "The files come to 'Intake and Assignment'—that's old Charlie DeWitt—where they're classified 'Standard' or 'Special Attention' and then assigned out to an investigator. The S.A.'s have a blue sticker attached to the front of the file. An S.A. is any executive-level hiring, executive-level promotion, or any person who will have access to that company's confidential information or trade secrets.

"We have to do the standard application cheaper than their own personnel departments could, so don't go crazy on these things. Just verify the address, check with the last employer, maybe call a reference or two. If the applicant is stupid enough to admit to a criminal record, check it out. Theft, dope, or sex charges—red-flag it.

"Obviously, the S.A.'s get special attention. We bill these by the hour, so be thorough. Do some legwork. Check out their finances. If the subject is living above his means, we want to know where the money's coming from. Check out his politics and his personal life. No commies or homos. Our clients want to know who they're giving the keys to the executive washroom to, if you know what I mean.

"When you've completed an investigation, color-code it. That's enough for the 'Standards'; the S.A.'s require an accompanying report, especially if you red-flag.

"Office boys come around twice a day—ten and three—to pick up completed files from your out tray. That's the only way your files get back into the system, so don't deliver them yourself, or come in to discuss or anything like that, because it drives profitability to hell. Just write good reports and feed them into the machine."

So on this morning of Christmas Even, Walter typed two S.A. reports on innocuous future executives whose lives met the acceptable standards of bland conformity and placed them in the out tray. It was almost nine by then, so he lit a cigarette as he looked out the window and saw 16-C's light come on. He waved at 16-C, adding a mouthed "Merry Christmas," then started in on the stack of files in his in box.

There were four new files, delivered by DeWitt's "bats" on the overnight shift.

"Why 'bats'?" Walter had asked Dietz.

"Because they fly around at night dropping shit on you," Dietz had explained.

The first file was a standard application for a blue-collar supervisory job at a plastics firm. Walter phoned the landlady and found out that the guy paid his rent promptly, didn't drink heavily or beat up on his wife. Then he phoned the first reference, who turned out to be the applicant's high school football coach, apologized for waking him up, found out that the applicant was a team player and great drive blocker, and chatted about Sunday's Giants–Colts game.

Walter attached a green flag to the file and put it in the out tray. Time elapsed, seventeen minutes. A nice profit for Forbes and Forbes, Walter thought. He was also racing the clock because he wanted to be on the Howard file well before noon.

He had dispatched the next two files, both standards, in similar fashion when Dietz appeared in his doorway.

"You're in early," Walter observed. It was only ten-fifteen and Dietz usually didn't put in an office appearance until at least eleven.

"I have a matinee," Dietz explained.

Walter thought that Bill Dietz was what Huckleberry Finn would have turned into if he had grown up in New York and taken early retirement from the police department. He was a rangy redhead with a perpetual grin. Friends said that Bill had been wearing that same grin when he hauled some minor Mafioso into the backseat of his police cruiser and pistol-whipped him, thereby guaranteeing that sergeant was the highest rank he would ever achieve. Dietz pulled the pin a couple of weeks later and came over to the civilian side with Forbes and Forbes.

This morning, along with the grin Dietz was wearing a plaid sports coat with a pink shirt and a black tie. His red hair was greased into a pompadour, and there was a trace of ducktail behind. Perhaps it was a shared tonsorial sense that had started their friendship—Walter and Bill were about the only men at Forbes and Forbes who refused to wear the standard crew cut.

"That shirt . . ." Walter said.

"It's the style," Dietz said.

"Sadly."

"How's the slush fund holding up?" Dietz asked. "I got a house dick at the 'Easy Lay' who thinks it's Christmas just because it's Christmas. Greedy bastard wants a five every time he lets me up. I have half a mind to call a buddy in the Two-Three to give him a hard time about double parking."

The Easy Lay was Bill's nickname for the Hotel Elysee, famous for its brisk business in afternoon guests.

"It's liquid," Walter answered. He reached into his bottom left drawer and pulled out a manila envelope full of cash. "Although it could stand some replenishment."

Walter and Bill had created the slush fund through the discreet submission of phony expenses. Its purpose was to provide a ready flow of cash to assist in investigations. In short, it was for bribes.

There was an expenditure category in the expense report for Gratuities, but Forbes Jr. didn't like to see a lot of money recorded there. He thought that investigators should investigate, and not just purchase information from snitches. The investigators thought that Forbes Jr. had a naive view of the world.

It wasn't just professional snitches, Walter knew. It was desk clerks, bellhops, room-service waiters, concierges, bank tellers, landlords, landladies, building superintendents, bookies, numbers runners, prostitutes, cops, and doormen, to name a few. All born with a New Yorker's knowledge that information and access are marketable commodities.

And one needed cash to trade in that particular market. Walter handed Dietz the envelope.

"Why don't you transfer to Matrimonial?" Dietz asked. He took a five-dollar bill from the envelope. "Come have some laughs instead of sitting behind a desk."

"And leave my colored stickers?"

"If you could see the stuff I see . . ." Dietz leered, handing the envelope back to Walter.

I have seen the stuff you see, Walter thought. Over and over and over again. I have seen quite enough of it, thank you.

". . . get the action I get—"

"Ah, well, Bill," Walter began, "you are a robust man who can handle that sort of sexual stimulation. I, on the other hand, am a born paper pusher."

"You're a regular Wally Cox."

"There you are."

Walter knew that Dietz's sexual bravado was a smoke screen, a purposeful fiction contrived to keep the grin plastered on his face. He was completely faithful and utterly in love with his wife, Mary, and it was the central tragedy of his life.

"Whose turn is it to contribute to the fund?" Dietz asked.

"Yours."

"Shoot," Dietz said. "Can I borrow a receipt?"

"On the sole condition that you will then leave and let me get back to work," Walter answered. He selected a pre-signed Pennsylvania Railroad slip and gave it to Dietz.

"Merry Christmas, Walter."

"Merry Christmas, Bill," Walter said. "And to Mary, please."

"I'll pass that along."

Dietz left and Walter had just turned his attention to the next file when his intercom buzzed.

"Withers. Personnel Security."

"Mr. Withers, Mr. Forbes would like to see you in his office right away. If it's convenient."

It's not at all convenient, thank you, Walter thought as he closed the new file and stood up to put on his jacket.

Forbes Jr.'s office did have a view of the Christmas tree. And Rockefeller Plaza, the skating rink, and the NBC Building.

Forbes Jr. was staring out the window, trying to get his pipe lit, when his secretary, the inimitable Miss Bradley, ushered Walter in. Forbes Jr. waged a constant battle with the science of thermodynamics as it related to pipe tobacco. It seemed to Walter that in every one of their personal encounters, the owner and chief executive officer of Forbes and Forbes was struggling with that pipe, his thin cheeks sucking, his large Adam's apple bobbing, his skinny fingers incessantly tamping. The man just could not keep his damn pipe lit.

"Withers," he inhaled. "Thanks for coming by. Sit down, please."

Walter chose a black leather and chrome Eames chair that was every bit as uncomfortable as it looked.

"You're doing a fine job for us," Forbes Jr. said, his jaw clamped confidently on the glowing pipe. "Personnel Security's rising young star."

Forbes Jr. folded himself into a chair behind his desk. Now that Walter really thought about it, Forbes Jr.'s body resembled a pipe cleaner, albeit a pipe cleaner dressed in gray flannel, with a gold watch and a crew cut.

Forbes Jr. sucked on the pipe, pretended to inhale

smoke, and asked, "You have the Howard file in your tray, don't you, Withers?"

"Literally in my tray," Walter answered. "I'm afraid I didn't bring it with me."

Forbes Jr. gave up the pretense that the pipe was lit, tamped the tobacco down again, struck a match, and held it into the bowl of the pipe. He inhaled, then said, "That's the potential V.P. at A.E., right?"

"Bingo," Walter answered. Michael Howard was being considered for a promotion to vice president in research and development at American Electronics, one of Forbes' biggest clients.

"Well, we certainly don't want to let that drop," Forbes Jr. said.

"I'm just about to start surveillance," Walter said.

"Something suspicious?" Forbes Jr. asked.

"Not really," Walter said. "Just trying to be thorough."

American Electronics' major competitor had beaten it to the punch on two new products in the past eighteen months. The ugly scent of suspicion was seeping into the corporate offices.

"Well, you're busy, then," Forbes Jr. said unhappily.

Walter said, "You have the look of a boss who needs to ask an employee to come in at night."

Forbes Jr. brightened. "I hate to play Scrooge, Withers, but I wonder if you have plans for this evening."

Merely a reservation at The Rainbow Room, Walter thought.

"Nothing special, chief. Why?"

"Do you know Carter from Personal Security?"

"Just from around the water cooler."

Forbes Jr. let a stream of smoke escape from his mouth and said, "He had an assignment for tonight but seems to have taken ill."

Which is only to be expected, Walter thought. "I'll be happy to fill in," he said.

"I'd do it myself, but . . . family obligations, you know."

The pipe had gone cold again.

Walter wondered how a man so seemingly inept could have created an organization as successful as Forbes and Forbes. Forbes Jr. was the sole Forbes of Forbes and Forbes. There was a Forbes Senior, but he had been an army surgeon. Forbes Jr. had left the army with the rank of captain and used his experience in the military police to launch himself in the private investigation business. He thought that Forbes and Forbes sounded more prestigious than just Forbes. Most of the employees called him Mr. Forbes or Mr. Forbes Jr., but Dietz insisted on referring to him as "And Forbes."

"We bachelors expect to be pressed into service on the holidays," Walter said. "What's the job?"

"Security for a little party at the Plaza," Forbes said.

"I'm hardly what you'd call a tough guy."

And there must be a baker's dozen of muscle-bound bachelors in Personal Security, Walter thought.

"Just so," answered Forbes. "This particular assignment requires not muscle so much as, shall we say, sophistication?"

"Who's the client?" Walter asked.

Forbes smiled what he doubtless meant to be a coy smile and pushed a newspaper across his desk. There among the tombstone headlines of Castro's progress in Cuba and a hideous school fire in Chicago was a pleasant photograph of a handsome couple happily Christmas shopping on Fifth Avenue.

Senator Joseph and Mrs. Madeleine Keneally.

Walter had always thought of them as the "Prince and

Princess of the Democratic Realm" under the somewhat monarchist theory that if a nation didn't have a royal couple, it would nominate one.

The chosen prince was an Irish broth of boy whose buccaneer family had made an immense fortune in bootlegging that they now sought to legitimize. He was a war hero, as behooved a prince, and a Democrat, and above all, young. The Senator, Walter thought, was perhaps the first candidate to market sheer youth as a political commodity.

And the King is old, Walter thought. Ike is old—his two terms are up—and the Prince wants to be the king. Funny how no one thinks, could *ever* think, of Dick Nixon as a prince, even though he's the officially anointed.

No, the young Democratic senator is the Prince, Walter thought, and that is largely due to the fact that he married a princess. She came not from bootleggers but from old money. The buccaneer prince had plucked her Rapunzel-like form from her father's seaside castle in Newport. Courted her in storybook fashion, wed her in high society. Catholics both—a genuine problem for a would-be king in a Protestant land—but hers was an aristocratic French Catholicism that muted the Irish priest-ridden image. The bootlegger prince had conquered the old money in the classic way, by sweeping it off its feet and carrying it to his bed.

Not that Walter objected. He rather enjoyed the archetypal aspect of this secular fairy tale, and coming from old money himself, he knew it could stand a breath of fresh air. Besides, he was himself a Democrat, perhaps the only employee in the albeit brief history of CIA who had used his absentee ballot to vote for Adlai Stevenson. He'd vote even more enthusiastically for the Prince—if the Prince managed to seize the nomination, that is—because the

Prince was young and the Prince was a warrior who wanted to do battle with the Bear.

As did Walter.

"I would have thought Keneally would have his own security," Walter said to Forbes as he pushed the paper back across the desk.

"He does," Forbes said. "They're in town for the holidays, and they're hosting this little soiree for a hundred or so of their closest friends. And in any case he wants us for the lady."

"He wants us to keep an eye on his wife?" Walter asked.

"He does," Forbes said. "And further informs us that she prefers a 'light touch.' "

"Well, that's me," Walter said.

Positively famous for being a light touch.

Forbes Jr. sucked on the pipe and said, "It should be a breeze. Give Miss Bradley your sizes and she'll get you geared out with the necessary black tie. Eight o'clock for drinks, buffet, dancing. They want the guests out by midnight."

Before their coaches turn to pumpkins and their footmen to mice, thought Walter. "I have suitable clothes," he said.

Forbes cocked an eyebrow, then said, "You see, I think you might just be better than Carter for this job. You have the background."

That I do, Walter agreed.

Forbes Jr. set the pipe down, opened his desk drawer, and handed Walter a small envelope.

"Sorry to mess up your Christmas Eve," he said. "This is a little token of appreciation for being such a good sport about it."

"That's not necessary, Mr. Forbes."

"Two tickets for Sunday's Giant–Colts game in Yankee Stadium?"

"But I accept," said Walter. "Football is one of my few passions."

"You live a sheltered life," Forbes Jr. said.

From your lips to God's ear, thought Walter.

Noontime on Christmas Eve on Fifth Avenue, Walter thought as he walked down that street. In the heart of the day in the heart of the town in the heart of the world. The imperial city on the best day of the year.

Fifth Avenue at noontime on Christmas Eve had an almost palpable air of good-natured frenzy. Last-minute gift buyers, their arms laden with overstuffed shopping bags, their chins tucked into their coats, their eyes focused straight ahead in fierce concentration on the next purchase, darted from door to door. Husbands and boyfriends on this last possible lunch hour paced uncertainly on the edge of the foot traffic and hoped to see inspiration shine from a window display in the form of *the* gift. The Santas and Salvation Army soldiers stool like islands in the stream and hoped that flotsam of capitalist surplus would wash up on their flooded shores. The clank of change in their buckets punctuated the canned, sentimental music that changed from storefront to storefront but didn't change at all. Shoes lunging for taxicabs crunched on packed, dirty snow. Friends had unexpected meetings with other friends and exchanged intelligence on what was left in what stores. Anxious eyes peered over the crowd to search out a loved one late for the luncheon rendezvous, and through it all Walter Withers happily tailed Michael Howard.

Happily, because Howard was tall and easy to see above the crowd. Happily, because Walter was glad to be out from behind the desk. Happily, because Walter could now make out the distinctive vibrato of the Three Chipmunks singing (singing?) "Christmas, Christmas time is here ..." this year's hit seasonal song. (For reasons neither he nor anyone else could fathom, Walter liked the Three Chipmunks, especially the one called Alvin, who was always being yelled at.) Happily, because it was Christmas Eve at noontime on Fifth Avenue, and there was no other place in the world that Walter would rather have been.

Happily, because there is an art to moving along a crowded city sidewalk.

Well, perhaps "art" is bit much, Walter admitted to himself, but definitely a craft. One has to spot the openings before they open, anticipate the holes in the traffic, and move into position to fill them. One has to turn sideways to take advantage of that narrow gap and then turn full front for speed to accelerate through the next one. One has unwitting blockers in front of one and would-be tacklers coming on, one has to be skilled, cunning and fit, and I am all of those things. I may have lacked the weight to start at Loomis and the talent to play for Yale, but I am the Frank Gifford of the sidewalk rushers.

Nor is Michael Howard any slouch, Walter observed as he struggled to keep up with him. What he lacks in style he makes up for in stride, the athletic bastard.

Walter had played tennis against such as Michael Howard, tall, muscular types with no finesse but great reach. Baseline straddlers with beautiful serves and high overhand smashes. But drop some top-spinners at their ankles and their game falls apart. They lack the nifty footwork.

And Michael Howard was all straight ahead today. No window-shopping, no eye for an empty lunch table, no glance at stylish women. Michael Howard was *headed somewhere* on a straight line, which is the shortest distance between two points, a simple strategy on the gridiron of midtown Manhattan.

Is it the straightforwardness of the innocent or the haste of the guilty? Walter wondered, mindful of the common wisdom that Christmas Eve is for wives and Christmas Eve afternoon for mistresses. Or, in the words of Dietz of Matrimonial, "I do more matinees around Christmas than the Rockettes."

Which is why Walter had made such a point to be loitering in the lobby of American Electronics' Forty-ninth Street office building well before lunchtime.

It had been there in the paperwork, as it always was. Ninety percent of investigative work was paperwork, the tedious, painstaking, detailed examination of documents. And right there in Howard's documents, in his updated résumé, was the first small slug in the otherwise flawless fabric.

It wasn't that Howard belonged to a health club. That was a bit unusual but not suspicious, and he certainly was the athletic type. What caught the eye was the location of the health club. The small, somewhat obscure Gramercy Gym on Twenty-third and Park, and Walter had wondered why a busy, ambitious executive would bypass several better, more prestigious, *closer* clubs for that quick lunchtime workout.

And as Howard led him down Fifth Avenue at a torrid pace toward Gramercy, Walter thought that nobody, not even the most fanatic Charles Atlas devotee, gave an hour on Christmas Eve to lifting weights.

So Walter was not surprised when Howard turned onto Twenty-third and strode right past the Gramercy Gym.

And now we are in the open field, Walter thought, and

he let a little more space develop between himself and his mark as they walked into a residential neighborhood away from the crowd. This is the tricky phase of the tail, because if Howard's destination is illicit, he will have a look around before going in, and we must not let ourselves be caught, as it were, flat-footed.

So when Howard turned south on Lexington, Walter crossed over to the east side of the street before heading downtown, figuring that he could parallel his mark for two blocks until Gramercy Park blocked his view.

The park will be a problem, Walter thought. If Howard is going to make a move, that's where he should make it. Give it a once-around-and-back-through, and the tail either has to back off or get pinned. So make a decision. Go the sound end and stay there even if he doubles back uptown. Let him go and wait for another day.

Settle down, Walter told himself. Your man's an amateur, perhaps a businessman on the take, but not a pro who knows his street craft. The chances are, he's just heading for a romantic assignation. A hurried exchange of bodily fluids and other gifts before heading back to the office Christmas party, the train to Darien and the regulation wife and two children, and a Christmas Eve of wrestling a Lionel track together and inserting a different tab A into a different slot B.

Then Howard turned east at the park and headed straight for Walter.

Coming to the net, so to speak, Walter thought. A bold choice for a base-liner, and you've caught me moving the wrong way. I can't just stop and I certainly can't spin on my heels to follow you, so it's your point.

Walter kept walking south on Lexington and let Howard cross east on Twenty-first Street behind him. He walked half the block and stopped.

The smart thing to do would be to give it up for the day, Walter thought. Try it again and have a couple of men waiting in the neighborhood so the next time Howard came to the net, he'd be *in* the net. But that would be expensive and risky on its own right, because if Howard had truly spotted him, and was involved in industrial espionage, he would surely change the meeting spot for the next time.

No, the best course is to assume that Howard is the oxymoronic innocent adulterer and try to pick up the tail again.

Walter hurried back uptown on Lexington and turned east on Twenty-first just in time to see Howard let himself into a brownstone on the downtown side of the street between Lexington and Third. Walter hurried to the uptown side of the street and trotted to the point where he could see the front of the brownstone from an angle. A blind was pulled in a window on the west side of the second floor.

For privacy, Walter thought sadly as he walked back to the corner.

He stood there for over an hour, switching his weight from one leg to the other, stamping his feet, his hands buried in his coat pockets. Every minute or so he glanced impatiently at his watch and searched the oncoming traffic as if looking for a ride that was very late.

He hoped that Howard was with a woman. Bad news for Mrs. Howard but good news for American Electronics.

But maybe not—if the company was infected with a mole, it would be better to find out quickly.

Walter knew that there were few things worse for any company than the fear that it had a traitor inside. That stench of suspicion was a poison gas that choked the life out of an organization. Colleagues became afraid to talk with one another; product information became restricted to an ever tightening circle of people, thereby cutting off the flow of fresh ideas and in itself arousing more suspicion. More and more of the company's energy went into uncovering the mole, less and less into its real work until professional paranoia became the rule of the day. Then there was no longer such a thing as bad luck, or sloppy work, or just plain being bested by the opposition. Everything became sabotage, and the ultimate result was a guarded collection of fearful individuals and not a company at all.

Walter thought that if he really wanted to kill an organization, he would plant not a mole but the rumor of a mole. A mole could be tracked down and destroyed; a rumor was forever illusive and immortal.

The thought kept him standing in the cold within view of 322 East Twenty-first Street until Michael Howard finally came out and caught a cab at the park.

Walter waited for another twenty minutes to see if anyone else came out of the apartment. He was almost grateful when nobody did, because it tended to indicate that a lover was lounging in post-coital languor inside. A debriefer would have waited about ten minutes before bailing out.

There was also the possibility that the apartment was a drop, that Howard had spent the hour transferring his information on an untraceable typewriter or over a secure telephone.

Walter got the shivers for a second. Not from the cold but from the old days, from the thought that perhaps the opposition had baby-sitters for Walter's mark. If so, they would still be in the neighborhood, and they would have made him easily.

He flirted with the idea of phoning Healy in Operations

to request a couple of boys to screen him as he went in. But it was Christmas Eve, the office party was doubtless in full swing, and he didn't want to get a reputation for being a nervous Nellie.

It's New York, he told himself, not Berlin or Vienna or even Copenhagen. And the opposition is Electrics Dynamic, Inc., not the Soviets or the Czechs or the East Germans. Nobody's going to get killed over the latest toaster technology.

Still, he was sweaty under his coat as he walked back along Twenty-first and hopped up the steps to 322. He opened the door and stepped into the foyer, which would be the worst place in the entire world to be if the opposition had their people on the street.

First a quick look at the lock. A sliding bolt, no protective metal shield.

Then to the mail boxes. Second floor, only two apartments. Memorize the names and try not to listen for the sound of feet coming up the steps behind you.

2A—Rubinsky, Mr. and Mrs. Possible but not likely. It's not a name one makes up.

2B—or not to be. *H. Benson*, the first initial a dead giveaway of a woman living alone. But maybe she's not lonely. Maybe she has Michael Howard.

He stepped back out on the street and walked east this time. Nobody was following him. He looked at his watch and saw that it was only two-fifteen.

He could easily get to Bill Dietz's apartment and have some time with Bill's wife, Mary, before Dietz got home.

Bill's sister answered the door.

"You shouldn't be here," she said.

She was as handsome as Bill. Flame red hair framed a strong face and tired blue eyes.

"I thought you might need some time to yourself," Walter answered. "Last-minute Christmas errands, that sort of thing. May I come in?"

The apartment was dark, but most apartments in the massive Tudor City complex were. The living room window shades were open, though, and Walter could see the East River and a bit of the United Nations building. A small artificial Christmas tree, beautifully decorated, stood on an end table. The apartment was overheated and stuffy. A television set cast a bleak, flickering light in the room.

"What are you watching?" Walter asked.

"*The Verdict Is Yours,*" Sarah chuckled.

"And what's your verdict?"

"I haven't really been paying attention."

"Ah."

"You must have things to do yourself," Sarah said quietly.

"Not really. I signed out on a surveillance, so I can watch Mary for a while."

He could see her hesitation, the struggle between her sense of duty and the offer of a small bit of freedom. She fought the same battle every time he came over.

"I'll be offended if you say no," he said.

"I do have a few things . . ."

Small wonder, he thought, what with a husband and a kid at home. Her mother looked after the child when Sarah was nursing Mary Dietz. The domino theory of illness.

"Do them," Walter answered. "Go for coffee. Go for a drink. Go for a walk. Go."

"Is it cold out?" she asked, easing her way into accepting his offer.

"Freezing."

He took off his coat and hat and laid them on the sofa as if to settle the matter.

"Would you get out, please?" he asked.

She took her own coat—red cloth—from the closet.

"She's sleeping," Sarah said.

Walter gently opened the door to the bedroom. Mary Dietz was propped up against three pillows. Her black hair was sweaty, and strands of it clung to the pale skin of her face, skin that looked translucent against the sharp outline of her bones. Her eyes were closed, but she didn't look peaceful. A grimace twisted her mouth, although Walter couldn't tell whether it was from pain or a symptom of the disease.

"It tests your faith, doesn't it?" Sarah asked from over his shoulder.

"It does."

"Are you a Christian, Walter?"

He nodded. "A bad one."

"Is there any other kind?" she asked. "She's had a rough day. I don't know how much longer Bill can keep her at home. Even with my coming over . . . I meant to wash her hair this morning, but—"

"You do a marvelous job, Sarah."

She buttoned her coat and put on her hat.

"An hour?" she asked.

"Two if you like," he answered. "Honestly, I have nothing to do."

When she left, he took off his shoes and walked into the bedroom. Pictures of Bill and Mary in happier days covered the top of the bureau. The photographs showed a striking woman. Then the disease had robbed her of the use of her legs, then her arms, and now it was at work on her spine and lungs.

Walter had heard the story from Benoit in Operations,

how Bill sat in that room nursing her and holding her hand, and how his sister took over for him when he was at work.

So one afternoon when he was sure Bill was on a case, Walter had gone over to the apartment and introduced himself to Sarah. After some doing, he finally persuaded her to take a break and swore her to secrecy.

"Why?" she'd asked. "Why are you doing this, and why a secret?"

"Bill's a colleague," Walter explained. It seemed sufficient.

Mary had been a little better then, and Walter would spend an hour or so two or three afternoons a week reading to her. Now she was asleep more often than not, but he would usually read aloud anyway.

"Hello, gorgeous," he whispered as he took a towel and wiped the corner of her mouth. He went into the bathroom and ran a face cloth under the tap, fussed with the water until the temperature was right, then went back into the bedroom and gently wiped her face.

A faded print of Jesus, soft light in his eyes and a faint, benevolent smile on his lips, hung over the head of the bed.

"Happy birthday," Walter said to the picture. "But you should have stuck around a little longer, chum."

Then Walter got down on his hands and knees, pulled a book from way under the bed, and sat down in the rocking chair.

"Where were we, Mary?" he asked. He found his place in the yellowed paperback copy of Spillane's *One Lonely Night* and said, "Oh, right. We're starting a new one."

He coughed rhetorically and then gave his best dramatic rendering as he read, "*Chapter One: Nobody ever walked across the bridge, not on a night like this. The rain was misty enough to be almost fog-like, a cold gray curtain that separated me from the pale ovals of white that were faces locked behind the steamed-up windows of the cars that hissed by. Even the brilliance that was Manhattan by night was reduced to a few sleepy, yellow lights off in the distance."*

He read for only a few minutes before he laid the book in his lap and fell asleep.

Walter awoke from his nap at Dietz's shortly before Sarah came back, chatted with her for a few minutes, kissed Mary on the cheek, and dashed out. He made it to the office in time to have an eggnog with Mallon and the boys, then dashed home to shower, shave, and climb into his black tie.

And telephone Anne.

"Sorry, darling," he said when she came on the line, "but I have to work tonight."

"Don't be sorry. I have to work tonight, too."

"But I wanted to be there."

He explained about the party at the Plaza.

"So you'll be guarding the young prince and his princess," she said.

"Strictly speaking, just the young princess."

"From the young prince?"

"Maybe," he laughed. "If I'm supposed to be her bodyguard . . ."

"Talk about closing the barn door," Anne said.

"Retract those claws."

"The young prince is a bastard," she said.

Walter thought that Anne's penchant for non sequitur came from spending so much time singing popular song lyrics.

"Is the party still on, and am I still invited?" he asked her.

"It is, and you are."

A Christmas Eve celebration at The Cellar among the Village hip crowd.

"I'll be wearing a dinner jacket," he warned, thinking about her bohemian friends. "Unless you think I should stop home and change."

"Don't. They'll think you're delightfully camp."

"I'll get there as soon as I can," he promised.

He made it to the Plaza Hotel by seven.

He had the cabbie drop him on the corner of Fifth Avenue and Central Park South because the drive in front of the Plaza's main entrance was jammed with town cars, taxis, and limousines. Besides, the view of the Plaza from that corner was one of Walter's favorite sights, especially on a sparkling, celebratory evening.

To his right the park glistened with new snow, and to his left silvery water gushed from the fountain in Grand Army Plaza. Straight ahead the Plaza Hotel itself presided like a queen over subjects who were arriving to greet her in their best holiday finery. The whole scene looked like one of those magic globe toys that drop artificial snow on pretty toy buildings.

And the sounds: the honking of horns, the hum of voices, the steady *clop-clop* of the carriage horses as they took excited children and dreamy lovers for rides under the trees in Central Park.

A gentle snow on Christmas Eve is the first and best present, Walter thought. It softens an otherwise hard day.

He had no trouble recognizing Keneally's personal security, three thick paddies from South Boston who stood on the Plaza steps stamping their feet, smoking cigarettes, and looking as comfortable and happy as three sailors in Sunday school.

Small wonder she wanted someone with my unquestionable *je ne sais quoi* to work the room, Walter thought with a self-indulgent chuckle. The boyos might be pretty handy at persuading a county registrar to get out the dead vote, but they'd stick out like the hackneyed sore thumbs in a party room at The Plaza.

The man who stood with them was something different, however. Ferret thin, well dressed in black tie and overcoat, his eyes scanning the approaching crowd for sign of friend or foe. This boy, Walter thought, could get things done in any room, particularly a back one.

Walter walked up and introduced himself.

"Walter Withers," he said, offering his hand. "From Forbes and Forbes."

The three guards kept their hands jammed in their pockets and gave him a grudging nod.

The thin young man stuck out his hand and said, "Pardon the lack of manners. I'm Jimmy Keneally."

"The brother," Walter said.

The famous, or infamous, depending upon your point of view, younger brother of Joe Keneally. His chief of staff, adviser, confidant, and fixer. He had none of his brother's blarney, charm or bluster, but he was cool and efficient.

"The brother," Keneally laughed. "These bums are Callahan, Brown, and Cahill. Callahan's the chief."

Callahan was built like a block of stone. He had a boxer's shoulders with a brawler's face. He looked Walter up and down, then asked, "So you going to make sure no one pockets the silverware, that it?"

"Something along those lines," Walter answered.

Callahan snorted, which seemed to give Brown and Cahill permission to smirk.

"Forbes give you the specs?" Jimmy Keneally asked.

"Sure."

"What you're basically wanted for is to ease out any uninvited guests. Quietly," Jimmy said. "I'm expecting a nice dull evening, but you never know."

"You shouldn't have shit to do," Callahan answered. "We'll cover the building. Something happens, you call for us. Got it?"

"Got it."

"I'll go upstairs with you," Jimmy said. "Get my party face on."

In the elevator, Jimmy asked, "You've never worked for us before, have you?"

"I haven't had that pleasure."

"I think I would have remembered you," Jimmy said. He gave Walter a long look, then said, "Yeah, you'll do all right."

I'll do just fine, thanks, Walter said.

Madeleine Keneally had thought it would be fun to be in New York for the holidays.

There was the shopping, the theater, and so many dear friends lived in the city.

"And Newport is so windy," she explained to Walter. "And the Cape is so . . . windy. And try as they might, they both have this dreary Puritan ambiance that they just can't seem to shake. Do you know what I mean?"

"I know exactly," Walter answered, "because *I* have this dreary Puritan ambiance that *I* can't seem to shake."

"Do you try, though, Mr. Withers?" she asked.

He raised his glass.

"Until I drop, Mrs. Keneally."

He couldn't tell if she was laughing from genuine amusement or a social skill she had practiced at Miss

Porter's School. That went along with the rest of it. She had that way of making whoever she was with feel as if he were the only person in a crowded room and the most interesting character in a brilliant assemblage.

Brilliant it was, too. It seemed to Walter that half the stars in the New York firmament were competing to shine in that one small room.

The composer of *West Side Story* bent down to chat with the author of *Breakfast at Tiffany's*, creating in Walter's mind a musico-literary Mutt-and-Jeff combination that was being jealously watched at the moment by a sloe-eyed essayist, an American with a nevertheless Latin name that Walter could not recall. It wasn't Fidel, whose guerrillas were even then closing in on Havana, Walter thought, but some name like that. And Walter had a vague notion that he was some distant relative of Madeleine's. In another cluster the detestable gossip columnist—a profession that Walter had on a par with bill collectors— Dorothy Kilgallen held court to suitors hoping for a mention in her next dispatch. Looking on smirking—his eyes met Walter's in a brief sharing of disdain—was a television "personality" that Walter recognized mostly because the NBC Building was cater-corner to his own office. He was the current "king of late night," Walter knew, if indeed your late nights were composed of sitting in front of the television set watching one personality chat with another. Walter recognized a few prominent figures of the current arts and theater scene, a judge or two, a gaggle of politicians, some debutantes in waiting, and some New York ladies who were simply New York ladies. A statuesque blonde with a daring decolletage added a little dangerous sex appeal.

The room was as glittery as the guests. Someone had gone to a great deal of trouble to whip it into a winter wonderland. Big lace snowflakes hung from the ceiling, and wreaths of spray-painted silver decorated the walls. The tables were draped in white linen with white plastic bells pinned to it. Behind the tables, unhappy waiters dressed as elves sliced turkey and ham, while other elves walked about offering hors d'ouevres and champagne.

But the star of the party was Madeleine Keneally.

Walter had watched her—of course, that was his job— as she moved gracefully around the room. Tall and elegant, she smiled and touched, laughed at each witticism, her big brown eyes getting bigger with each anecdote. Her dress, remarkably simple for this gathering, was in that ineffable shade somewhere between silver and white, and it contrasted with her chestnut hair, which was cut severely at the base of her long neck. Occasionally he got a waft of her voice, breathy and soft.

Intimate, he thought. That's what it was. She gave each person the illusion that their conversation was intimate.

And now it was his turn, and he was impressed that she was just as warm, just as interested, and just as charming as she was with all the other guests, even though she knew he was one of the evening's hirelings.

"But you're drinking ginger ale!" she protested. "Let me get you some champagne."

"But I'm on duty, you see."

She put on a frown that stopped just short of being a pout. "Because of me, I'm afraid."

"Quite the opposite," he answered. "Because of me you're *not* to be afraid."

She suddenly looked so serious that it took him aback.

"Is that true?" she asked.

I meant it as a play on words, he thought, but it's true. He held up his right hand and said, "Puritan's oath."

She looked embarrassed and unsure of what to say next,

so Walter leaned in and whispered, "Shall I let you in on a professional bodyguard secret?"

She looked relieved that the social game was on again.

"Please do. I love intrigue."

"It is very hard," Walter said, "to guard someone when you're standing next to that person."

"Why is that?" she whispered.

"Because you can see only the person and not the danger," he answered. "This is especially true when the person is as lovely and charming and nice as you are."

He stepped back and mimed a professional bodyguard stance.

"What a graceful way of telling me to move along," she said. "I feel as if I should put my hand out to be kissed."

"Don't do that," Walter said. "I couldn't resist the temptation, and then your husband would get jealous and challenge me to a duel, and that would ruin the party, not to mention the peace of Christmas."

She turned to look at Joe Keneally as he worked the room. The senator did look dashing as he told what appeared to be a naughty joke to a small knot of people that included the television star and the statuesque blonde. He was tall and youthful-looking. His shoulders were heavy and rolled a little forward, the way a boxer's do when he's moving in for the kill. His brown hair, combed in a modest pompadour, had just a tinge of red to it. He *was* the Irish broth of a boy, but born to the manse rather than the cottage. He caught Madeleine's eye and smiled. A smile that promised mischief and romance.

"Do you think he'd do that?" she asked. "Fight a duel for me?"

"Any man would."

She turned to look at Walter again.

"Am I really 'nice'?" she asked.

A serious question.

"You really are, Mrs. Keneally," he answered.

"Madeleine, please."

She gave him a little curtsy and slid away.

As Walter watched her engage the next guests, he was sure of two things. One, he liked Madeleine Keneally very much. Two, she was in some sort of trouble.

That's when the ruckus began.

Sometimes the sound of trouble comes suddenly, like a crack of gunfire, and then all you can do in that horrible moment is know that you've fouled up and pray that your mistake isn't lethal.

But sometimes it comes gradually. You hear it coming and have a few gracious moments in which to prevent it, and that's what happened that Christmas Eve at the Plaza.

Walter heard it first, a choir of discordant voices from outside the party room. The sound was simultaneously muffled and reverberant, so he figured that it was coming from the stairwell below.

Which gives me blessed time, he thought, and a decent shot at containment. He set his glass down and moved casually toward the door. He was in the lobby when a loud drunken voice rose from the cacophony below, "Can the princess come out and play? Will Rapunzel let down her hair?"

Walter heard the party chatter soften behind him. The guests were doubtless aware of the intrusion now, so he didn't have much time. He made it to the stairwell door just as it opened and a man lurched into the lobby.

He was tall and well built. A shock of thick black hair hung down his forehead toward his broken nose. A blue denim shirt showed beneath his open naval pea coat. His chinos and work boots were wet with snow, and he held a bottle of beer and a knit watch cap in his right hand. He looked over Walter's shoulder at the scene in the party room and said, "Christ, it's Vienna in 1914."

The face was familiar, but it took a few seconds for Walter to remember where he had seen it before. Something to do with Anne. Her place in Stockholm. On the dust jacket of a book. *The Highway by Night*. Sean McGuire.

He had gained a certain celebrity since his book got a rave review in the *Times*, a review that labeled McGuire the avatar of the beat generation. The cultural press had coined the word *beatnik* to describe the latest anti-establishment movement. Walter had recalled that before McGuire had heard the call of the highway at night, he'd been a fullback at Columbia.

He weaved in front of Walter and said, "I'm here to deliver a poem."

"I had you as more of a prose writer," Walter said.

McGuire's blue eyes showed surprise.

"Same thing, poetry and prose," he muttered. "Should be, anyway."

"Ah."

"I'm here to deliver a poem," McGuire repeated.

Four more men came through the door behind him. Each of them dressed like working-class heroes. All drunkenly grinning. Walter recognized the skinny one from one of Anne's books of poetry. The other two he'd never seen.

"How many guys does it take to deliver a poem?" Walter asked.

McGuire grinned and said, "Depends on how many guys try to stop them."

Walter shrugged. "I like poems."

He heard the elevator slide open behind him and glanced over to see Callahan and Cahill step out. Why hadn't they stopped this downstairs? The bodyguards started toward McGuire but hesitated when Walter shook his head.

That didn't stop them. What stopped them was Jimmy Keneally brusque shake of *his* head.

"I'll tell you what," Walter said to McGuire. "Give me the poem and I'll deliver it for you."

McGuire lifted the bottle, took a swig, and shook his head.

"It's not *written*," he said with contempt. "It's not a written poem. It flows, like my lifeblood."

Which will start flowing liberally any moment if these Boston boys get their way, Walter thought.

"A poem for Madeleine Keneally!" McGuire hollered. "Madeleine, sad Madeleine, queen of the realm! She—"

"What's this all about?" Joe Keneally asked as he stood at Walter's shoulder.

Walter turned to see Madeleine in the doorway. Her cheeks were flushed and lips pressed tightly together. Other guest gathered behind her. The gossip columnist pulled a notebook from her purse as the photographer struggled with his flash.

"I'll take care of it, Senator," Walter said.

McGuire continued, ". . . dances with the king who sits on the western throne of Jefferson's lost country calling un-American every activity that isn't honeyed money—"

"Careful, now, that one almost rhymed," said Walter.

". . . while plastic Christmas sees plastic nails in bleeding Jesus crying 'Madeleine, Madeleine, Madeleine' . . ."

"You're starting to repeat yourself," Walter advised him.

From the corner of his eye he saw a few of the younger bucks at the part start to press forward, ready to defend Madeleine and the rest of their caste. He could feel Keneally's shoulders tense in readiness for a fight. As for the security boys, they were already embarrassed, so would delight in pounding these beatnik intruders and throwing them down the stairs.

The three closest to the door would be no problem. One feint of a jab and they'd run for their lives. But McGuire, well, he has those longshoreman's hands, the halfback's shoulders, and the broken nose. Not to mention the beer bottle.

"Madeleine, sad lane, sadly, madly Madeleine . . ."

There'd be hell of a row. All of which will look pretty ugly in tomorrow's papers and worse on my record, Walter thought. There's only one way to distract a writer in mid-flight of fancy.

"I'm a better poet," Walter said.

McGuire stopped and glared at him.

"I'm a better poet than you are," Walter repeated.

McGuire cocked his head and said, "Prove it."

Walter assumed a formal declamatory stance, loudly cleared his throat, and announced, "A poem for Sean McGuire! One that rhymes."

"Let's hear it," McGuire said.

Walter mimed grave artistic concentration.

" 'Twas the night before Christmas," he started.

A few titters and even McGuire got a goofy smirk on his face.

"And all through the Plaza . . ." continued Walter.

"Rhyme that," McGuire said.

"Some beat poets were stirring . . ."

Applause from McGuire's compadres. McGuire, ego challenged, was waiting for the rhyme.

As was Walter. He held the silence as he searched for a word.

"Disturbing *la casa*," he finally said.

Applause and cheers, Walter observed. Still a crowd scene, but at least they were his crowd now. McGuire smiled and graciously bowed to him. Walter returned the bow, then held up his hand for silence.

"The squares and the beats," he continued, "were all dressed up with care . . ."

Hoots and laughter.

"In hopes that Santa—or Sartre—soon would be there."

Walter eased toward McGuire, took the beer bottle from his hand, and took a long sip from it.

"Thirsty work, this poetry business," Walter said. He kept the bottle and walked toward the elevator. "When up from the lobby there came such a bustle . . ."

He pointed at the guards and winked at them.

"Two big Irish boyos to finish the hustle!"

Mock boos and cheers. Not knowing what else to do, the embarrassed bodyguards took a bow.

Walter stepped into the elevator and took a quick look at the board. The Hold button was down. Walter pressed Lobby and stepped back out.

"And so we announce as we edge out of sight," he said, dangling the beer bottle in front of McGuire like a shiny Christmas ornament.

McGuire moved to grab it, but Walter stepped back into the elevator. He knew McGuire wouldn't back down. Couldn't leave it looking like the fool. He'd try for the bottle.

"Quick enough?" he asked the writer.

Walter set the bottle on the elevator floor.

McGuire faked disinterest and started to turn away. Then he leapt for the bottle. When he did, Walter hit the hold button and the elevator doors started to close. Walter made it out, McGuire didn't. The elevator headed downstairs with him in it.

"Merry Christmas to all, and to all a good night," Walter said.

Laughter and applause.

McGuire's buddies headed down the stairs to find him.

"You'd better get down there," Walter said to Callahan. Then, sotto voce, "And you owe me one, so don't hurt them."

"Good job," Jimmy Keneally said to Walter a few minutes later. They were back at the party. Madeleine hovered over Keneally's shoulder.

"But I wish I'd had a chance to punch the son of a bitch," Joe said.

"That's all we'd need," Jimmy said.

"Drunken writers may want their pictures in the paper punching presidential hopefuls," Walter said. "Future presidents don't want their pictures in the papers punching drunken writers."

Joe Keneally's glare turned into a broad smile, "What makes you think I'm a presidential hopeful?"

"It's the season of hope, Senator," Walter answered.

Keneally turned to Madeleine and said, "Did you *know* that jerk, Madeleine?"

"I know his work," she answered. "I've read his book."

"That dope wrote a book?" Keneally asked. "Not a book of poetry, I hope."

"A novel," Madeleine said.

"He sure seemed to know you," Keneally said, staring at her.

Walter said, "That's what happens when you announce your parties in the newspapers, Senator. There's an inherent conflict: You want the publicity but not the public."

Keneally answered, "If that's the public, I sure as hell don't want them."

"But I hear the band tuning up," Walter said, "and your guests are waiting for you to dance."

Madeleine took Keneally's arm.

"Time to be the perfect hosts, darling," she said as she led him away. She turned back to Walter and mouthed the words, "Thank you."

"Aw, shucks, ma'am, just doin' my job," Walter muttered to himself.

"And doing it so beautifully," the statuesque blonde said to him. She held a champagne glass out to him.

"It's Christmas Eve in Manhattan, and beautiful women keep offering me champagne I can't drink," Walter said to her. "Your accent, is it Swedish or Danish?"

Her thick platinum hair hung over bare shoulders. Her white wraparound gown barely concealed her breasts, but still it was her face that caught your eye and held it. Perhaps it was because her dark blue eyes were set a little wider apart than would be considered perfect. Maybe it was the slight, un-Scandinavian curve of her nose. Or the high, sharp cheekbones on which a ship could crash and founder. Or was it the fullness of her lips with their promise of pleasures slow and tactile?

A winter wonderland, indeed, Walter thought.

"Both," she answered, setting the champagne glass back on the table. "Father was Danish, mother Swedish. I was raised in Copenhagen but went back to Sweden to do films."

Of course, Walter thought.

"If you cannot drink," she asked, "do you wish to dance?"

Profoundly, Walter thought. "It's not a matter of what I wish," he said. "It's what I am. I suppose the cat is out of the bag that I'm the bodyguard here."

Her tone dropped from the parlor into the bedroom.

"And whose body are you guarding?" she asked.

"Mrs. Keneally's."

"Lucky woman."

She looked over to where Madeleine and Keneally were waltzing.

"But she seems well looked after for the moment," she observed.

Keneally looked over Madeleine's shoulder, saw Walter with her, and gave him a male grin.

"Have you come to the States to do a film?" Walter asked.

"To try," she said. She held out her hand. "I'm Marta Marlund."

"Walter Withers."

"A pleasure."

"Yes, mine."

How is it, Walter wondered, that your skin smells like a spring meadow and warm, rumpled sheets at the same time?

"Have I seen any of your films?" he asked.

"How would I know that?" she laughed. "Have you seen many Swedish films?"

"Countless," Walter said. Not to mention endless.

"Then perhaps you have seen me."

"I'm sure I have."

"I'm flattered."

She held her hand over her breasts, an act of modesty contrived to draw attention. Transparent but effective, like the gown.

"May I be very frank?" he asked.

"Please."

"You're distracting me."

"Now I am the lucky woman."

"From my work," he added.

71

"When does your work finish?" she asked. "When Madeleine is safe in her bed?"

He nodded.

"You do not need to guard her body then?" she asked, eyes wide in mock innocence.

"Now, now," he scolded.

"She's very pretty, yes?"

"In an expensive sort of way, I suppose," he answered.

Marta didn't get it.

"I will let you get back to your work," she said. "But perhaps I will see you later?"

"I have found that this is a world of infinite possibilities," he answered.

When his eyes found Madeleine, she was staring at him.

A while later, Senator Keneally made his way to the front of the room and tapped a spoon against his champagne glass. When the music stopped and the party chatter settled into an expectant quiet, he held out his arm out for Madeleine, who stepped over to stand by his side.

"Madeleine and I," Keneally began, his broad Boston accent stretching the vowel out, "want to thank you all for coming. We're delighted to have had the chance to spend Christmas Eve with all our New York friends. We hope you've enjoyed the party."

He paused for the applause, grinned broadly, and added, "Especially the impromptu poetry reading."

The crowd laughed. Encouraged, Keneally added, "I can only hope that my wife will invite more distinguished poets to parties at the White House . . ."

The crowd laughed and cheered. As Keneally put his arm around Madeleine's shoulders, she said, "Darling, if you ever read any poets who are actually still alive, I'll be delighted to invite them."

"My wife thinks I'm a low-brow!" Keneally announced, and after the laughter subsided, added, "And she's probably right. We went to see some modern art earlier, and it's a good thing that she was there to explain it to me."

The man has genuine charm, Walter thought as he watched the assembled guests. They were drinking him in.

Keneally continued, "I also want to thank those of you who offered your support to our campaign." He paused with the professional timing of a stand-up comedian then said, "And for those who didn't—yet—you can leave your checks with Jimmy on the way out."

Madeleine gave him a gentle elbow in the ribs, and Keneally said quietly, "Seriously, Madeleine and I are warmed and heartened by your support and good wishes.

"A man shouldn't seek high office for what it is, but for what it can do. Nor should the people judge a candidate by what he is, but for what he can do. And that candidate should not just look at his country for what it is, but for what it can be. And there is much that we can do together to make this nation the country that it can be. A nation of opportunity, of justice, of freedom for all its citizens. A nation that will stand as a beacon of freedom not just for its own people, but for all the people of the world.

"That, I think, is the challenge for our generation. As we take the baton to run our part of the race, we must keep our eyes toward the goal and run bravely, and run well."

Walter saw that the guests had settled into complete, enthralled silence. They'd go out tomorrow and work for the man.

And so, Walter thought, would I.

Keneally went on, "Well, I'm sorry I turned this into a

political talk. What I really meant to do was to wish you all, on behalf of Madeleine and Jimmy and myself, a truly merry Christmas and a wonderful New Year. God bless you all."

The sophisticated Manhattanites answered in one voice, "God bless you."

Later, after most of the guests had left—a number of them having slipped an envelope or a check to Jimmy Keneally—the Senator approached Walter.

"I wanted to thank you for the fine job you did," Keneally said. "And I don't think we've actually formally met."

"Walter Withers, Senator. A pleasure."

"Joe Keneally."

"Yes, I know," Walter said as they shook hands.

"Well, Merry Christmas, Walter."

"And to you, Senator."

Keneally whispered, "There'll be a little something extra for you—"

"Wouldn't dream of it, Senator."

"A man of principle, eh?"

"Salaried, anyway."

"I see," Keneally said. "In any case, Merry Christmas again. And I wonder, as a final duty of the evening, if you'd see Mrs. Keneally to her room?"

Madeleine said, "Joe, I—"

"I have a little politicking to do," Keneally said to her. "Brandy, cigars, and deal cutting."

"Joe, it's Christmas Eve," she protested.

"I know. It never stops, does it?" he said. "So Walter, if you'd be so kind . . ."

Keneally kissed Madeleine on the cheek and ushered her onto Walter's elbow.

Outside her room, she said, "Well, good night, Mr. Withers. And thank you."

"I can wait in the hall until the Senator comes up," Walter offered.

She laughed, "No, thank you. It might be a long wait."

"I don't mind."

She lingered in the doorway for a moment, then said, "No. I'll take a pill and go to sleep. And I'm sure Joe's gentlemen from Boston will be up here any moment to keep the world out."

"I'm sure."

"And me in," she sighed. "Good night. Merry Christmas."

"Merry Christmas."

She started to shut the door, then changed her mind.

"How's your dreary Puritan ambience, by the way?" she asked.

"Considerably lightened."

"Then it's been a good party," she said, and closed the door.

Jimmy Keneally approached Walter in the lobby.

"Good work tonight," Jimmy said.

"Thank you."

"I've reserved you a room."

"Thanks, but that won't be necessary. I live in town."

"Yes, I know." Jimmy smiled a lopsided, embarrassed smile. "Would you mind just checking in anyhow, Walter?"

"May I ask why?"

"We need to have a little meeting away from prying eyes," Jimmy said.

And you need a sanitized room, thought Walter.

"So you want me to check in and then take off," he said.

"That's what I had in mind," Jimmy said. Then he added, "Forbes said that you were a team player."

That's me, Walter thought. The team player. He had a bad feeling about this, didn't really like his name being used for other people's subterfuge, even the Keneallys'. But Forbes had apparently made him available, and it was probably better just to do it and then take it up with him.

"All right," Walter said.

"Good man," said Jimmy. "I'll just wait for you in the lobby."

Walter went to the registration desk and checked in.

"Luggage, sir?" the clerk asked after he handed Walter the key.

"I travel light," Walter answered.

"He travels best," the clerk warbled as he took his hand off the bell.

Walter walked over to Jimmy and slipped him the key.

"Anyone asks," Jimmy said, "you slept here. Okay, Walter?"

Ah, duplicity, Walter thought. A condition of a man from which there is no escape. Not even in this best city in the world on the eve of the birth of our Redeemer.

"Sure," Walter said.

"We'll be calling you," said Jimmy as he turned and walked away.

Walter might have thought no more about it, except to believe that the Keneallys were meeting with some New York politico unready to give his public support. But Walter suddenly fancied a solitary drink in the Oak Room before joining the doubtless hysterical party in the Village.

A quiet drink in an old dark bar sounded good, and it

would give him a chance to wish the bartenders a merry Christmas as well. So he trundled off to the venerable Oak Bar to contemplate life, politics, love, and the beauty of a single malt.

Would have enjoyed it, too, except that Joe Keneally was huddled in a dark corner with a few cronies in a cloud of clichéd cigar smoke. And Marta Marlund sat alone at a table across the darkened room. Walter saw Jimmy Keneally walk by her and leave the key on the table.

And he saw Joe Keneally look up and smile.

Walter decided to skip the drink.

The guitar player smiled and nodded as Walter edged his way into The Cellar.

Elvin Page was Anne's sideman on her recordings. He provided the crisp cords around which her voice could swirl, wander off, and then return on his downbeat. Now he was on the small stage doing a solo, his long fingers sliding across the strings and up the scale. He preferred not to use a pick, feeling that he got a better sound with his thick, callused thumb. As always he was sharply dressed, tonight in a rich blue suit with a white shirt and a blood red tie. His fat brown face shone with sweat.

Walter waved as he struggled out of his coat. He looked for Anne in the packed club but didn't see her.

The Cellar was crowded with the denizens of the fringe. Black was the color of the season with the East Coat avant-garde, and the poets, musicians, and artists looked like shadows in the thick haze of cigarette smoke. The group was cosmopolitan, Walter would give them that. Celtic expatriates in tweedy jackets brooded over mugs of ale while trying to seduce romantically emaciated folk types with straight hair and turtlenecks. Smartly dressed Negro jazzmen in dark suits, white shirts, and narrow black ties listened patiently as denimed remnants of the Old Left engaged them in earnest conversation about civil rights. Some artists, their shirts ostentatiously stained with paint, drank cheap wine and eyed the sleek college girls in their black leotards and tights.

The Cellar matched their deliberate drabness. The plaster had been knocked away to reveal bare red brick. A few movie posters—*The Bicycle Thief, Rebel Without a Cause, Jules and Jim*—had been glued to the walls at carefully haphazard angles. The chairs and tables were literally junk, scavenged off the city's trash piles and given a reprieve with a little wood stripper and varnish. The low ceiling was water-stained, the rotten plumbing dripped, and the exposed wiring threatened mass electrocution at any moment. It was the East Coast version of the American underground, and the fact that it was in a basement was just serendipitous symbolism.

Walter shucked his disdain, though, and concentrated on the sound as Elvin Page cut with clean, precise notes through the cacophony of political chatter, pick-up lines, clattering glasses, and the whir of a blender concocting some vile sort of mixed drink.

"Where's the bride?" Mickey Evans asked, noticing Walter's dinner jacket.

"I left her on the cake," Walter answered. He shook the sax player's hand. "Merry Christmas."

"Ho-ho-ho," Evans answered.

Walter had always thought that Evans was the most unlikely musician he'd ever seen, the one you'd never pick out of a lineup if the charge was "jazz saxophone player." He was tall, skinny, blond white guy who came from the sun-baked farmland near Bakersfield. His wrists were big and lumpy, his face weathered from a youth spent plowing, stringing barbed wire, and throwing bales of hay to the cattle. He had picked up the sax for his high school marching band and discovered that he couldn't march and hated high school. But he sure did love that saxophone.

"California," he said to Walter.

"Yes?"

"It's warm there."

Walter looked at Evans's eyes. They were as empty as the desert. The man was stoned on heroin.

"And the sun sets over the ocean," Walter said.

"So?"

"On the East Coast it rises," Walter explained. "You have to get up at dawn to see it."

"Or catch it on your way home," Evans said.

"There's always that," Walter admitted. "Have you seen Anne?"

"She's around someplace."

Walter didn't like her being around someplace. He preferred her under a baby spotlight in a classy room. Or out on a stroll along the river. Or at a quiet dinner for two. Or in bed.

But not lost in the crowd.

It scared him for some reason that he couldn't put his finger on. He got a vodka from the bar and leaned back to listen to Elvin and watch for Anne. Maybe she'd gotten tired of waiting for him and left.

Elvin returned to the melody.

Walter recognized it as "East of the Sun, West of the Moon" just as he spotted Anne edging her way out of the narrow hallway that led to the lavatories and the rear exit. She was chatting to a young woman behind her, a short Negro girl in a leotard and skirt.

Anne spotted him and waved, talked to the girl again, then kissed her on the cheek and started to make her way through the crowd to the bar.

Walter noticed that she was still wearing her nightclub garb, a low-cut red satin dress, but had taken off the usual earrings and necklace. She looked terrific, a devastating blend of innocence and sexuality. She had the performer's glow, too, and must have killed them at the Rainbow Room.

"Looking for a date, sailor?" Anne asked as she sidled up to him.

"Sorry, but I'm meeting someone."

They kissed.

"How are you?" she asked.

"Tired," he answered.

"You're not going to be a party poop, are you?"

"Never let it be said."

Not of Walter "Last Call" Withers, he thought. Who closes the bar, goes out to breakfast, and orders champagne with the orange juice. Who can return a wicked serve, stir a decent martini, and get back for the lob shot. Who knows what evil lurks in the hearts of men.

Talk about your kings of late night.

He whispered, "Let's go to your place."

"Down, boy," she laughed, then added, "But out of curiosity, which did you have in mind, sex or sleep?"

"First one and then the other," he answered. "In no particular order."

"Flattering."

"Ah, well," he said. "Are you singing?"

"I've done sung," she said. "A *très* sweet set with Elvin and Mickey. Mickey was very out tonight."

"Out" of the melody as opposed to "in." Walter had learned some of the jazz jargon from Anne. A musician who played his improvisations fairly close to the melodic line was in; one who took it away from the main tune was out.

"He thinks he's Coltrane already," Anne added.

"He's not Coltrane."

"Nobody is," Anne said. "He's annoying the other musicians, though."

"Why do they play with him?"

"He's tapped into a source for fixings," she answered. "It's hard to get clean needles these days, or so I'm told."

"Well, Mickey is doped up tonight," Walter said.

"Why should tonight be different from any other night?"

"Wrong holiday."

"He'll be riding with Contessa soon," Anne said sadly. She took his arm and laid her head against his shoulder. "Anyway, I'm sorry you missed our set. After three sets for the squares at The Rainbow Room, it was a kick to sing some real jazz."

"I like The Rainbow Room," Walter said. "And the songs that you sing there. But then again, I'm a square."

"Well, you can be a square again on New Year's Eve," she said. "They're giving me a big band for the big night. You'll be there?"

"I'd be nowhere else in the world," Walter said. "Now, how about you buy me a drink?"

She bought him a vodka and tonic and led him to a table near the stage. Elvin finished his solo on a crisp chord and passed the melody off to the bass player, Ronald Henson, a tall, thin, light-skinned Negro who sported a pencil mustache and dressed like an Oxford don in a Harris tweed jacket, twill trousers, and knit tie. Elvin left the stage and went over to the bar ostensibly to get a drink, although Walter recognized this as a way of deflecting attention to the bass solo.

Walter suspected without the slightest animosity that Anne had a thing for Ronald Henson. Indeed, the bass player was movie-star handsome and sophisticated, and

Anne had once observed to Walter that, of all musicians, bass players seemed to make love to their instruments when they were playing. Walter speculated that was because, of all instruments, the bass most resembled a woman's body. And he could easily picture lovemaking as Henson cradled the instrument against his chest and his long fingers alternately plucked and slid across the strings, eliciting long, deep, low moans. Yes, he could easily imagine lovemaking.

As apparently could the drummer, Les Blake, who sat behind his traps with his eyes closed, rubbing his brushes across the cymbals in a sibilant rhythm. Les, who backed up Anne on all her recordings with brush work as soft as a summer kiss. Les, with wiry red hair and thick jowls and a complexion the color of vanilla.

"So how's the royal family?" Anne asked.

"The Keneallys?"

"Who else?"

"She made a charming impression," he answered. "He made a lovely speech."

"You're gushing!"

"I'm not gushing," he said. "Thirty-three-year-old men from Connecticut don't gush. In fact, we are known for our fine sense of understatement."

"Keneally is a bastard."

"So you've said," Walter purred. "Nevertheless I think I'll vote for him."

Anne looked seriously shocked. "Have you forgotten HUAC?"

The aptly named House Un-American Activities Committee, which she pronounced "whack!" What was it that Mort Shal had said? Every time the Russians thrown an American in jail, the committee throws an American in jail to show them they can't get away with it?

He said, "I was overseas during the committee's heyday. Now that I think on it, so were you."

"Okay, how about the Senate Internal Security Committee?" Anne asked. "Keneally sits on that. Not then, darling, *now*. Same thing as HUAC, just a different name."

"Yes, SISC," Walter answered. "Maybe we should call Joe Keneally the Cisco Kid. I can be Pancho."

"I don't think it's funny."

"Apparently not," Walter answered. "Listen, we can nominate Adlai again and make Nixon president."

"It is to puke," Anne said.

"Or Lyndon Johnson," Walter drawled.

"I'll take Adlai."

"And lose."

"Better to lose with Adlai," she said, "then to win with a red-baiting cold warrior like Joe Keneally."

"I'm a cold warrior," Walter said.

"Baloney."

He shrugged, sipped on his drink, and turned his attention to the band. He didn't want to be drawn into a spat with Anne on Christmas Eve.

"Anyway," Anne said, "Keneally's a dog."

"I thought he was a bastard."

"He's a bastard dog."

"Ah."

Anne said, "He's a pale of Jacoby's. He used to hang around the Angel trying to pick up the singers. Apparently he thought that getting laid came with the two-drink minimum."

"Did he try to pick you up?" Walter asked.

"As you pointed out, I've been in Europe."

"Then how do you know?"

"Girl talk," Anne said. "These things get passed around,

you know. When a girl works the clubs, she needs to know who's likely to poke his nose into her dressing room."

"His nose?"

"I was being diplomatic."

"New Year's resolution?"

They sat and listened to the music.

"Are we fighting about something?" she asked after a few moments.

"No, we're fighting about nothing."

"Shall we stop?"

"Absolutely."

They clinked glasses.

Elvin wrapped up the tune with a strum chord. Some people applauded and a few snapped fingers.

Street craft doesn't end at the sidewalk. Walter felt someone watching him, and he used the break in the music to sweep the room with his eyes and smile as if he were enjoying a room full of friends.

"Your pal doesn't like me," he said to Anne.

"Which pal?" Anne asked.

"The one you were talking with when you came in."

"Alicia?"

"She's staring at me,"

"Because you're so gorgeous in your party threads."

Walter didn't think so. It was an angry glare, as if she were asking questions and already didn't like the answers.

"What does Alicia do?" he asked.

"She's a poet."

"Have you known her long?"

"She's around the scene. She waits tables at Good Night."

"Has any of her work been published?" Walter asked. "What's her last name? Maybe I've read her."

Although he hadn't read a poet since Owen and Sassoon, found Eliot incomprehensible, and thought that Pound should have been outright shot as a traitor.

"You're not at work, darling. Stop asking questions."

"Just trying to show an interest," he said.

"You're going to make me jealous if you keep asking about her," Anne said.

He lightened it up. "Well, darling, she is very pretty."

"She is, and if you touch her I'll break your arm," she said sweetly. "Are you ready to go?"

"I was ready to go when I got here."

She gave him a dirty look.

"Sorry, sweetie," he said. "It's just not my crowd."

"It's my crowd," she shot back. "And I didn't mean go home. I have to drop in at a party at Good Night. Oh, look! Is that Sean McGuire?"

Only this time he had a coffee mug in one hand and a rumpled sheet of paper in the other. His pea coat was draped over one arm. He looked sober, almost solemn.

The crowd quieted as McGuire, followed by Mickey Evans, stalked up to the stage.

McGuire shook Elvin's hand, then sat on the bar stool and faced the audience.

"I have a poem for you," he said quietly.

A few beats snapped fingers, inspiring in Walter an urge to snap their fingers in a different sense.

" 'American Fall,' " McGuire said.

Wishful thinking? Walter wondered. But at least it appears to be a written poem.

"In American fall the field from emerald green turns brown," McGuire read.

His sober voice was an improvement, soft and low as opposed to the hoarse stridency of his drunken ranting.

"As windblown stallions gasp for crisp autumnal air."

Evans blew a sharp, high note, then bent it up.

"*And I watch the horses stagger and stumble . . .*"

Another riff from Dantzler.

"*American Fall.*"

Do I detect an actual meter? thought Walter.

"*In the American fall foreign names tumble,*" McGuire continued, "*like cards from the tables on Ellis Island . . .*"

Walter thought Sean looked sad, as if he were considering something precious that he had lost. The denim shirt and chinos didn't look pretentious now. They looked like the clothes of an oversize child.

"*Olszewski, Nomellini, Gonzaga, McCord . . .*"

On Donner, on Dancer on Prancer, on Blitzen, Walter thought. But he wasn't making fun, he was starting to enjoy the poem.

"*Modzelewski, Blanda, Unitas, Rote,*
Foreign names tumble onto American ground
Becoming American as they fall
American Fall."

McGuire raised his mug to Dantzler, who took the cue and launched into a plaintive sob.

"I like it," Anne whispered, "but I don't have the slightest idea what it's about."

"Football," Walter answered.

"Sean McGuire writing about football?!" Anne asked.

I wonder if I'm the only person in the house other than McGuire who knows that he played halfback for Columbia until he broke his leg, Walter thought.

"*I have watched the stallions gallop in the coliseum*
Crooked thumbs down for them and me
Run far but not far enough,
Crossed the line enough to win but not enough to win,
The horse I ride falls short
And we both fall."

American Fall."

He's lost the crowd, Walter thought. They don't get the imagery.

McGuire paused and stared at the page as if he were trying to make out the words. He looked exhausted, neither drunk nor exactly sober, but . . .

Well, *beat*, Walter thought. That was the word for it.

"*But still I love to watch the horses snort the crisp autumnal air,*" McGuire recited.

"*The chargers stomp the dirt and charge*
Back and forth across the tilted field.
I charge with them,
I stomp and snort and run,
But you can never run far enough,
You can never run away
In the American Fall."

McGuire dropped his head and looked at the floor during the confused applause. He leaned over so far that it looked like he was going to topple over and collapse. Then he set the mug on the stage floor, straightened up, and walked out the back way.

And Walter had an idea about what might be frightening Madeleine Keneally.

The acrid smell of marijuana scorched Walter's nose as Anne held the cigarette up to him.

"Boo," she croaked, holding the smoke in her lungs.

He shook his head. "No, thanks."

They were back at her apartment on Washington Square East. Her place was small, invariably described as "cozy" by first-time visitors. Solid oak bookcases stood floor-to-ceiling against three of her living room walls. The fourth had French doors that opened to a small balcony looking out on the Arch of Triumph in Washington Square Park.

From the living room a narrow hallway led off to the small kitchen. A bathroom and two bedrooms came off the hallway. She had converted one of the bedrooms into a studio, where she had an upright piano, a hi-fi system, her records, and disorderly piles of sheet music. Her bed was a four-poster, some of her many hats hanging from the posts. Some Impressionist prints—Anne had a thing for William Merritt Chase—were hung from the off-white walls. Thick blue drapes kept out the sun so that she could sleep into the afternoon when she was working in clubs but not recording.

But now they sat in the living room, trying to find their way into a decent fight.

The fight had really started at the party at Good Night, where Anne often performed after hours, trying out her more avant-garde stuff for "the boys and the girls."

"What?" Walter had asked the first time she had used the expression.

"Come on," she'd said. "The boys and the girls. The boys who go with boys and the girls who go with girls."

"Ah."

"Ah," she'd mocked, enjoying the fact that he'd seemed nonplused.

Good Night was a two-story redbrick on West Fourth Street, and Walter had known it when it was still a leftover speakeasy called The Peppermill. The first floor was a conventional bar with a small stage—more a platform, really—just large enough for a piano and a singer. But the second floor was anything but conventional. Up the back stairway—an architectural fact which led to many a bad joke—was a large room that served only the boys and the girls and their invited guests.

The upstairs was presided over by a distinguished old Southern queen by the name of Jimmy Benoit, who was the ostensible owner. The truth, Walter knew, was that Good Night, like every other "fag joint" in the Village, was owned by the Mafia.

The peculiar economics of vice, Walter thought. Be it gambling, prostitution, drugs, or sodomy, whatever bit of human behavior society doesn't want to acknowledge, it is forced underground, where the Mob takes it over and adds a surcharge.

As did the vice squad. Walter knew that the cops were well paid not to go up the stairs at Good Night.

Walter and Anne had trooped over to the club shortly after McGuire finished his poem. They began one of those longtime-couple silent fights from the moment they climbed the stairs, because she immediately fell to hugging and kissing everyone in the room, and he repaired to a martini and a stance of aloof courtesy.

It wasn't the predominant homosexuality of the guests, or the fact that some of them were in drag—and very good drag at that—or even the open kissing between men.

Yes, it was, he admitted to himself. It bothered him. Odd, because it had not bothered him in Europe, not after stints in Amsterdam and Copenhagen, certainly not after his own expeditions through the male brothels of Hamburg, shopping for young talent with which to bait the honey traps.

But homosexuality seemed somehow un-American to him. Not in the sense of *anti*-American, certainly, and perhaps *non*-American was the more accurate phrase. It seemed more of a European vice, somehow at odds with America's aggressive fertility. Perhaps because it's more open in Europe, more accepted, there was an Old World lassitude about it. But driven underground here, homosexual Americans had the slightly hysterical energy of the confined. Walter knew the godawful pressure of keeping secrets, the constricting necessity of hiding yourself so deeply that even when you're safe you let it out only in short, manic bursts.

That clichéd homosexual shrillness, Walter decided, was the whistling of steam from the boiling pot.

And the pot was whistling merrily this Christmas Eve.

The room itself was beautifully done in the Art Deco style that was Walter's personal favorite. A long bar dominated one wall, the mandatory banquettes were upholstered in plush black, as were the chromed tables, and an enormous mirror ran floor to ceiling on the brick wall. Pin-spot lighting created an interior chiaroscuro effect, highlighting the tiny stage in front of the mirror and the tables, shading the booths and the small door behind the mirror that led to the infamous baths and steam rooms, in which, as Walter imagined anyway, all manners of faggotry were indulged. The place had the feel of an elegant speakeasy, and it was every bit as done up for Christmas as was the party room at the Plaza.

Only more tastefully, Walter thought, laughing at his stereotype. But it was accurate. The white, black, and silver Art Deco motif had been carried into Christmas with tinsel, aluminum Christmas trees, and black cardboard silhouettes of Santa's sleigh, various reindeer, toy soldiers, and dolls. An elaborate model railroad was set up on a long buffet table in the center of the room, and the locomotive and its cars chugged merrily around the trays of meats, cheeses, breads, and salads. The coal car carried olives.

Nor were the assembled celebrants any less sparkling. Unconstrained by a black-tie dress code, they were a stylish motley, from the dark tweeds of the writers—Walter recognized one of the year's hottest novelists and a powerful critic—to loose silk shirts of emerald green or fire engine red over tight black chinos favored by the stage crowd. A few wore ties, more sported ascots or neckerchiefs, most were open collars.

The lesbians dressed more formally. There were several dinner jackets replete with black tie, one tuxedo, and even some ruffled shirts. A few dressed like English scholars with frumpy dresses and sensible shoes.

"Are you Anne's Walter?"

A tall, thin older man took Walter's hand and asked the question.

"I am Anne's Walter," Walter answered. "Walter Withers."

"Jules Benoit," the man said. "I am so glad that you've finally mounted these stairs."

"Anne loves the place," Walter said.

"And the reverse is true as well."

"She'll be glad to hear that."

"Walter, you're very welcome here," Jules said. "We just ask that you be discreet."

"Of course."

I am in fact known for my discretion, Mr. Benoit.

"I'm surprised Paulie's not here, though," Walter added.

He enjoyed watching the skin pull a little tighter on Jules's face.

"Paulie never comes upstairs," Jules said. "How do you know Mr. Martino?"

Walter shrugged an everybody-who's-anybody-knows-Paulie shrug. Paulie Martino was a soldier in the D'Annunzio family, a bookie who laundered money by investing in places like Good Night. And it was a good thing to let Jules know just how discreet he could be.

"You're not one of the boys," Jules mused. "Are you a gambler, Walter?"

"I place a football bet from time to time," Walter said. "But I hope you'll be discreet about that."

"Well, enjoy the party, Walter."

"I like the train."

Jules sighed. "I just go crazy at Christmas time."

The conversation that drifted back and forth in front of Walter was electic. He eavesdropped on the usual New York artsy chatter about books and plays, restaurants and bars, who was sleeping with whom, who was no longer sleeping with whom, and who was about to sleep with whom.

He was surprised to overhear the essayist he'd seen at the Plaza discussing the upcoming Giants game with a younger chap who had the look of a Broadway actor.

"Sports are the essential ingredient to a democratic society," the essayist remarked. "They're the great leveler. Everyone can talk about a football game, more importantly, everyone does. Rich, poor, left, right, hetero, homo. It's an icebreaker for democratic discourse."

This led to a spirited debate on whether a football game was a homoerotic event, during which discussion Walter observed that most football players were not, after all, homosexuals and was corrected by the essayist, who informed him that he might be surprised.

"I mean, good Lord—" the essayist said. "What's your name?"

"Walter."

"Good Lord, Walter," the essayist said, "there you have an entire line of men squatting in presentation position, and the quarterback reaches under, into the *crotch* of one of them, and emerges with the *ball*, Walter, and then they all try to achieve penetration of the other men's line. I mean, good Lord, Walter, it's suppressed homosexuality

sufficient to make Freud! And—and please don't misinterpret this, but don't I know you from somewhere?"

"Possibly the Plaza."

"*Definitely* the Plaza, and you're the clever one who
handled Sean McGuire," the essayist said. Then added,
"Speaking of football players . . ."

"Anyway," Walter said, "who do you like in the
game?"

"Darling, I like them all, but if you're asking me who I
want to win, then it's the Giants. Speaking of Freud . . ."

So Walter had a good time, except that he could not figure out why Anne was sending him icy stares. In fact, the
better time he seemed to be having, the icier the stares became. And when she was called upon to sing, she took an
almost savage glee in announcing that she would only
perform a duet with *her* boyfriend.

He picked up this gauntlet and joined her at the piano.

It was a silly little number they'd started doing one wet
night in Beaulieu sur-Mer, when he'd joined her on stage
to prove that he couldn't sing, and this night at Good
Night he did the same thing, providing the "doop-doo-de-
doops" under her head line.

The crowd loved it when she sang the opening.

> "*Why don't you come and join the group?
> It's better than being a party poop.*"

and Walter responded with.

> "*Doop doo de doop
> do de doop do dee doop de doop*"

with a Stan Laurel expression and a deadbeat, inept little soft
shoe. And they were positively charmed when Anne trilled,

93

"Say you love me, really love me, say you love me true"

and Walter answered with an off-key but heartfelt

"I love you."

Although Anne was anything but charmed, Walter knew. He could feel her dagger eyes underneath her performer's facade even as the number finished and he took a blushing bow.

And when out in the street, he'd raised his arms to the night sky and hollered, "God, I love this city!" and she'd said nothing, he knew she'd find some revenge for whatever it was he had done to make her mad.

He didn't have to wait long. The second they'd taken off their coats, she'd taken the stick of tea from her purse, lit it up, and sat on the floor.

He tried not to let it get to him, but it did.

"Is this a new habit?" Walter asked, nodding at the marijuana cigarette.

They both thought that he looked ridiculous, standing there like some indignant bluestocking Sunday school teacher.

"It's not a habit," she said. "Try some."

"Where did you get it?"

"Alicia gave it to me."

"Alicia," he said. "Is that what you were doing when I came into the club? Out in the alley smoking tea with Alicia?"

She took another drag, then teased, "Yes, Aleeesha. I know what you're thinking, Walter. Exotic, oversexed Negresses with voodoo potions leading innocent white girls into—"

"That's ridiculous."

"Watcher Withers," she croaked, holding the smoke in her lungs. "That's what your name should be, 'Watcher' instead of 'Walter.'"

"And why is that?" he asked, although he knew.

"Because you stand outside and watch," she said. "No, not outside, *above*. You stand above it all, in all your moral superiority, and sneer at us poor, carnal mortals who *do* the things you watch."

In vino veritas, he thought. In marijuana, what?

"What, may I ask, have I not done now to provoke this assault?" Walter asked.

She shook her head back and forth. "That's just it, that's just it. You just did it. You use words, your snotty, condescending, superior intellect to keep people away, to distance yourself so you can have the space to look down and watch."

"I see."

"And sneer," she added. "You're so damn establishment! You leave that nouveau riches, fascist trash at the Plaza and come down to where I live and sneer at my friends."

"I'm not sure that the Keneallys' *riches* are all that nouveau," he said. "Nor do I think they had anything to do with either Mussolini or Hitler. And I wasn't sneering."

"You were sneering on the inside. Only you're too damn polite to do it openly," Anne said. "You sneer by being even more polite, more charming, more witty, more perfect. Saint Walter."

"Isn't that Saint Watcher?"

"It's even your job," she said. "You watch people. That's your job, to watch people."

He sighed and said, "I will plead guilty to working for a living, yes."

"Don't you hate your job?"

"As a matter of fact, I like it."

"Watching people," she insisted.

"That what's I do," he answered.

"Take a break," she said, offering the marijuana again. "Join the party."

"It isn't lit," he said.

"So light it."

He'd left his lighter in his coat, so he grabbed a book of matches from a bowl on the side table. The matchbook was pink with a silhouette of a medieval knight on horseback, lance a-tilting. The words GOOD NIGHT were emblazoned in a black arc.

He lit the match and held it to the cigarette. She sucked it until the tip glowed and then handed it to him.

He inhaled deeply and handed it back to her.

"Happy?" he asked. "Merry Christmas? I love you again, Walter?"

"I love you very much."

She handed the stick back to him.

"Why does this mean anything to you?" he asked, inhaling on the cigarette.

"Because you hide behind doing everything right," she answered. "You hide behind your self-control."

"I don't know that self-control is such a bad thing, Anne."

"Please don't be a saint, Walter," she said. "I get afraid that I don't measure up."

Saint Judas, he reflected, thinking of Joe Keneally and Marta Marlund in bed. And Michael Howard and H. Benson. Madeleine Keneally and Sean McGuire. And Anne. And himself.

He sat on the floor beside her, held her by the shoulders, looked into her face, and said, "*Je t'aime*."

"*Je t'aime aussi*. But I'm afraid of letting you down."

"You couldn't."

"You don't know me, I—"

He put his finger to her lips and shook his head.

"It's Christmas," he said, "and soon it will be the new year. The time for new beginnings and fresh starts."

"Do you think so?"

"I never quite know what I think," he said, "only what I hope."

For you, and me, and God and the forgiveness of sins.

When they went to bed, she took him inside herself quickly, with few preliminaries and little foreplay. When she kissed him it was wet and deep, and she inhaled his breath as if she were trying to suck life . . . not *out* of him exactly, never that . . . but *from* him. And when she came, she turned her gray eyes to his and stared as if she were trying to find an answer to an unasked question.

He lay awake afterward for a long time, thinking of her and Christmas and the new year, and he stroked the golden down on her forearm and watched her sleep.

For you, and me, and God and the forgiveness of sins.

CHAPTER TWO

Blue Monk

Thursday, December 25

Walter woke up early on Christmas morning after a short, bad night's sleep. He slipped out of bed, put on a robe, and from the stoop retrieved the pamphlet that was masquerading during the strike as the *Times*. He had his first glorious cigarette of the day as he brewed a pot of coffee and looked at the news.

I must be getting world-weary, he thought as he scanned the headlines, because I am weary of this world. Gromyko was threatening to blow the so-called Free World to smithereens over Berlin, and the Pentagon was boasting that we'd have the Atlas intercontinental ballistic missile ready "for combat use" in a year. Ike claimed that was proof that there was no missile gap, Keneally said it was proof that there was, and Walter was put in mind of another Mort Sahl bon mot, that we should give the Russians all of our scientific secrets so that *they'd* be two years behind. In a more positive vein, the barricades had been taken down in Jerusalem "under the brilliant December sun" in honor of the holy day. Walter was pleased to note that Israeli policemen and Jordanian soldiers "mingled casually in No Man's Land," but was bemused that the only thing that allowed for Jews and Moslems to "mingle" was a Christian holy day evolved from German pagans.

Well, I am world-weary, indeed, and the barricades will doubtless be back up tomorrow, Walter thought.

And speaking of up . . .

"Good morning," he said to Anne as she trundled into the kitchen. "You're up early."

"Has Santa come?" she asked. Her eyes were puffy slits, her hair a tangled mess, and her robe could have been charitably described as frumpy.

"Come and gone," Walter said. "But he made coffee."

"Darling Santa," she mumbled. "I always knew there was a reason I liked that jolly old fat man."

"Why *are* you up so early?"

"Drive upstate," she mumbled. "See the parents."

"You're sure about Greenwich?"

"Sure."

Walter poured her a cup of coffee and laced it heavily with cream and sugar until it resembled *café au lait*. Then he found a loaf of French bread in the pantry, sliced it lengthwise, then across, laved it with butter, and handed her half. She sat down at the counter, dipped the bread into her coffee, and seemed to come to a little bit.

"Merry Christmas, darling," she said.

"Merry Christmas."

"Shall we open presents?"

"Let's do."

They sat on the floor in the living room and looked at the presents they had set under the small tree earlier in the week. She had carefully wrapped his in shiny red paper with big, hand-tied bows. He had relied on the kind ministrations of wrappers at Saks, Bonwit's, Bergdorf's, and Brentano's.

"You first," he said.

"We'll take turns."

He gave her a pair of pearl drop earrings, a long silk scarf, a pair of winter gloves, a brown man's fedora, two of the large pins that were the current fashion, copies of Ferlinghetti's *A Coney Island of the Mind* and Cheever's *The Housebreaker of Shady Hill* and a renewal to her subscription to *The New Republic*. Her gifts to him were a tweed sports jacket, a money clip, a sweater, a subscription to *Sports Illustrated*, and record albums *Mahler's First Symphony, Coltrane and Monk, The Modern Jazz Quarter*, and *Ahmad Jamal at the Pershing*, which she said was the jazz recording of the year.

Something else: a reel-to-reel tape.

"What's this?" he asked.

"Some cuts from my sessions," she said shyly. "I wanted you to have a tape, because some of them aren't commercial enough to make it on the album. I hope you like it."

"I'm delighted."

She looked at the gifts stacked on the floor.

"We're certainly conventional," she said, "for a couple of bohemians."

"*You're* a bohemian."

"And you're the corporate man," she answered. "I'm sorry we fought last night."

"Me, too."

She said, "I think it's being back in America. The pressure to conform sharpens our differences."

"Are we in America?" Walter asked. "I thought we were in New York."

"New York's not America?" she asked.

"It's a magical isle in a sea of conformity."

"Is it?"

"It can be."

"I don't know."

He leaned over and pulled the knot of her robe. It opened and he reached for the center of her and parted her legs just enough to touch her there.

"It can be," he repeated.

He gently pushed her down, and the sound of Christmas wrapping crumpling underneath her sounded like the crackling of a fire as they made love.

"You look tired, Walter," his mother said as she passed him a plate of turkey. "Have you been getting enough sleep?"

Mothers, Walter thought, are the one constant in an otherwise unpredictable world. And to tell the truth, Mother, I woke up at Anne's, kissed her on the cheek, threw on my rumpled dinner clothes, found a Jewish taxi driver, and went home to take a shower and a shave. Then I picked out a decent Christmas suit, got the M.G. out of the garage, and violated all the speed laws of two states to get here for a sherry before dinner.

But he said, "Yes, Mother. Why, do I look tired?"

His sister Elizabeth rolled her eyes.

"And how is Anne?" Barbara Withers asked. "Are you still seeing her?"

The maternal radar. Subtle, accurate, deadly.

"Just last night, as a matter of fact," Walter answered.

His brother-in-law Roger, irritating even by brother-in-law standards, actually smirked into his mashed potatoes. The jealousy of the shackled man, Walter thought. On the receiving end of my sister's sharp leash hand.

"Too bad you didn't bring her along with you," Elizabeth said.

"She's spending the day with her family," said Walter. So you'll have to find other entertainment.

"And where are they?" his mother asked.

"Somewhere upstate."

"Well, we'd love to see her," Mrs. Withers said with benign insincerity. Mrs. Withers didn't dislike Anne, not at all, but she simply couldn't see her son with a nightclub singer. Even though he had become a private investigator.

Barbara Withers had always fulfilled the role of a patrician wife gracefully. Included in this responsibility was the obligation to *age* gracefully. Since her husband's death some five years earlier and the additional burden of family leadership, she had picked up some of Sam Withers' gravitas, without, however, his acerbic temper. On this Christmas morning her snow white hair was perfectly coiffed, her gray dress svelte, the predictable strand of pearls no less stylish for being predictable.

Barbara Withers shared with her husband the belief that people had a right to expect certain things from other people, that otherwise society was impossible and "we all might as well just climb back into the trees and throw fruit at one another."

Barbara Withers also knew what was expected of a patrician Connecticut wife and more so of a patrician Connecticut widow.

"A wife," she had once told her family, "may flirt at the country club Christmas party. A widow may not—it might be taken seriously."

So Barbara Withers knew that a mother may hint to her thirty-three-year-old son that he is having an affair with the wrong woman, but she must never come out and say so or even ask. That sort of direct interference may be expected well south of the Mason-Dixon line, but certainly not in suburban Greenwich. Besides, she had refrained from asking her son too many questions since the day Sam had taken her aside and told her that their son had entered government service but that it was best simply to tell friends that young Walter was "in business."

"How's the private eye business?" Roger asked, again with a smirk. He was the assistant principle at the local high school. That, coupled with Elizabeth's trust fund, allowed them to live comfortably, and he never bothered to hide his smug amusement at Walter's being a "private eye."

Walter was tempted sometimes to point out to Roger that his principal occupation in life was to contribute sperm for Elizabeth's principal occupation in life, which was dressing up their three children like department store mannequins. The kids, Roger Jr., Eleanor, and Margaret, had gotten the hint and pretty much behaved like plastic children, although they could be amusing and even charming when their parents allowed them to be kids.

"As the name would indicate, it's private," Barbara answered for him. "Would you pass the potatoes please, Roger?"

Which was New Englandese for *We do not discuss what Walter does for a living. Not then, not now, not ever.* A bit hard on dinner conversation, perhaps, but it comes with the trust fund.

We are good at secrets, Walter thought of his family. We do them well. We have not only the New Englander's innate regard for privacy but also the experience of two generations of covert service, which means by necessity also a covert life. He had only heard about his own father's World War II exploits as rumors during his own training. The Company veterans hinted about it, about Withers Sr. and manipulation of Spanish currency to make sure that country could never even think about getting off its back and joining its fascist soul mates against the Allies.

So when his mother said, "It's nice to have you home for Christmas, Walter," he knew that she was welcoming him home from his war in Europe.

A Cold War perhaps, but still a war, Walter thought. One comes home without medals or commendations, but with a résumé cut from whole cloth and phony references ready to back it up.

Even their house seemed to keep secrets, Walter thought, seeing it anew with a veteran's perspective. Indeed, it had been built in the days when a house was designed to keep the world out, not let it in. There were no picture windows, no sliding glass doors, no patios for the house in which he had grown up. No, the Withers home was an old, solid, two-story rectangle with solid doors and a stone foundation. A house safe for secrets.

"And it's nice to be home, Mother," Walter answered.

They passed the potatoes around, and the turkey, the dressing, the peas, and the carrots. Then there was the pumpkin pie, the apple cobbler, and the plate of Christmas cookies, and they cleared the table and did the dishes themselves, because Barbara would not let the help leave their families on Christmas Day.

Then they repaired to the living room, where Roger reengineered the fire while Barbara settled in with a cup of tea, and exchanged presents. The kids had already opened theirs in the morning, of course, except for ones from Grandma and Uncle Walter.

As usual, Uncle Walter had combed Manhattan for the messiest and noisiest presents possible. He had spent happy hours in Schwartz's choosing gifts that were bound to cause the maximum disturbance and chaos at the Kenner household, and now he was slyly delighted at the expression on Elizabeth's face as her children opened up the drums, cap guns, three Hoola Hoops, a You Can Be a

Painter kit, a Kid Detective fingerprint kit, and a chemistry set that veritably warbled of stubborn, unsavory aromas, and floor-refinishing bills. To the thrilled cries of "Thank you, Uncle Walter!" he responded with a modest smile, shrugs, and "Well, I just hope you get a lot of use out of it," as Roger gave him disapproving looks.

He gave Roger some very good pipe tobacco from Dunhills, his sister perfume from Sakes, and his mother an antique pin he'd found in the Village, a copy of *Breakfast at Tiffany's*, and a scarf.

As for Uncle Walter, he received some argyle socks "for those gum shoes" from Roger and Elizabeth, a portable chess set from the kids, and a cashmere blazer from his mother.

"Looks like Batista's finished," Roger observed after the gifts had been exchanged and the kids had settled into the serious business of examining their new possessions. "It looks like Castro's going to waltz right into Havana . . . or should I say 'samba'?"

"And you disapprove, Roger?" Walter asked.

"Of Castro?" Roger asked, giving Walter his very best wry, pedagogical eyebrow. "The man's a communist."

"More of a socialist," Walter said.

"Same thing."

"In either case, so what?" Walter said.

"Are you turning pink on us, Walter?" Roger teased.

"I think communism is a lovely idea," Walter said.

"Good God, Walter . . ."

"He's teasing you, Roger," Elizabeth said.

"No," Walter said. "I really do think it's a lovely idea. Or ideal, I should say. I think it's a tragedy that it's not practicable."

"Well, which is it?" Roger asked, his lips twitching in irritation. "Are you for or against it?"

"Communism?"

"Yes."

Because he knew that it would annoy Roger, Walter answered, "Both. I think that it's a beautiful ideal that won't work because it flies in the face of human nature, more's the pity."

Roger assumed the demeanor of a headmaster browbeating a recalcitrant middle-school boy and asked, "Just what aspects of human nature do you object to?"

Walter gave the question some serious thought, then said, "Selfishness."

"Selfishness?" Roger repeated.

"Yes," Walter said. "Simple greed. An absence of Christian charity."

"Communists are atheists, Walter," Roger patiently explained with a sidelong glance of amused condescension to his good wife.

"Nevertheless," Walter answered, "if Christ were to come back today, there's no question in my mind that he'd be at least a socialist, if not a raving Trotskyite."

"Walter!" his mother gasped, although he could tell that she was thoroughly enjoying herself.

Elizabeth said, "Your son spends a few nights in Greenwich Village and turns into Dorothy Day."

"Walter would never make a Catholic," Mrs. Withers said. "Cheap wine gives him a headache."

"What's wrong with Dorothy Day?" Walter asked.

"She's a Catholic and a communist," Elizabeth said.

"But communists are atheists," Walter said mildly. "Roger said so."

"I did and they are," Roger insisted.

"Have you dug your bomb shelter yet?" Walter asked.

His mother gave him a censorious look.

"We're putting one in," Roger said seriously. When he

saw Walter's amused smile, he said, "We are! And it's a prudent idea, Walter! You should have one, too."

"I live in an apartment building," Walter answered. "But I'm sure you'll invite me into yours."

"I wouldn't be so sure," Roger muttered.

Later, when the Kenners were loading their dubious loot into the station wagon and Walter had a private moment with his mother, he asked her, "Are you disappointed in me?"

She looked startled and answered, "Not at all. Of course not."

"In my occupation, I mean," Walter said. "Are you disappointed I didn't join Father's firm?"

She laid a maternal hand over his and said, "Walter, your father knew that he was a very strong, very successful man, and it worried him. Not for himself, but for his children. He worried that you and Elizabeth would be afraid that you could never match up to him. Your father was your father. He was very proud of you. So am I. Is something wrong?"

"No, nothing."

"You're not letting that foolish Roger get to you, are you?" she laughed.

"A little bit," he admitted.

"He doesn't know that there's a world beyond his nose. But you shouldn't bait him the way you do."

"I know, but I can't resist," Walter said. "Why don't you come into the city soon? Sardi's and the theater? I'll get tickets to *Sunrise at Campobello*."

"A play about FDR?" She recoiled in mock horror. "Your father would spin."

"*Flower Drum Song*, then."

"Sounds wonderful, either one."

"It's a date?"

"After the holidays."

He gave her a kiss and a hug, said his good-byes to sister, brother-in-law, nieces and nephew, hopped into his car, and went back to work.

The Howard home was new, one of the recent generation of suburban designs that aspired to be more than tract housing. The house was long and low, one sprawling floor with large picture windows, a parking bay, and a two-car garage. The house looked expensive, looked like a big down payment and a hefty mortgage. On the other hand, Howard made a good salary at American Electronics.

The family was out in the front yard.

Walter could watch them easily from where he was parked, across the street and a little down from the house.

He had driven over to Darien from Greenwich because it was close and this was a good opportunity to look at the house and maybe get a glimpse of the family without using up half a day commuting.

The kids wore shiny snowsuits. The little boy's was pulled over what looked like a new football helmet, and he clutched a football in his arms as he waddled around his father toward a goal line of imagined glory. The little girl had several big dolls and an enormous plastic horse piled onto a sled and was trying to give them all a ride. One of the dolls kept falling off.

Mrs. Howard was getting it all on the 8mm film camera. She could get Michael and the boy to stop and wave, but the little girl was stubborn in her concentration and wouldn't look up.

To Walter's surprise, Mrs. Howard was a looker, a really handsome woman with dark brown hair, full lips, and a striking face. What is it, Walter wondered, that she can't or won't give him . . . or he can't ask . . . that sends him to 322 West Twenty-first on those secret afternoon jaunts?

And she doesn't know, Walter thought. That was clear when she walked over to her husband and put her arm through his and rested her head on his shoulder as they watched their children play. She was smiling and laughing, believing that her happiness was safe.

This suburban idyll, Walter thought. This new American dream, neither city nor country but a banal melange of the two. A society connected by television and automobile and little else except the desperate delusion fostered by the tube that we all want the same thing: a house in the suburbs.

Or perhaps I'm the deluded one, he thought, clinging to my fantasy of a New York that no longer exists, that's being choked out of existence by the ever thickening suburban sprawl.

A few more years and the clubs will be dead. The customers who once lived in town and would stop in for a quick drink, a couple of songs, and a few laughs now live in the 'burbs. And it's a long drive, parking, and maybe a baby-sitter, so it's easier just to turn on the television and watch the same performers who used to play the clubs ply their trade for Jack Paar or Steve Allen or Joe Pine instead. The cabaret has become the living room—or what's the dreadful expression Elizabeth and Roger have: the "family room"? And when the clubs die out, I suppose I'll be one of the few mourners at the wake. The rest of America will be in their suburban bomb shelters, sitting in the televised glow of the seemingly endless parade of cowboy shows.

In the meantime my magical isle sinks into the sunset.

So here sits Mrs. Howard, neither city mouse nor country mouse, and her husband a suburban mouse by night and a city mouse by day, and he has his own city mouse tucked away in a secret city nest.

And here sit I, watching her.

Merry Christmas, Mrs. Howard, Walter thought.

And Merry Christmas to me.

He sank down in his seat and waited for them to go back inside. When they did, he pulled out and headed back for the city.

It was dark when he got back to Manhattan.

He garaged the car, went up to his apartment, and opened the present from Forbes and Forbes. He poured a stiff measure of twelve-year-old scotch onto some ice cubes, put some Chopin on the hi-fi, and sat down to do some seriously self-indulgent brooding.

Walter's apartment had the pristine look of a place in which the inhabitant didn't spend much time. It had a fairly large sitting room with a double-windowed view to Thirty-sixth Street, a deep-cushioned sofa that his mother had picked up and Walter had duly accepted, two matching wing-back chairs and an oak coffee table, all of which sat on a rectangular Persian carpet of faded reds, blues and golds. One of the bone white walls contained a floor-to-ceiling bookcase, the shelves of which Walter had re-arranged to hold his new Webcor hi-fi system and his blossoming collection of jazz albums from Prestige, Blue Note, Riverside—and Anne's label—Verve. He had them alphabetized—Basie, Blanchard, Blakey, Coltrane, Davis, Ellington—and wrapped in special plastic liners that he purchased from a serious little shop near Sheridan Square. The bookcase even held a few books: Robert Ruark's *The Old Man and the Boy*, Hemingway's *The Sun Also Rises*, Maugham's *Of Human Bondage*, and the complete, and to

Walter's mind tragically truncated, works of F. Scott Fitzgerald.

But except for these few well-leafed volumes, Walter cheerfully admitted that he wasn't much of a reader. He preferred magazines, especially the photographic ones, and his magazine rack spilled over with old numbers of *Life, Look, Time,* and especially *Sports Illustrated*. He had a subscription to *The New Yorker*, enjoyed the cartoons and a few of the short stories, picked up *The Atlantic Monthly* when the whim struck, and had lately taken to buying the new *National Review*, because although it annoyed Anne to no end, Bill Buckley was a fellow Yalie and by far the wittiest writer in New York since Robert Benchely and a good guy to have a drink with at the White Horse.

The door to the left gave access to a narrow kitchen, a classic bachelor kitchen with a barely used stove and never used oven, a white porcelain sink, and a brand-new Frigidaire—Walter always cringed at the name, it brought to mind some unresponsive French woman—that at this particular moment contained a dozen eggs, two sticks of butter, a bottle of orange juice, three fifths of Stolny vodka, and several bottles of precious Scandinavian aquavit. The cabinets were filled with neatly lined rows of the new glasses and dishes he had purchased on his return to the States, a box of corn flakes, enough wineglasses for a small party, and the few French champagne flutes that had survived the transatlantic shipping.

His bed and bathroom were on the other side of the sitting room. Walter figured that he spent most of his scant time at home in one or the other. The bed was basic, a wood-frame job with an oak headboard that contained a shelf and two small cabinets. The walls were papered with some subtle print that his mother had selected to match the royal blue bedspread and pillowcases that she had also selected.

The bathroom floor had octagonal black-and-white tiles, an old white sink, and a shower-bath, although Walter had never used the bath. His medicine cabinet, behind the shaving mirror, contained shaving cream, a bottle of Old Spice, a safety razor with Schick blades, some Band-Aids, a stiptic pencil, a bottle of Bayer aspirin, Listerine, Vitalis, the all-essential packets of Alka-Seltzer with the drawing of the smart-ass little cretin who never had a hangover but smirked at yours, a toothbrush, and a tube of Colgate.

The apartment was tidy because Walter had a lady who came in once a week to basically straighten up after Anne, and because Walter was rarely there. He was up to work early, out late socializing, and spent most weekends down in the Village with Anne.

But on this somewhat melancholy Christmas night he was on his third scotch and had just resolved to join Albert Schweitzer in Africa when the doorbell rang.

"I got your address from the desk clerk at the Plaza," Madeleine Keneally said. "I hope you don't mind."

She was wearing a bright red coat and a black beret. She looked stunningly beautiful standing there in the hallway.

"I brought you a present," she said. She held out the package like an offering.

"Would you like a drink?" he asked as she took off her coat. He hung it in the closet and she sat on the sofa.

"Have you been drinking, Mr. Withers?"

"Yes, and please call me Walter," he answered. "Should I open his now?"

It was a box of Godiva chocolates. Doubtless someone had given it to her and it was all she could think to bring.

"She's beautiful," Madeleine said sadly. "And very sexy, like a movie star."

"Who?"

Her eyes got angry. "Your Marta."

"I'm not so sure she's my Marta," he said.

"Is she wonderful?"

"What do you mean?" he asked.

"You know what I mean."

"Chopin's nocturnes," he said, nodding his head toward the hi-fi speakers. "Do you like them?"

They sat and listened to the music for a few moments.

"How did you get away on Christmas day?" he asked.

"I just said I was going to give Walter Withers a present," she said. "Everyone thought it was a wonderful idea."

"Did the Senator?"

She looked puzzled. "Yes. Why have you been drinking, Walter?"

"I find Christmas night rather sad."

"All the presents have been opened and here you are all alone?" she asked.

"Something like that," he said. "Why are you really here, Mrs. Keneally?"

"Madeleine."

"Why are you really here, Madeleine?"

"I told you," she said.

Please don't be here to ask me questions about your husband and Marta Marlund. I am too drunk to lie but not drunk enough to tell the truth.

"Maybe I wanted to hear you say that I was a nice person again," said Madeleine.

"You're a nice person again," he said. "And maybe you wanted to tell me about you and Sean McGuire."

She bit her lip. "Is it so obvious?"

"Don't worry," he said. "Only the Shadow knows."

He got up, went to the kitchen, and opened a decent bottle of red wine. He poured a glass for her, another two fingers of whiskey for himself, and came back into the sitting room.

"It hasn't had time to breathe," he said, handing her the wine. "The booze notwithstanding, please don't mistake me for a priest."

"I didn't come for absolution."

Nevertheless, she told him all about it.

She had been an art student when they met, come to the city to escape the castle tower, to shake her young limbs free of the golden chains for a while. Shake them she did, slumming at being bohemian, shifting from Smith College teas to ratty coffee houses, from Newport drawing rooms to Village pads. To Sean McGuire's bed.

"I loved him," she whispered to Walter. "He was handsome and dangerous and didn't play tennis. We had our affair on bare mattresses in borrowed lofts."

"I really don't want to hear the—"

"And then he got in a car and left and broke my heart, and I felt like a fool," she said. "When Sean came back—two years later—I was with Joe, but he wanted me back. I told him it was over. He said he loved me. I told him that I was in love with Joe. When he showed up last night . . . I'm afraid of him."

"Have you told the Senator?"

She shook her head. "I'm afraid he suspects," she said. "If he *knew* I'd had an affair with Sean, I don't think he could stand to stay with me."

Walter was tempted to tell her the truth about Marta but decided against it. Neither she nor Keneally would appreciate the symmetry.

She added, "And I'm afraid of what he'd do."

"To you?" Walter asked.

"To Sean," she said. "I'm afraid Joe would beat him up, or—"

"Have him beaten up?" Walter asked.

Or worse, he thought.

Madeleine started, "And then I'm afraid . . ."

"What?"

"I'm ashamed of being afraid of this . . ."

"You're afraid," Walter said, "of this bit of your past catching up with you."

She nodded.

He continued, "Because there's no such thing as a private life for you anymore. If the Senator wins the nomination—and we both think that he will—then you'll be exposed to the scrutiny of not only the press but—"

"The FBI."

"Funny you should say that, because they were the next letters out of my mouth."

As a good CIA man, even a prematurely retired one, Walter despised the FBI. A turf battle, he supposed—two rival colonies of ants fighting over the same pebbles—but he detested Hoover personally. While both agencies had similar methods (after all, who was the great Scandinavian Pimp and Deadly Recruiter to cavil over sexual blackmail?), Walter believed that CIA at least tried to serve the country, whereas the FBI served first and foremost the Director himself, the loathsome toad. And Jedgar (for this is how Walter usually referred to the revered Director) would have a ball with knowledge like this, Walter thought. He would be in a frenzied transport of delight as to whom to blackmail and how. He could keep Keneally from even seeking the nomination, or he could let Keneally run, let Keneally win, and then own him.

Which is, after all, why I am probably still registered as a guest at the Plaza.

"Hoover hates Joe," Madeleine said, then added, "But not as much as he hates Jimmy."

"And do they reciprocate?"

"They can't wait to throw him out on his ear," Madeleine said. "And Sean is mad, you know, he—"

"Mad in the sense of angry or insane?"

"Both, I think," Madeleine said. "He's ruled by impulse. I'm half afraid of showing up as a character in his next novel, or mentioned to a columnist, or seeing a billboard on Times Square declaring his undying love, or . . ."

Pity the poor people who were not raised as spies. They write things down.

"Did you exchange love letters?" Walter asked.

"Yes."

"Erotic in nature?"

She forced herself to look straight at him. "I was in love with him."

"Of course," he answered. "But you understand that they present a problem."

"Oh, yes."

"If he's saved them—"

"I'm sure he has."

"Not to offend your feminine ego," Walter said, "but if Sean has saved them, and if Hoover gets a whiff of your affair, the Director would do *anything* to get his fat little fingers on them. I don't mean to frighten you."

"Will you help me?"

Because of me you're not to be afraid, Walter thought, recalling what he'd said to her just the night before.

"Maybe McGuire can be bought off," he said.

"Money doesn't mean anything to Sean," she said. "And with the success of his book . . ."

116

"He's doing more drinking than writing," Walter said. "I imagine we could buy the letters."

She finished her glass of wine and set it on the side table.

"I don't have the money," she said.

"Your family—"

"—has property, not money," she said. "There's a difference. In fact, my family has very little money at all. My father is a more talented drinker than he is a gambler."

"The party last night cost a pretty penny," Walter objected.

"Money attracts money." She held up her ring finger. "I might be my father's most lucrative piece of property."

"Ah."

Keneally *père* is broke and needs an infusion of cash. Joe Keneally wants to be president and needs an appropriate first lady. And future first ladies do not have affairs in their pasts, certainly not well-documented affairs with famous beatnik writers. Madeleine's impassioned writings could queer the deal.

She added, "I do love Joe."

"Of course."

"Can you help me?"

"What makes you think I can?"

"You handled Sean last night," she said. "I was hoping you could handle him again. I can't pay you very much."

Walter made a quick, curt gesture that dismissed the notion of payment. "I'll talk to Mr. McGuire," he said.

"But you won't—"

"Hurt him?" he asked. "It's not my style."

"There's something else."

Good Lord.

"Something else?"

Madeleine Keneally was close to tears. "Can you save him?" she asked.

"*Save* him?"

"He's lost something," she said. "I saw it at the Plaza. There used to be a light in his eyes, and it wasn't there. He looked heavy and puffy and . . . dead in the eyes."

"He was drunk."

"It was more than that and you know it."

"What makes you think I can 'save' him?"

I'm not so sure I can save myself.

"Instinct?" She shrugged. "Besides, as my knight errant you are obligated to try."

"Then I suppose I have no choice."

"How can I thank you?"

He took the lid off the box of candy and carefully selected a chocolate truffle. "You've already brightened an otherwise drab and lonely Christmas night," he said. "What more could I ask? You'd better go now, before people start talking about us."

He held her coat for her and saw her to the door.

"Try not to worry," he said. "I'll take care of it."

She kissed him on the cheek and left.

But how do I take care of it? Walter asked himself. And isn't that always the question?

Someone had beaten the unholy hell out of Sean McGuire.

Walter could tell that even from the sliver of face he saw behind the chain lock. The eye that glared out from behind the door was purple and narrowed in pain. His lower lip was swollen and cut.

"Merry Christmas," Walter said.

"I don't have the money," McGuire mumbled.

"I'm not from Martino," Walter said. "May I come in? I'd like to talk with you."

"I don't feel like talking."

McGuire started to shut the door.

"You know me from Christmas Eve at the Plaza," Walter said.

The door shut and opened again. McGuire shuffled over to a bare mattress on the floor and slowly let himself down. He leaned back against the wall, tipped back a bottle of Knickerbocker, and stared at Walter.

"That's it," McGuire said. "I thought you were a little small to be muscle for Joe Keneally."

Walter said, "I'm afraid I'm confused. Are we in trouble with Paulie Martino or Joe Keneally?"

McGuire shrugged.

"What makes you think that Senator Keneally uses hired thugs?" Walter pressed.

McGuire snorted. "I grew up in Massachusetts. In a shithole mill town. I know the Keneallys."

Walter lit two Gauloises and handed one to McGuire.

"So what are you doing here?" McGuire asked.

Walter took off his hat and coat and laid them on the cleanest part of the grimy kitchen counter. The apartment was a typical Barrow Street pad, a combined kitchen, sitting, and bedroom with a small bathroom. The place was also filthy and smelled like dried sweat.

"I came to tell you," Walter said, "that as amusing as your little stunt at the Plaza may have been, you'd be better advised not to repeat it."

"Keneally send you?"

"I sent myself."

"Yeah? How come?"

"I'm your guardian angel," Walter said. "You remember me from the Plaza. You don't remember that I was also at the Cellar."

"I was drunk."

Walter said, "You read a poem. I may have been the only person there who understood it. I was certainly the only person who knew that Paulie Martino has two broken thumbs. By the way, do you know how they got that way?"

"No."

"Well," Walter began, "when Angelo was just a little shylock, Albert D'Annunzio sent him to break the thumb of a gambler named Angelo Gagliano, who was behind in his payments. Angelo and Paulie were pals, so Paulie merely gave him a stern talking-to. When Albert D'Annunzio found out that Paulie had disobeyed his instructions, he doubled Angelo's punishment and gave it to Paulie. I imagine it hurt, don't you?"

"How do you know all this?" McGuire asked. "You don't look like a hood."

"I was losing football bets before you ever carried a ball for Columbia," Walter answered. "Who beat you up?"

"Two of Martino's boys."

On Christmas Day, Walter thought. It made sense, however. Mob boys tended to get bored on holidays. They were not really family men and would have been looking for an excuse to get out of the house after dinner.

"How much do you owe?" Walter asked.

"Two thousand."

"How much of that is vigorish?" asked Walter.

"A little over half."

"And growing every day."

"And growing every day."

"Football players make rotten football bettors," Walter said.

"Is that right?"

"So it would appear," Walter said, smiling. "In fact, the only people who are worse gamblers than athletes are writers."

McGuire laughed and took another swallow of beer. He fished in his pants pockets and came out with a couple of red pills.

"I'm not much of a writer these days, either," McGuire said. "You want to know the best and worst thing that ever happened to me?"

Not especially.

"Sure."

"The *New York Times* called me a genius," McGuire answered. "The voice of my generation. The beat generation. That was the best and the worst thing. The real critic was on vacation, did you now that? Some replacement wrote about my book. A goofy accident. Made me famous, finished it."

"Finished it?" Walter asked.

McGuire said, "When the *Times* gets around to seeing something, the something is over. The book is like the light from a distant star, man. By the time you see it, it's already dead."

So you had to find a way to lose, Walter thought. You write a book about being beat, and the book is a huge success, and the contradiction is unbearable. You become an establishment star for being an anti-establishment rebel, and what do you do next? All an honest man can do is to take the money and lose it on a foolish bet.

Get beat again.

"So how come you're here?" McGuire asked.

"I read your book," Walter answered.

An answer that only a writer would accept, Walter thought. It takes an author's ego to believe that a moth is attracted just by the bright light of his talent.

Walter added, "It changed my life."

Meaning that it had injected several hours of tedium into what might have been an otherwise pleasant Sunday evening.

McGuire looked at Walter's tweed, polished Bancroft shoes, and Gordon tie and smirked, "Yeah, it changed your life."

Walter added, "I'd like to help."

"You got two grand for me?" McGuire asked.

"No," Walter said.

"Then how can you help?"

Spoken with scorn, Walter noted, but still with the faint hope of a drowning man who believes the next wave might bear a spar on which to cling. And writers, God bless them, believe in possibilities. Believe in the justice of their own redemption. Believe in the reality of illusions. And the first illusion of this particular writer is that scribbling a novel the literary equivalent of an extended act of onanism gives him certain rights. The first rule of recruiting the opposition is to find out the nature of his illusions and never disappoint him with reality. Until, of course, you have no further use for him.

So Walter said, "I know how to get it."

McGuire popped the Dexedrine pills into his mouth and washed them down with the beer.

"I could use a guardian angel," he said. "All the angels I know are hopeless poets, beat musicians, and Buddhist saints with growling stomachs and a heroin jones."

Walter smiled appreciatively. The speech could have come straight from his book. But that was just fine: First you must get the mark to perform for you, show you his best party trick, try to please you. Then you reward him.

"Have you had dinner?" Walter asked.

"Man, I haven't had breakfast," McGuire answered. "Unless dexies and beer count."

Still performing, Walter noted.

"Is there some place around here?" asked Walter, who could recite the words etched on every window in every joint in the Village.

"There's Harry's, but I don't think it's your kind of place."

"But is it your kind of place?" Walter asked, playing the role of pilgrim. Harry's was a greasy spoon, picturesque if you liked that sort of thing, classic Village cheap chic.

"Martino's boys took every penny I had," McGuire said.

Walter answered, "Please, it would be an honor."

He opened the refrigerator, found some ice, cracked a few cubes into a dish towel, and held the cloth up to McGuire's swollen eye. He had read McGuire's book and knew that the man believed in angles. One must above all play one's expected role, he thought.

Now the Harry's in Venice, Walter thought, there was a Harry's. He could almost taste the chicken soup that Hemingway liked so much, washed down with a half bottle of red and a genuine espresso. But this joint in the Village, as much as Walter loved Village joints, had the aggressively downbeat ambience of the self-conscious underclass. Not to mention lousy food.

McGuire scarfed it down, however: a plate of scrambled eggs with onions and green pepper and two thick slices of buttered rye toast. McGuire sucked down three cigarettes and as many cups of coffee during the short meal while making just enough conversation to justify the bill.

The sadly predictable behavior of indigent scribes, Walter sighed. Like actors, they will always sing for their supper.

But there was business to conduct, so Walter interrupted to say, "The Giants are three and a half point underdogs Sunday."

"They can't lose," McGuire said. "Not with that defense. Hell, they shut out the Browns last week."

So Walter raised his eyebrows to signal "Draw your own conclusion" which McGuire did.

"Paulie's shut me out everywhere," McGuire said. "I can't get a bet down."

"But I can."

There is a look that the true gambler has, a certain gleam that reflects from the shiny star of the "sure thing." You never see it in the professional gambler; his is the cold stare of the resolute mathematician. But the *real* gambler is the guy who believes in the concept of fate, his own fate, and when he sees his star . . . well, his eyes shine. As did Sean McGuire's in the soft neon of the diner on this Christmas night.

"I can place a bet," Walter repeated.

"I don't have any credit," McGuire said.

"I do."

"You'd do that for me?" Sean asked.

For you, to you, whatever.

"It would be my pleasure," Walter said.

"Let's get the bet down."

"No," Walter said, "we'll wait and see if the spread changes. We might even get another point or two."

McGuire looked alarmed. "It might even up, though."

"Which would be valuable information in itself," Walter said.

People who make decisions at the first possible moment are usually called decisive, Withers Sr. used to say. I call them foolish. Never make a decision until the last *possible moment, which is when you have the most information with which to work.*

Walter's cab was just pulling up to Anne's when he saw her come out of her building, look left and then right, and then hurry into a waiting taxi.

"I almost hate to utter these words," Walter said to the driver, "but follow that cab."

It would be a small but delightful joke. Anne had apparently changed her mind and was heading up to his place. He would pop out of the cab behind her and have a laugh about it.

Except that her cab turned not east but west on Fourteenth Street. Away from his place.

And there had been something about her as she came down the stairs. Innocent when he first saw it, but now it became suspicious. The sharp glances to see if anyone saw her? Her uncharacteristic haste—Anne never hurried anywhere—to get inside the cab? The look on her face, which could only be described as furtive?

She had, Walter regretfully decided, a Michael Howard look about her. The look of the unfaithful.

And so now he would follow her, just as he'd followed Michael Howard, albeit in an overheated cab.

He sat low in the seat and felt like a guilty fool during the long trip over to Sixth and up to Broadway, then all the way up into the nineties.

The driver's fat face grinned in the rearview mirror.

"Your girl seeing a spook?" he asked.

"Shut your filthy mouth," Walter said.

The driver frowned and said, "I ain't going much farther uptown, chief."

"You don't have to. Pull over here."

Anne was getting out of her cab on the downtown corner of Ninety-fifth and Broadway. Walter paid the driver, added an insulting tip, and ignored the driver's muttered "Merry Christmas."

He watched as Anne crossed Broadway and walked west on Ninety-fifth. The marquee on the Thalia Theater read ORSON WELLES' A TOUCH OF EVIL, with CHARLETON HESTON in smaller letters beneath. She looked small and fragile under the soffet lights as she bought a ticket and went inside.

He crossed Broadway himself and waited on the downtown corner. Five minutes later, he saw Alicia, Anne's pretty Negro pal from the Cellar, wrapped in a gray cloth coat far too big for her, stride down the uptown side of the street, cross in the middle, and buy a ticket. Walter waited until she was well inside before he went up to the box office. Then he stood outside until he was sure that the film had started.

The theater was crowded. Walter wasn't sure what it was that drove people to the movies on Christmas night. Perhaps they needed to see something larger than life, or maybe it was the last piece of magic left in the day, or maybe it was just a convenient time to go out. But movie theaters always did a booming business on Christmas.

He stood behind the partition in the back and let his eyes adjust to the glimmering dark. Anne and Alicia were sitting in the third row on the right aisle of the center section.

He recalled exactly how he had asked about Alicia at The Cellar.

"Have you known her long?"

"She's around the scene. She waits tables at Good Night."

Lies of omission, Walter thought.

"You're going to make me jealous if you keep asking about her."

Sins of commission, but which sins? And why? Walter asked himself.

Anne doesn't want to see you and goes to a movie with a friend, so what? So she said she was spending the day with her family upstate and didn't mention she had a date with Alicia. She doesn't have to tell you everything. So she buys a ticket and meets her friend *in*side the theater, it's cold outside.

"Your girl seeing a spook?"

"Shut your filthy mouth."

He took a seat in a back corner of the theater and watched the film until it looked like the climax was coming up. Then he eased himself up and out of the movie house. He waited around the corner, and the cold added to his resentment, even though he wasn't quite sure what it was he was resentful about.

He was surprised when Alicia came out alone. He'd expected Anne and her to go for a drink or coffee, but Alicia turned uptown at the corner. She was edgy, too. She had that slightly stilted, nervous walk, the gait Walter's CIA instructors had called "the turkey trot," fast, up on the toes, but stiff.

One of the instructors, a moon-faced giant named Fischer, had a different expression, his maxim having been, "Hot hands, cold feet. When you're holding something guilty, an infection spreads from your hands straight to your feet. The hotter your hands, the colder your feet get. The solution, like everything else, is in your head. You have to forget about what's in your hands, or the opposition will have your ass."

But Alicia hadn't had the benefit of Fischer's wisdom, and whatever she had in her hands—and all Walter could make out was the same plain bag she'd arrived with—it was very much on her mind. He hoped to God that Anne wasn't foolish enough to be buying marijuana and dispensing it to her friends.

He followed Alicia to 110th Street, where she turned east and entered a building between Broadway and Amsterdam. He watched until he saw a light come on and Alicia's silhouette appear behind a thin blind on the fourth floor.

There was a coffee shop directly across Broadway from the building, and he was lucky enough to get a booth by the window. The coffee was vile, as were the ham and eggs, but it was warm inside and he could watch Alicia's apartment. Walter finished his meal and went to the pay phone in the back.

"Is it too late to be calling?" he asked Anne when she picked up.

"Never too late for you, darling."

"You sound out of breath."

"I just got in."

"From?"

"From upstate, silly," she said. "I told you. I went up to see my parents."

When will amateurs ever learn to bury a single lie under a thousand truths? he asked himself.

"Hello, Walter?" he heard her say. "Are you there?"

"I'm here."

"Where's 'here'?"

"Some coffee shop," he answered. "I got hungry and didn't feel like cooking."

She said, "Listen, I'd invite you over but, frankly, I'm exhausted. You must be, too."

"I'm beat," he said.

"And I have a 'day' tomorrow," she said. "I'm in the studio all day and then the Rainbow Room. Can you come?"

"I'll try."

"Do try, please." A pause. "Well, Merry Christmas."

"Merry Christmas."

Walter hung up and went back to his booth. He swallowed the last dregs of bitter coffee, left a quarter on the table, and walked out into the cold. Seeing no cab, he stepped down into the subway station at 110th, bought a token, and walked down the platform.

Why lie? he thought. Why lie about a movie date with a friend?

It troubled him deeply because he knew what all good investigators know: It's not the substance of the lie that's important, it's the motive for the lie.

Christ, he thought, "motive." Now I'm thinking of Anne and using words like "motive." Christ.

The station was empty late on Christmas night, and Walter heard their footsteps before he saw them.

There were two of them, two white guys with the albino look of the hopelessly addicted and the silly smirk of the terminally stupid. And they were the usual big-small combination of the predatory duo, the smaller just smart enough to be a sycophant, the bigger one just dumb enough to believe it.

No finesse, either, Walter thought. Not on a deserted platform late at night. They're just coming straight on. Why waste the time and effort to be subtle?

They were six feet away when the smaller one flashed

the blade, a wicked butterfly knife with a cross-hatched handle.

Please go away, Walter thought. Please. I'm just not in the mood.

The small junkie waved the blade in Walter's face as the bigger one stepped around behind him.

"Give me your wallet, I might let you live," the smaller one said.

Walter didn't answer.

The junkie slashed the knife an inch from Walter's nose.

"Did you hear me?"

Walter didn't answer.

The junkie jabbed the blade at Walter's throat. Walter stepped back and grabbed the man's wrist with his left hand, then brought his right hand across the top and pushed down. The junkie's wrist snapped and the knife clattered to the floor. Walter pivoted, grabbed the man's hair, tilted his head until his neck was stretched, and raised his own hand like an ax.

"Run away or I'll kill him," Walter said.

The big junkie stared at him. His friend's eyes bugged out in fear and pain.

"I'm in an unfortunate mood," Walter said. "I repeat: Run away or I'll kill him."

"You're a goddamn animal," the big junkie said. Then he turned and ran.

Walter could hear him piling up the subway steps. He let go of the small man's hair, and his head hit the platform floor. The man curled on the ground. Walter walked farther down the platform but could still hear him whimpering when the train pulled up.

Walter got on board and sat down.

At home he poured himself a stiff drink, showered, listened to some quiet jazz, and went to bed.

The dream that night was similar to what it usually was. He was lying on the edge of a cliff above the dark, cold waters of the North Sea as his marks clung to a rock below. And one by one the waves came, and swept them away one by one. The only difference was that in the dream this Christmas night Anne appeared on the rock, and she was the last to go.

CHAPTER THREE

What's New

Friday, December 26

Bill Dietz held forth at the water cooler.

"You wouldn't believe," he was telling a small gaggle of investigators, "the sounds coming out of this place. I didn't know if I was on Fifth Avenue or at the frigging Bronx Zoo . . ."

He paused as one of the secretaries walked past. She smiled and gave a knowing look.

He continued in a lower voice, "The guy's making noises like a gorilla, she's howling like one of them laughing . . . what-do-you-call-thems—"

"Hyenas?" Walter suggested.

"Thank you, professor. Hyenas," Bill said. "I'm telling you, I'm out there in that hallway, I don't worry I'm getting it all on tape, I worry the microphone's going to crack."

"But you got it?" Moodie, an accountant from Fraud and Embezzlement, asked salaciously.

"I got it," Dietz said. "Tell you what, when her old man hears this, he won't know whether to take her to court or straight into the bedroom."

"A word with you, Bill?" Walter approached Dietz as the group started to drift away.

Dietz followed Walter into his office and shut the door.

"What's up, sport?" Dietz asked.

Walter briefed him on the Howard file and told him about following Michael Howard to the apartment on Twenty-first Street.

"I'd like to put it down as an extramarital affair and forget about it. I don't want to hurt anybody," Walter said. "But there's always the chance that it's something else."

"Ninety-nine times out of a hundred it's sex," Dietz said. "Either they got some honey in a love nest, or they're picking up pros at the Tap Room."

"I saw him with his wife yesterday," Walter said. "They looked happy."

"He is." Dietz grinned. "Hell, she probably is, too. Either she doesn't know, so what the hell, or she does know and she's grateful someone else is doing her duty for her."

"Doing her duty?" Walter asked.

Dietz shrugged. "I dunno, they Catholic?"

Walter sighed and said, "I have to go in, don't I?"

Dietz nodded. "You want some backup, sport? Operations owes me a couple."

The lights came on 16-C's office. He waved and Walter waved back.

"What are you, queer for that guy?" Dietz asked.

"Not at all, William," Walter answered. "I'm queer for you."

Dietz dropped his hand to his fly and said, "Hold on. I have something for you."

Walter's intercom buzzed. "Saved by the bell," he said. "Later, darling?"

"Another time, sweetheart," Dietz said. "Let me know about that backup. Nothing to be ashamed of, Walter."

He chucked Walter on the shoulder and left.

"Mr. Forbes would like to see me?" Walter asked into the intercom.

"How did you know, Mr. Withers?" the feminine voice answered.

"Who knows what evil lurks in the hearts of men, Miss Bradley?" said Walter. "Only the Shadow knows."

He was rewarded with her deep, low laughter.

Forbes Jr. is a lucky man, Walter thought.

Forbes Jr. had his pipe stoked up like a kitchen stove when Walter came in. "How was your Christmas, Withers?" he asked.

"I had an interesting Christmas Eve," Walter answered.

He watched Forbes Jr. blush. The reddened skin made an interesting effect against the silver hair.

"Joe Keneally's an important client," Forbes Jr. said.

"Apparently."

"He wants to use you again tonight," Forbes Jr. continued, watching a graceful skater etch figure eights on the rink below. "They're going to the theater, dinner at a club afterward."

And so it goes, Walter thought. And so it goes.

Walter said, "I'll bet Keneally's arranged a date for me, so I don't stand out like a sore thumb."

"We all do all sorts of things for the firm," Forbes Jr. answered. He struck a match and held it to the bowl of the pipe.

"Miss Marlund?" Walter asked.

"There are worse fates, Withers."

"At least Keneally's faithful in his infidelities," Walter said. "I'll take a pass on this one, if you don't mind."

Forbes stood up and went to the window to get a better view of the skater. The move also had the benefit of putting his back to Walter Withers.

"I'm afraid I do mind," he said.

Do I try again, or would that be pushing it too far? Walter thought.

"If it's for the good of the company, Mr. Forbes . . ." he said.

Forbes Jr. declared victory on that issue and moved ahead.

"How are you coming on the Howard file?" he asked.

"I'm just about to nail down a couple of loose ends," said Walter.

"I won't keep you, then," Forbes Jr. said. "We need that report."

Knowing a dismissal when one was issued, Walter got up, resisted the temptation to tug his forelock, and made for the door. Forbes Jr. had already settled behind his desk and was pretending deep concentration on some piece of paper-work.

A shabby way, Walter thought, to treat your best whore.

The locks on H. Benson's place opened like flowers to the sunshine. Nevertheless, Walter wished he'd taken Dietz up on his offer of some backup.

Temper, temper, temper, he chided himself. Temper is the undoing of the impetuous man. He had stalked out of Forbes' office, grabbed his coat, hat, and burglary tools, and headed straight for H. Benson's apartment. He was still thinking about his irritation at Forbes while he picked the lock—the instructors at the Company were right, it *was* like riding a bicycle—and into the apartment. But once he was inside, the operational nerves cooled him off. Chilled him, in fact.

It was not his field, really, this operational stuff. He'd done precious little of it at the Company, his specialty hav-ing gone more toward expensive dinners. He chuckled at the memory of the old joke often told during his training days—Question: What is Withers' best course? Answer: Dessert.

Nevertheless, he had learned his stuff and here he was inside H. Benson's apartment feeling the pins and needles of fear. As opposed to the slings and arrows of outrageous fortune, he thought.

He also recalled the first maxim of breaking into opposition territory: Infiltration is simple, extrication can be complicated. Or in simple English, as every burglar, rented spook, or self-styled Lothario knew, getting in is easy, it's the getting out that's hard.

So the first thing he looked for was an alternate exit. The fire escape came off a window in the kitchen and would do if H. Benson, a snoopy neighbor, or a cop showed up unexpectedly. Then he went into the bathroom, which as any unspeakably vulgar party guest will attest, is the quickest way to find out about one's hosts.

The first thing Walter noticed was the absence of certain items. There were no woman's cosmetics, no hair spray, no perfumes. No chichi towels, no pink bars of soap, no nylons hanging to dry.

No woman lives here, Walter thought.

Two toothbrushes—one blue, one red—in the rack.

He opened the medicine cabinet. A bottle of aspirin, a tube of toothpaste, a small bottle of mouthwash. Two razors and shaving cream. He slid the shower curtain back. No razor on the bath shelf.

Walter felt his calves start to stiffen. No turkey trot, he thought as he took a deep breath. No imaginary footsteps on the stairs. Work fast, work clean, do your job and leave.

In the bedroom closet he found a couple of sports coats, size 42, a pair of gray twill trousers, a pair of cordovan loafers, and some old gym shoes, all consistent with Howard's frame.

More interesting were the clothes that didn't fit Michael Howard: a black leather jacket, size 38; three pairs of dungarees, 32 waist, 34 length; black high-top Keds, size 8. A few white shirts, 15 collar, 34 sleeve. Men's clothing.

Howard's lover was a man.

Walter searched the bureau drawers. Bottom drawer empty. Middle drawer, men's underwear, socks, some T-shirts. T-shirts medium, too small for Howard. Top drawer more of the same, but large.

It's a classy business, he thought as he felt around under Howard's intimate clothing, grateful that at least Howard wasn't in them at the moment.

"But it's a sad and mistrustful world," he said to himself as he saw a thin leather wallet. He pulled it out with thumb and middle finger, then flipped it open.

The driver's license said HOWARD BENSON, but it described Michael Howard. Six foot two, brown hair, brown eyes. And the signature was consistent with the handwriting on Howard's job application. The "Howard" on each was identical.

The signatures on the American Express card and Diner's Club card told the same story: Howard Benson was Michael Howard.

When, oh when, would amateurs become a bit more creative in their choices of aka's? Walter wondered. There are certain responsibilities that come with a covert life, among them the obligation to make a decent effort. Howard Benson, indeed.

Jack in the city and Ernest in the suburbs, Walter thought, appropriately thinking of Oscar Wilde. *The Importance of Being Ernest*.

The importance of being duplicitous, he thought. Especially in America in the waning days of 1958. Well, neither Michael Howard nor Howard Benson was getting the big promotion, Walter thought. Homosexuals were persona non grata in the executive dining room. Unfortunately, the possibility that Howard was involved in industrial espionage had not been completely ruled out, so he would still have to locate Howard's lover and confirm that the relationship was merely sexual.

Merely sexual, Walter thought. There's the chuckle for the day. Merely sexual.

But thou shalt not pause to think, Walter reminded himself. Nor shalt thou take time to analyze, for he who hesitates on enemy ground is lost.

So on to the sitting room. Remarkably unremarkable. Sofa, chairs, coffee table. Single bookshelf of best-sellers. A few volumes revealing possible interest in the popular theater.

Nobody lives here, Walter thought. This is a place of assignation.

But there was something on the coffee table, what was it?

Matchbooks in a glass bowl. A flash of pink caught his eye. A silhouette of knight in the tilts. Good Night.

Walter fished through the bowl. Not one book of matches from Good Night but four.

A place frequented.

And not just by Michael Howard/Howard Benson either, Walter thought. By Anne, and Alicia, who works there. And if you had come to the Christmas party, Michael Howard, you might have spared me the trouble of breaking into your apartment. But you were in the suburbs with your family.

He listened for sound in the hallway before letting himself out, then stopped at a phone booth and called the office.

"Forbes and Forbes, how may I direct your call?"

"Vice squad, please."

"Mr. Withers, is that you?"

Walter always made a point to give Agnes, the erstwhile receptionist, a chuckle.

"None other, Agnes."

"You want Matrimonial?" Agnes asked. "You just missed Mr. Dietz. He came through about ten minutes ago."

"Heading where, may I ask, Agnes?"

"Jersey, and he wasn't happy, let me tell you."

Walter thanked her, hung up, and dialed Bill Dietz's home number.

Sarah answered.

"How's your day?" Walter asked, even though he could tell from the sound of her voice that she was having a rough time. "Could you use a break?"

Two minutes later he was in a taxi heading for Forty-second Street.

Mary Dietz was awake this afternoon, awake but exhausted in the aftermath of a bad attack, and Sarah was just putting a syringe away when Walter arrived. The bedroom was foul with the smell of tortured sweat. But she was glad to see him. Gave him her best smile and wished him a good afternoon and listened with what was left of her pleasure to his melodramatic rendition of the trashy book.

"*That night the nation got a report on the 6:15 P.M. news broadcast,*" Walter read from *One Lonely Night*. "*There had been a leak in the State Department, and the cat was out of the bag. It seemed that we had had a secret. Somebody else was in on it now.*"

The drug did its work quickly, however—mercifully—and she slipped into sleep as his words became a drone. He read on anyway because sleep wouldn't come for him even in the stuffy, soporific room.

He could use a nap, too, because he had a big night coming up.

A night on the town.

The big night started, as Walter supposed big nights should, on Broadway, and if there was anything not to love about Broadway, Walter didn't know what it could be.

Although Broadway ran the entire length of the city, when Walter thought of Broadway he usually had in mind the section around Times Square: the theater district, the Great White Way, the Broadway of the sparkling lights.

The lights in that holiday week of 1958 shone with the full brilliance of the American theater. Sauntering down Broadway on that particular night, Walter, Marta, Joe, and Madeleine strolled beneath lights proclaiming *Music Man* at the Majestic, *West Side Story* at the Winter Garden and *My Fair Lady* at the Mark Hellinger. Judy Holliday was starring in *Bells Are Ringing* at the Alvin, Lena Horne was in *Jamaica* at the Imperial, and John Gielgud made his own kind of Shakespearean music in his solo *The Ages of Man* at the Broadway.

Walter had the theater listings virtually committed to memory and knew that within these few blocks one could see on stage Henry Fonda, Anne Bancroft, Helen Hayes, Jason Robards, Jr., Kim Stanley, Don Ameche, Elaine Stritch, Joseph Cotton, Eddie Albert, Vivian Blaine, Robert Morse, Christopher Plummer, Rosemary Harris, Eli Wallach, Maureen Stapleton, Walter Slezak, Jayne Meadows, Imogene Coca, Cyril Ritchard, and to Walter's great delight, Claudette Colbert and Charles Boyer. The very names of the theaters held a certain magic for Walter: the Helen Hayes, of course, and the Martin Beck, the Lyceum, the Bijou, the Broadhurst, the Belasco, the Booth, and the Barrymore, and two dollars and thirty cents got you through the doors and into the cheap seats.

If you were truly serious about theater—as Walter wasn't but Anne was—you could wander off-Broadway to see Brendan Behan's *The Quare Fellow* at Circle-in-the-Square, or *Look Back in Anger* at the Forty-First Street, or *The Power and the Glory* at the Phoenix. Down in the Village *The Threepenny Opera* had been running for four years at the Theatre de Lys, *The Boy Friend* played at the Cherry Lane, *The Crucible* at the Martinique, and it was *The Time of the Cuckoo* at the Sheridan Square Playhouse.

And that was just the live stage.

For a movie buff like Walter (he refused to call them "films" as did the artsy crowd at the Cellar) New York was a celluloid paradise. At the pretty Paris Theatre—cater-corner to the Plaza—Alec Guiness looked into *The Horse's Mouth*, Rosalind Russell was *Auntie Mame* at Radio City Music Hall, while at the small but distinguished Sutton Theater—on Fifty-seventh off Third Avenue—Leslie Caron, Louis Jourdan, Maurice Chevalier, and Hermione Gingold starred in *Gigi*, which Walter had now seen five times.

At the first-run houses on Broadway a buck got you into the Odeon to see Jimmy Stewart and Kim Novak in *Bell, Book and Candle*, or into the Translux for Leslie Caron and Dirk Bogarde in *The Doctor's Dilemma*, or into the Victoria, where Susan Hayward shouted *I Want to Live*, or into the Astor for Burt Lancaster, Deborah Kerr, Rita Hayworth, and David Niven in *Separate Tables*.

Walter had a bad case of Broadway. The street had a tendency to turn him into Walter Mitty Withers, and he would have cheerfully traded his whole career for one small but tasty role in a big musical. Would have, too, he thought as he squired the trio toward the Majestic Theater, except that I can't sing and neither can I dance. But other than that . . .

Ah, but I shall have to settle for walks among the shades of Cohan, Runyon, and Broun, for steaks at Donovans, whiskeys at Toots Shors and martinis at Sardi's. And to sit as I do in the audience—usually alone as Anne is elsewhere warbling Porter standards to the club crowd—and watch in awe the performers on the stage.

But I could haunt the theaters, he thought. Become one of those mysterious and pathetic stage door Johnnies who wait in the alley with a bundle of flowers and an invitation to dinner or a weekend in the country. I could become a professional annoyance to every long-legged chorus girl in New York and have a great time doing it, too. Become a hanger-on, waiting for the reviews at Sardi's, showing up at casting calls with helpful suggestions, greeting directors by their nicknames—God, I would be brilliant at it.

And maybe I should do it, too. Or be an errand boy who goes for coffee and bagels, runs out for cigarettes and half pints of booze, fetches taxis in the rain. Cheerfully servile and without present responsibilities such as . . . well, here I am with Joe Keneally. With his mistress on my arm and his wife at my side, but on Broadway, nevertheless.

A street, Walter mused, on which you can see most of the sights at least twice at the same time. Where the neon, the flashing lights, and the large plate-glass windows combined to create an enormous outdoor hall of mirrors. A funny house where one could stop and pause and see not only yourself—bathed scarlets, silvers, and ambers—but also what was behind you, or down the block, or across the street.

Such as the two serious types doing a bad job of trailing them, the same two who had been following them since they left the Plaza for their walk to the show. Walter was familiar with the term *ham-handed*, but he often thought of the Bureau's men as "ham-footed," and that's why he thought that these boys were two of Hoover's humorless agents. Their unsubtle technique was typical of security agencies that got to do their work in the same country in which they were the final authority. They lacked the paranoid skills of those who worked on enemy turf, those for whom a moment's clumsiness might mean a quick arrest or a quicker death.

"Ham-footedness," as Walter styled it, was just the arrogance of power. And these boys, in their regulation gray overcoats, crew cuts, and polished black shoes, clearly thought that they were the home team.

But you're not the home team, Walter thought. I'm the home team.

"Broadway," he announced as they waited for the light on Forty-fifth, "is where people come and pay money to watch other people's dreams."

Madeleine said, "Walter, I can't tell if that remark is deeply cynical or completely charming."

"Or both," Keneally observed.

"It was said in admiration," Walter answered as they crossed the street. "It's one reason I believe in God, country, and the ultimate nobility of mankind."

"Why is that?" Madeleine asked, laughing, enjoying the game.

"Because," Walter said, looking back at her, although really to check that the two men were still following, "it's proof of a deity that creates a creature who uniquely laughs, cries, sings, and likes to watch its soul mates prance around in silly costumes, and who collectively suspends its awareness of grim realities to pretend to believe that a flimsy construct of wood and painted muslin is, for instance, River City."

"Is this species," Marta Marlund asked, "the same one which will not spend a penny to help juvenile delinquents in bad neighborhoods but will spend millions to watch actors *play* juvenile delinquents a few blocks away?"

You're smarter than I thought, Walter observed. And those same words could easily have come from Anne Blanchard's mouth. And the two grim boys are still with us.

But for whom? For Keneally? For Madeleine? Which act of congress, pun intended, had Hoover sniffed? And on whose carnal trail had he set his hounds?

Ignoring Marta, Madeleine asked, "You've covered God and the nobility of man, what about country?"

"It's simple, isn't it, Senator?" Walter asked. "You have a country that not only allows a Broadway but encourages it."

"Bravo, Walter. Bravo."

"But shouldn't art serve society?" Marta asked.

"In that society pays for what it wants," Walter said, "Broadway serves it nobly."

"Even if what it wants is pretty pictures?" Marta pressed.

"Especially then," Walter said. We can have ugly pictures on our own, without any professional help, thank you. One of the men was tall, skinny and young. Hatless and short-haired. The other was older, mid-forties, Walter guessed, and stocky. Thick-faced, florid now in the cold.

"But art should educate society," Madeleine said.

"To what?" Walter answered. "Itself?"

"Beautify it, then," Madeleine insisted.

"I've nothing to say against beauty," Walter answered. "Present company *in*cluded."

"You missed your trade, Walter!" Keneally laughed. "You should become a diplomat!"

"Is that a job offer, Senator?" Walter asked.

Keneally laughed.

"And isn't it just a *little* premature?" Walter added.

Keneally's handsome face flushed with pleasure. His skin looked golden under the warm lights of the Majestic Theater.

"Well," he said, "I don't think the party will go 'Madly for Adlai' three times in a row. And as for certain Texans, well . . ."

"Do you think America is ready for a Catholic president?" Marta asked.

Except in her dialect it came out "Cat to lick precedent," Walter thought. And judging by the look in Keneally's eye, he doesn't like the question.

But the smile stayed fixed on his face as he said, "I think Americans would elect the *pope* if he could end the recession. Five million Americans are unemployed, one third of our industrial centers are—"

"Darling," Madeleine stopped him with an uxorial hand on the elbow. "You're not compaigning tonight. And besides, Walter's escort can't vote."

"And Walter's escort needs to use the little escort's room," Marta said with a poisonous simile at Madeleine.

And we have trouble right here in River City, Walter thought as he opened the door for them.

The two men didn't follow them in.

But even the Bureau, Walter thought, would have trouble getting tickets to *The Music Man* during a holiday week. Nor would Hoover's bean counters pay the ten bucks for fifth row center.

Walter enjoyed the show, thought Robert Preston was terrific in the title role, and was in a generally cheery frame of mind as they stepped back out onto the street.

Keneally whistled "Seventy-six Trombones," his breath

145

visible in little puffs of steam in the cold air. He paused long enough to ask, "What do you kids want to do now?"

"The Stork Club?" Walter suggested. "Or Sardi's? '21'?"

"They all sound wonderful," Marta said.

"They do," Madeleine said, "but do you know where I really want to end the evening?"

A true princess, Walter thought, issues her commands in the form of a question.

"Where?" he dutifully asked.

"The Rainbow Room!" she announced.

Do you know where I really *don't* want to end the evening? Walter thought.

"Done!" Keneally said.

As is the king's perogative.

A taxi—treacherously, Walter thought, given that taxis were at a premium at curtain time—appeared, and they climbed in. Leaving the two grim boys shivering in the lurch, scrambling to find their own cab.

And leaving me, he thought, in a no less uncomfortable situation, heading—in the company of Joe Keneally and Madeleine Keneally and Marta Marlund—toward the Rainbow Room and Anne.

The Rainbow Room epitomized New York City for Walter Withers.

Sixty-four stories above Rockefeller Center, the nightclub seemed to float in the air on its own power, as if the laws of gravity that applied to the rest of the natural world were, as it were, suspended for the Rainbow Room. Most clubs were on street level—you stepped out of your cab and the doorman swung open the door and there you were, in a classy joint that was still very much a part of the street. Other clubs, those speakeasy remnants of Prohibition, were in cellars—you stepped down into their cool basements and literally became a part of the city's underground. But the Rainbow Room was in the sky, the only place it could be, really, and it sat above the city, not part of its earth or its street, but of its air.

"It's quite literally ethereal," Walter had once said about the Rainbow Room, describing it to out-of-town friends. "It lives in the ether of the city. You step off the concrete into an elevator that whisks you upward. You step out and you're in this magical room in the sky. I'm convinced that if the Greek gods returned, it would be to Manhattan and that the Rainbow Room would be their new Olympus, only with better booze."

And the room itself was full of New York paradox. In the first place, having ridden up sixty-four floors, you stepped down to get into the room. It was classic Manhattan, really, because you could stand on the landing and survey the crowd for a moment before walking down the curved staircase with its polished chrome handrail, a walk that took you behind the bandstand so that your entrance became a part of the performance.

The room itself was the unique Manhattan blend of warm and cool. Its circular, polished wooden dance floor was ringed by three levels of black and chrome tables and chairs. The ringside tables were draped in silver tablecloths that looked like ice against the warm wood of the dance floor.

And that floor was made for dancing. Its parquet was pieced together in a complex mosaic of interlocking circles that came together in a black star in the center. It was a floor made to defy the gravity of friction, to let lovers glide as if on air, free from the drag of the earth and their own earthbound awkwardness. And the lovers' faces shone, as did Madeleine Keneally's on this particular night, reflected by the thousand crystals of the chandelier that sparkled like a shattered star in the orbed ceiling above the room.

"Would you not like to dance?" Marta asked Walter, reflecting in her broken syntax Walter's exact state of mind. He would not like do dance, would like, in fact, to not dance, would like in fact to leave and go home with the singer.

Anne's sharp tones cut like a razor tonight, Walter thought. No, not a razor—an icicle. A brilliant singer, not a belter or a crooner but a vocalist, can sing any words and make them mean anything she wants. Walter was sure that Anne could sing the Manhattan white pages and make them sultry. Conversely, she could take a love song like "April in Paris," which she was singing right then, and turn it into an indictment.

Walter knew what the counts read, too. Guilty in the first degree of being with Marta Marlund, a tall Nordic beauty with blue eyes and a big chest, most of which was bared this evening for public viewing.

It was unfair, Walter knew, this jealousy. Unfair after her betrayal of Christmas night—had it been a betrayal?—but the feminine sense of fairness had little if anything to do with moral symmetry. No, a woman's sense of justice is more circular, less linear. It was all right for Anne to be with another woman, quite another thing for Walter. Perhaps, he thought, if I was with another man she would not be so angry.

And it's the particular woman, too, isn't it? Walter thought. Marta Marlund was the sort of woman who made other women angry just by coming into the room. Nor did she settle for that. Rather, she filled the space around her with a threatening sexuality, a refusal to soften the erotic edge that bordered the narrow frontier between men and women. There was no mask, no screen, no compromise. Marta was always in bed.

All the more so this night. She was wearing a silver dress that seemed like it could slide off her body as easily as rain. When she leaned forward, as she often did—consciously, unabashedly in a parody of sexuality that was no less sexual for being a parody—her breasts seemed to pour forth like milk itself. And when she caught a man looking—and men looked—she smiled an *I can't say I blame you, yes, isn't sex wonderful* smile that promised nothing but possibilities. Every man knew that when it came to bed—if it came to bed—Marta Marlund would throw herself wide open, would invite a man into every part of that full, milky, misty, hot, cold body.

Anne Blanchard knew it, too, and it made her furious, and when she shot Walter another frigid look, it was enough to make him think that enough is enough and he said, "Yes, let's cut a rug."

Marta's look of confusion at the idiom was deliberately charming, and he took her by the hand and raised her to her feet.

The champagne had hit her harder than he'd thought. She was tipsy—it made her seem all the more available—and it seemed as if the whole room was watching as he led her to the dance floor. Certainly Madeleine glanced over. She feigned a smile as Joe turned her and grinned a lupine grin.

The smile seemed to make Marta angry, and she pressed to Walter like wallpaper. Her breasts flattened against his chest, and she made small, subtle circles against his crotch and smiled when she felt him harden.

"You are alive after all," she whispered. "I was beginning to wonder."

"Wonder what?" Walter asked.

"If even you liked me," she answered. "If even you liked women at all."

Because in your mind, a man has to be queer to turn you down, Walter thought.

"Don't flatter yourself," he said. "Just call it a reflex reaction."

"Then I am all the more flattered," she said.

"Stop it."

"You don't want me to stop it."

She pressed tighter against him. "If the music ended now," she teased, "everybody would see that you do not wish me to stop it."

She rubbed against him.

She whispered, "You feel good. You would feel better inside me."

"No, thank you."

She smiled. "No matter. It can happen this way, and only you and I will know it."

"You can keep it to yourself, thanks."

But his voice was thin and tight, and they both heard it.

"But I can't, really, you know," she said as her hips ground slowly against him.

She closed her eyes, smiled, and sighed.

"The real thing?" Walter asked. "Or just a *frisson?*"

"She can't do what I do for him," she said suddenly.

"But he's married to her."

"But he *screws* me."

"Your English is improving, anyway."

The music stopped. Marta smiled at him and stood close for a few seconds before stepping away. She let him lead her back to the table, where she sat down beside Madeleine and said, "Your husband is a wonderful dancer, it seems."

"Yes, he is," Madeleine answered.

"I'm an oaf," Keneally, said, "compared to Walter Withers there."

Keneally smiled, but the look on his face warned Marta that she was stepping a little too close to the line.

"Where did you learn to dance, Walter?" Keneally asked.

"My mother made me go to one of those awful classes when I was a boy," Walter answered. "It was sheer torture, of course, all the more so when I was partnered with a red-headed girl with green eyes. Her name was Jill, and she was my first love."

"And did she break your heart?" Madeleine asked.

"Of course. Her family moved away after that season. We exchanged a couple of letters and then . . ."

The waiter came, and Keneally ordered another round: champagne for the ladies, a scotch rocks for him, a martini for Walter.

The drummer hit a rim shot, and Anne's voice broke into "Ask me how do I feel / Now that we're cozy and clinging," the opening lyric of an up-tempo "If I Were a Bell."

"I'll bet you've done some heartbreaking of your own," Madeleine said to Walter.

"I'm afraid not," he answered. "No, I'm fated to be the second lead in the movies. The other guy gets the girl."

"Always the bridesmaid, never the bride?" Keneally asked.

"Something like that."

Madeleine looked pointedly at Marta. "You're not going to break his heart, are you?"

"No, I think he's going to break mine," Marta said. "I don't think he loves me at all."

"Walter, you cad!" Madeleine said.

"The singer's terrific," said Keneally.

"Isn't she?" Walter asked.

And looks smashing to boot. A black sheath classic chanteuse dress, a string of pearls we bought together in Nice. Hair a shimmering gold. And she will break my heart.

> *"And if I were a bell / If I were a bell,*
> *If I were a bell I'd go*
> *Ding-dong ding-dong ding."*

The last notes hung crystalline in the air.

"Ding-dong ding."

As if the evening was not riddled with quite enough tension, Keneally invited Anne over to the table after her set. She came, bearing the glass of chilled grapefruit juice she always drank between sets, and said with a frigid smile, "Hello, everyone. Hello, Walter."

"Hello, Anne."

"You two know each other?" Madeleine asked.

"Everyone knows Walter," Anne said. "He's a man about town. A man of the world, as a matter of fact."

"We're old friends," said Walter.

"Why didn't you say something?" Madeleine asked.

Anne looked at her incredulously, looked at Marta, and asked, "Really?"

Keneally, sensing a fellow cad in trouble, jumped in with "You're a terrific singer. It's a pleasure to meet you."

"I wish I could reciprocate, Senator."

And there's the bell for round one, Walter thought.

"You don't think I'm a terrific singer?" Keneally asked.

"It's not a pleasure to meet you."

"Anne—" Walter started, but Keneally's laugh stopped him.

"Are you a Republican, Miss Blanchard?" Keneally asked.

"I'd rather swallow my teeth," she answered. "No, I just hate what you and your gang are doing to the country."

"My gang?" Keneally asked.

"Your committee," Anne clarified. "The Senate Internal Security Committee?"

"And what are we doing to the country?" Keneally asked.

"Your witch hunts," she said. "They hurt people."

"We're pikers compared to Uncle Joe Stalin."

"Excuse me, but I think he's dead, or haven't you heard?"

"Khrushchev's no better."

"Than McCarthy?" Anne asked.

"Excuse me, but he's as good as dead."

"How about Nixon, then?" Anne said. "Or Keneally?"

Keneally laughed again, held up his hands, and said, "Jesus, don't put me in the same boat with Dick Nixon!"

"You hopped in on your own, Senator."

"I don't believe they allow discussions of politics or religion in the Rainbow Room," Walter said. "Something about making the champagne go flat . . ."

He saw a photographer steaming over from the stairway. The camera held low, beneath table level, but visible all the same from the way the little man's shoulder was hunched. Walter got up and stepped into his way. Close so the man couldn't raise the camera without hitting him with it.

"Not tonight," Walter said. "Private party."

"Private party in the Rainbow Room?" the photographer said. "This is as pubic as it gets, friend."

"All the more need for some manners, then."

"I got a job to do."

So do I. And I'm not sure it includes having this little tableau spread all over the Saturday papers.

"Please give them their privacy," Walter said.

"The Shining Knight and his Lady Fair out on the town? Are you kiddin' me? With a blonde looks like that? Come on."

"It's okay, Walt," Keneally said.

No, Senator, it's not okay. It's not okay at all, if you don't mind. But he stepped back and sat down next to Marta.

Who leaned over and kissed him on the cheek just as the flashbulb went off like an explosion.

"Could I have names?" the photographer asked. He had his pad and pen out. "The Senator I know, of course, and Mrs. Keneally. But Miss Marlund, who's the gentleman?"

"My escort for the evening," Marta cooed.

"Does he have a name, or is he a man of mystery?"

"Oh, a man of of mystery."

"Walter Withers," Marta said.

Thank you very much, Marta, thought Walter.

"Are you in show biz, Walt?"

I'm in the no-show biz, as a matter of fact, Walter thought.

"I'm just in regular old biz," he said. "And I think that's about enough," Walter said.

"Cool it, mystery guest," the photographer chirped. "Do you have something you want to tell us, Mrs. Keneally?"

"Yes, that I'm having a lovely evening! Now, you will excuse me, won't you, dear?" Madeleine asked the photographer. "I have to powder my nose."

"Yes, myself as well," Marta added.

And off they went.

"In the course of things I suppose I should toddle off with them," Anne said. "But my nose isn't shiny, and I don't have to pee."

"I do," Keneally said, getting to his feet. "Nice to meet you, Miss Blanchard. I still like your music."

"Well, we have that in common," Anne said.

Keneally worked his way through the room, smiling, pointing, and shaking hands. The photographer followed, snapping his pix.

"That was charming," Walter said to Anne.

She shrugged. "I'm not their guardian angel."

"And a good thing, too."

She leveled a gaze on him and asked, "So did you bring

pitons and rope with you tonight? To scale the heights of the Marlund's snowy peaks?"

"Nice."

"A question, awaiting an answer, my good sir."

"In that case," Walter said, "the only climb I had hoped to make tonight was into your bed."

"Tonight?" she asked. "As in *this* night? As in the remaining hours between now and morning?"

"I think you have it bracketed," Walter said. "Tonight."

Her gray eyes turned flinty. "Spend it with your Stockholm whore," she said before turning and walking back to the bandstand.

Well, Walter thought, she's not mine, she's not actually Swedish, and as for being a whore, that's a matter of interpretation I would rather not make. And I don't want to spend the night with her. But other than that . . .

Joe Keneally came back to the table.

"What keeps women so long in the can?" he asked.

"They're probably comparing notes about you," Walter answered.

"You have a mean streak in you, Walter," Keneally said.

"Let's say that I'm less than entranced by the situation," Walter answered.

Keneally said, looking sheepish and proud at the same time, "Come on, Walter. I'll make it worth your while."

"Impossible."

"Then do it for Madeleine."

Walter gaped. "I have to hear this," he said.

"I'm going to screw Marta anyway," Keneally began. "And if Maddy found out it would hurt her. She saw you and Marta flirting—"

"Did you arrange that, too?" Walter asked.

"Marta's a good sport," Keneally said. "Anyway, you're a bachelor, what's the harm?"

Walter answered, "The harm is that I find it extremely distasteful."

"Forbes said you'd do it," Keneally countered.

Of course he had.

"Did he?" asked Walter.

"He said you were a good company man."

Walter stopped to light a cigarette.

"Christ, she's good in the sack," Keneally said. "Shame to dump her."

"Are you dumping her?"

"Have to," Keneally said. He leaned forward in his chair and added, "She thinks she's in love with me."

"And I take it you don't reciprocate."

"I love to screw her, that's for sure."

Walter winced, whether at the vulgarity or the bluntness or both, he wasn't sure.

"But she isn't the only lay in the world," Keneally continued. He laughed, leaned across the table, and whispered, "Marta wants me to divorce Maddy and marry her. I told her I'd rather be president."

"And you love Madeleine," Walter cued.

"And I love Madeleine," Keneally repeated. "Marta threatened to go public so I'd *have* to marry her. Of course she was drunk. Had a real load on."

"In vodka veritas."

Keneally said, "So tell her, will you?"

"Sorry?"

"Be a sport and tell her, will you?"

"Tell what to whom?" Walter asked, although he knew.

Keneally said, "Tell Marta it's over."

"No, thanks."

"Be a pal."

"I'm not your pal."

"You could be," Keneally said. "There are advantages to being a pal."

"I know Marta's enjoyed it."

"It'd be better if she heard it from you," Keneally said, and damned if his eyes didn't look compassionate.

"No, it would be better if she heard it from you."

"She likes you,"

But she loves you, Walter thought.

"Take care of it, Walter," Keneally said. "Tonight, after I leave your room. That's what you're paid to do, isn't it? Take care of things? So take care of it."

The ladies appeared, suitably freshened, back at the table.

"I want to find out how much Walter learned in dance class," Madeleine said. "Do you mind, darling?"

Keneally smiled and said, "Of course not. Just don't break his heart."

"I would never break sweet Walter's heart."

"Or mine," Keneally added.

She blew Keneally a kiss and held out her hand for Walter. The band started up, and they hadn't danced for more than a few bars when Madeleine leaned in and asked, "Have you had a chance to talk to him?"

"McGuire?"

"Don't be mean," she said. "Of course Sean."

"I talked with him."

"And?"

And of course Keneally and Marta were on the floor. Walter wondered if Keneally was getting the same pseudo-orgasmic treatment he'd had. Keneally was laughing and so was Marta, and were they talking about what they would do later?

"And he has problems," Walter said.

"Did you talk to him about me?"

"Not yet."

"*Walter.*"

"It's premature."

"I'm dying."

"I'll handle it," Walter said.

If it all goes well, he thought.

"Sweet Walter. You dance very well."

We all dance very well, sweet Maddy, in the Rainbow Room. On a sparkling night in the capital of the world in the closing days of the Year of our Lord 1958. As I dance with the wife, as the mistress dances with the husband, as my beloved glares at me and sings.

We dance and change partners and dance again.

Walter was smoking a cigarette and nursing a whisky in Jimmy Keneally's room at the Plaza when Jimmy came in and sat down on the bed.

"May I take this to mean that the carnal act has been completed?" Walter asked. "Madeleine safely locked in her chaste room? Your good brother and your gooder self huddled in a political meeting that just couldn't wait for the morn?"

"I've often said that the one thing standing between Joe and the White House is his dick," Jimmy answered. "You're an educated man . . ."

"At least so says Yale." Walter shrugged.

"Then you know that every hero has his fatal flaw," Jimmy said. "Women are Joe's."

"His Achilles' heel is located somewhat farther north," Walter observed. "I must say he has enormous energy."

"He doesn't sleep," Jimmy said. "Two, three hours a night, maybe. I honestly don't know if it's the sex he craves or if he's just desperate for company."

"In the dreaded small hours," Walter said.

"It's the pills," Jimmy added.

"The pills?"

"For the pain in his back," Jimmy said. "He takes pills for the pain, pills to sleep, pills to stay awake . . . I shouldn't be telling you this."

"We were followed tonight," Walter said.

Jimmy's eyes showed just a flash of alarm before settling back into the normal cool gaze.

"By?" he asked.

"I didn't ask them," Walter said. "But I'd put my money on the Bureau."

Jimmy nodded. "Goddamn Hoover. I swear the bastard can *smell* sex."

"I went up to the room with Marta and sat while she drank," Walter said. "There was no one in the hallway when the Senator came a tiptoeing."

"Thank you."

"Not to be rude, but just for the record," Walter said, "you're not welcome."

"I understand," Jimmy said.

"My boss signed me on for a job, and I'll finish it," Walter said. "So it's between me and him. Monday morning I'll go into his office and tell him I won't work for you again."

Jimmy sighed. "She has to go, Walter. Now."

"You're the fixer," Walter said. "You're famous for it."

"I can't tell her, Walter."

"Why not?"

"I'm afraid to."

"*Please,*" Walter snorted. "You're a guy who walked out on Joe McCarthy, and took on the unions, which in this town means taking on the Mob, and you're afraid of Marta Marlund?"

Jimmy stared at the floor. "Afraid of myself and Marta."

"Ah."

Jimmy smiled. "Ah."

"Have you . . ."

"Not yet," Jimmy answered. "Another reason she has to go *now*."

Walter finished his drink and said, "Then I suppose I'll just go and give her the happy word, then."

"You're a sport, Walter."

Yeah, a sport.

Marta was on the bed. Her diaphanous nightgown hid none of her considerable charms. She gripped a glass of what seemed to be vodka in her left hand. On the side table a cigarette burned in an ashtray. Next to it, a prescription bottle.

"That's dangerous, smoking in bed," Walter said.

"Joe is safely tucked in?"

Voice thick, words slurred, Walter thought. She's well into her cups.

"The Senator is in the arms of Morpheus," he said.

"Whatever that means."

"He's asleep."

"Lucky Senator."

She raised the glass to her lips. Some of the vodka— Walter could smell it now—went into her mouth. Most of it ran down her chin. A small drop trickled slowly down her long neck.

"Can't you sleep?" Walter asked.

"Did he tell you how wonderful I am in bed?"

"No, I just take that as an article of faith," Walter said. He took the glass from her hand and set it on the side table. "I think you've had enough."

"Don't take that away unless you have something to replace it."

"Are you in love with him, Marta?"

She nodded. "Stupid, yes?"

"The head and the heart . . ." Walter shrugged. "Anyway, he's a bastard."

"A bastard," she agreed.

And yet you love the bastard. A strange and comic species are we.

"It's over," he said.

"Do you think?"

He shook his head. "I know. He sent me to tell you."

"Brother Jimmy did, you mean."

You can actually watch a drunk thinking, Walter observed. The thought process is just that much slower, and you can literally see it.

"Don't think about making trouble," he said. "Don't even think about *thinking* of going to the press. Cry your eyes out, pack your things, go to Hollywood. I'm sure he'll make financial arrangements for you . . . open a few studio doors . . ."

"I can ruin him."

"You don't know these people," Walter said. "You have no idea."

"No. *You* have no idea . . ."

He didn't stop her when she reached for the vodka again and drained it.

"I'd better be going," Walter said.

"Now that you've delivered your message," she said. "Am I supposed to tip you, or does Joe take care of that, too?"

"Good night."

"Are you any better in bed than he is?!" she asked as he reached the door.

"Honestly, Marta, I wouldn't know."

"Come and let's see."

She posed. A studio publicity version of seductiveness:

on her side with one leg tucked up, her head resting on a cocked arm, a knowing smile on her lips. Pathetic, and oddly seductive.

"I will shower, if that's what's bothering you," she said. "I'll wash him off me, *out* of me, if you are so delicate. Or jealous."

"Marta—"

"Or frightened?" she asked. "He'll never know."

"That's not it."

"Come on," she cooed, stroking herself, her long fingers gliding back and forth between her legs.

Silk on silk on silk, Walter thought despite his best efforts.

"I need . . ." she said. "Come on, do me. I want you to do me."

"Try to get some sleep."

"Do me. Please do me. Isn't that what men like to hear? 'Please do me.' Doesn't that make you hard? Always it did him."

"Good night, Marta."

He turned to open the door.

"*Don't leave me like this!*" she yelled.

"Please keep your voice down."

"I can't stand to be left like this!"

Then talk to Keneally, he thought. Stagger down the hall and pound on his door. Scream his name, until the flashbulbs start exploding like the Fourth of July.

But that would never do.

Not with the two feds doubtless in a room somewhere down the hallway.

He had one foot out the door when she yelled again.

"Your friend Morrison knew what to do with a woman!" she hurled at him.

I beg your pardon? Morrison?

Walter kicked the door shut and whirled around. He strode to the bed, grabbed her by the shoulders, and pushed her up against the headboard.

Thinking it had worked, she smiled and continued, "*He* was wonderful in bed! *He* did me until I wept!"

"You're lying!"

"Wouldn't you like to think so!" she yelled into his face.

"How do you know Morrison?"

It's not a de-accelerant. It's a complete deflator.

"Until I wept!"

Spend it with your Stockholm whore.

"How do you know Morrison?" he repeated.

"Until I wept . . ."

She slumped in his hands. He laid her on the bed, rolled her onto her side so she wouldn't choke. He put out her cigarette, and then the Great Scandinavian Pimp and Deadly Recruiter took the back stairs out of the Plaza Hotel.

It was from a phone booth in the lobby of the St. Moritz that he called Morrison. Having traded a crumpled ten for eight bucks worth of dimes, and charmed the long-distance operator, and waited until her voice chirped, "Your call has gone through," all while his heart pounded and a sick feeling settled in his stomach, he finally heard Morrison's voice, thin and reedy across the transatlantic line.

"Walter? Walter Withers?"

Was there just a trace of paranoia in the voice? Is it him or me? Or both?

"Michael, how are you?"

"Cold and lonely without you, sweetheart. What's up?"

And the tone asking, Why are you calling? And why on this line?

"A little personal business, Michael."

A pause.

"Shoot."

"Do you know a woman named Marta Marlund?"

"The actress Marta Marlund?"

"The same."

Another pause. Trying to recall the truth, or trying to come up with a lie?

"I met her at a party once, Walter."

"Are you sure?"

Morrison laughed. "Have you ever seen her, Walter?"

"Actually, yes."

"Then you'd know that I'd remember if I met her."

"Michael," Walter said, "this is a tad embarrassing, but I have to ask. Did you sleep with her?"

"Your lips to God's ear."

"Did you?"

"I'd give my left testicle, but alas . . ."

"You're certain?"

"I'd have had my dick bronzed," Morrison said. "Why, may I ask with an agonizing sense of impending envy, do you want to know?"

Walter made himself chuckle a locker room chortle and said, "I just like to know that I'm not about to jump into a friend's bed."

"I can't answer for the rest of her personal history," Morrison said, "but sadly, I can assure you that her sheets are unsoiled by the personal fluids of Michael Morrison. But will you promise to call me back and tell me all about it?"

"No."

"You can reverse the charges."

"No."

"Well, then can I have Anne?"

"Michael . . ."

"This is costing you a fortune, sweetheart," Morrison said. "Good luck, and I hate you."

"Thank you, Michael."

And you make me weep.

Sweetheart.

Anne answered the door in a blue flannel robe. Her eyes were sleepy.

She said, "Walter, it's obscenely early and besides, I told you—"

He slid past her into the apartment. She shut the door and turned around to face him.

"Why is Marta Marlund a 'Stockholm whore'?" he asked again.

She shook her head.

He grabbed her arm. "Why," he asked, "did you call Marta a, quote, 'Stockholm whore'?"

She looked as if she was going to cry.

"I was angry that you were with her," she said.

"You knew her before."

"No."

"Yes," he insisted. "Maybe at a party at Morrison's?"

"That's how *we* met," she said, the tears starting. "Let go of me."

He let go and walked across the room.

"God, you look like you hate me," Anne said.

"I love you," he said.

"If you love me, stop asking these questions!"

"I can't."

"Please!"

"Why—"

She turned and walked toward the kitchen. He reached out, grabbed her, and pushed her against the wall.

"Walter!"

"Why did you call Marta a whore?"

"Walter, please . . ."

"Why did you call Marta a whore?"

"Walter . . ."

She started to slide down toward the floor. He straightened her up and pressed her against the wall.

"Why did you call Marta a whore?"

"Because she is!"

"How do you know?!"

"Because she is!"

"How do you know?"

"Because I slept with her!"

He let her go and her back slid against the wall. She squatted, her face hidden in her hands.

"You . . . ?"

"I slept with her," she said tiredly. "More to the point of your question, I paid her to sleep with me."

"More than once?"

"Oh, yes," Anne said. "You know what she's like."

"No, I don't."

She looked up at him with what? Walter wondered. Was it surprise? Gratitude? Disdain? Disgust?

"Saint Walter," she said.

"Go to hell."

"I'm there, Walter."

He wanted to lift her up and hold her. Tell her that nothing had changed, that he loved her, wanted her. But something stopped him, something as chill and harsh as a New England winter, so he just stood there looking down at her and heard himself ask, "While we were together?"

"Yes."

"How about Alicia?" he snapped. "Are you sleeping with her, too?"

She looked up at him, gray eyes so sad, and said, "Maybe."

And he just stood there.

"Leave now, Walter," she said after a minute or so. Her voice sounded so tired. "Will you just get out now? Please?"

"Will you be all right?"

"Out."

And the forgiveness of sins, Walter thought as he softly closed the door. And the forgiveness of sins.

CHAPTER FOUR

Ill Wind

Saturday, December 27

Walter Withers lurched out onto the early morning streets, where the darkness was broken only by the faint cones of light from the street lamps. The Arch of Triumph loomed eerily from Washington Square like a mocking ghost from his and Anne's happy Parisian days. No triumphant march now, he thought. No sunny April afternoon but a cold New York morning.

He tried to take the revelations in the order in which they had come to him: Keneally and Marta. Marta and Morrison. Marta and Anne.

Keneally and Marta. Obvious enough on the face of it. The Senator is quite the swordsman, he's married, and he's running for office. So he keeps the affair secret, and when the affair threatens to become public, he ends it.

Nothing extraordinary there. Almost mundane in its sad predictability, save for the celebrity of those involved.

Move on. Marta and Morrison. Morrison a would-be swordsman who claims, however, that his steel lacks the necessary tensile strength. Droops at fear of the honey trap. But Marta says quite the contrary. Morrison made her weep. Yet Morrison said he never had the pleasure, as it were. And as any good investigator knows, *it's not the substance of the lie as much as the motive for the lie.*

But what motive? Why would a man lie about his sexual prowess? Why would a single young man deny having bedded a starlet like Marta Marlund?

And then Walter thought, as he strode through the Village streets among the early morning city sounds of garbage cans clanging against the pavement and the engines of delivery trucks coughing in the cold air, about the painful couplet: Marta and Anne.

Marta and Anne.

Is it, he asked himself, just the infidelity that is so painful? The sexual *concurrency* of the affair? That at the same time she was sleeping with you, she was sleeping with Marta? *Paying* to sleep with Marta? And is the homosexual aspect of the affair equally or more troubling? Is it better or worse that she cheats on you with a woman rather than a man?

And what else? Irksome now to you . . . troublesome . . . *distasteful* that we are now all relatives of a sort. That there is now a carnal connection—you to Anne, Anne to Marta, Marta to Morrison. So you, my boy, and callow Morrison are related through sweat and intimate tissue and gasps and moans and cries.

As are you and Keneally, too, for that matter, by an identical bridge. Via Anne via Marta we are all in the same bed.

And that makes you angry, Walter observed to himself. And what else?

Apprehensive.

He stopped, took out a cigarette, and cupped his hands against the wind to light it.

Apprehensive? Why?

Coincidence.

Too damned much of it.

He walked to the all-night diner on Second Avenue and Sixth Street to get out of the cold. He sat at the counter, ordered a cup of coffee, and replayed his unfortunate scene with Anne.

How about Alicia? Are you sleeping with her, too?

Maybe.

And maybe not, Walter thought. They went to the movies and then left each other right afterward. No coffee, no drinks, no lovemaking, even though Alicia's apartment was nearby. And then Anne lied about where she'd been. Lied not about a secret tryst but about a movie date.

And Alicia left the movie with a serious case of the turkey trots. Had something hot in her hands and was in a hurry to get it home.

Are you sleeping with her, too?

Maybe.

But you *were* sleeping with Marta, Anne. Who is sleeping with Senator Joe Keneally.

We are all of us washed ashore on the sleek Scandinavian fjord that is Marta Marlund.

So who is she?

He left a buck on the counter and walked back into the cold.

He hailed a cab and rode up to Seventy-sixth and Fifth. He walked into an elegant lobby decorated in expensive *chinoise* and approached the doorman, who sat behind a small desk.

"Is Mr. Koenig in?" Walter asked.

"Herr Koenig is in residence," the doorman purred with just the slightest corrective emphasis on *Herr*.

"Would you ring him, please?"

"And who may I say is calling on him?"

"Herr Withers."

"Is he expecting you?"

"No."

"A moment, please."

The doorman spoke quietly into his telephone and then announced, "Herr Koenig said to send you right up."

Dieter Koenig came to the door in his terry cloth robe. He peered over the chain and said with complete insincerity, "Walter, how nice to see you."

"How about asking me in, Dieter?"

"I'd love to, Walter, but it is a bit early to receive visitors."

"Send him away," Walter said. "Send him to the Met, send him to brunch, send him to Saks to buy himself a present."

Dieter frowned.

"*Sofort, bitte,*" Walter said. *Now, please*. Saying it in German seemed to have the desired effect.

Dieter slid the chain open and ushered Walter into the hallway. Dieter's blond hair was tousled. He pulled his robe more tightly around his short, slim body and said, "Would you mind waiting in the sitting room for a few moments?"

"Do you mind if I smoke?" Walter asked.

"I don't mind if you burn," Dieter answered, finishing their ritual joke. "I'll be just back."

Walter sat down in a Second Empire chair by the window and looked out at Central Park. The big oaks stood out in stark black against the clean snow of the large meadow. Just across the street the sailboat glittered with ice. Across the park, the Gothic towers of the Dakota rose in a clear blue winter sky.

God, but I do love this city, Walter thought.

He took a cigarette from its case, lit it with a heavy enameled lighter from a side table, and listened to the sounds of Dieter shooing his latest young lover from the bedroom.

Dieter had redesigned the apartment since Walter had last been there—what was it, perhaps three years ago. Then it had been cluttered with expensive objets d'art and pricey gewgaws. Now he had concentrated on a few good pieces of furniture and a couple of really good paintings. The walls, then a cloying peach, were now a stark white.

"You really are a pain in the ass," Dieter said when he came in.

"Stop whining and get me a coffee," Walter answered. "I need one."

Which was true enough, but the purpose of ordering Dieter around was to get him back into the habit of service.

Dieter understood that perfectly and answered, "Yes, I would like a coffee myself. In fact, I had just put some on."

To show me that he's willing to be hospitable but not servile, Walter thought. We do fight our battles on strange ground.

Calling from the kitchen, Dieter reminded him, "I haven't heard from you in quite some time, Walter! Actually, I had heard that you were no longer in the business!"

"What business is that, Dieter?"

Dieter laughed and came in from the kitchen with a silver tray bearing a small glass coffeepot and two small cups.

"Black still?" he asked.

"Still."

Dieter poured two cups of the thick coffee, then said, "You're missed in Hamburg, Walter. The man we deal with now is businesslike but crude."

"But still he pays in dollars."

Dieter waved a hand at the paintings and smiled. "Yes."

It was useful to remind Dieter that he was after all a pimp. A high-priced pimp, but a pimp nonetheless. In Walter's days as the Great Scandinavian Pimp and Deadly Recruiter he had often purchased high-priced bait for his honey traps from Dieter's Hamburg stable.

"How was your Christmas shopping?" Walter asked.

Dieter shrugged. "Mediocre."

Dieter annually brought a few German youths over for the American market and returned to Hamburg with a few fresh young American cowboys.

"You've always had the best coffee," Walter said.

"Zabar's." Dieter shrugged. "Jews."

"I need some information," Walter said.

"Anything," Dieter said, meaning anything that could be paid or bartered for.

"*Iche stelle gerade fest,*" Walter said, lapsing into German again, "*wie fremd ich in meinem eigenem Land bin.*" It has just struck me how much a foreigner I am in my own country.

"A problem unique to Americans," Dieter said.

Walter ignored the jibe and said, "I know my way to every flesh pot in Hamburg, but in New York I am a virtual stranger."

"Nevertheless, you found your way to my place."

"It's a well-trod path."

"More than you know." Dieter's eyes brightened.

Walter recognized the challenge. Dieter had found some powerful new protector and was waiting to be asked who it was so that he could demur. Walter let it drop.

"The Good Night club . . ." Walter began.

"Sorry," Dieter snapped. "I can't help you there. I'm strictly PNG."

"PNG?"

"Persona non grata."

"Then do you know a man named Michael Howard?" Walter asked.

"No."

"Also known as Howard Benson?"

"No."

Walter described Howard physically, omitting any reference to American Electronics. "I don't suppose he's a client of yours," he said.

Dieter asked, "Who are you working for these days, Walter?"

"Is he?"

Dieter smiled charmingly. "Would I tell you if he was?"

"Are you familiar with the phrase 'undesirable alien'?" Walter asked.

"I have connections of my own."

There it is again, Walter thought. And we're in a standoff.

"In any case," Dieter said, "it is not an issue. I don't know this man."

"I'm trying to find his lover."

"He is not one of my boys."

"Oh, well."

"I sell mostly to old queens at Regent's Row," Dieter said.

"You are an old queen, Dieter."

"Then, I know what they like," Dieter said. "Anyway, if your friend is a habitué of the Good Night club, it is not likely that his lover is a professional."

"Really?"

"You are betraying your own background, Walter. Not everyone is a client or a whore. It could be something else."

"Such as?"

"Love," Dieter said. "You have been upstairs at Good Night?"

"Once."

"No whores allowed," Dieter said. Then, pointedly, "No procurers, either. I'm surprised they let you in."

"Well, it was Christmas Eve."

"Sentimental, then."

Walter looked out the window. A young couple were briskly pushing a baby carriage along the sidewalk. The baby wasn't visible, just the blue blanket. Stockbroker, Walter thought. Nanny's day off. On Saturdays the proud papas push the prams.

"You are working the other side of the fence now?" Dieter was asking. "Once the blackmailer, now you are concerned about the possibility that your man is being blackmailed?"

"Maybe."

"Maybe," Dieter scoffed. He was really enjoying this. "Listen, truly, I know nothing about this. I suggest to you that it is purely romantic. But if you want to ask around, there are several places . . ."

"And you'll give me a character reference?"

Dieter laughed. "I'll be delighted to say that I positively know you to be of low character."

He listed a few bars and clubs, then they made a few minutes of safe small talk before Walter got up to excuse himself. Gesturing to the pricy appointments in the apartment, he said, "You're doing well these days, Dieter. Prospering."

"Just doing my part in the German economic miracle."

"New York 'vice' hasn't come sniffing around?" Walter asked. "When they smell success, they usually want a taste."

Dieter slashed the air with his hand, a Teutonic gesture of dismissal. "I do not worry about the local police," he said.

Probably not, Walter thought. Not for Dieter the pink triangle and the concentration camp. He had survived the Gestapo, the Stasi, and the whole Cold War alphabet soup, all by finding and servicing the private needs of powerful patrons. He could probably handle the NYPD.

But who have you found now, Dieter?

"You are being careful, aren't you?" Walter asked, feeling a sudden, inexplicable protectiveness for the diminutive pimp. Something about old times, he guessed.

"Always," Dieter answered. "And you?"

"The same." Then he added, "But you're in a dangerous business."

"You are implying I have a choice?" Dieter asked. "Why did you really come, Walter?"

"I told you."

"And I heard," Dieter said. "But I really do think that when you wake an old friend up early on a weekend morning and make him send away a beautiful young man that you owe the friend at least some approximation of the truth."

"Do you know a Marta Marlund?"

"Yes, certainly," Dieter said. "Film actress."

"More?"

Dieter paused before answering.

"Whore."

"Whose?"

Dieter wrinkled his thick blond eyebrows and frowned. "Please, Walter, you should know."

Walter shook his head.

"Yours," Dieter said.

"I'm retired," Walter answered.

"Your successor, then."

"The crude one."

"Yes," Dieter said impatiently. "Morrison."

Dieter must have been surprised when Walter laughed.

"You are amused, Walter?"

"More surprised, really."

Although why I should be is a good question. Why should I be surprised that the Company is running an operation on Joe Keneally?

And why should I care?

"Well, take care of yourself, old friend," Walter said.

"And you."

I shall, Dieter.

Or I'll try to, anyway.

Walter grabbed a cab, got out in Washington Square Park, and hurried to Anne's apartment.

He rang the bell, waited, and rang it again. Waited, then held his finger down on the button and listened to hollow chimes inside the apartment.

Come on, come on, come on. I know you're asleep, but please come to the door. Please.

Please be asleep. Please be in there asleep.

He let himself in.

Her bed was empty.

Anne was gone.

He went out and looked for her, pacing the streets of the Village, where he had walked so many Saturday afternoons with Anne. The Village, ersatz Berlin, faux Paris, the most European part of this most American of cities.

Saturday afternoons, mornings really for a chanteuse and her lover, sweet, sleepy post-coital strolls for coffee and croissants, in winter to hustle shivering into the warmth of a dark old café, in the summer to sit at a sidewalk table lingering over cigarettes and newspapers and watching the neighborhood walk past. Busy Italian women on the way home from their shopping, their arms full of newly ground sausages, fat tomatoes, and fresh bread. Old Jewish men in a studied pace, deep in conversation or argument, faces as old as their diaspora itself. Earnest young artists with a day to create, young Mafiosi with trouble in mind, a married couple walking a dog. And Anne, lips pursed at some story in the *Village Voice*, her fingers twined around the cup handle, slowly negotiating the blind trip to her lips, the lips that he had so lately sucked. The first delicious cigarette of the day.

And the sounds. His shoes in rhythm with Anne's. Good-natured debates between greengrocer and would-be buyer at the vegetable stands. *I'll buy down the street! So go ahead!* A soprano practicing an aria from a third-floor walk-up. A radio at the newstand droning about Mantle and Maris. Shouts of kids playing *ringolevio*. A half-dozen languages, half a hundred dialects. And her voice, Anne's voice, talking with him about the news, about politics, music, the people they saw, the food they ate, their love-making. Or trying on him a new phrasing for the line of a song.

Sweet pushcarts slowly glide by.

And the Village was *smells* to him. The crisp smell of freshly washed green beans on the stand. Or peaches. Or the wonderfully acrid scent of green onions. The fecund aroma of an Italian bakery. Or in summer, the sour smell of garbage on the sidewalks as the concrete heated up. The waft of cigar smoke from an old Italian man at a sidewalk café. Smells in shops: rich coffee, delicate teas, tobacco in Village Cigars. And the scent on Anne's neck—vanilla, had it been?—on that July afternoon when walking down the sidewalk on Barrow he leaned over suddenly to kiss the nape of her neck.

And tastes. Italian ices on a hot day. Or spaghetti in marinara sauce. Thickly buttered bread. Sharp espresso, sweet red wine. In Chinatown fresh dim sum and steamed bread. And the last lovely cigarette of the afternoon.

And tell me what street compares with Mott Street . . .

And the sweet and musty taste of her as he sipped her later that summer afternoon on her sun-drenched bed.

These things were the Village for him and seemed gone now, on this gray, merciless morning. Be careful, he thought, of the streets on which you stroll with one you love, for they are never your own again.

And Anne was nowhere to be found. Not in the coffee houses or in the bars. Not paging through French magazines at Village Cigars, not buying fresh bread at La Patisserie. Not sitting on a bench in Washington Square, not window-shopping the boutiques on Sullivan.

Not there.

Perhaps, he thought, she's at the Plaza, he thought bitterly, seeking comfort in the arms of Marta Marlund, actress, mistress, and Company whore. And wouldn't Anne be shocked if she knew that she'd been in bed with the Company? In Marta's embrace?

Or, for that matter, mine?

He could never tell her, of course, when he was still with the Company. And she had seemed to believe, or at least never questioned, his cover story about ScandAmerican Import/Export. After he had left, his marks swept up and washed away, there seemed little point in telling her his past.

That's not true, he thought. You were afraid to tell her, just as she was afraid to tell you about her other side. And now both our secret pasts come back in the person of Marta Marlund.

Who Michael Morrison made weep. Michael Morrison, breaking all the rules by sleeping with the hired help, then lying about his impotence to cover his guilty trail, the lying dog.

As are you, he thought. And you should tell her. Casually drop it over drinks at the Duplex, perhaps. *Darling, isn't the music wonderful, and did I ever mention that in our European years I was a CIA spy, and would you like an espresso?* Right, that should do it. Then add, *By the way, your sapphic sometime lover is a Company whore, so you might want to be a tad discreet about your pillow talk.*

Yes, you should tell her. Just in case Marta *is* on a job for Morrison and the Company. But of course you can't tell her without also telling her how you know these tawdry things. Tell her that your life with her has been largely a lie.

But that's not entirely true, either. The love was not a lie. The love was real.

And you never took another woman to your bed. Or another man either, if that's the more accurate comparison.

You never betrayed her.

Walter walked down to Hudson Street, to the White Horse Tavern. The White Horse, Walter thought, where Dylan Thomas had his last drink before staggering ungently into that good night. The old pub was quiet. Within its old, wooden walls a few Irish longshoremen knocked back beers, and a couple of young Village intellectuals sat in a booth discussing whatever it is, Walter wondered, that young Village intellectuals discuss these days. In this case, as Walter overheard, it was Brigitte Bardot.

And God Created Woman, indeed, Walter thought. Didn't he just, the humorous old coot.

Walter took a stool at the bar. There are only a few things, he thought, that a man can do when he has woman troubles: Drink, work, or go fishing. Walter Withers didn't have the time to drive upstate to find an open stretch of trout stream, so he started to work on a bottle of Jameson's.

Walter's life heretofore had been based on a strict self-control, keeping the lid on, as it were—*tightly*—so that the very act of taking the lid off the bottle was symbolic in itself. He was aware of this, of course. When someone has kept himself under such tight control for so many years, he notices even the slightest relaxation of discipline, and drinking on the job was not slight.

It's a paradox, his father had told him. Enormous self-discipline brings with it enormous freedom. A tyranny of the spirit allows for freedom of action. The undisciplined never choose their actions, the disciplined always do.

Very well, thought Walter Withers on this cold, gray Saturday. I choose to drink. To drink and be ugly. To drink and be cruel.

After all, he thought, the bloody aftermath of Christmas—uncelebrated lest it ruin the sentiment of the season—was Herod's slaughter of the innocents. And Joseph and Mary smuggled the real boy—God's resource, if you will—across the hostile border, slipped him back in when it was safe, and kept him dormant for thirty years. A sleeper, living his cover as a carpenter. Oh, there was the odd slip: water into wine and overly precocious remarks in synagogues and the like, but basically it worked until God had use for him; then up the sleeper pops for a three-year run that ended as it always does: a show trial, torture, execution, and no one finds the body. And if God's own agent didn't stand a chance, who among them did?

No matter how tight one keeps on the lid.

Just ask Michael Howard.

Of course, Walter would have to confirm it, make sure that Howard kept a homosexual lover in a Gramercy pied-à-terre, be certain that it was just that—just that?—and not *two* betrayals, one of his wife and the other of his company. And of course, that would be Walter's happy job, to identify and locate the lover and confirm that he had nothing whatsoever to do with the electronics industry, and why had Anne insisted I come to the party at Good Night? To taunt me? To court discovery? To ease me into the fact that she loved women as well as men, as well as me? More than me?

He poured his second whiskey.

Cover. Michael Howard doubtless thought that his own was secure, but then again he wasn't a sleeper. To the contrary, his fatal flaw was that he was too good at his job, had become promotable, had attracted attention. He'd have done better to stay mediocre, to find himself a nice, safe spot in the middle of the herd and stay there.

Ah, well. His hubris, his problem.

And another whiskey gone.

And Sean McGuire here.

The writer hung his pea coat on the coat stand and took the stool next to Walter's. He was wearing an unbuttoned plaid wool shirt over a white T-shirt. His hair was greased straight back, and his face was puffy. Not from the beating he'd taken, either, Walter noticed, but from drink.

"You mind?" he asked Walter.

"Glad for the company."

The bartender set another glass down, and Walter poured Sean a drink.

"Dylan Thomas died in this joint," Sean muttered.

"I was just thinking that," Walter answered. "Although actually he died in the street outside. Why, do you have similar ambitions?"

"I could do worse."

"You could, indeed."

"Baltimore has a hell of an offense."

"Yes, they do."

"Johnny Unitas."

"Lenny Moore."

"I dig Lenny Moore," Sean said. "He runs like jazz. He runs like Bird blew."

Walter lifted his glass. "To Charlie Parker."

"To Charlie Parker."

"To Lenny Moore."

"To Lenny Moore."

"To Dylan Thomas."

"To Thomas."

Walter refilled their glasses.

"To F. Scott Fitzgerald," he said.

"Oh, man," Sean said. "To Fitzgerald."

"You know what I love to say?" Sean said a few moments later. "I love to say, Jim Katcavage. Man, that's a name for a defensive end. Katcavage."

"Because it rhymes with savage," Walter said.

"You think so?"

"Sure."

"I'll bet you're right," Sean said. "Gonna be a hell of a game, man."

"Are you going?"

" 'Course I'm going."

"Well, watch yourself," Walter said. "The Keneallys will be there, too."

"Yeah?"

"Yeah. I'll be with them."

McGuire stared into his glass for a minute, then asked, "Why should I watch myself with the Keneallys, Walter?"

"I don't think you're their favorite person."

"You get the bet down?"

"Not yet."

"What are you waiting for?"

"The last possible moment," Walter said. "Always make your bet at the last possible moment."

"This is my last bet," McGuire said.

"Famous last words."

"Behan's in town," McGuire said. "I saw him last night, drunk as a sailor on Third Avenue. Puked in the gutter and passed out on the sidewalk. Another Celtic writer drinking himself to death."

"Well, I suppose there are just some responsibilities that go along with being a Celtic writer."

"To Brendan Behan."

"To Brendan Behan."

"To Jim Katcavage."

"Katcavage."

"To the entire Giants' defense," Sean toasted.

"To the entire Giants' offense," Walter offered.

"To Charlie Conerly," Sean said. "Did you know he's the Marlboro Man?"

"No, I didn't."

"The truth," Sean said. "Charlie Conerly, quarterback of the sainted New York football Giants, was the model for the original Marlboro Man."

"Is that your way of cadging a smoke?"

"It isn't, but . . ."

Walter pulled his cigarette case from his jacket pocket, lit two à la Boyer and handed one to McGuire.

"Do you know what I did with my whole advance for *Highway*?" Sean asked.

"You drank and gambled it away."

"I drank and gambled it away," McGuire laughed. "Now I'm broke, man, I'm beat."

"You have a best-seller," Walter objected. "You must be making money."

McGuire shook his head. "You know how publishers pay, man?"

"No."

"*Slooooooooooowly.*"

"Well, if you don't have it," Walter said, "you can't drink it and gamble it away."

"There's that."

"There's that."

"Why do you drink?" McGuire asked.

Walter thought about it for a few moments, then said, "I have troubles of the heart."

"I have troubles of the heart," Sean said.

Walter didn't want to hear a word about Madeleine Keneally, so he offered a toast to close the topic. "To troubles of the heart."

"To troubles of the heart."

They sat in the shared male silence that came with troubles of the heart, then Sean said, "Anne Blanchard is your chick, huh?"

"I'm not sure I'd phrase it exactly that way," Walter answered. "But yes, and how do you know?"

"Big city, small scene," Sean said. "Anyway, I've heard her sing. I dig her, man. She's a jazz angel. That voice don't come from *this* world."

"To Anne Blanchard."

"To Anne Blanchard."

"Walter?"

"Yes?"

"You gotta let people be what they are, man," Sean said. "You gotta let people be what they are."

Walter tossed five bucks on the bar.

"Finish it," he said to Sean.

"I'm only telling you, man—"

"Thanks."

"—what I tell myself all the time."

Walter walked outside. The sky was one of those that Walter thought of as thin, a fragile blue that could turn to steel in an instant. And cold, too; that wet, heavy cold that reminded you that New York was a port city, that with the ocean liners and freights also came the gray damp.

I'll take Manhattan
The Bronx and Staten Island, too. . . .

Warmed by the whisky, Walter left his overcoat unbuttoned and let his scarf hang loosely around his neck. He stuck his hat on his head at what he thought was a jaunty, devil-may-care angle and hit the streets.

For the next few hours Walter Withers worked his way through Dieter Koenig's list of New York's homosexual hangouts and imbibed at least one drink at each one of them. He told himself that it was part of the job, part of blending into the environment.

But it was about Anne, of course. Anne and anger, to be alliterative about it. Anne and anger, but why? Was it just the fact of betrayal, or betrayal with a woman? Would it have been better if it had been a man? Or worse?

And there it was. The guilt. The guilt that he was happy that it was a woman instead of a man.

But why *that* woman, why Marta Marlund? God damn it, *why that woman?*

That was the question that kept him drinking through his tour of the bars and clubs, the gyms and the steam rooms. The question that made him sidle up to the bar and order a drink, then ask about Howard Benson and get a negative response. Then order another drink and, ignoring the hostile glares and suspicious stares, sit there and drink it—sip it if he chose.

He knew he was behaving badly—offensively—but wanted to misbehave, wanted to offend, wanted to drop—

for just a day—the subtle courtesies of his profession and personality.

Drop them he did, to the point where by the cold gray-brown of the late afternoon he would simply lurch through the door, ask the question, grin at the silent stares, then lay his cash on the bar, and silently dare the bartender to refuse it. Then he would sit, drink, and watch the patrons either freeze into a sullen tableau or flee on the assumption that he was a vice cop, an error he did nothing to disabuse.

It was behavior, he knew, that was based on his power and their lack of it. Behavior that was no different from the worst Southern sheriff throwing his weight around in a Negro honky-tonk. It was black-shirt behavior, jack-boot behavior, behavior that Anne would despise and abhor, and that was the point, wasn't it?

Saint Walter.

By the time he worked his way back to Good Night—as he knew he was going to do, as he knew was inevitable, as he drunkenly knew was the point of this whole stupid exercise—he was wickedly drunk.

A heavily muscled doorman dressed in a slate gray blazer, white button-down shirt, and skinny black pants blocked the stairs.

"Are you a member, sir?" he said.

"I'm going to assume that's not some sort of hideous pun," Walter answered.

"Huh?"

"I am not a member, my good man," Walter said. "I *have* a member, but I am not a member, nor do I know the password."

"This is a private club."

"Which is a redundancy, isn't it? In any case, I have business here."

"What kind of business?"

Sort of "find the homosexual in the woodpile" business, Walter thought, but didn't say. Instead he asked, "Do you know a man named Howard Benson? Athletic, tennis-playing sort of fellow?"

The doorman glowered at him and repeated, "This is a *private* club."

"Discretion is an admirable quality in a doorman," Walter said. He took a five-dollar bill from his pants pocket and offered it.

The doorman pushed the money back, saying, "Shove it up your ass."

"As Freud spins," Walter mumbled.

"Funny."

"Actually, I've been upstairs before," Walter said. "Christmas Eve. A bright star had appeared in the east, three wise men gathered, and I was the guest of the oh-so-stylish *chanteuse* Anne Blanchard. I had a good time, too. Better than I expected . . . to have . . . had."

"Why don't you go somewhere and get yourself a cup of coffee?" the doorman asked.

"Why don't I go upstairs and have a cup of coffee?" asked Walter, producing another five.

"Because it's a private club and you're not a member."

"Is Howard Benson a member?" asked Walter. "You see, I'm not used to this. Doormen usually like me. Even my own doorman likes me, which you'll admit is extraordinary, familiarity breeding contempt and all, although some people would have it that familiarity just breeds, period. Not even a laugh? Are you made of stone, man? Not even a chuckle or a chortle?"

"C'mon, chief."

The doorman grabbed him by the elbow and started to move him toward the outer door.

"No, no, no, no, no," Walter said. His laugh now had a

distinct edge to it. "Kindly remove your hand. I do not allow strangers to handle me."

It's a bad habit, once started difficult to stop, Walter thought. The very edge of the slippery slope.

Something in Walter's eyes made the doorman take his hand away and merely hold open the door.

"Thank you, " Walter said.

"My pleasure."

"And not entirely unpleasurable to me," Walter said, "to see a man do his job despite financial inducement to do otherwise. One sees less and less integrity these days. By the way, I'm a personal friend of Jules Benoit. Would that help?"

"Mr. Benoit isn't here today."

"Also, I'm a relation of sorts to one of your waitresses," Walter added. "Lovely girl named Alicia. Do you know her?"

"You're related to Alicia?"

"Shhh." Walter put his fingers to his lips. "It's a secret. Very hush-hush. Great grandad in the slave quarters type of thing. Anyway, is she here?"

"I don't know."

"Need to talk to her. Really need to talk with her."

To find out, Walter thought, if her relationship with Anne is of a business or personal nature. Or an intimate nature. Or all of the above.

"Sorry, chief."

"Need to go upstairs."

"No can do."

"I'm also a personal friend of Paulie Martino's," Walter mumbled darkly.

"It's all right, Ben," said a cultured voice behind Walter. "Mr. Withers is my guest."

Walter turned around and saw the sloe-eyed writer from

the Plaza, the essayist with whom he'd discussed football. The man was dressed in distinguished-writer Saturday afternoon garb: a tailored tweed jacket, cotton twill trousers, suede shoes.

"Thank you," Walter said. "Embarrassed I don't recall your name."

"I don't know that you ever learned it," the writer said. "In any case, my name Julian. Julian Hidalgo."

Walter stuck out his hand.

"Shall we go upstairs?" asked Julian.

"We shall."

The room seemed considerably duller than it had on Christmas Eve. Gone were the decorations, the tree, and the bright tablecloths. Gone, to Walter's disappointment, was the train.

The club was far from empty, however. There were a number of drinkers at the long bar, some congenial groups laughing in the banquettes, and a few couples dancing to the jukebox, which to Walter's ear was knocking out some pop tune repetitively proclaiming that something was or was not happening "at the hop hop hop."

Michael Howard Benson wasn't in the room.

Nor was Alicia.

"You seem," Julian said, "to have an inordinate degree of curiosity about the establishment. May I ask why?"

"Business and personal."

"Kindly keep your business out of here," Julian said. "As to the personal . . . Well, I'd otherwise be interested in indulging your curiosity, but, you see, I have a date."

"You misunderstand me."

Julian eyed him for a long moment and smiled. "Do I?" he asked. "I wonder."

"Don't trouble yourself."

"It's no trouble."

The dreadful "hop" song stopped. The jukebox clicked and whirred, the needle scratched a new disk, and Tommy Edward's voice began "It's All in the Game." The couples on the dance floor embraced and started moving gently to the slow song.

"It's no trouble," Julian repeated. "In fact, perhaps you'd like to join us?"

"Join where?"

"Behind the mirror."

In the infamous baths.

"No, thank you," Walter said.

"Does your lovely Anne know?"

"Know?"

"That you have these . . . urges."

"But I don't."

"Again, I wonder."

Walter pulled his cigarette case from his jacket and offered one to Julian.

"Gauloise," Julian said.

"I acquired the habit in Europe."

"As did I."

"I'm talking about the cigarettes."

"I'm not," Julian said. "Wouldn't you just like to come back and see? Later you can say you were drunk. It's true—you are."

Perhaps Michael Howard Benson is there, Walter thought. In flagrante delicto as it were. That would about do it in the old report. And pay the joint back. Back for what? he asked himself. For Anne and Alicia? For Anne and Marta? Betrayal for betrayal?

"Call it professional curiosity," Walter said.

"Call it whatever you want."

He followed Julian behind the mirror, through a small wooden door that led to the back, a changing room just off a corridor that was cheaply partitioned with pinewood walls into small cubicles.

Julian stripped, wrapped a towel around himself, and looked at Walter.

"I'll stay dressed if you don't mind," Walter said.

Julian shrugged. "We'll be in number three."

Walter sat on a bench, his head whirling from the surfeit of booze and the steamy heat. The pinewood partitions did little to mute the sounds of assignation coming from the baths—the laughter, the sighs, the occasional moans. A short, sharp, climactic cry.

Despite himself he listened for feminine voices, not really expecting to hear any in what seemed a male domain. Not really expecting to hear Anne's voice, yet hearing it in his head.

Despite his better nature he got up and walked down the corridor, feeling like hell for looking into the first two cubicles at the naked men who clearly, even through the hazy steam, were none of them Michael Howard Benson.

He stood at the open door of number three at the smoothly muscled back of Julian Hidalgo as it rose from the steaming water. Looked at the strong hand that gripped the back of Julian's head where it bent to an intimate kiss.

Sean McGuire's head was tilted back in pleasure. When he looked up again, he saw Walter looking at him. Julian halted his ministrations and looked over his shoulder.

They were the three of them frozen in this tableau until Walter turned and walked away.

You gotta let people be what they are.

Walter made his way back to the long bar in the main room.

"Top of the afternoon," he warbled to the bartender in a stage Irish brogue that Barry Fitzgerald would have blushed at.

"Afternoon," the bartender answered.

He was too handsome to be just a bartender, Walter thought. He was actor handsome, stage handsome, tending bar between auditions. Were there no professionals left in what had once been an honorable trade?

"Jameson straight up, if you'd be so kind, my good man," Walter said.

On the jukebox the Everly Brothers were playing "All I Have to Is Dream," and the place had crowded up even in the few minutes Walter had been in the back. Probably, he thought, the Saturday matinee crowd just getting out.

The bartender poured his drink, slid it across the bar, and said, "That's a lousy dialect."

"Well, let me give you a straight line, then."

"A straight line?"

"You know what a straight line is."

"Sure."

"Okie-dokie, here we go," Walter said. Then he pronounced in a clumsy actor's fashion, "I'm looking for a man."

"Why don't you finish your drink—quickly—and leave?"

"No, no, no, no, no," Walter clucked. "I give you the straight line, and you give me the punch line. You say something like, 'Aren't we all,' or 'Well, you came to the right place.' "

"You came to the wrong place," the bartender said. Then he got busy wiping glasses.

"That's more like it," said Walter. "Wrong line, of course, but more in the spirit of things. Let's try it again. 'I'm looking for a man.' "

Heavy silence as the entire room listened and feigned indifference.

"A man by the name of Howard Benson."

"Look somewhere else."

This from a voice at a corner table. Walter turned on his stool to see a young man in a red flannel shirt over khaki slacks. A thin but muscular young man. Not barbell muscles or football muscles. Not boxing muscles.

"I have been looking somewhere else," Walter said. "I've been looking everywhere else."

"Try the precinct house," the young man said. "You might be surprised."

Brown hair, cut short. Green eyes, shiny with anger. A gym bag at his feet. White lettering on black vinyl: ANSONIA STUDIOS.

Whatever that is, Walter thought. But doubtless the answer to the muscles.

"And what would your name be?" Walter asked.

"None of your damn business."

"How do you spell that?"

The young man held up his middle finger, "Like this."

"And do you know a Howard Benson?"

"No."

"How about Michael Howard?"

"No."

Forthright people make such bad liars, Walter thought. And the other clothes in Michael Howard Benson's apartment would probably fit you. You've made a mistake, my brave young man. An admirable error born of good character, but an error nevertheless. You ought not have stood up for your friend or yourself. You should have stayed quiet, stayed in the shadows. There is after all a reason it is the sin that dare not speak its name. If you had not been so brave, I would not have known. I would have gone away thinking the afternoon was a sick, drunken failure.

But schooled in deceit as we are, decent people do not stand the chance of the proverbial snowball in hell.

"Oh, well," Walter said.

"Now get out."

"I'll leave when I'm ready."

"I think that you're ready now," said Jules Benoit's slow Southern voice. "Walter, you've abused our hospitality. I'll have to ask you to leave, please."

Walter slid off the stool and addressed the young man, "See, it's the 'please' that makes all the difference."

"And not come back," Jules said.

Walter laid a hand on Jules' shoulder. "I'm sorry," he said.

"You should be ashamed."

"I am."

"Good-bye, Walter," Jules said.

"Good-bye."

The air outside was heavy, the sky dark and threatening to snow.

When he got home, his apartment door was cracked open and someone was inside.

Walter pushed the door with his foot and saw a tall, be-spectacled man in a cheap gray overcoat thumbing through a book on his shelf. The man turned around when the door opened and asked, "Walter Withers?"

The man was tall and skinny with a round face and a head that looked too heavy for his thin neck to carry. His glasses were bottle-thick with ugly brown frames. His black hair was slicked straight back and needed a trim. Under the overcoat he wore a cheap black suit with the de rigeur white button-down shirt and black tie.

"And you are?" Walter asked.

A badge came out. Gold, flashing dimly in the lamplight.

"Detective Zaif, NYPD. Come in."

"Thank you."

Walter shut the door behind him.

"You were banging a woman named Marta Marlund?" Zaif asked casually.

"A gentleman doesn't answer that question," Walter answered as he hung up his hat and coat.

Christ Jesus, what is this about?

"In Room 512 of the Plaza?"

"The specific location doesn't alter the obligations of chivalry," Walter said casually, even though alarm jolted from his heels to his head.

"You were registered in Room 512 of the Plaza," Zaif said.

"That is true."

"That's where the body was."

Walter felt the pins-and-needles electricity of fear.

"Whose body?" he asked.

"Marlund's," Zaif said, annoyed, as if the answer was obvious.

He was waiting for a reaction.

"My God," Walter said. "What happened?"

What happened is, Walter thought, that I made a phone call to Michael Morrison and now Marta's dead. What happened is that I went to see Anne and now Marta's dead.

Zaif stared at him for a few seconds before answering, "It looks like she croaked herself."

Walter sat down and put his head in his hands.

"That's what it *looks* like," Zaif said. "But I'm not sure I buy it."

"What do you mean?"

Another pause. A you-tell-me pause.

"I think maybe she had some help," Zaif said.

"Why do you think that?"

"Where were you all day?" Zaif asked. "By the way, have you been drinking?"

"That's where I was all day."

"Where?"

"Drinking."

"No, I mean *where*," Zaif said.

"Here and there."

"Hither and yon?"

"Hither and yon."

Zaif wandered over to the shelf that held Walter's record collection. "You have some nice music here."

"Do you like jazz?" asked Walter.

"I'm more of a classical guy," Zaif said. "You know, your basic Jew. My parents wanted another Heifetz." He held up the long fingers on his big hands. "I have the equipment but no ear. Anyway, I just started to get interested in the new stuff. Brubeck, Getz, Desmond. You have a lot of this Blanchard singer. I don't now her. Who is she?"

Good question, Walter thought, but answered, "Among other things, she's my girlfriend."

"Uh-oh," Zaif said. "Did she know about Marlund?"

That she's dead? Walter wondered.

"They've met," he said.

Zaif smiled. "You have balls, Walt."

"Why do you think—"

"What do you do for a living, Walt?"

Among other things, Walter thought, I'm a beard for Joe Keneally.

But he said, "If we're going to be on a first-name basis, Detective, let's even it up."

"Sam. Not Sammy."

"Walter. Not Walt. And I'm an investigator at Forbes and Forbes."

Zaif's hand edged under his coat. "You have a gun license, Walter?" he asked.

"Yes."

"Are you carrying a gun now?"

"I don't own a gun."

"Answer the question I asked you."

"I do not at present have a gun on me."

Zaif's hand came back out in the open. "Do you play chess?" he asked.

"No, I find it almost preternaturally tedious," Walter said. "Why?"

"Because I don't want you playing chess with me. I just want you to give me straight answers to straight questions."

There is not now, nor has there ever been, such a thing as a straight question, Walter thought.

"I'll cooperate in any way I can, Sam."

"So let's go."

"To . . . ?"

"I blush at the cliché," Zaif answered. "Downtown."

"Why don't we just talk in the relative comfort of my apartment?" asked Walter.

"The answer is inherent in the question, isn't it?" Zaif said. Then he added, "Talmudic scholar."

"I gathered."

Zaif took Walter's hat and coat from the rack and tossed them onto his lap.

"A coffee for you, a tea for me," Zaif said as he set the cardboard tray down on the small metal table in the interview room.

Ink from Walter's fingers smudged the cardboard cup as he picked it up and sipped the hot, if otherwise vile, delicatessen coffee. A radiator hissed and crackled along one wall. The room was oppressively hot—Walter knew that that was the idea—but he stubbornly refused to loosen his tie, unbutton his collar, or even take off his jacket. Being unshaved and unshowered this late in the evening was already a humiliation, and it was necessary to maintain some dignity. So he stayed buttoned up, as it were, and sweated beneath the clothes.

He took some satisfaction from the fact that Zaif was sweating, too—his glasses kept slipping down his nose—but had kept on his own jacket and tie in a sartorial battle of wills. His sleeves were a tad too short as well, Walter noticed as the detective laid his big hands and lumpy wrists on the table.

"So tell me about Marta Marlund," Zaif said.

"If you have specific questions, I'll try to answer them," Walter responded.

That bit from the training days. Don't talk, elicit questions. Glean from the questions the direction that the asker wants to go, then take him somewhere else.

"Okay," Zaif said. "Where did you meet?"

"I don't recall."

"You recall," Zaif said. He carefully tore two packages of sugar, poured them into his milky tea, and stirred. "Nobody forgets where they met a woman like that."

"Perhaps it was Paris."

"What's that, a song title? 'Perhaps it was Paris,' 'Maybe it was Moscow' 'Could It Have been Copenhagen'?"

"It could have been Copenhagen," Walter admitted.

"She was Danish, right?"

"I believe so."

"You should have heard the jokes when we found her passport," Zaif said. "You know, 'I'd sure like piece of *that* Danish.' 'Wouldn't you like some of that with your coffee in the morning?', that sort of thing. So how is it a schmucky P.I. like you gets to *schtupp* a movie star?"

And here we go, Walter thought.

"I'd hardly call her a star," he answered.

Zaif said, "I've seen a couple of her movies. My girlfriend likes those art films. I'm telling you, Marlund was the complete fantasy shiksa. The hair, the eyes, the pistols . . . fucking Brunhilde with sex appeal. So how is it?"

"I beg your pardon?"

"So how is it a schmucky P.I. gets to *schtupp* a movie star?"

"There are three questions there, aren't there, Sam?"

"There's a hell of lot more than three, Walter," Zaif said. "Quit stalling."

Walter pulled his cigarette case from his jacket, offered one to Zaif, then lit one for himself.

"Jesus, what is this?" Zaif said when he took a drag.

"Gauloise," Walter answered. "French. I get them in the Village."

"They taste like shit."

"An acquired taste," Walter said. He took a long drag on the cigarette and added, "You're right. They do taste like shit."

"You know, Walter," Zaif said, "now is about the time that one of my shanty Irish colleagues—less refined and cultured than myself—would probably bounce your head off that nice metal desk and tell you to answer his fucking question."

"Are you going to bounce my head off this nice metal desk?"

"No, I'm too Jewish," Zaif answered. "I'm going to nag you."

Walter sat back in his chair and said, "Once again you are making the assumption that I was having intimate relations with Miss Marlund."

"Just because we found her lying on the bed in your hotel room, as good as naked in a filmy negligee . . ."

Information received for none given, Walter thought. Patience is a virtue, and is even occasionally rewarded. And yet the image was troubling, tawdry, and sad. A lonely woman in her come-hither costume, exposed to the ungentle touch of strangers.

"I think I met Marta at a party in Copenhagen," Walter said. "When she came to New York she looked me up."

"What were you doing in Copenhagen?" Zaif asked.

"I worked for ScandAmerican Import/Export, based in Stockholm. Copenhagen was a place we went for weekends sometimes."

"I don't get it," Zaif said.

"What don't you get, Sam?"

"You were working in international import and export, and now you're a private investigator?"

"I was in charge of security for ScandAmerican."

"Okay," Zaif said. "How was it you quit?"

"I just wanted to be in New York."

Zaif blinked beneath the glasses. "You missed what?" he asked. "The Automat?"

"As a matter of fact, yes," Walter answered. "And Sardi's, and the Stork Club, and Broadway shows, Times Square at night, hot dogs, pretzels with mustard, Italian food, football games—"

"—the Plaza Hotel . . ."

"—not to mention the Waldorf."

"How is it you get a room at the Plaza, Walter?" Zaif asked. "You live, what, ten minutes away? How is it you don't take her to your place?"

"As you said, she's a movie star."

"*Was* a movie star," Zaif said. "The Plaza's expensive. How does a P.I. afford the Plaza?"

"I have a modest private income," Walter answered.

"Are you rich, Walter?"

"I have a modest private income."

"Enough if you've got a Danish actress can ball, you can do it in style, right?" Zaif asked.

"In theory I suppose that's true."

"When was the last time you saw Marlund?"

Walter recognized the technique. The classic interrogation is shaped like an inverted pyramid. It starts with broad questions and then narrows down to specifics. They were now approaching the narrow part, working their way down to the apex.

Walter answered, "Early this morning. I left to go to work."

"What time?"

"I don't recall exactly."

"Of course not," Zaif snapped. "How about approximately?"

Because you think you have a time of death, Walter thought.

"Eight?" he said.

"Are you asking or telling?"

"I'm approximating," Walter said. Zaif was picking up the pace now, asking for facts, bringing his questions closer to the circumstances of Marta's death.

"Where'd you go?"

"To work."

"In the office?"

"In the field."

"What do you mean 'field'?" Zaif asked. "What were you doing, picking cotton?"

"In a manner of speaking."

"But earlier you told me you'd been drinking all day."

"That's right."

"But now you say you were working."

"They're not necessarily mutually exclusive," Walter said. "Ask your shanty Irish colleagues—less refined and cultured than yourself."

Zaif chuckled and asked, "You can give me names and places?"

"I can give you places."

He told Zaif about The White Horse, then named a few other bars that he frequented but hadn't been that day. More likely than not, the bartenders would say if asked that he had been there, memory being an imperfect and fluid thing.

Zaif pushed his glasses back up on his nose and asked, "What was Marlund drinking?"

"Why?"

"Vodka?"

"It could have been vodka, yes."

Tell them what they already know, the book said. That way you elicit more questions based on what they know. Every question they ask is an answer for you. And it must have been an overdose, Walter thought.

"Were you drinking with her?"

"No."

"You're sure."

"Yes."

"Did she get drunk?"

"She was somewhat in her cups, yes."

"Did you ever tell her she'd had enough? Take the glass from her hand?"

Father, take this cup from my hands?

"No, I regret to say that I didn't."

"Is that your style, Withers? Get the girl a snazzy hotel room, get her loaded, get in her panties?"

"I'll assume that's a rhetorical question," Walter said.

"Pills?" Zaif asked.

"I'm not following you."

"Did you give her pills?"

"No."

"Your room looked like a pharmacy."

And now, Walter thought, we're at the phase when the interrogator stops asking questions and starts making statements.

"Marta mentioned that she had trouble sleeping," Walter answered.

"And you helped her out with that."

Vodka and sleeping pills, Walter thought. But why does he think she had help?

"No," Walter said.

"No?"

"*No.*"

"But you *saw* her take pills," Zaif said.

"No, I said she told me that she did."

"And I'm asking you if you saw her take any," Zaif pushed.

"And I'm telling you that I didn't," answered Walter.

"But you saw pills."

"I think so."

"What kind?"

Nembutol, Walter thought. But he said, "I don't know."

"You don't?"

"About three times a year, Detective, I get a headache and take an aspirin," Walter said. "That's about the sum of my experience with pills."

"Nembutol," Zaif said.

"Is that what killed her?"

"I don't know. Is it?"

"I don't know, either."

"See, I think you do."

Which didn't seem to Walter to call for a response, so he drank his coffee but otherwise kept his mouth shut.

After a bit Zaif said, "See, we find Marlund lying on the bed like this, with her right hand hanging over the edge. On the floor just below her hand is a hotel glass lying on its side and some vodka spilled on the carpet."

"She dropped the glass."

"That's what we think, too," Zaif said. "Guess what's in her left hand."

"A sleeping pill."

"Nembutol, to be precise. So what it looks like is that she was eating these things like M&M's and washing them down with vodka."

That's what it looks like, Walter thought. It looks like she was brokenhearted and hopeless and desperate and alone and she took her life. That's indeed what it looks like. But that's not what you think, Detective Zaif, and you're about to tell me why.

"The problem is . . ." Zaif began, then took the trouble to push his glasses up again so he could look Walter straight in the eye. "The problem is that your fingerprints are all over the glass."

Yes, that is a problem, Walter thought. Another problem is that it's virtually impossible to kill yourself by washing Nembutol down with alcohol. If you take too much at one time, you vomit it up. If you take them one at a time, you pass out before you can ingest a lethal dosage.

"Why," Walter asked, "would I want to feed Marta Marlund a lethal dose of sleeping pills?"

Zaif answered, "That's what I don't understand. If I had a motive, I'd arrest you right now. But as the old cliché goes, don't leave town."

"New York's the town for me," Walter said.

"Berlin?"

"Porter."

"Anyway, don't leave town."

Oh, I won't, Detective Sergeant Zaif. I most definitely won't. Because I share your suspicion that Marta Marlund was helped into her terminal sleep. And if that is true, someone had a reason, and that reason is most interesting to me.

When Walter got home, he tried to call Anne, but the phone rang until her answering service picked up. He left a message asking her to call, took a shower, and then tried to get a few hours' sleep.

The dream came that night in shattered shards of images. But in the most vivid he was no longer on the sea cliff looking down, but on the rock itself. Engulfed by the ocean, the bodies of his marks washing against the cliff and the wave was rising like a wall of water.

Straight toward him.

CHAPTER FIVE

Scrapple from the Apple

Sunday, December 28

Football, Walter Withers thought as he finished shaving, is the American game.

While it might be true that baseball is the American pastime, football is the sport that typifies the country itself. Americans may pass time in the gentle, leisurely rhythms of baseball, idling with a beer and a hot dog at the park or listening in half attention to the hypnotic drone of a radio broadcast, but it is football where the American psyche, the American energy, the sheer American passion for struggle, plays itself out.

Baseball is a game played under warm and sunny skies, football a contest waged in the harshness of all weathers. The baseball season starts with the new warmth of spring and finishes in the soft twilight of early fall. The football season begins in the crisp air of autumn and ends under the unrelenting sky of winter. They play football in the rain, snow, and cold, and the fans share at least that part of the game's challenge. While the baseball fan sits back in his seat, face to the sunshine, sipping his beer, the football fanatic more often than not *stands,* packed shoulder to shoulder with his comrades, passing a flask of hard liquor to fight off the cold. The football fan is not the sunshine soldier but the winter patriot.

Baseball is a game of skill and grace. Football is a contest of wills.

Of *team* wills, he distinguished. While baseball is a game designed to match individual against individual in a series of showdowns—the beautiful coordination of the storied double play the exception rather than the rule—football subordinates the fierce American individualism to a common goal, or goal post, as it were. Each man has his role, each is dependent on the other. The teamwork is epitomized in the offensive line, anonymous and unheralded save to the true cognoscente. The linemen labor in what appears to be brutal chaos but is in fact brutal precision that requires immaculate timing and rhythm. In the offensive line, thought Walter, is the essence of football and the essence of the country.

Yes, he punned, baseball is the national pastime whose time has passed. Baseball is the game of the farm, football the game of the factory. Baseball is a game of peace, football a game of war.

Even when it's a Cold War, Walter thought. Because we will never truly be at peace again.

He washed the lather from his face, patted some Old Spice on his cheeks, then went to his closet to get his Sunday go-to-football-game best. The feel of a starched white shirt against his skin revived him more than the scant hours' sleep he'd had. He slipped into a pair of gray wool trousers, then sat on the bed to put on some argyle socks and brown Churchills.

He chose a maroon knit tie that matched his heavy tweed sports coat and again thanked the fates that New York was still a town that dressed for occasions. Finding the silver flask he'd had since Yale (Boolah, boolah, and Beat Harvard and all that), he filled it with single-malt scotch he'd been saving for, once again, an occasion. Tempted to take a drink, he quickly screwed the lid on lest he "Oscar ('I can resist everything but temptation') Wilde" the situation.

No, Walter thought, you have had your day of despair. Now is the time to take yourself back in hand and get to work.

"A four-in-hand means the man's in hand," he said to himself as he ran the tie through his collar. This was one of his father's more tortured aphorisms, but the point was adept. *Clothes do* not *make the man, his father had said, but are an outer reflection of the inner man. They say* exactly what *they seem to say.*

Accordingly, he dressed carefully, then fixed a pot of strong coffee and smoked a single cigarette while waiting for the coffee to perk. He scanned the headlines of the Sunday *Times* until the bubbles started to *plop* in the glass top, then drank the coffee and ate two slices of heavily buttered toast.

Nembutol, he thought. The trade name for the drug pentobarbitol, a common barbiturate. Zaif was sharp, all right, but hadn't figured out yet that something was missing. It all depended on how thorough and knowledgeable the medical examiner would be, and Dietz would let him know about that. Dietz hadn't been thrilled to get Walter's three-in-the-morning phone call ("William, in the words of F. Scott Fitzgerald, 'In the dark night of the soul it is *always* three a.m.' "), but after a few cheerful obscenities had been cooperative enough. Dietz was always ready to help a buddy and defend the good name of Forbes and Forbes, even if it meant paying a visit to the morgue and hitting up a few old connections. ("And William, and Fitzgerald didn't say this, but find out if there was a needle mark.")

And if there is a needle mark, Walter thought, then Marta was murdered. If so, by whom?

It would be quite useful right now, he mused, if my role

in the Company had been that of an investigator rather than a pimp. But I do seem to recall—from Spillane, was it?—some hoary old test about motive, means, and opportunity.

All right, then, motive. Who had a motive? Joe Keneally, for one, if he thought Marta was going public with their affair. But he wouldn't have done it himself. He'd have arranged it through Jimmy. So Jimmy Keneally, the aide-de-camp, the chief of staff, the *fixer,* might have fixed this situation. He wouldn't have delegated it to Callahan, Brown, or Cahill. It was too important and required some subtlety.

Who else?

Madeleine, of course, speaking of subtlety. Cliché, perhaps—the jealous mate—but possible.

Then there's Anne.

He dialed her number again, again reached her service, and again left a message. Where the hell could she be? Marta was dead and Anne?

He put on his hat and coat and headed out the door.

Perhaps he'd find some answers with Clan Keneally at the game.

When he stepped outside, the two Bureau men were crouched in a black sedan. The car started and trailed him to the subway, where one of them jumped out and followed him down.

The train rumbled under Harlem. Packed elbow to elbow, the jammed celebrants nevertheless managed to pass flasks among themselves and take small, democratic sips before passing them on again, often to strangers. The smell of booze, aftershave and cigar-smoke-imbued clothing filled what air there was, along with sounds like "Conerly" and "Gifford" and "red dog" and "home field."

Walter loved it: the crowd, the friendly jostling, the tilting of the train, the nervous chatter, the hopeful anticipation of the Big Game.

And a big game it would be. The two teams were evenly matched: Weeb Ewbank's Colts had a powerful offense averaging almost forty points a game while Joe Lee Howell's Giant defense allowed an average of twelve. But more than that, Walter thought happily, it would be a game of great talents and great personalities.

On the Colts' side there was Johnny Unitas, rescued from a life of sandlot ball and now one of the best quarterbacks in the sport. His prime receiver was the perfectionist Raymond Berry, who'd had his new bride throw footballs to him on their honeymoon and who ran the cleanest, most precise pass patterns in the league. When Unitas wasn't throwing to Berry, he was looking for his flanker, Lenny Moore, number twenty-four, who was a terrific runner either off the pass or taking a pitch-out wide to either side. The fullback was Alan "The Horse" Ameche, all 240 pounds of him, and he was never going to take it outside but straight up the middle behind the huge offensive line, especially Joe Parker, six-three and 275 pounds.

But Walter was even more concerned about the Baltimore defense. They were big and mean. On the left side were Gino Marchetti at end and Art Donovan at tackle, and together they made up the most vicious pass rush in football. They weren't especially fast, particularly "Fatso" Donovan, a squat little mick from New York who weighed 275 after a steam bath, but they were relentless and loved to hit quarterbacks. And Giant QB Charlie Conerly was thirty-seven years old. A tough thirty-seven, but thirty-seven nevertheless, and Walter didn't know how many licks he could take from Donovan and Marchetti and keep going.

On the other side of the Baltimore defensive line was Don Joyce at end, and playing tackle was the biggest man in the NFL, Eugene "Big Daddy" Lipscomb. At six-six and 290 pounds, nobody ever called him Eugene.

Lipscomb was a story, Walter knew. His mother had been stabbed to death when he was eleven years old, and the boy had gone to live with his grandfather. As a kid he worked as a dishwasher and laborer until he was old enough to join the marines, and it was at Camp Pendleton he discovered that he could play football. He'd been bounced by the Los Angeles Rams and picked up by the Colts for $100, and now he made it just damn difficult to run up the middle on Baltimore. Not with Lipscomb backed up by the middle linebacker, Bill Pellington, who was not all that big but just plain crazy.

The problem, Walter knew, was that you didn't really want to run left on them, either, not into Donovan and Marchetti, and so what remained was the right side, pitting Giant tackle Roosevelt Brown against right end Don Joyce. And Joyce had just beaten up on Brown in their meeting earlier in the season, a game the Giants had been lucky to win 24–21. And that was with Unitas on the bench, injured.

No, the Giants' offensive coach, Vince Lombardi, had his work cut out for him, Walter thought, maybe even more than Tom Landry, who was in charge of the Giants' defense.

But that was one sweet defense. Not as physical as the Colts, perhaps, but smarter and more disciplined. The Giants' defense didn't crush a team as much as they smothered it. Landry had them in an outside 4–3, with Andy Robustelli and Dick Modzelewski on right end and tackle Rosey Grier and end Joe Katcavag on the left. Sam Huff anchored the middle, with Harland Svare on his right and Cliff Livingston on his left. They were a *reading* defense, Walter knew, who counted on their football sense whether to rush into the gaps to plug a run, or slide out to avoid the trap block. They cued off Huff, who took his own cues from the offensive center and guards. They were a great defense, statistically the best in the league, but Walter didn't know if they could stop Unitas, Berry, Moore, Ameche, and the Colts' offensive line.

It was going to be a great game, all right, greater than the oddsmaker had it. The line was now running at three and a half to four points with the New York bookies and four and a half to five in Baltimore. Which meant to Walter one of three things: Someone knew something about the Giants, someone knew something about the Colts, or someone had laid one hell of a bet on Baltimore, driving up the spread to attract New York bets and cover the book.

When he got to his seats—on the forty-yard line about twenty rows up—the teams were going through their final warm-ups on the field and the Keneallys were already seated. The young Bureau man who had stood in such misery on the crowded train backed off then, kept walking up the aisle to a section of standing room on the railing above.

Madeleine Keneally wore a heavy black cloth coat with a fur hat and a huge scarf wrapped around her neck. She was also wearing dark glasses and sat slumped in her seat, looking cold and miserable.

Callahan, Cahill, and Brown sat in the seats directly above the Keneallys.

"Well, if it isn't Cerberus," Walter said.

"Who's that?" Callahan asked.

"The three-headed dog that guards the gates of Hades," Walter answered.

"You got a smart mouth," Callahan mumbled.

Jimmy Keneally got up to shake Walter's hand. As he did, he leaned in and asked, "What did you say to the police?"

"Nothing about the Senator," Walter said, smiling.

Jimmy smiled broadly. "That's good, Walter."

Joe Keneally stayed seated but stretched a hand up to Walter. "Hello, Walter. Sorry to hear about your friend!"

"Thank you, Senator!"

Madeleine stared at them.

"Hello, Walter," she said as he sat next to her.

"Mrs. Keneally."

"How are you?"

"Just awful, thank you," he answered. "And you?"

"We shouldn't be here," she said.

"But there are appearances to keep up," said Walter.

"It's so cold-blooded."

Walter turned to look at Senator Keneally, who looked for all the world as if he didn't have a care in the world. Hatless, light winter coat, ruddy-faced. Vigorous.

"Well, Walter," Joe Keneally said, "it's not exactly Harvard–Yale, but I suppose it will do. You're a Giants fan, I take it?"

"And you're cheering for—what are they called—the Colts?"

"Are you a betting man, Walter?"

"From time to time I've been known to lay a wager."

"Five bucks on the Colts."

"You're on."

It would be good, Walter thought, to beat the Senator at something.

The Giants were behind 14–3 at halftime.

The game had started off well enough. Lombardi neutralized Donovan and Marchetti by placing Gifford on the right side as if he were going to get a pitch-out, then having Conerly roll left, away from the Baltimore pass rush.

"Donovan looks like a sack of potatoes!" Joe Keneally

had screamed to Walter, and certainly it didn't look to Walter like the fat man would be able to chase Conerly all day long if this kept up.

So Conerly threw to Kyle Rote and Frank Gifford and occasionally handed off to fullback Alec Webster for a few yards up the middle to keep the Colts honest. No big gainers, just enough to move the ball and keep it out of Unitas' hands.

Then they broke one, a pitch-out to Gifford on the left side. Roosevelt Brown let Don Joyce slip inside, then blocked up and took out the linebacker, Don Shinnick. This opened a hole for Gifford to break into the open field. As the crowd cheered and Joe Keneally screamed, "Get him!" Gifford cut inside, weaved through their secondary, slipped tackles, and slashed forty-three yards to the Baltimore eighteen.

"God, I love to watch that man run!" Walter yelled.

"He's a genius!" Jimmy hollered back.

Madeleine said, "I hate football!"

But the big Colt line shut them down then, and on came Pat Summerall for the field goal, and it was Giants up by 3–0.

"Three points isn't going to do it for you, Walter!" Keneally yelled.

The Giant defense held, the Colts punted, and the Giants took over on their own twenty. Conerly played it safe and handed off to Gifford, who stepped through a hole right of center, blew past Donovan, and fumbled. Big Daddy Lipscomb fell on the ball.

"Your genius just dropped the ball," Joe said to Jimmy.

"It happens to geniuses," Jimmy answered.

"Which is why I don't want them around," Joe said. "Doesn't look good for you, Walter!"

Unitas ran Moore outside, Ameche inside, Moore outside

again, and they were on the Giant two-yard line. Parker smothered Grier on the next play, and Ameche bulled into the end zone.

Joe and Jimmy stood up and applauded. There were a couple of thousand Colts fans in the crowd, but most of them were down by the twenty-yard line, so the Keneallys stuck out.

Colts 7, Giants 3.

Joe spotted another lonely Baltimore fan a few rows down.

"Isn't that Rosenbloom?" he asked Jimmy.

"Sure is."

"We should make a point to say hello at halftime!"

That's odd, Walter thought. Why wouldn't the Colts' owner sit in the press box with the other bigwigs?

"Your team doesn't look so good right now!" Joe yelled to Walter.

"We can't give you a twenty-yard field," Walter answered. "We'll be okay if we don't fumble, and Gifford's had his fumble for the day. Gifford doesn't fumble twice."

But he did, not his own twenty this time, but on the Baltimore fourteen, a soul-killing fumble that Don Joyce picked up, ending a long Giant drive that was on the verge of exhausting the Colt defense.

Instead it brought Unitas onto the field. Throwing short out patterns to Berry, he moved the Colts to the Giant fifteen, then threw a touchdown pass to a double-teamed Berry in the corner of the end zone.

Colts 14, Giants 3.

Halftime.

"You're looking bad, Walter," Jimmy said.

Walter answered, "Our defense has to get more aggressive. We're just sitting back and letting Unitas pick us apart."

Walter unscrewed the lid of his flask, took a substantial drink of whiskey, and handed the flask to Jimmy. Jimmy passed it to Joe, who took a swig and passed it back.

"What about me?" Madeleine asked.

"I didn't think it was quite your style," Walter said.

"I'm freezing," she said. She took a sip and made a face.

"I want a hot dog," Walter said. "Would anyone like a hot dog?"

"I'll come with you," Jimmy said.

"What you need is a *red* dog," Joe laughed.

He has a point, Walter admitted. Landry might want to consider loosing the red dog, the blitz, sending Huff through the middle on passing downs to try to get to Unitas before he could get it to Berry. It would be risky, of course, leaving only one defender on either Moore, Berry, or Mutscheller, but the Giants had to do something to slow down Baltimore. They can't play the second half inside their own twenty.

He and Jimmy edged out of the row onto the steps and made their way toward the concession stand.

"Do you think the FBI boy would like a frank?" Walter asked Jimmy.

"Where is he?"

"About four steps below us," Walter answered. "You didn't notice him?"

"That's your business," Jimmy said. "Goddamn Hoover would jump all over this if he got anything."

They walked past the concession stand to an alcove by an entrance ramp.

To his credit, Walter thought, Jimmy Keneally looked hesitant and abashed when he asked, "So are you going to keep your mouth shut, Walter?"

"Jimmy, about three hundred people saw the four of us out together Friday night," Walter said. "We were at a

Broadway show and the Rainbow Room. Don't you think the police can find that out?"

"Let me worry about the cops," Jimmy snapped. "Anyway, the coroner's already confirmed it's a suicide. The cops aren't going to waste their time on a suicide. So there's no reason to bring Joe's name into it."

Unless there's a needle mark, Walter thought. Then the New York City police might be the least of the Keneallys' worries. And mine.

"Goddamn Joe," Jimmy was saying. "He doesn't realize people get hurt."

Doesn't he? Walter wondered.

"Hoover's boys might come after you," Jimmy said. "Can you hold up?"

Walter nodded. Until or unless I find out that you had Marta killed, he thought. Then all bets are off.

"We'll make it up to you," Jimmy said. "When this blows over."

"I don't want your money."

And I don't know that this is going to blow over.

The Giants didn't play the next half inside their own twenty—they played it inside their own three. Four times—*four times*—the Giant defense held inside their own three-yard line. Four times, as Joe Keneally moaned and Walter screamed his voice hoarse and the crowd started a chant that had never before been heard inside a football stadium—*Deefense! Deefense!*—the undersize and outweighed Giants kept the Colts from putting the game away. All the more impressive because the Colts had moved down the field with the cool precision of a superior offense. When the Giants blitzed, Berry read the defense and ran short, precise hook patterns that allowed Unitas to dump the ball quickly. When the Giant linebackers stayed back,

Unitas had time to find Berry and Moore on long sideline passes.

But on the goal line the Colts ran out of room to maneuver. Down there it was nothing fancy, just line against line and the Giant line held, and held and held and held again, as the crowd shouted *Deefense! Deefense!* and Walter thought, *This is football, this is the clichéd game of inches, this man against man and will against will and there is no room to retreat,* and he felt moved to the point of near tears as the outmanned Giants *willed* themselves to hold.

And something else. Curiosity? The inveterate football fan's proclivity to coach from the stands? The bettor's second sense? But why had Baltimore not kicked field goals on fourth downs? Walter wondered.

Maybe the first time it was confidence that they could punch it over. Arrogance and stung pride on the second and third times, perhaps. But it was that fourth try—first and goal at the Giant three-yard line midway through the third quarter—that Walter Withers found so troubling.

The afternoon sun had faded by then, and the Giant end zone was in cold, deep shadow. That more than anything, Walter speculated, was what saved the Giants, for Ameche took two successive handoffs and slipped both times on the icy field before he could get started. Unitas went up the middle himself on third down, surely thinking that he could walk three yards behind Nutter and Parker. But Grier dug down beneath Nutter and took his legs out, and Modzewleski shot in and snagged Unitas from behind. Huff smacked him head-on, and Unitas fell at the one.

"God damn it!" Joe Keneally yelled.

Madeleine scolded, "Honey—"

"I don't like losing!" Keneally yelled.

But you're winning, Walter thought, and still Ewbank didn't call for Bert Rechicar to kick what had to be an almost automatic field goal, which would have put the Colts up by two touchdowns. A safe lead with the Giants offense seemingly stagnant against the Colts *berserker* defense.

But Rechicar didn't come out, Unitas went back into the huddle, and 64,000 Giants fans screamed *Deefense! Deefense!* as the Giants stood in their sweat-stained dark blue jerseys, hands on hips, not talking or conferring, but just waiting.

Then the Colts line came up over the ball, the game literally on the line, and the Giant linemen bent into their four-point stance, dug their feet into the hard ground behind them, jammed their hands—blood seeping through the tape on their knuckles—into the ground in front of them. Unitas barked the signals, and Walter gasped as the right side of the Baltimore line opened a gaping hole in the middle. Everyone saw it, everyone except Ameche, who took the pitch and ran *out*side, and Walter thought his heart would stop as the Giant linebacker Cliff Livingston dived sideways, hit Ameche across the ankles, and dumped him for a four-yard loss. And the Giants' hopes, faint as December sunshine, were still alive.

"Damn it!" Keneally yelled. He was red in the face, and his lips were turned into an angry sneer.

"Ameche ran the wrong play!" Walter yelled, but he knew that Keneally wasn't analyzing the game now. As the Giants' offense came out on the field, Walter saw that Keneally had more than five dollars invested in the game. It had somehow become personal, something between him and Walter, twisted up with Marta and Madeleine.

"You want to make it a hundred, Withers?" Keneally asked.

Madeleine quickly said, "Honey, I don't think—"

"A hundred's fine, Senator."

"Walter," Madeleine said, "you don't have to—"

"A hundred's fine."

Conerly handed off to Gifford, who took it five yards, then to Webster for three, and the Colts defense was playing for a run because it didn't look like Conerly had any arm left.

Then suddenly there was Conerly—the Marlboro Man himself, old legs pumping for his life as Marchetti closed in—looking for a target, and then Kyle Rote was open, just for a second, and Conerly's tired arm zinged a bullet past the defender who was going for the interception and Rote was off, straight down the sideline as the Colts secondary desperately tried to catch him.

Walter was on his feet with the rest of the crowd, screaming like mad, and Madeleine was leaning on his shoulder, jumping up and down and screaming, and Rote was on the Colt twenty-five when Sample hit him from behind and the ball popped out of Rote's hand and hit the ground.

Walter heard himself literally groan, and Madeleine covered her eyes and so missed it when the ball bounced up into the hands of the slow Giant fullback Alec Webster. He held on and rumbled, the Colt defense hanging off him like hyenas on wounded prey, but Webster kept his legs churning to the fifteen, the ten, the five, and finally he fell out of bounds at the Baltimore one.

"It's fate!" Walter hollered, and he could almost believe in fate at the moment and all the more so when the Giant offensive line surged and Mel Tripplet went in behind them and the crowd—and there was no other word for it—*roared.*

Summerall kicked the extra point.

Colts 14, Giants 10.

Keneally glared.

"You're alive," Jimmy said to Walter. "You have a chance."

"This is a *game!*" answered Walter.

The Giant defense seemed to gain courage from the score. Four minutes left in the third quarter, Colts with the ball and a four-point lead, and the Giant defense now found a savage strength. Katcavage, Modzelewski, Robustelli, and Grier attacked the Colt line, crushing the pass pocket inward, and Huff sliced through the middle twice to crumple Unitas.

Walter saw that the Baltimore center Buzz Nutter was tipping off Huff on the passing plays, not consciously, of course, but in his stance. For as his confidence waned, he started to cheat on the passing plays, setting back a little bit over the ball. Huff was reading it, signaling his line, and they were just charging forward, unconcerned about covering the run. So Unitas was crashed into the frozen ground and Baltimore had to punt and the old man was back on the field and now it was the fourth quarter.

Conerly reared back and threw a forty-six-yard bomb to Bob Schnelker, then hit him long again, then lofted a pass at Gifford, who didn't fumble this time but held on and not only held on but carried the defender on his back and fought his way into the end zone.

And the redemption of sins, Walter thought.

Giants 16, Colts 14.

The conversion, as the crowd howled its joy at the winter sky.

Giants 17, Colts 14.

And then it was simply a battle. Unitas passing, the Giants blitzing, Berry faking and getting open, Huff smashing into Unitas's sore ribs, the ball wobbling incomplete. Or Unitas throwing over a leaping Huff, Berry reaching for the ball with his fingertips, grabbing it as he placed his toes an inch inside the sidelines. The Colts fought down to the Giant thirty-eight, where the defenders finally stopped them.

They'll try for the field goal now, Walter thought, because the rules of a championship game called for a sudden-death overtime in case of a tie, and three points will tie. Now they'll take the field goal they spurned earlier.

But the field goal fell short, and the Giants got the ball back.

And fumbled. Substitute halfback King, fresh legs, fresh lungs, and cold hands, muffed the handoff, and the Colts had the ball on the Giant twenty-seven.

The crowd groaned a collective groan, then rallied with their cheer of *Deefense! Deefense!* as the Giant defenders pulled their helmets back on and shuffled onto the field.

"You're finished, Walter!" Keneally crowed. "Your boys are too tired!"

But to Walter's vast admiration they held again. This time it was Katcavage and Robustelli, who crushed the pocket from outside rushes and threw Unitas for long losses outside of field goal range.

The Giants took over on downs.

And now they don't have to score, Walter thought. All they have to do is to keep the ball for four and a half minutes. One first down and the game is over.

As it must in a game like this, it came to a third down. Third down and four yards to go on their own thirty-nine, and Walter's heart raced and the stands were oddly quiet as Conerly took the snap and handed off to Gifford. He swung wide right, cut back behind a block, and was on his way to the first down when Gino Marchetti desperately lunged and grabbed Gifford's ankles. Then Donovan wrapped him up around the shoulders and dragged him to the ground just as Lipscomb piled in, stopping Gifford from inching forward.

Marchetti's ankle had snapped, and he rolled off the pile in agony. They were carrying him to the sideline as the officials came out with the chains to measure.

"I can't breathe," Madeleine whispered.

Nor can I, Walter thought as the officials stretched the chain. The crowd sucked in a collective breath and then groaned as the linesman held up his hands a few inches apart. Then the crowd regained its courage and cheered for the Giant offense to make it on fourth down, then groaned again as punter Don Chandler trotted out.

"No!" Madeleine screamed. "No!"

Despite himself Walter silently screamed the same. For it was a failure of nerve, he thought. A loss of nerve at a time when only nerve mattered, and even though the punt put Baltimore on its own fourteen with one minute and fifty-six seconds to go, Walter knew that New York courage lost was Baltimore courage gained and that the defense was tired.

For there are those moments, Walter thought. There is, as Shakespeare's Cassius observed, a tide in the affairs of men that when taken at the flood leads on to fortune. And if that is true, then the inverse is true as well: When the tide is not taken at the flood, then the tide recedes, and fortune with it, and that is what his beloved Giants faced then, the immutable recession of the tide.

Unitas seized the moment. He lost four seconds on an incompletion to Dupre, but hit Moore for eleven on his next throw. Ninety seconds left, ball on the twenty-five.

A heavy rush, nobody open, but Unitas managed to throw out of bounds. Eighty-two seconds.

The crowd quiet now—the ball back on defensive ground and the clock ticking as slowly as a glacier. Time refused to move.

Nutter snaps the ball, Unitas fades back, the Giant line rushes with the desperate savagery of a wounded lion. Berry breaks for the sideline. Huff fights through his block and smashes into Unitas a second after he releases the ball. Unitas crumples to the ground, but Berry catches the pass.

Complete for twenty-five yards. Ball on the fifty.

Another snap, another rush, tired line fighting tired line, Berry runs along the sideline again, then cuts in toward the center into the seam between the backers and the secondary. Unitas throws it on a frozen rope for sixteen yards. Ball on the Giant thirty-four.

A gasping spell as Unitas takes his team into the huddle. Huff gestures to his teammates—*jump, jump, block the pass*—and the Colts come up again. The snap, Unitas back, Katcavage plows over Sandusky, Robustelli wrestles with Parker, Grier and Huff charge up the middle, Unitas throws over Huff's straining fingers, and a leaping Berry grabs it for twenty-one yards.

Ball on the Giant fourteen, fifteen seconds left in the game.

Then the clock seemed to start again, relentless now, as not Rechicar but Myhra comes out for the field goal. Along with Donovan and Sherm Plunkett and the Colts' biggest linemen to block against a Giant block. The clock ticked and there were just seven seconds left as Walter watched and Madeleine looked through spread fingers and the crowd held its single breath and Marchetti sat up in his stretcher and Grier and Katcavage high-lowed Donovan as Huff jumped over the top and Myhra hit the bill and the linemen heard the *plunk* and turned to watch as the ball sailed through the darkened sky and the uprights, and the game— after sixty minutes of ferocious struggle—was tied.

Walter bent over in exhaustion, glanced over, and saw that Joe Keneally was doing the same.

"It's a game, Withers," he said, not meaning *just* a game, meaning it's a *game*.

"Sudden death," Walter said quietly, for he could speak quietly just then and be heard, for the crowd was silent.

"I'm already dead," Keneally answered.

The Giants won the coin toss, the crowd's enthusiasm muted by the strange ritual in this first ever sudden-death game. But the Giant's first play was stuffed at the line. On second down Conerly missed Schnelker by inches. On third and long, Conerly faded back but couldn't find an open receiver. He tried to run, tried gamely, but thirty-seven-year-old legs wouldn't give him the speed and Pellington drove violently into his knees, then Schinnick wrapped him up and took him down. Inches short of the first down. This time there was no question: Chandler punted and Unitas, Moore, Berry, Parker and company took the field.

Ball on the Baltimore twenty as the Giants defense pulled their helmets on once again.

"Do your boys have it in them?" Keneally asked.

No, we don't, Walter thought, but he held the thought.

And the Giants held, driving the Colts into a third and fifteen.

But it was just a respite. On the next play the Colts offensive line gave Unitas an eternity. He had Moore, faked to him, and then rolled out, dodged a charging Modzelewski, and spotted Berry—more important, spotted the defender covering the receiver slip—then motioned Berry to keep going, then hit him long.

The Giant defense dug in on the next play and readied to charge. Walter saw the Baltimore center lean back over the ball—a sure sign of the pass. The Giant defense was geared to it, too, and Modzelewski shot in on the snap and was trap-blocked as Unitas handed off to Ameche, who ran through the hole Modzelewski had left and streaked ahead for twenty-three yards. With the Giants back on their heels, Unitas hit Berry again on the New York nine-yard line.

"They'll kick the field goal now and I win!" Keneally hollered.

Baltimore by three, Walter thought, and your bet is safe. But there isn't going to be any Baltimore field goal.

Myhra stayed on the sidelines, and Unitas came up to the line. He handed it to Ameche, who plowed up the middle and was stopped by Huff and Katcavage. Ball on the seven and the crowd half expected them to kick it then. But Unitas came up again, the Giant line dug in to stop the anticipated run up the middle, and Unitas tossed a flare pass to Joe Mutscheller in the flat. Mutscheller headed for the goal line but slipped on the ice and fell on the one-yard line.

"I can't believe he put the ball in the air!" Keneally wailed.

I can, Walter thought. I absolutely can. They didn't take the field goals before, and if they take it now, they win by three. But three points loses if you've put a ton of money on the five-point spread. And if you're the owner and you've done that, you can even sit in the stands and pass signals.

Third down on the one, an almost certain field goal to win the championship, and indeed, Myhra started for the field.

"That's it, Walter!" Keneally yelled in triumph. "An automatic field goal and you owe me a hundred bucks!"

"Two thousand there's no field goal," Walter said.

"What?"

Madeleine looked shocked. "Walter, what . . . No!"

"Two thousand they don't kick the field goal," Walter repeated.

"From the one, Withers? Are you nuts?"

"No guts, Senator?"

"Two thousand."

"Right now. Take it or leave it."

Keneally grinned. "You're on."

Myrha stepped on to the field.

"I hope you're good for the money, Withers," Keneally said. "I intend to collect."

Then Myrha trotted back, for Unitas was bringing his team back to the line.

"What's he doing?!" screamed Keneally.

What he's told, thought Walter. By the owner in the stands. Win by six or else.

For the last time the Giants braced for a goal-line stand. For the last time, as darkness gathered and the crowd resumed its chant, they hunched down in a hopeless last stand, and Walter loved them nonetheless for the hopelessness, loved them more perhaps in imminent defeat. For these his champions were human with all the human frailties and limits, and they had done all those limits would allow, and if that meant defeat, then defeat had its own sad beauty.

The ball was snapped and the Colt line blocked down and Mutscheller trapped Livingston and Ameche put both hands over the ball and rumbled through the hole and it was over.

Colts 23, Giants 17.

The Giants had lost the best game Walter had ever seen.

"You sandbagged me," Joe Keneally said.

"I hope you're good for the money," Walter answered. "I intend to collect."

Keneally glared at him. He said, "Jimmy'll see that you get it."

Walter shook his head. "I want it from you, Senator. Personally."

"It's Sunday."

Walter shrugged. "Whenever it's convenient."

"The Senator and I have a meeting," Jimmy interjected. "Walter, would you mind escorting Mrs. Keneally back to the hotel?"

In the limousine Walter joked lamely. "We have to stop meeting like this."

She looked so fragile and so fresh with her long cloth coat of British scarlet and her fur hat. Makeup so subtle it was nigh invisible except to the practiced eye.

"I thought you enjoyed covert rendezvous."

"What do you mean?"

"Are you still protecting him?" she asked. "Even now that the poor Marta woman is dead?"

He looked so surprised she continued, "Of course I knew, Walter darling. Women always know."

"And does Senator Keneally know that you know?"

"I suspect that he does," she answered.

"Then why bother with me?"

She said, "I think you were there more to protect me from public humiliation than to protect him against wifely discovery. He's had her for months, and before her—"

"Why do you stay married to him?"

A shrug and she said simply, "I love him."

As if that answers everything, Walter thought. As if it doesn't.

"There are many magnificent things about Joe Keneally," Madeleine said. "Fidelity is not one of them. He'll find another one to nail."

"Where did you learn such language? Not at Miss Porter's."

"It *was* at Miss Porter's," she answered. "What do you think we girls talked about at night?"

"Kindly don't rekindle my adolescent fantasies," Walter said. "Why don't you dump him and marry me?"

"But I think you're spoken for," she answered, "by the

lovely and talented Miss Anne Blanchard. Oh, please, Walter, it was so obvious."

"Was it?"

"You're a darling man, but almost as stupid as every other man."

"Speaking of which, I think I have your problem solved," he said.

"By your foolish wager?"

"Not so foolish."

"But it's your money."

"I couldn't enjoy money that came from a Giants' loss," he said.

She squeezed his hand and mouthed, "Thank you."

They rode in silence until she added, "Besides, Anne told me."

"Pardon?"

"Anne told me that you two were involved," she said. "After persistent questioning on my part, of course."

For a moment Walter felt as if his heart might crack like a block of ice. He tried to keep his tone conversational as he asked, "When did you speak to Anne?"

"Yesterday morning," she answered. "Before all this horror."

"You did?" he asked lightly. "Where?"

"I bumped into her in the lobby of the Plaza."

"At the Plaza?"

"I was coming in and she was going out, so we shared a little girl talk."

And of course, not living a life of unending duplicity and suspicion, thought Walter, it never occurred to you to ask what she was doing there. But mine is such a life, and I do want to know what Anne was doing at the Plaza the morning that Marta died.

*   *   *

Walter chose a dark spot on the southwest side of Broadway and 116th Street where he had a clear view of Alicia's apartment. Most people, he mused, look to find the rays of light in the darkness, but we covert types search for those slivers of darkness in a city of light. And we are amazed by how much darkness we can find in this neon city.

Especially uptown, near "The Jungle" as Dietz (not Upton Sinclair) called it. Columbia, Barnard, and the Jewish Theological Center formed a scholarly archipelago that struggles to stay afloat in an ever more turbulent ocean of poverty and crime. (You're allowed, he thought, especially in personal musings, to mix metaphors when you're trying to keep your mind off the cold while standing stock still. It could be first a jungle, then an ocean. Perhaps a jungle island.) Here the lights were not as bright, here a number of types roamed the nights streets unnoticed—the thoughtful scholar, the lovesick student, the restless junkie, the would-be mugger, the insomniac, the madman, the wishful wistful would-be retired spy.

Praying—although his hands were not laid prayerfully together but clenched in his coat pockets—that he had not already missed it. Praying not for the forgiveness of sins but for their potential redemption.

Whoever was behind this would move fast. They would be edgy now, seeking to redeem an operation that had probably ended prematurely but could still come up a winner—a big winner, really—and that would take time. That's what Walter was counting on, that little logistical delay that would allow him to be here in time, and here came Alicia—a prayer answered—down the steps and down the sidewalk. If ever Walter had seen the turkey trot, he was seeing it now. The poor girl was hot, was frightened, was in danger, and to Walter it looked like God's mercy itself.

He would know in moments, he told himself, what level of operation it was. If she goes alone, he thought, it's still a mid-level affair and I have a chance. If escorts pick her up now, slip seamlessly into the stream of her movement and like guardian angels keep her safe and warm, then we are looking at something else altogether.

But if the angels were there, they were very, *very* good, and while street craft had not been his particular strength in his training days (God, what *had* been?), he still thought he could spot them if they were there. Or they would have spotted him, and he would already be lying dead in an alley, doubtless in a sliver of darkness, his lifeblood drained by a blade to his heart and his wallet and watch gone. With this cheery thought in mind he measured his distance from Alicia and kept it constant. When it happened—if it happened—it wouldn't be all that close to her apartment. So he had time to give space for a bit, which was a good thing because Alicia had the Swivels, which Walter recalled from his training was the only thing worse than the Titanic.

When a subject is carrying something hot, the instructor had said, he or she may develop one of "two extreme postures of the head": One is the Titanic: The subject sets his head straight for the destination and will not move it until he crashes into the iceberg. The other is the Swivel, in which the subject's head never stops turning from side to side. The Titanic subject won't allow himself to see any danger; the Swiveler sees nothing but.

And Alicia was Swiveling now, though trying to control it. But espionage had never been a good business for amateurs and dilettantes, regardless of how committed they might be. Of course, you didn't ask them to jump into the deep end of the pool right from the start. No, it was all harmless toe dipping at first—an errand here, a favor there, until before the poor mark knew it, she was in over her head. First it's "Someone will drop something off at your apartment, someone will pick it up. You don't even have to know what it is." Then one sickening night it turns to "Listen, there's no other choice, really. Just take the package, drop it where we tell you, and forget about it." And the mark says no, and you say, "All right. It's your choice, of course. But you wouldn't want them to find this stuff in your place, you really wouldn't. I mean, the best thing we could be talking about will be years in prison, and that's the *best* thing. Just throw it out? After all we've done for you? You can't do that, darling, because then I'd have no other choice but to make a few calls and then they'd come for you anyway and the best thing we could be talking about will be years in prison and that's the *best* thing. No, really, what you want to do is just drop it at . . ."

Walter knew how it worked, having done it so many times himself. Had seen the fear and the helpless resentment cross the mark's face like a cloud over one of those blank Swedish skies, and then the mark would say, "Okay. Just this once," and you'd say, "Good, just this once." Until the next time. And the next, and the next until finally the mark screws up and gets caught, and it's not as if we've lost an actual agent, is it?

Some recruits do it for money, some for the cause, and others from simple blackmail. Walter had a feeling that Alicia was a true believer, a romantic who loved the cause and wanted to do something romantic for it. How romantic did she feel now as she crossed west on 106th and headed like a greyhound for Riverside Park?

Walter picked up his own speed and found to his dismay—a bit more time on the tennis courts, a bit less in the nightclubs, my boy—that he had to struggle to stay with her. She was headed for the home stretch now, and it had gone all right so far, so she was racing to get it over with.

They had probably had her do a dry run—to lull her into doing the real thing, if nothing else. ("Listen, I'll tell you what. If you're nervous about this—and who wouldn't be—we'll make a dry run at it. You go to the drop first—nothing on you—and if they're there, they have nothing. And you'll know exactly what to do for the real thing.") So she knew where the drop was, wouldn't have to slow down and look for it, and would do it fast.

And that's where things will start to get tricky, Walter thought. That will be the bad and scary moment, between the drop-off and the pick-up. That is when you will have to be at your most nimble, clever, and resourceful.

Because the best thing we could be talking about will be years in prison, and that's the best thing.

He could feel sweat start to run beneath his heavy clothes and wondered if it was the exertion or nerves. He tried to judge the distance, far enough to remain unseen, close enough to get to the package. Before someone else does.

And get away, there's that part, too.

I should have become a banker, he thought. Happy, boring days spent with numbers. Quiet evenings of domestic fornication. Weekends at the club. And why does everyone I tail these days have to be an athlete? He sped up and tried to match his pace with hers so his footsteps didn't strike her ears like the rat-a-tat of a drumroll as they entered Riverside Park.

The park was strip of green lawn, ball parks, playgrounds, and basketball courts that flanked the bluffs of the west side. Steps led down from Riverside Drive into the park and onto a broad, tree-lined promenade. Walter was counting on two things: One, that she would drop the package hot-potato-like and keep moving, and he felt fairly confident about that. Two, that the pick-up man would watch the drop from a distance, not wanting to be trapped too easily in any net that might have been thrown over her. He'd need both those things even to try to make this work out. There was no point in wasting any more energy thinking about them because they either were or weren't, and if they weren't, he'd be dead and that would be that.

Down the steps. A landing and she can go left or right. Doesn't matter, you can spot her either way. Guess and lay back.

To the left she does, downtown, pacing under the big trees along that broad promenade that reminded him so much of Europe. The Hudson off to their right, and beyond that the lights of Jersey. The high wall to their left, broken here and there by a staircase, scalable in spots by a skilled climber, was otherwise a trap. Park benches. All empty, thank God, all devoid of that wino or psycho who was probably neither.

And Alicia has her head down now. The horse is headed for the stable. She sees the drop.

Good Lord, a trash can? How clichéd, Walter thought, how trite.

He felt his own legs start to turkey trot underneath him as he closed the distance. This is no time, my boy, he told himself, to give counsel to your fears. Close it way up now. If she hears your footsteps, she'll think it's them, not you. She'll want to believe that. Her arm looks like a stick as she reaches into her coat for the package, pulls it out, and—poor thing—so awkwardly, so stiffly, drops into the trash can, looped by a metal band to a tree. And keeps moving, running almost, which gave him the time he needed to grab the package.

His own arm felt fairly wooden—his legs leaden, his

mouth dry, his heart hammering—as he reached in, picked up the paper bag, and turned to head back uptown.

Now *move,* he told himself. Get those legs pumping and move.

Then he heard the muffled feminine scream and knew that the pick-up man—men, as a matter of fact, two of them—had waited close to the drop site indeed. To kill her, according to plan, and now—because the plan had gone wrong—to kill him as well.

Walter Withers ran.

It was probably the fact that killing him was outside the plan that gave him a chance. Those four or five seconds that the opposition took to think about this new factor bought Walter the distance to make an opening move. To exercise, as they would say in his training days, some initiative.

Initiative, Walter Withers gulped as he ran. Easy to come up with on the academic turf of the training ground, harder to produce when you are any second expecting a bullet in the spine that will send you tumbling helplessly to the frozen ground to await a bullet in the head, but mustn't think that way. Initiative, then. Escape and evasion in the open field, or Riverside Park, and what can I recall? Create distance, then turn, not sideways, but *diagonally. A diagonal angle of escape simultaneously creates the maximum distance for you and the maximum uncertainty for your pursuers.*

So he ran hard while the boys were thinking it over, then jogged obliquely right, eastward, that is, toward the high stone wall. Which would seem to be a bad move, trapping him on the one side, but would make him much harder to see—gray coat, gray stone wall, all cats gray in the dark—and there would be a staircase coming up soon, but he was damned if he could remember where it was.

They had made up their minds now, and he could hear their feet pounding hard behind him. Nothing subtle here, no cat and mouse, just flat-out pursuit. Catch him if they could for the swift and silent knife; if not, get close enough for the shot.

Make them run, he thought. Make them expend the oxygen so that they would be huffing and puffing, and their meaty hands would be shaking when they tried to take steady aim on the center of your back. It is indeed hard to hit a moving target, harder still when you yourself have been running and the slightest quiver of the barrel can send the bullet far astray.

Walter ran along the base of the wall, thought briefly of trying to scale it, realized that he would be plastered against it like a Kentucky squirrel, and ran on. He started to panic as he realized that one of the boys was sprinting and the other one had settled back into a job. It was a good tactic because they would switch off while making him run full speed, and that game would have to end soon.

The sprinter was already gaining ground.

And me in street shoes, Walter thought, slipping and sliding and gaining neither purchase nor the precious distance. A ridiculous and savage state of affairs, that I might be simply too slow to survive. And out of shape as well, already running out of air.

I could turn and fight, he thought, try to dispatch the sprinter quickly, get his gun, and then shoot his chum. But these boys are professionals, not surprised subway junkies, and even in the unlikely event that I should disarm the first, I would doubtless miss the second. Was it Morrison who had actually pinned the drawing of the barn onto the target at the training range, and roared when I missed it?

So Walter ran on, praying for the staircase that would give him at least a chance to emerge onto Riverside Drive, still in desperate trouble but at least alive.

For the moment, he thought, until they use the well-lit street to gun you down like a convict in the yard. The only advantage you have just now is darkness, and it is darker down here in the park, so use it.

They'll expect you to break for the street, he thought as he came close to a staircase. So he sucked for air and hit the stairs running hard. Reaching the first landing just as his pursuer made it to the bottom of the steps, Walter lunged across the landing and flung himself down the opposite steps back into the park. Then he dashed across the broad promenade to its west edge and dived under some shrubs that clung to the low stone wall.

No footsteps came. The sprinter was up on the street, and the plodder had stopped.

The plodder has seen something move across the promenade but wasn't sure just what or where, Walter thought. The sprinter is just figuring it out and is on his way back down.

They can't see you, he told himself. Do not panic, do not flush, they can't see you. Try to remember that.

They hadn't given up, he saw. They were good, well trained and in no hurry. Each edged his way west to form a widening V shape. Next they will move toward each other, closing the open top of the V until one of them spots you.

They're moving carefully, he thought, heads low in case you're armed, their own guns out now. And you're running out of time. And space. And I profoundly wish I had spent more time in this not unlovely park so I'd know my options. Know what is on the other side of this wall that will soon be my only protection.

Walter reached his left hand up and felt along the wall.

It was only about three feet high here. He tucked the package into the waistband of his trousers and tried to get up in one smooth move, but the branches snagged him. The bush rustled and he knew they'd heard it, seen it perhaps, and now he had even less time as he laid himself flat along the top of the wall. He threw his right leg over, felt along the stones for a foothold, found one, and dug in as he reached his left leg over and did the same. The stones were icy and slippery as he forced himself to take first one hand, then the other off the top of the wall and find a grip along its side. There he was as the boys closed in, clinging to the side of an icy rock wall, his hands quivering with strain, his fingers burning with cold. A ridiculous position, really, as the plodder reached the spot first and slowly—glacially, perhaps—eased his head over the wall to see what he could see.

They looked at each other for a second, this nameless killer and Walter, and exchanged a foolish glance before Walter's grip gave way and he pushed with his feet and hoped that it wasn't too far to the ground.

It was only about fifteen feet, but it was fifteen feet of vertical darkness that saved is life as he landed in the right field of the softball field below. He managed to take most of the fall on his feet and remembered to roll, although his left ankle would from thereon be the weak spot in his tennis game. He rolled over backward, landing in an undignified thud. The air was driven from his lungs, so he lay helplessly for what seemed like an eternity before he could start to crawl away.

But the boys apparently weren't keen on leaping into the darkness. They stood along the top of the wall, trying to spot him but couldn't, and Walter crawled along the base of the wall, then raised himself into a pre-hominid sort of ambling crouch and started back downtown, looking for one of the tunnels that led from the West Side Highway back onto Riverside.

He heard one of them behind him make a heavy thump on the hard ground and could only assume that the other one was trying to run a parallel course above them. If he could make it into the tunnel before the chaser could catch up or the other one could find a shooting angle, perhaps they might miss one. Run right past him and right over him, and he could make it back onto the street with enough time to get clear or . . .

The mouth of a tunnel opened up in front of him. He was just into it when he heard the purr of an engine behind him and felt a car pull up.

I should have known, he thought. I should have thought of it. Of course they'd have a car. They always do.

But too late to think of it. He was trapped now, his escape route a trap, and the long white car coming up like a ghost in the night.

He heard a window roll down.

They can't miss at this range, Walter thought.

"You look bad, man," the Negro voice said.

Theo, the Contessa's chauffeur, cruising the streets on her sanding instructions.

"I'm beat," Walter said honestly.

"Hop in, man."

Walter flung open the door and crouched down on the seat. He could see the sprinter in the side mirror. Theo saw him, too, stepped on the gas. The big car roared out of the tunnel and down Riverside.

"You shouldn't cruise for dope in *this* park, man!" Theo laughed. "It's dangerous!"

"I'll keep that in mind."

Walter lay down on the backseat and closed his eyes. He was asleep seconds later. When he woke up, they were pulling up in front of his building, and he could see Anne's silhouette behind the shade.

She was curled up in the big chair, his terry-cloth bathrobe wrapped around her shoulders. She woke up when he came through the door.

"I let myself in," she said. "I hope you don't mind."

"It's why we had the keys made."

"I mean *now*," she said.

"I don't mind," he said. "Where have you been? I've been worried."

"Upstate at my parents," she said. "I left after my last set last night. I wanted to wake up on the farm this morning. Take a walk and think."

"About us?"

"Among other things," she answered. "Why were you worried?"

"You went to see Marta yesterday morning," he said. "After our little scene."

"*You* created the scene."

"You went to see her."

"Yes."

The voice tentative. A decidedly defensive tint to the inflection.

"Why?" he asked.

"Why do you think?"

"Why?" he repeated.

"I told her that I'm in love with you," Anne said. "That I wasn't going to see her again."

A half truth? Walter wondered.

Lies of omission.

"How was she?" he asked.

"How do you mean?"

"Was she drunk?" he asked. "Sober? Cheerful? Depressed?"

"She was stoned," Anne said. "And she'd been crying. She actually loves that bastard."

Loves, Walter thought. Present tense. She doesn't know.

Or she's pretending not to know.

"She told me about you," Anne continued. "Told me that you were Keneally's messenger boy. And his beard. After that I wasn't so sure I loved you, Walter."

"But here you are."

"Here I am." She looked him over and said, "You look like hell. What have you been doing?"

"Working."

"For Keneally?"

"For myself," he answered. "I could use a stiff drink. How about you?"

"I'll even fix them." She disentangled herself from the chair. "How about putting some music on, Walter? The silence in here is positively sodden."

She went into the kitchen.

"Why don't I put on your tape?" he called.

"You haven't listened to it yet?"

"I've been a tad busy."

He threaded the tape onto his machine and let the spool fast-forward until he heard the Three Chipmunk squeal of voices. Anne stepped back into the room just as the sounds of lovemaking came through the speakers.

She stood still and stared at Walter. With the two drinks balanced in her outstretched hands she looked tipsy like a tightrope walker.

"Here, let me take those before you spill them," Walter said. He gently pried the glasses from her hands, set one on the coffee table, and drank from the other. The smoky scotch warmed him for what seemed like the first time all day.

Marta's recorded voice groaned in a chant of pleasure that seemed to him unfeigned. Keneally grunted in a masculine backbeat.

"How did you get that?" she asked.

"More to the point," he said, "how did *you*?"

"Walter . . ."

"Don't bother thinking up a lie," he said. "Marta gave them to you, and you handed them off to Alicia. The first one on Christmas night at the Thalia, the second one sometime Saturday. Was it before or after you told Marta you loved me, by the way?"

"It has nothing to do with you."

"Really?" Walter asked.

"Marta asked for my help."

"That's too simple."

"That bastard is hurting friends of mine."

"The committee?" Walter asked.

"Yes, of course the committee."

"And you thought you'd blackmail him?"

"It was Marta's idea."

"You don't know what you're doing."

"I know *exactly* what I'm doing!"

No, you don't, my beloved liar. You don't know that Marta is being run by someone. Someone who in turn wants to run Keneally. Someone who killed and killed again to get it done. You don't know. God, I hope you don't know.

The lovemaking on the tape started to build.

"Please turn that off," Anne said.

Marta's voice rose to a throaty keen.

"I'd say we're just about to the end of an episode,

wouldn't you?" he asked. Then despite his better nature added, "Of course, you'd know better than I."

"Please turn it off."

"Why?" Walter asked. "Christ, you're not *on* one of these, are you?"

She sat down on the couch and put her head between her hands. He watched as he ran her fingers into her hair.

"No," she said quietly. "Why are you being so cruel?"

"Why am *I*?" he asked.

Marta was calling the Senator's name, over and over again, and then adding the single word *yes,* as Walter and Anne listened in silence. He turned off the tape, sat beside her on the couch, handed her her drink, and said, "So Marta came to you . . ."

"Weeks ago," Anne said, "and asked if I would do her this favor, and it seemed like such a simple thing, and I didn't know that you—"

"That I *what*?"

"That you would get involved," she answered. "Horrible coincidence, isn't it?"

Except that I don't believe in coincidence, Walter thought, horrible or otherwise.

She set down her drink, got up, and took her coat from the rack.

"Where are you going?" he asked.

"I can't imagine you'd want me to stay. You're working for Keneally," she said. She jutted her chin toward the tape player. "Congratulations. You did your job. The secrets are safe, and the prince will become king."

"Do you think that this is over?"

"I think *we're* over," she said. "We're just on different sides, Walter."

She stood there waiting for him to deny it.

He wanted to, but his mouth wouldn't form the words.

"You can't stay here," he agreed. And not for the reason you think. Not because I hate you now, not because I work for Joe Keneally, but because they'll be coming. One side or the other. For the tapes, for you, for me.

"No," she agreed. A small, cynical smile played at the corner of her lips. "I can't stay here."

"And you can't go home," he added. Not if what I suspect is true. If what I suspect is true, they'll snatch you up in a moment, one side or the other.

"Is that right, darling?" she asked. Then in mock horror. "Am I in *danger*?"

"Marta's dead."

It was remarkable to him how much he hated to see pain come into her eyes.

"My God," she said. "How?"

"The coroner says suicide," he answered. "The trite but true combination of booze and pills."

"They killed her," Anne said.

"Who?"

"The Keneallys."

"Why do you say that?"

"You do their dirty work," she said. "You should know."

Her gray eyes filled with tears.

"God, Walter, you didn't . . . ?"

"Kill her?" he asked. He shook his head. "But thanks for asking."

"I'm sorry."

"Gosh, don't be," he said. "I'd say it was a completely reasonable question given the circumstances."

"Can you please stop being glib?"

"No, I don't think I can."

"Lose control . . ."

He chuckled. "Definitely not that."

"It's the way you punish people."

"I suppose it is."

"God damn it, I did what I did for a reason!"

"I know that!" he shouted back. "So did I!"

"I know mine," she said. "What's yours?"

"I . . ."

"What?" she asked. "Tell me. Tell me. What's your reason, Walter? What keeps you going? What keeps the shoes shined and the tie knotted and that cheerful, superior smile on your face? What's the secret? What's the dream? What is it that makes you scream in the night?"

You, he thought. You do.

"No answer?"

"Theo's waiting for you downstairs," he said.

"You think of everything, Walter," she said. "You even arrange my ride with the Contessa. What happens then, Walter? I get suddenly ill and the doctor doesn't come?"

"I think you should stay with her until . . ."

"Until they come for me?" she asked. "Who will it be? The cops? The Bureau? Keneally's thugs?"

"Anne . . ."

"You?"

"Anne . . ."

"Je ne regrett rien," she said. "Unlike your dear self, Walter, I know my reasons. I know what a person does in this world."

"I do know."

Standing in his doorway, she said, "No, you don't. You just hold your nose, lace on your shoes, and march."

"Perhaps that's what a man does."

"A company man."

She tossed her scarf around her neck with a deliberately

246

theatrical flourish, then said, "Well, Rick, at least we'll always have Paris."

"Je taime," he said.

But she was out the door.

McGuire wasn't sleeping, of course. He was up, steamed on Dexedrine, and he showed really very little surprise when he answered the door to see a disheveled, scratched, and pained Walter Withers standing there.

"Rough game, man," McGuire said. "I'm dead."

Walter shook his head. "I put the money down on Baltimore by five."

"You bet against your own team?"

"You believe in poetry," Walter said. "I believe in trap blocks."

"Jesus, man."

"So you're off the hook with Martino."

McGuire stood in the middle of the floor, shaking his head and scratching his hair. "Jesus, man."

"Do me a favor?" Walter asked.

"Anything."

Walter pulled the brown paper bag from his overcoat and handed it to McGuire.

"Just keep this in your place for a few days," Walter said. "I'll be back to pick it up."

McGuire looked dubious for a second, shook his head, and said, "If this is pot, man . . ."

McGuire took the package, the audiotapes of Senator Joseph Keneally's trysts with poor dead Marta Marlund, Swedish starlet and Soviet spy, the audiotapes that Marta had given to Anne and Anne to Alicia, and put them under his mattress.

Then he studied Walter for several seconds and said again, "You bet against your own team?"

*　　*　　*

In the dream that night, Anne slipped from his grasp and off the rock into the black water. But in this new dream he was not on the cliff above but on the rock with her. He woke up as the next wave rose and came toward him.

CHAPTER SIX

But Not for Me

Monday, December 29

Walter arrived at the office at seven a.m. sharp.

"Good morning, Mr. Withers," Mallon said.

"And to you, Mr. Mallon."

The doorman gave Walter his coffee and Danish and observed, "You look a little tired today, Mr. Withers. Tough night?"

"You might say that," Walter answered.

"Shame about the Giants."

"Did you go to the game?"

Mallon shook his head. "Saw it on the television. Thought we had it won."

"Ah, well. Next year."

"There you go, Mr. Withers."

Walter went up to his office, set the coffee and pastry on his desk, and stood at the window for a moment. He waved to 16-C, then poured his coffee into his mug, ate the Danish, then settled into the daily expense report and wondered just how many of Saturday's drinks he could rightfully—prudently might be the better word—apply to the Howard file.

He'd just decided that the proper answer was none when Dietz, uncharacteristically early, came into the office and shut the door.

"How'd you know?" Dietz asked.

"About what?"

"Needle marks. On your dead broad."

Walter asked, "Marks, plural?"

"The M.E. found a single puncture between the middle toes on her right foot," Dietz answered, "so mark singular. Did I say marks?"

"Yes."

"Sorry."

"Not at all."

Dietz pulled from his overcoat a newspaper folded to the gossip page and laid it on Walter's desk. To his horror, Walter saw a grainy photo of himself and Marta Marlund at the Rainbow Room. Keneally and Madeleine had been cropped out of the picture, doubtless due to a word between Jimmy Keneally and an editor. The caption read, *Sexy starlet Marta Marlund frolics at Rainbow Room with mystery date Walt Smithers the night before her suicide.*

"Broad's all over you," Dietz observed, not without a certain sadistic pleasure. "Good thing you gave her a phony name, you dog."

"Funny."

"So how was she in the sack?"

I might be the one person in my circle of acquaintances unable to answer that question, Walter thought.

"Toxicology?" he asked.

"Is going to take awhile."

But we know what it's going to show, Walter thought.

"Walter," Dietz said carefully, as if he was approaching an awkward subject, "you got a situation here you need some help with?"

"Everything's fine, William."

"Yeah, okay," Dietz said. "Do you want to keep the paper for a souvenir? Have it framed, hung on the wall?"

"I don't think so."

"You mind if I take it?" Dietz asked. "Proof that I work with a real celebrity?"

Walter smiled back and said, "I don't mind if you stick it up your ass."

"Don't get me all hot. I have a full day's work ahead of me."

"Really? And when did you change jobs?"

"Good-bye, mystery date."

"So long, sweetheart," Walter said. "And thank you."

Dietz waved and opened the door just as Sam Zaif was about to knock on it.

Dietz looked at him and said, "If it isn't B'nai Brith."

"Don't hit me, Dietz," Zaif answered. "I'm not handcuffed."

"I'm not circumcised. Want to see?"

"You gentlemen don't mind if I do a little work, do you?" Walter asked.

"I got a little work to do myself," Dietz said. "Walter, you need anything—"

"I will let you know," Walter said.

Dietz paused long enough to give Zaif a look that an anthropologist might describe as territorial.

"You be nice," he said.

Zaif shrugged and shook his head. Dietz held the stare for a second longer and then moved off down the hall. Zaif came in and plopped down in the chair in front of Walter's desk.

"You take a nice picture," Zaif said.

"They captured my good side."

"Not as good as Madeleine Keneally or Joe Keneally," Zaif went on, "but you're still a good-looking guy. I went to the newspaper office and got the negative. Then I went over all my notes from our interview, and I couldn't find one single itty-bitty reference to the fact that you and Marlund were double-dating with America's most enchanting couple. Did you just forget to mention that, Walter?"

"Apparently."

"Apparently," Zaif mumbled. "I get called into my lieutenant's office this morning. He tells me to wrap Marlund up as a straight suicide. And I say words to the effect of 'Not so fast, Lieutenant,' and he says words to the effect of 'Faster.' So I go back to my desk and I'm a little troubled because I wonder what's the big rush, and I get a cup of tea and crack open the paper and there you are. I go get the negative, and now I think I'm starting to understand what the big rush is. You sandbagged me, Walter."

"Sorry."

Zaif shook his head.

"One-word answers this morning, Walter?"

"Unintentionally," Walter answered because he couldn't help himself.

"So how is it you happen to be buddies with Joe Keneally and/or Madeleine Keneally?"

"My mother knows Madeleine's mother," Walter said. "I guess they were chatting on the phone, and Mrs. Keneally said that Madeleine was going to be in New York and my mother said that she should look up her son Walter. I suppose Madeleine invited me to her Christmas Eve party by way of stopping any further maternal nagging."

Zaif had already found out about the party at the Plaza, Walter thought. He continued, "So I asked Madeleine and Senator Keneally out for an evening on the town to reciprocate lest my mother be embarrassed by my lack of manners."

"Your mother knows Madeleine Keneally's mother," Zaif said.

"They went to school together."

"What school?"

"Ethel Walker."

Zaif said, "Now see, *my* mother knows Jerry Lewis' mother."

"Really?"

"But I never got to meet him," Zaif said.

"Sorry."

"That's all right. I don't even think he's funny."

"The French love him," Walter offered.

"They eat snails, too," Zaif said. "The point is, I don't think that even Jerry Lewis could make a few calls and squelch the investigation of an unattended death."

"Well, maybe in France . . ." Walter said.

Zaif looked genuinely angry when he said, "But I'm getting heat to call Marlund's death a suicide."

He stared at Walter until Walter said, "I don't have any heat, Detective."

"But Senator Keneally does."

"I would imagine he does."

"It doesn't take much imagination," Zaif said. "Joe Keneally bobs his curly red locks, and every Harp in the department wets himself. Well, I'm no son of the ould sod, and I don't march in anybody's St. Paddy's day parade."

"Yes, you've made that point," Walter said.

Zaif nodded his head a few times, then pushed his glasses back up on his nose and said, "You never screwed Marta Marlund."

"For the last time . . ."

"Because you're a homosexual."

Walter raised an incredulous eyebrow.

"I found a matchbook from that club Good Night when I was in your apartment," Zaif explained, "and did some checking around yesterday. The doorman there knew you well."

There is a God, Walter thought, and retribution is swift.

"You were seen at half the homo hangouts in Manhattan Saturday," Zaif said.

"Only half? It seemed like a longer day."

"So I don't think you ever laid an inch of hose to Marlund," said Zaif. "I think you were Joe Keneally's beard."

"You have a fevered sexual imagination," Walter answered.

Zaif got up, leaned over the desk, and said, "So screw Senator Keneally, screw my lieutenant, and screw you."

"Then you have a busy day ahead of you, Detective," Walter answered.

Zaif turned around and walked out.

Walter was pondering the ramifications of the visit when the intercom buzzed and summoned him to Forbes Jr.'s office. He bumped into Jack Griffin in the hallway.

"Geez, Walter," Griffin moaned.

"Could you be more specific, Jack?"

Griffin's rabbit face looked almost tearful as he whined, "That's awful about that Marlund. Such a waste."

Walter put a kindly hand on Griffin's shoulder. "She was a troubled woman," he said.

"Yeah, but I mean, here you were getting to nail a woman who looked like that, and she goes and kills herself!" Griffin said. "What a waste."

"Thanks for the sentiment, Jack," Walter said, disengaging to get to Forbes Jr.'s office.

"Walter!" Jack called after him. "I thought your last name was Withers!"

"The newspaper got it wrong!"

"Geez . . ."

Forbes Jr.'s pipe was puffing smoke like the Little Engine That Could as Walter was ushered into his office.

"Damn shame about Marta Marlund," Forbes said stoically, jaw manfully clenched on the pipe. "I assume the police contacted you."

"Yes, sir."

"Did you . . ."

"I saw no need to mention the Senator."

"You have a future at Forbes and Forbes," said Forbes.

"I hope so, sir."

"You can count on it," Forbes said. "You've handled yourself very well, Withers. Just know that the firm appreciates it."

"Thank you."

"You might try to stay out of the papers, though."

"Right."

"You've become the office celebrity," Forbes said. "The girls are all agog."

"I'll try not to take undue advantage."

Forbes Jr. blinked, then understood it was a joke and attempted his best version of a comradely chuckle. He recovered from this hilarity sufficiently to ask, "How's the Howard file coming?"

"I'm just wrapping it up, Mr. Forbes. One or two details . . ."

"Nail them down and write it up," Forbes said. "Although what we do is investigation, what we get paid for are *reports*."

So Walter dutifully sallied forth, metaphorical hammer in metaphorical hand, to nail down confirmation of Michael Howard's homosexuality so that he could write a report on it. A report that would doubtless be labeled with the career-ending red flag but nevertheless contribute positively to the ledger sheet at Forbes and Forbes.

Because it was important now to play it cool, to play it like a normal working day until he could make contact. Let the wheel spin around him, as it were—which it was, which it would—and stay calm in the hub.

Just another working day.

Frugal with Forbes' money (although Walter somehow considered it more Dickless Tracy's money; he remembered well the morning the old accountant had walked the corridor like a town crier, wailing, "Too many taxis! Too many taxis!"), he took the subway to Seventy-second and Broadway, a traffic island that the city thought of as Sherman Square and everyone else knew as Needle Park. This triangular oasis in the broadest part of Broadway contained a concentration of heroin higher than, say, downtown Istanbul. Its citizens wore either the frenzied look of the desperate or the glassy-eyed gaze of the enraptured. They were people who existed either in heaven or hell and knew no earthly middle ground, but waited for their angels in the doughnut shops and lunch counters that bordered the east side of the park like entrance gates. It was Walter's considered opinion that when ten or twelve emaciated pilgrims stand outside a Chock-Full-of-Nuts at six in the morning, waiting for it to open, they are not doing it for a cup of coffee and a chocolate doughnut, but rather for that moment of deliverance when Al, or Phil, or Chick—the angels, the pushers—arrive with that morning's glassine envelope full of paradise.

A convenient spot it was, Needle Park—removed from the tourist centers, across Central Park from the wealthy East Side, way uptown from Little Italy, where the heroin importers lived with their wives and kids. No, it was a good deal for everyone—from the city fathers to the Mob, to the cops to the addicts themselves. A sensible arrangement, Walter thought as he eased himself down on a bench next to a lady junkie whose indifference to her new neighbor was total. Although he did look a bit out of place in his heavy overcoat, gray fedora with a sporty red feather, and polished Bancrofts. But heroin addicts are a democratic lot, not noting differences of class, race, or sex. Their eyes are too firmly fixed on heaven.

Not Walter's. His gaze was directed across Broadway to the west side of the street, to the second floor of an enormous yellow brick building, where a sign in one of the floor-to-ceiling windows read: ANSONIA STUDIOS. There—for the windows generously gave an almost complete view—was the first piece of good luck Walter had received in many days, for in black leotard a wiry, muscled young man joined a dozen other wiry, muscled young men in a grueling and synchronized drill back and forth across a polished wood floor.

It was the young man who had challenged him in the bar on Saturday, the man who had reacted so severely to the mention of Michael Howard. A young man who had yet to learn that when you have something to hide, you have to hide everything. And therefore not carry gym bags advertising your probable whereabouts.

He is beautiful, Walter thought as he watched the man move with practiced grace, and if my gate were hinged that particular way, it would swing toward such as this young dancer.

Then again, Walter Withers could cheerfully sit through three consecutive showings of any Fred Astaire movie, and he actually loved ballet. He considered dance a rare blend of athleticism and art and found the mixture enchanting.

He did even on this cold December morning, huddled on a bench with junkies and watching the dancers work out through the windows. He couldn't hear the music, or the teacher's cadenced bark, but he could see it all in the dancers' rhythmic motions. He could see the sheen of sweat glisten on the faces and bare arms, silent testimony to the effort it took to make something appear effortless.

The kid was strong, Walter observed, with a dancer's long shoulder muscles and wide chest. He'd be no easy pickings in a fight, and Walter made a note to give him plenty of room when he—as he inevitably would—followed him to his next appointment.

To the Winter Garden, as it turned out, and Walter wasn't surprised—only a tad dismayed—that the kid wanted to walk the twenty-seven blocks to the theater. Walter's ankle was unsteady and tender, and it wasn't a matter of giving the kid room but of hustling to keep within visual distance, and Walter vowed that when this thing was all over, he would play tennis at least three times a week and cut down on booze.

The Winter Garden was closed, of course, on a late Monday morning, but there was a long line at the box office because *West Side Story* was a smash. And as the kid went through the stage door, Walter wondered if he was a Jet or a Shark and decided that the haircut made him a Jet all the way.

Walter waited a minute or so and then approached the guard at the stage door.

The guard took a stubby cigar from his mouth and grunted, "This is the stage door."

"Right you are," Walter said, taking a five-dollar bill from his pocket, "and a young man just went through it and I'd like to know his name."

It turned out to be Tony Cernelli.

Walter took out his pad and pen, scribbled a quick note, attached it to another five, and asked the guard to deliver it for him.

The guard put the bill in his pocket and asked, "No flowers or nothing?"

You know you're in New York, Walter thought, when you tip a fellow ten bucks and he implies that you're cheap.

"Just the note, please," he said.

It was a short distance back to the office and the exercise was helping his sore back and legs, so he decided to keep walking. Through the Midtown canyons of skyscrapers that in the days of his youth had been elegant brownstones.

The city he had known was fading. Le Ruban Bleu, once the haunt of such as Cole Porter, Moss Hart, Noel Coward, and Marlene Dietrich, long torn down for the antiseptic Corning Glass Building. Downstairs at the Upstairs demolished to make room for the Time/Life Building. The whole magical isle disappearing to be replaced by names of corporations. Cold, giant glass and steel boxes wherein crewcut, buttoned-down drones labored until they marched to their trains for the suburbs to watch their cowboy shows on television and dream of freedom. Park Avenue, once a boulevard of warmth and elegance, now a column of Mies van der Rohe monstrosities. Glass buildings reflecting other glass buildings.

When he got to his desk, there was a stack of phone messages: Madeleine Keneally, Joe Keneally, Jimmy Keneally, Sam Zaif, and Dieter Koenig. The one that really interested him at the moment was the one from Koenig, because among other reasons it was an invitation to lunch and it was in code.

Only Dieter, Walter thought, would put out an urgent call for a meeting and schedule it at the Russian Tea Room.

Dieter was already at his table when Walter got there. The German pimp looked almost prim, sitting up very straight, his hands folded on the white table, his blond hair slicked straight back. He had chosen a charcoal gray, double-breasted suit with a discreet chalk stripe, and a blue silk tie.

"This is very nice," Walter said as he slipped into his chair and pushed his legs under the long white tablecloth. "But very extravagant."

"It has been too long since we have had a really good lunch together," Dieter answered.

His voice had its usual elegant timbre, but there was a quaver of something else. Nerves? Sadness?

Walter said, "Well, it's very nice."

"Live well, die well."

This said as the waiter came up and was dispatched with a call for two martinis. There followed slivers of fresh salmon, chilled cucumber soup, a hot, peppered quail in a sauce as impenetrable as it was delicious, new potatoes . . . all served and consumed amid the pleasant cacophony of a crowded restaurant. The ring of crystal, the clatter of china and silver, the hurried footsteps of frenzied waiters, the loud whispers of book deals and stage contracts, the happy chatter about shopping expeditions, the sotto voce observations about who was being seen with whom.

For Walter and Dieter the conversation was casual. Dieter had something to say but wasn't ready to say it yet, and the courtesies must be observed, so they talked about the theater, Willy Brandt, Castro, Pier Angeli, the excellent food, *Doctor Zhivago,* their relative tennis games, and then the coffee was there, and Walter offered cigarettes and Dieter mentioned casually, "I saw the doctor this morning."

"Oh?"

Walter felt nauseated, a sickening fear deep in his stomach.

"A Jew," Dieter said, "but . . ."

". . . the best."

Dieter nodded.

"Not good news," he said.

Walter suddenly realized that Dieter had summoned him

to inform him that he was dying. Had summoned him to a valedictory lunch.

"Dieter, if there's anything I can do . . ."

"A prayer from time to time."

"Every day."

"What do doctors know?"

"They're fallible."

The bill arrived. Walter made no effort to pick it up or argue to pay his share, as Dieter would have been greatly offended. He paid in cash, they retrieved their coats, and were walking west on Fifty-seventh Street when Dieter said, "Walter, I worry about you."

"You know I left ScandAmerican."

"But still I worry."

Dieter was walking very close, the sleeve of his coat brushing against Walter's.

"About what?" Walter asked.

"Mir ist etwas zu Ohren gekommen."

The literal translation: Something came to my ear. German for: I hear things.

Again Walter felt a sickening stab of fear.

"What do you hear, Dieter?"

"About you and Senator Keneally," Dieter said. "About you and Marta Marlund."

"A tough assignment, that's all."

There on the sidewalk of busy Fifty-seventh Street. Traffic noise immense, human noise immense, no microphone in the world could pick them up, Walter thought.

Dieter said, "The FBI is very interested in Senator Keneally."

"Which is to say that he's a U.S. senator," Walter answered casually. But not feeling at all casual, for if the two grim gentlemen he saw on the night before Marta's death were indeed with the Bureau, then he was in a race.

"And maybe president someday," Dieter added.

"Maybe."

"So Hoover's very interested in his sex life, *ja*?" Dieter laughed.

"You know J. Edgar," Walter said. "He does like to sniff people's sheets."

"Including yours."

Walter felt his blood run cold. He'd never understood the expression before, but it was an accurate one. His body really did feel distinctly chilled.

"Yes?" he asked.

"I hear things."

And then Dieter's hand was in Walter's coat pocket. Holding Walter's hand, something cold and metallic pressed between their warm skin. A good-bye squeeze and then the hand was gone.

And a whisper from Dieter, "Promise me. Only if you *need* it. It is too dangerous otherwise."

"All right."

"*Versprich es.*" Promise.

"*Versprochen.*" I promise.

Dieter stopped walking and said, "I'm going the other way, actually."

"Well, thank you for lunch."

"Pleasure," Dieter said. "I'm flying back to Germany tonight."

"So soon?"

"It's time."

"Well, then . . ."

And again Walter wanted to cry, because Dieter looked so fragile standing there. Like the finest crystal and china, so fragile.

Dieter shook his hand and said, "Take good care of yourself, my friend."

"*You* take good care of *your*self, my friend," Walter said. "And thank you."

A dismissive wave of the hand and Dieter turned and walked away. Walter stood for a moment and watched him go, watched the back of his coat blend into the scores of others on the crowded sidewalk, watched him fade into the city.

Walter returned home to find that his apartment had been ransacked.

Nothing had been taken, of course, nor had the slightest effort been made to make it even look like a burglary. Whoever had searched the place didn't care that he knew it, although Walter wished that they had gone the entire distance and left a calling card, there being so many parties interested in the priapic would-be president Joseph P. Keneally.

No, Walter had expected this to happen. The only thing that seriously annoyed him was that the searchers had felt it necessary to remove all his albums from their jackets and leave them strewn over the floor, doing God only knows what damage to their vinyl surfaces. So as he was sorting Miles from Monk and Bird from Bean, the doorbell rang. It was Detective Sergeant Sam "not Sammy" Zaif of the New York Police Department.

"Another cultural stereotype exploded," Zaif said as he surveyed the wreckage. "About homos being fastidious."

"I don't know that I'm really in the mood for your brand of comedy this afternoon, Sergeant."

"Keneally's boys toss your place?"

"Or for your Bogart imitation."

"Touchy this afternoon."

"What do you want?" Walter asked. "If you can find it, help yourself."

Zaif knocked some books off a chair and sat down. Walter continued trying to reorganize his jazz collection as Zaif started. "I checked with the M.E. again. He found only slight traces of barbiturates in Marlund's stomach."

"Uh-huhh . . ."

"Don't you get it?" Zaif asked. "How could she have swallowed a lethal dose of Nembutol and not have it show up in her stomach?"

The answer to this riddle, Walter thought as he gently put a precious Oscar Peterson L.P. back into its dust jacket, is that the Nembutol was injected directly into the bloodstream, bypassing the digestive system.

"I asked the M.E. the same question," Zaif said, "and the schmuck basically says words to the effect of 'I dunno.' Then he mentions he found what might be a puncture mark between her toes, and I ask him why he didn't tell me this before and he answers words to the effect of 'You didn't ask.' So I say, 'You can't still be calling this a suicide,' and he says, 'Sure I can. The woman gave herself an illegal injection' . . . an 'illegal injection,' like we're going to charge her . . . 'and died as a result.' And I say, 'Doc, that's wonderful, except we didn't find any syringe,' or words to that effect. So he starts to dig his feet in, says something like, 'The woman was known to have combined alcohol with barbiturates, and that always has the potential for a deleterious occurrence.' 'Deleterious occurrence?' I ask. 'Like death?' and he says death is certainly one possibility and I say, 'Possibility, my ass, Doctor. The only thing we know for sure is that she's dead.' "

"If you'd like to pause for a breath or something, don't mind me."

"No, I'm fine," Zaif said. "So I ask the doctor if there's any way that we could determine if she had been killed by a lethal injection—either self- or shall we say other-inflicted—and he says, 'Sure. Check her liver, it oughta show up there.' And I say words to the effect of 'Swell, open her up again,' and he says he can't do that. I get a little pissed off at this point and ask, 'Who do I have to talk to to get this done?' and he says—you're going to love this, Walter—he says, 'Try the attorney general or whatever in Denmark, because that's where she is,' and those are his exact words. The body was shipped out this morning."

"What did you want?" Walter asked. "To stuff her and mount her, so to speak?"

"You're regaining your sense of humor," Zaif said. "That's good. No, what I figure is that someone either poured booze down her until she passed out, or put something in her Smirnoff that knocked her out, then pumped her full of liquid pentobarbitol, which is pretty smart because Nembutol is just the trade name of pentobarbitol. So it looks perfect, right? Unhappy actress goes for the long good-bye with booze and pills, speaking of cultural stereotypes."

Which is about the way I have it, too, Walter thought. I just haven't nailed down precisely who. Soon, though.

"But now you'll never know," Walter said, "because you can't have another autopsy performed."

"Oh, I'll know because you're going to tell me."

"Really?"

"Because it's the only option you have left, Walter," Zaif said. "Christ, Keneally had a beautiful woman like that killed, just think what he'll do to you, and he wasn't even fucking you. At least I don't think he was. Was he?"

Walter found the new Ahmad Jamal recording, started to put it in its sleeve, then changed his mind and put it on the record player instead. He selected the "Poinciana" cut, and a second later Vernel Fournier's exotic drum solo filled the apartment.

"I decided your next soliloquy deserved some background music," Walter explained. "Now tell me please why Senator Keneally had Marta Marlund killed and why I am in the same mortal danger."

"This is very strange music."

"It's a strange tale you have to tell."

"Keneally was banging Marlund, don't even try to deny it," Zaif said, "and he's using you as his beard. Keneally knows he's going to dump Marlund, Marlund sees the handwriting on the wall and decides to blackmail Keneally. Who does she get to help her with the technical stuff but a sleazy private you'll-excuse-the-expression *dick* such as yourself? So she gets photographs, she gets tapes, she gets, I don't know, a plaster of Paris mold of his big Irish *schlong*. And she says to Keneally words to the effect of 'Not so fast, Joey boy. How would you like the papers to get hold of this stuff?' and she might as well be saying 'Please kill me' because it has the same shall we say deleterious effect. But Keneally still has the problem of the photos and/or tapes . . . or maybe home movies . . . and he figures if Marlund didn't have them, who does? Walter Withers, that's who! So he sends his little leprechauns over here to find them, except I know that you're not dumb enough to keep them here, Walter, so why don't you just tell me where they are and save yourself a beating from Keneally's thugs?"

Walter stared at him for a moment, then asked, "Have you considered psychoanalysis, Sam? A year or two on the couch would do—"

"I can offer you protection, Walter," Zaif said. "You try to blackmail Joe Keneally, and all you're going to get is dead."

"Thanks for dropping by, Sam."

"Who's the pianist? He's pretty good."

"Ahmad Jamal."

"Some kind of Arab?"

"A Negro."

"Think about my offer," Zaif said. "If you'll testify I can make a case."

"There's nothing to think about. It's a fabrication. Brilliant but a fabrication."

Zaif got up. He handed Walter a card and said, "My number at the station. Think it over. I'd hate to be investigating your murder."

"Yes, me too."

Walter was still listening to the Jamal trio and straightening his apartment when Anne called.

"Alicia's dead," she said.

I know that, too.

"Your friend from the Cellar?" he asked. "My God, what happened?"

"She was raped and murdered in Riverside Park last night," Anne said. "The bastard raped her and then slit her throat."

Actually, the other way around, he thought. The thorough sons of bitches. Blond actresses die from booze and pills in swank hotels. Negro girls are raped and stabbed in parks.

He said, "That's terrible. Are you all right?"

"I suppose . . . I don't know . . ."

The soft sound of her crying. For her friend, for her lover, for herself? Walter wondered.

After a bit she murmured, "It seems like everyone's dying."

"It can seem that way sometimes."

Then, in a burst, as if she had to blurt it out before she lost her nerve, "Walter, I—"

"Don't say any more."

For God's sake, don't say where you are. We've enough recordings to last a lifetime, short though our lives may be, and we don't need another.

"Don't," he repeated sternly, sharply, "say any more. And hang up now."

She cried again, then asked, "Can you come over?"

"Sorry, I can't."

Because this needs a little more time to work itself out, he thought. But he heard the misinterpretation in the coldness of her voice. It was the unmistakable tone of a lady who perceives that she is being dropped.

And betrayed.

"Okay," she said. "I'll see you when I see you, I guess."

"Soon," he said casually.

"Whenever," she answered, and hung up.

He found the Coltrane-Monk album, her Christmas gift to him, and put it on the hi-fi. Then he lit a cigarette, sat down, and listened to Coltrane lay down the plaintive melodic line of "Ruby, My Dear" and felt as if he was going to cry. God, I'm getting to be just a soppy old queen myself, he thought as he felt a hot tear flow down his cheek. I have to put things back into boxes.

It was a memory from training, one of the few useful items he'd picked up. *Take whatever you don't have to handle at the moment, they'd taught him, and put it into a mental box. Lock the box and forget about it. When you've mastered that discipline, you've organized yourself into a number of little, locked boxes that you only open when the time is right. Then you deal with one box at a time.*

He admired that technique and used it often, but now it seemed to be slipping on him.

I have so many boxes, he thought in a moment of glorious self-pity. I have my Keneally box, and my Madeleine box, my McGuire box, my Morrison box, and my Dieter box. And my Anne box, which is the one that needs to be locked and locked right now. That's the dangerous one, that's the one with the love and the fear in it. That's the one that could make me slip, make the fatal mistake. Haven't I killed enough people this week without killing the one I love, and that's just the sort of thing I'm talking about—put it away in a box and lock it up.

So he finished his smoke, then went into the bathroom and washed his face and gargled with Listerine. By the time these small rituals were done, he had locked his emotions into a small mental box labeled "Anne" and opened the box filed under "Howard, Michael" and steeled himself to do what he had to do.

Which in this case meant going to Sardi's.

Tony Cernelli recognized him as soon as he came in. "You're the creep from the bar," he said.

"That's an accurate enough description," Walter said. "May I make it up to you by buying you dinner? Although I'm not sure that Sardi's food is exactly compensatory."

"I'm particular about who I share a meal with," Cernelli answered. "Now what is it you want?"

"Right now I want a table," Walter answered.

They got one along the wall, beneath a caricature of Alexander Woollcott. It was early and a dark night in the theaters, so the place was unusually empty. An unenthusiastic waiter took their orders for a martini, a Coke, and an order of french fries.

"You want an order of fries?" the waiter asked Walter.

"Please."

"An order of fries," the waiter repeated.

"An order of fries."

"You just want fries."

"Which is why I ordered them."

"With a martini you want french fries."

"Right," Walter said, adding, "with vinegar on the side, please."

The waiter paused for a moment to make sure that everyone understood that his time was being wasted, then went off to get their order.

During this exchange Tony Cernelli sat in sullen silence. He had dressed for the occasion, however, Walter noted, in a blazer and a tie over his chinos and loafers.

"Thanks for meeting me," Walter said.

"What's this all about?" Cernelli asked. "Your note said it was a matter of importance to Michael."

"What's the nature of your relationship with Michael Howard?" Walter asked.

"What gives you the right—"

"Is it of a sexual nature?"

"—to pry into—"

"Who is Howard Benson?" Walter asked.

"—people's private lives, and—"

"Or is Howard Benson simply an alias for Michael Howard?"

"—go around asking questions—"

"By the way, does Mrs. Howard know?"

"As a matter of fact, yes, she does." Cernelli glared at him.

The waiter chose this moment to return with the Coke, the martini, and a steaming plate of thick, fat fries. Walter took a swallow of the martini, then poured vinegar over half the plate of fries. He stabbed one of the thickest fries with his fork and put it into his mouth. "Sorry about this," he said. "It's very rude, I know, but for some reason I'm starving. Grab a fork and help yourself. Do you like vinegar?"

Cernelli sipped his Coke.

"Either you tell me who you are and what this is about, or I'm leaving," he said.

"Sure," Walter said. He swallowed the potato and said, "My name is Walter Withers, and I work for Forbes and Forbes Investigative Services, Personnel Security Division. I'm doing a background check on Michael Howard for his potential promotion to vice-president."

"And you want to know if he's homosexual," Cernelli said.

"No," Walter lied. He took another bite and said, "I want to know if he's involved in industrial espionage."

"Michael?" Cernelli laughed.

"When a man keeps an apartment under a different name, he leaves himself open to all sorts of suspicions," Walter said.

Cernelli started to get up.

"Sit down, please, Mr. Cernelli," Walter said. "If you want to help your friend."

Cernelli slowly lowered himself back onto the seat.

"Look," he said, "you've already 'caught' us. Congratulations. You're a great 'homo hunter.' So just write your little report and—"

"Settle down," Walter said. "I don't have to put anything about you in the report as long as I know that you're not involved in stealing trade secrets from American Electric. As long as I'm assured that your little love nest is just that and nothing more, then as far as I'm concerned the matter is finished and I can write a clean report. Otherwise, I'll have to write up the apartment, the alias . . ."

"We love each other," Cernelli said.

"So your relationship is of a personal nature?"

"Yes."

"Sexual?"

A pause before the terminal jump off the cliff.

"Yes."

"Do you have any business relationship of any kind with Electric Dynamics, Inc.?" Walter asked.

"I own a toaster."

"Help me out here, Tony."

"No," Tony sighed, "I have no business with Electric Dynamics, Inc."

"Has Michael Howard ever revealed any confidential business information to you?"

"He talks about the office."

"Say no, Tony."

"No," Cernelli said. "Anything else?"

"Would you like to order now?"

"Go to hell."

Cernelli got up and walked out.

Well, Walter thought, that about nails down old Michael Howard.

He finished the french fries and the drink, left enough cash to cover the check and a large tip, and headed back to the office to type up a report red-flagging Michael Howard as a sexual deviant.

Because what we get paid for are reports.

He was on Forty-eighth Street nearing the office when a limousine pulled alongside and Joe Keneally hopped out. Walter kept walking.

"I'm used to people returning my phone calls," Keneally said, walking beside Walter.

"I'm sure you are."

"This cop keeps bothering me—"

"Nice fellow named Zaif?" Walter asked. "Tall, very smart, needs a better tailor?"

Keneally's face was red. "He thinks you're blackmailing me," he hissed. "He thinks you have tapes of me and Marta."

"Yes, he told me."

"He also thinks you may have killed her," Keneally said. "Jesus, Walter, when I said get rid of her—"

"Please try not to be any more ridiculous than you already—"

Keneally grabbed him by the elbow and turned him around.

"Did you?" he asked. "Did you kill her, Withers?"

"No, Senator. Did you?"

"No!" said Keneally. "This cop also said that another woman's prints were all over the room. He wants to fingerprint Madeleine!"

"I wouldn't allow that, Senator," Walter said calmly. "The prints will probably match."

Which set Keneally back on his heels. He was positively wide-eyed as he asked, "What the hell is this all about?"

Walter answered, "I'm not entirely sure yet, but I'll let you know. In the meantime, keep your boyos out of my apartment, try to keep your fly zipped, and talk to your wife. And do you have my money?"

Keneally took an envelope from his pocket and jammed it into Walter's chest.

"Watch yourself, Withers."

"Not to worry, Senator."

Ah, but you've been a busy bee, Detective Sergeant Zaif, Walter thought as he left Keneally standing on the sidewalk. Buzzing around cross-pollinating your suspects until one of the flowers opens up and blooms with a story. Tell your pal Walter that you think Keneally had Marta killed, then tell Keneally you think an out-of-control Withers killed Marta and then decided to blackmail him. See who talks first. A busy bee.

He stood inside the building for a moment, decided that the Howard report could wait until morning, then went back out on the street and took a cab to the corner of Carmine and Sixth.

There was no doorman outside the Parma Social Club, just the usual gaggle of tough guys in their black overcoats and polished shoes. And one of them was Paulie Martino.

"Walter Withers!" Paulie yelled. "The hell you been?"

"Out and about, Paulie."

They shook hands.

"Paulie, you have paper on a fellow named Sean McGuire?" Walter asked.

"A big mistake," Paulie said. "Never carry writers. They think they're allowed to write themselves a different ending. Why, you know the guy?"

"Can we go inside?"

Paulie walked Walter through the door and said to the bodyguard, "It's okay. He's with me."

"I know Walter Withers," the bodyguard said.

"Hello, Carmine," Walter said.

Carmine Badoglio had been around Albert D'Annunzio for a long time. He'd been younger then, and a little less thick around the middle some twelve years before when a college kid had persuaded an idiotic bookie to lay him two grand on the Yale–Harvard game and then lost. And Albert, who in those days still took a personal interest in such details, thought he was going to have to send somebody to the far reaches of New Haven to hold the kid upside down until his money fell out and then write it off, because college kids at Yale had a habit of not paying their debts. Carmine liked to tell the story about when young Walter Withers, dressed in a gray flannel suit, a Yale scarf, and drunk to boot, came rolling up to the door with twenty-two hundred in cash and said he had to deliver it to Signor D'Annunzio personally. The dumb little bookie had urine running down his leg, but Albert took the cash, and then this kid pulls another grand out of his pocket and gives it to Albert as "security against future losses," but says it in Italian, no less, and invites Albert to his club to play tennis sometime. Everyone was waiting for Albert to twist this kid's head off his neck and fucking *eat* it, but Albert looked around, smiled, and said, "Who is this kid? He's got style."

So Walter was welcome in the Parma Social Club, and in the intervening years a couple of Albert D'Annunzio's superiors had expired of natural causes—multiple gunshot wounds being about as natural in that particular profession as anything else—and Albert had risen to a high executive position in what was now a national concern with offices in the greater New York metropolitan area, Las Vegas, and Phoenix, Arizona. But the old club on Carmine Street was still Albert's choice of personal location, and it was here that he could usually be found if you could get inside the door.

"I'm done with writers and artists," Paulie said. "They're a scummy class of people."

"I'm swearing off writers myself," Walter said.

"You make out okay on the game?"

"I survived."

"That's good."

"I figured Mr. Rosenbloom had serious money on a five-point spread."

Paulie grinned. "A lot of guys didn't figure that out."

The club hadn't changed much since the last time Walter had been there. The same bad murals of Mt. Etna, bloody red lava spilling incontinently down its slopes, filled the otherwise chalk white walls. The small round tables still had white tablecloths on them, and the bar was still a dark mahogany with ornate carvings of Sicilian hunting scenes, except that they were hunting stags instead of each other, which Walter thought was deceptive.

"Two wines," Paulie said to the bartender. "I'm not even going to read books anymore. They just give you ideas, you know?"

"I know," Walter agreed.

"The fucking 'highway by night,' " Paulie snorted. "A couple more weeks he'll be *under* the highway by night, know what I mean?"

Walter pulled the envelope from his jacket pocket and handed it to Paulie. He looked at the bills and asked, "The hell is this, Walter?"

"McGuire's debt," Walter said. "Minus a little of the vigorish."

"Close enough," Paulie said. "*Salut,* Walter."

"*Salut,* Paulie."

Walter downed the thick red wine and said, "I need to have a word with Albert if I could."

"He's in the back," Paulie said, then lowering his voice, added, "Eating. That's all he does anymore, Walter, is eat. His life is one long continual meal. I don't know when the guy has time to take a dump, for crying out loud. He's always at the table. The waiters here can't keep leather on their shoes, they're always walking back and forth bringing him pasta, bringing him sauces, bringing him ravioli, meatballs, sausages, cheeses, and the pastries. . . . You know that bakery on Minetta?"

"Sure."

"The owner bought a boat last week, was going to name it 'The Albert,' except some of the guys talked to him, told him maybe that might offend, you know?"

"So what did he call it?"

Paulie shrugged. "I dunno. Probably named it after his wife, except she ain't exactly Audrey Hepburn, either. You want me to go see if Albert has a minute?"

"Please."

"Forget it. I owe you."

So a few minutes later Walter was seated at Albert D'Annunzio's private table in the back room, watching the obese mobster consume a platter of fettucine carbonara with side orders of squid and sliced prosciutto.

"You had dinner?" Albert asked as Walter sat down.

"I ate," Walter said.

Albert said, "Paulie's a good kid, I never should have let him take those classes at NYU. All he wants to do now is read books and ball Jewish girls. Anyway, I'm glad it worked out. But I told him, no more writers."

"I think he got the message."

"I hope so," Albert mumbled through his food. "Now, what's with you?"

"I came to ask a favor," Walter said.

Walter asked and received, they exchanged a little more small talk, and on the way out Walter said, "Paulie, there's a little something else I need."

When he heard what it was Paulie said, "You gotta be fucking kidding me, right?"

But Walter wasn't kidding, and Paulie was on the spot, figuring he owed Walter and all, so Paulie said he'd make it happen and Walter thanked him profusely.

Then Walter had one last errand to do. He went to Village Cigars and bought a packet of Juicy Fruit gum. Then he got into the subway at Sheridan Square and wrote a short message on a piece of note paper: *Battery Park at dawn. . . . Bring terms.*

He got off at Ninety-Sixth Street, walked to the Thalia, bought a ticket, and sat in the same seat that Anne had on Christmas night. He took the note from his pocket, the gum from his mouth, and used the gum to stick the note to the bottom of the chair. He watched *Touch of Evil* for a few minutes, then got back in the subway and made his way home.

He had one quick nightcap—a scotch and water—and collapsed in bed. Tomorrow would start early, be a long day, and quite possibly his last.

He was eager, though, to see who would answer the note. Whoever it was had killed Marta and Alicia, and would probably try to kill him.

His sleep that night was dreamless.

CHAPTER SEVEN

Ruby, My Dear

Tuesday, December 30

Dawn, then, in Battery Park.

Walter sat on a bench on this southernmost tip of Manhattan as the sun rose, more silver than gold in the winter mist, over Brooklyn. He felt this slight warmth on his back, for he was facing west—as arranged in his message—toward the Statue of Liberty, that lonely lady looking faint, small, and distant in the black and choppy waters of the bay.

Battery Park at dawn, he had written. *I'll be on a bench facing west. Bring terms.*

Letting them know that they could make a safe approach. Himself sitting out in the open on this barren stretch, the perfect sitting duck if that's what they wanted, gambling that it wasn't.

And if it is, I'll never know, he thought. Not in this world, anyway. I'll just hear the footsteps of approach, then a short silence, and then the world will go black.

To wake up in heaven, no doubt, he thought cheerily. Well, some doubt. Considerable doubt if God is more just than merciful.

At least hell is warm, or so the brochures say.

Battery Park, Walter thought as he shivered from cold

and fear. I had to pick the coldest damn place in New York City for this rendezvous, this "live drop," as they say in the trade. A Siberian wind whipping down the Hudson and joining with the wintry gusts from the ocean to blow right through my good Republican cloth coat. Inside of which this good Democrat is freezing, thank you very much.

Battery Park, Walter mused, where Manhattan Island finally narrows to a single point and gives the lie to Kipling. *East* (Side) *is East / And West is West,* he recited, *And never the twain shall meet. Except at Battery Park / At the bottom of South Street,* Walter added, making up doggerel because there was nothing else to do but shiver and be terrified, especially when he heard the footsteps behind him.

It's the Plodder, Walter thought with some surprise. I would have thought they'd have gotten the bloody bastard well out of here by now. But then there are practical issues, I suppose, and they probably think that the police aren't going to expend a great deal of effort to find the murderer of just another Negro woman. And they are probably right.

Walter sensed the presence of the large man standing close behind him, then felt the cold metal of a pistol barrel press into the base of his skull.

> *Our Father, who art in heaven*
> *Hallowed be thy name*
> *Thy kingdom come . . .*

Walter recalled the old expression about "blowing someone to kingdom come" and understood it for the first time as he imagined the Plodder's finger tightening on the trigger.

> *. . . Thy will be done*
> *On earth as it is in heaven.*
> *Give us this day . . .*

Well, give us this day, that's all.

Then a large manila envelope dropped into Walter's lap. He felt a wave of relief, then a bolt of pain as the pistol butt smashed into the back of his neck. Hard enough to double him over—his hand grasped for the edge of the bench to keep him from toppling over, his eyes watered, his stomach threatened to erupt—but not enough to knock him out. Just enough to keep him occupied as the Plodder disengaged.

And perhaps just a touch of revenge for the chase in Riverside Park? Walter wondered.

He opened the envelope.

Photographs of himself and Anne in various European cities. Otherwise innocuous pictures of a shopping trip in Paris, a stroll along an Amsterdam canal, an artsy afternoon in Brussels. A particularly painful shot of him on the steps of her apartment in Skeppsholmen. Then a new set of photos: Anne and Marta in bed. The same grainy quality of a cheap stag film, but the images are clear enough, Walter thought. Anne's petite body looked even smaller enveloped in Marta's long limbs. Her fingers splayed on the broad field of Marta's back. Her eyes wide, her lips open, Marta's hair flowing across the tops of her thighs. Suckling on Marta's breast. Walter could *hear* Marta's cries, could hear Anne's. . . .

Enough.

Walter turned to the documents. Dry stuff, but more than enough to convict Anne of espionage. And treason. A years-long record of faithful service to the Party, replete with dates and places. More than enough to send her to one of the Old One's secluded cabins in the mountains where the company psychologists, pharmacologists, and just plain old-fashioned interrogators would work on her until they drained her.

She'd been a typical young idealist, Walter inferred from the documents, a born-to-the-breed fellow traveler. Father a trade unionist, mother a socialist. The usual memberships in the usual, dreary catalog of organizations: Young People's Socialist League, Fair Play for Russia . . . Vocal support for our gallant Russian ally in its struggle against German fascism ("A second front now!"). All of which Walter already knew. All sadly naive, he thought, but also sadly typical as well.

No, it did not get interesting, didn't get dangerous, until Anne started traveling to Europe. On tour—a built-in reason to move from city to city. For the "Cause" then, could she deliver a message here, a signal there, this film canister, this small bundle of cash? To a comrade in Vienna, to a comrade in Oslo, to a comrade in Nice, comrade? All well documented.

And of course McCarthy was back in the States, blowing apart lives and careers, and it's easy to understand, Walter thought, how she would fall for all of this. Hard to know in those days who was the real enemy. Easy to be confused, easy to betray one's country if one believed in the workers of the world, you see, and the withering away of the state, and HUAC was blacklisting most of one's friends.

Then in '56 the gallant Soviet ally sent its tanks into Budapest to machine-gun students in the streets, and the refugees started pouring into Vienna with stories of glass tubes shoved up penises and then shattered, and women raped with bayonets, and old friends just disappearing. Anne's confusion grew and her enthusiasm dimmed, and a smart handler would have said yes, okay, no problem. The People thank you for your service, and no hard feelings. In fact, I'm giving a little party in Stockholm on the Fourth. . . .

So her career as a courier was over, *just* over, by the time she met you, by the time the Great Scandinavian Pimp and Deadly Recruiter fell into bed with a Soviet mark who was also sharing a sapphic bed with another Soviet spy who in turn came to the wildly democratic bed of Joe Keneally and got it all on tape.

Which is the point, of course, Walter thought. Not that Keneally is screwing around, but that he's screwing around with—*inter alia multa*—a Soviet agent. The sweetest, stickiest honey trap of all time, this one. A United States senator—maybe a United States president—in a long-term affair with a KGB whore.

But of course Anne wouldn't know all that. Wouldn't know about Marta, so when a courier was needed, well . . . *the best thing we could be taking about will be years in prison, and that's the best thing.*

And me with her. Because they'll never believe you weren't in on it. Never believe that your lovers' rendezvous were not in fact the assignations of espionage. And even if they want to believe you, they'll have to make sure, and that could take years of interrogations. That is, if they don't just take you out somewhere and shoot you, as you thought they might that dank night in Hamburg.

At least they want to make a deal, Walter thought. Or want me to think that they do, to lull me into negotiation while they set up the kill.

Which, Walter thought, brings us to this melancholy moment. Which brings us to the note in the manila envelope: *Bring the tapes to the Boat Basin tonight at nine.* Followed by a few logistical details. No need to spell out the or-else. Or else this packet goes to CIA and FBI, and you'll spend the next few years in those mountain cabins. So just do us this little favor, Walter, and take the tapes to the Boat Basin tonight at nine.

Which I will do, Walter thought. Which I most certainly will do.

He didn't feel particularly angry. It was the business. But the smarmy postscript did rankle, he had to admit, the gratuitous, unctuous note that read: *P.S. It's not that she loved you less, but that she loved the People more.*

There were details to attend to first. Things to wrap up, responsibilities that must be met before he could take the tapes to the Boat Basin.

He got unsteadily to his feet, caught his balance, and found a convenient trash barrel. Spreading the incriminating documents under yesterday's newspaper—the front page featured a photo of ice skaters in Rockefeller Center, his own office building in the background—he lit a cigarette, then touched the lighter to the newspaper.

As he walked away, a grateful bum came over and rubbed his gloved hands over the barrel, warming himself in the fire and the gathering dawn.

Walter walked up through the Wall Street district, alive now with commuters rushing to man the wheels of commerce, to buy and sell, and to trade. An appropriate setting, Walter thought.

He went to a phone booth and dialed the Contessa's number.

"My dear, are you mad?" she asked after answering on the seventh ring. "It's the middle of the night!"

Nevertheless she agreed to wake Anne, who came sleepily to the telephone.

Without prelude Walter said, "I know everything."

"What?"

"I know everything."

A long silence. A silence he had heard, so to speak, from

so many marks after just being told the bad news. *Our unsmiling boys will drop a word to your unsmiling boys. . . .*

"Who *are* you?" she asked.

In lieu of an answer he asked, "Do you love me?"

Another silence before she answered, *"Oui, je t'aime."*

"Do you trust me?"

"My God, do *you* trust *me*?"

"Do you trust me?"

To how many marks had he put that question? On how many park benches, in how many cafés? On how many long and soulful walks through how many city parks, along how many rivers? How many times on the banks of the black, cold, and angry Skeppsholmen in those bitter Stockholm days? *Do you trust me?* Said in such a way that the mark couldn't say no.

"Yes."

"Then stay put. Do you understand?"

"Yes."

"Stay where you are," he ordered. "Don't go out, don't let anyone in, don't come to the phone unless it's me."

Funny, he thought, how even over a telephone line you can feel hesitation.

"What?" he asked.

"I go back to work tomorrow night," she said. Then added, "The Rainbow Room."

Tomorrow it will all be over, he thought.

"Stay put until you hear from me," he said.

"I—"

"Do you trust me?"

"Yes," she said. "Do you hate me?"

"No," he said.

"Je t'aime."

"Je t'aime aussi."

As I do, he thought as hung up the phone.

My dear traitor.

"You're in early, Mr. Withers," Mallon said. "I'll send the coffee and Danish up."

"You are a prince among men," Walter said.

"Not to be nosy," Mallon said, "but do I see blood, Mr. Withers?"

"I dropped a razor blade this morning, stooped to pick it up, and forgot that I was underneath the sink when I straightened up," Walter said.

"Ouch."

"Stupidity has its price," said Walter.

"You should get that looked at."

"If you're saying that I should have my head examined, you have a point."

Mallon laughed, then said seriously, "Anything I can do for you, Mr. Withers?"

Walter started to demur but said instead, "Just have an eye for strangers, would you?"

"Strangers?"

"Anyone who doesn't seem to have business here."

Mallon gave him a practiced doorman's skeptical gaze. "Dropped a razor blade," he said.

"A Schick, yes."

"Treacherous things."

"As are sinks."

Then up to his sliver of an office feeling empty-handed *sans* morning coffee and pastry, head throbbing, but also feeling strangely . . . *elated* was too strong a word . . . *re-signed* perhaps. Content, anyway, to settle into the soothing drill of paperwork for a few hours.

He stepped over to the window, took in his partial view of Saks and St. Patrick's, and watched as 16-C made his unenthusiastic entrance to his place of work. He didn't wave at 16-C this morning and the man looked—from a distance it was hard to tell, but it seemed anyway that the man looked offended. 16-C looked at Walter for a moment, then shyly raised his cardboard cup in what might have been a greeting or a salute. But Walter didn't wave back, just stared for a moment and pulled shut his Venetian blinds.

He settled in to work, for even though he probably would not be back the next day, the work doubtless *would* be, and it would be unfair to stick his successor with incomplete files. No, he thought, your personal problems are exactly that, your personal problems, and ought not be the worry of your friends and co-workers.

So he picked up a blank daily expense report, entered the Sardi's tab, and attached the receipt. Then he fished out a blank Nedick's receipt from his collection and filled it out for nine bucks and change to cover his ten-dollar bribe to the charmer at the Winter Garden.

The DER completed, he picked up his daily activity log, which was a bit tricky given the situation. So he gave himself an extra couple of hours on the Howard file and fudged a little on the hours he'd devoted to the various amours of the Keneally family and called it even.

One of Mallon's minions arrived just then with the breakfast, said that Mallon would scalp him if he accepted the proffered tip, and made a hasty exit out of the office.

The phone rang while Walter was bolting down his breakfast.

"Withers, Personnel Security."

"Zaif, Assisted Suicides. Guess what?"

"Keneally confessed to the Lindbergh kidnapping?"

"Better," Zaif chirped. "Madeleine Keneally won't consent to having her manicured hands messed up with nasty fingerprint ink. She went absolutely ape when I suggested it. Started to cry and everything. Next thing I know, Jimmy Keneally's in my lieutenant's office looking like he's about to hemorrhage! I couldn't exactly read his lips, but words to the effect of 'that dirty Kike' and 'dog patrol in Benson-hurst.' I'm telling you, Walter, this is doing wonders for my persecution complex."

"I'm happy for you, Sam."

Zaif continued, "Keneally storms out giving me a look like he's going to punch me out right there, and then the lieutenant calls me in. He looks like he's been sodomized with a telephone pole and starts off with, he actually says, 'Listen, you smart-ass Jew'—'Smart-ass Jew?' I repeat, and he says, 'That's what I said, you smart-ass Jew,' then words to the effect of if I ever contact Madeleine Keneally or Joe Keneally again, he's going to rip off my testicles and feed them to the polar bears in the Central Park Zoo. I mean, is this guy Freudian or what, Walter? Then he tells me he's reassigning Marlund to Keegan, who 'knows how to close a suicide when he sees one,' and I say, 'Well, Keegan sure knows the words "closing time," that's true.' So what I'm saying, Walter, is that it's not too late."

"For closing time?" Walter asked.

"For you getting on board," Zaif said. "I have to tell you, Walter, the Keneally brothers are pissed at you."

"Why?"

"I told Joe that you went belly up," Zaif said. "Well, not him directly but Jimmy, because Joe wouldn't take my call. I just said words to the effect of 'Tell the Senator that Walt Withers went belly up on him and is delivering the tapes and everything to me tonight."

"But that isn't true."

"It could be, Walter," Zaif said. "It better be. Because Keneally is gunning for you now, and you've got no place to run except into my loving arms. Who killed her, Withers? Was it Keneally? His wife?"

"I believe you told Keneally that *I* killed her," said Walter.

"A ploy," Zaif answered. "To lull him into false complacency."

"It didn't work."

"No," Zaif agreed. "And I said 'might.' I told Keneally that you *might* have killed her."

"Or words to that effect."

"Or words to that effect," Zaif echoed.

And indeed, Walter thought, my actions may well have had a causal effect in the death of Marta Marlund, so in a certain respect it isn't unfair to say that I might have killed her.

"But I don't think you did," Zaif said. "I don't think you're the killer type."

"But you think I'm the blackmailing type," Walter said.

"I think you're the *dead* type unless you come in out of the cold."

As I am planning to do, friend Sam, this very night.

Misinterpreting Walter's silence as hesitation, Zaif said, "If you were involved in this somehow, Walter, the time to come forward is now. You know the old saying: The first person in gets the witness chair; the last person in gets the electric chair."

"I'm not familiar with that old saying. I think you just made it up."

"I did," Zaif said with the pride of authorship. "But it's true."

Walter did Zaif the courtesy of pretending to think it over, then said, "I believe I'll just have to take my chances, Detective."

"Your chances are zip, Withers."

"Zip Withers," Walter said. "Sounds like a crusty old football coach at a small Midwestern college."

"You know what it's going to say on your toetag? 'Walter Withers: Sucker,' " Zaif said. "Which is too bad, because I'm beginning to like you."

"Yes, our relationship has been brief but intense."

"Like my career."

True, Walter thought. Zaif needed to beat incredible odds and make some kind of case against Keneally, or he truly would be netting fugitive pooches in Queens.

"Ah, well . . ." Walter mumbled. Then he added, "I can put a good word in for you at Forbes and Forbes if you'd like."

"Yeah? They hire smart-ass Jews?"

"It would be quite useful to have someone who doesn't mind working Christmas," Walter said.

"I'll think about your offer," Zaif said, "if you'll think about mine."

He hung up. And rather abruptly, Walter thought.

So it was back to wrapping up loose ends, including, Walter thought—and no hideous pun intended—Michael Howard. He hauled out the Underwood, slipped a carbon between two sheets of paper, and fed them into the roller. He checked the corners to make sure the pages were even, then began to type his investigation report.

SUBJECT: HOWARD, MICHAEL, A. FILE #:AE 576809
INVESTIGATOR: Withers, Walter DATE: 12/30/58

This investigator observed the subject over the course of a period including 12/24/58–12/29/58. While a background check of subject revealed no negative information, live surveillance of the subject revealed that subject maintains a second residence at 322 E. 21st St., Apt 2-B, Borough of Manhattan, City of New York, under the alias "Howard Benson." Further surveillance of the subject revealed that subject frequents establishments known to cater to a homosexual clientele. Further surveillance and an interview revealed that subject shares the above-referenced residence with a Mr. Anthony Cernelli, an admitted homosexual. Mr. Cernelli admitted in an interview with this investigator that his relationship with the subject is of a "romantic" and "sexual" nature. Mr. Cernelli further stated that he has neither solicited nor received confidential business information from the subject and that he would have had no reason to do so. As Mr. Cernelli's profession is that of "dancer," it would be reasonable to believe that his statement in this regard is credible. Nevertheless, the subject's covert sexual activity precludes any security classification other than that of High Risk (Pls. refer to Memorandum 328-F, 3/19/55, American Electronics, Inc. to Forbes & Forbes, "Security Risk Classifications"). If we can be of any further assistance in this matter, or provide any further clarification, please do not hesitate to contact our office.

And that should put the bullet in the back of Michael Howard's head, Walter thought. He paper-clipped the report to Howard's file, then attached a red tab to the top right corner and set it in his out tray.

It's a pity, he thought, bearing no ill will toward Michael Howard personally. But the rules of the job are the rules of the job, and if you can't accept them you shouldn't take the job. It applied equally to Michael Howard and himself.

He then checked his in tray and saw that the bats had left him a full load of fresh guano in the form of five new background checks, one of them an S.A. on an advertising executive. He made a few phone calls, checked a few references, talked with a couple of landlords and teachers, and cleared three of the four standard checks. Then he signed himself out on the S.A.—File #DD00023, Burbach, David

M.—and took a taxi to McGuire's place to wrap up another loose end.

McGuire looked bad. His face was pale and puffy, his otherwise white T-shirt stained with what looked like vomit, his khaki pants dirty and wrinkled.

Save him, Madeleine Keneally had asked. Save him.

"Having a Dylan Thomas day, are we?" Walter asked. He edged himself past McGuire into the apartment.

"Can't write."

"Small wonder."

"I can't write so I drink."

"But you will acknowledge that there's something of a horse-and-carriage problem there," Walter said. He lit a cigarette for McGuire, another for himself, and stood in the window looking out at the Village.

No glass-and-steel boxes here, Walter thought. Not yet, anyway.

"This city," Walter said, "has always been a magical place for me."

"All cities are."

"No," Walter said. "I really believe that every person has a city of his youth and that no other place is quite as magical."

"You sound like me," McGuire chuckled.

"Anyway," Walter said. "New York is the city of my youth. It's my city."

"Dig."

Walter turned from the window and said, "But it's not yours."

"No?"

"No. For some people this town is magic. For others it's poison," Walter said. "I think it's poison for you. In fact, I think you should leave."

"That's what you think, man?"

"I want you to leave now."

McGuire shook his head—not to gainsay but to clear it—and ran his fingers through his dirty hair. He took two bottles of Knickerbocker from the refrigerator, opened them on the kitchen counter, and handed one to Walter.

"I don't have any clean glasses," he said, plopping down on the mattress.

Walter sat in the kitchen chair in front of McGuire's old typewriter in which a blank page, pristine as a Vermont snowfall, was rolled.

Walter lifted his bottle. "To Jim Katcavage."

"Jim Katcavage."

Drinking on duty again, Walter thought as the cold beer sluiced down his throat. Ah, well, sometimes drinking on duty *is* the duty.

"What do you mean, man, you want me to leave?"

Walter nodded. "What I want you to do is to give me every letter, every photo, every scrap of paper that could connect you with Madeleine Keneally. Then I want you to leave town."

"Did Madeleine send you?"

"It doesn't matter."

"Did Keneally?"

"It doesn't matter."

"I need to know!"

So plaintive a cry, so resonant of my own situation, Walter thought. Yes, I can understand the need to know. So that tonight, when you drink in anger, as you will, your curses will have a name.

Walter lifted his bottle again. "To problems of the heart."

"To problems of the heart," McGuire toasted. "Who are you, man?"

"Among other things," Walter answered, "I'm the man to whom you owe two thousand dollars."

"But I won the bet."

"No, *I* won the bet," Walter said. "You won nothing. In fact, you would have bet on the losing team."

"You said I was off the hook," McGuire protested.

"Did you think it was a free ride?" Walter asked. "That you just stick your thumb out on the great highway of life and someone picks you up and carries you to wherever it is that you want to go? Do you really think that life is like that?"

"You set me up."

"Well, yes," Walter said as if it were the most obvious thing in the world. Which to Walter it was. "The road was so simple, wasn't it?" he added softly. "A pack of cigarettes, a full tank of gas, and an endless highway stretching west."

McGuire glared at him, then pushed himself up and rooted around his closet for a few minutes while Walter finished his beer. Then he handed him a shoe box full of papers and snapshots.

"This is all of it?" Walter asked.

"All of it."

"Just out of curiosity," Walter said, "may I ask why you held on to these?"

"Reminded me of a time when someone loved me." McGuire shrugged. "Not the idea of me."

"Do you love her?"

"No."

"You love the idea of her."

"I guess so."

McGuire sat back down on the mattress.

"She asked me to save you," Walter said.

"Save me?"

Walter nodded.

"Maybe you have," McGuire said.

"I hope so."

"How about you?" McGuire asked. "Your troubles of the heart? You figured that out yet?"

"Not quite."

"Well, if there's anything I can do . . ."

"As a matter of fact . . ."

Madeleine Keneally looked like hell. Her skin was pallid, her eyes red and puggy. Still, she looked elegant in a gray dress and pearls, as if she had expected Walter Withers to phone and say he was dropping by her suite.

"I don't know about you," Walter said as he looked around at the French decor, "but I think that the next time Germany conquers France, it should get to keep her."

She made a face of delighted horror and scolded, "What a horrible thing to say, Walter Withers!"

"You've been crying," Walter said.

"Is it that obvious?"

"Only in daylight."

"I won't go out until evening, then," Madeleine said. "Won't you sit down?"

He handed her the shoe box, saying, "I brought you a present to cheer you up."

She took the box, her hands shaking only slightly as she opened it and perused the contents. She looked at the letters for a long time, although lost in memory or regret Walter could not tell.

Finally she said, "Walter Withers, you dear man."

"Yours to burn," Walter said. "Don't fall into the sentimental trap of keeping them."

"How can I ever thank you?"

"You can tell me the truth," he said.

"About?"

But there was an edge to the question, an edge of fear, and what else was it, he asked himself . . . inevitability?

"You were in Marta's room the morning she died, weren't you?" he asked.

She nodded. Slowly, sadly.

"Why?" Walter asked.

Her voice was so subdued he had to strain to hear her as she said, "God help me, Walter, I think I killed her."

He said nothing, waiting for her to go on, knowing that one doesn't interrupt a confession.

"I went to have it out with her," she said, her tone as soft as the sunlight that filtered through the linen drapes. "I don't know why—Lord knows there have been other women—but she seemed more dangerous, more of a threat, more of a mistress than a fling, and while I felt I could tolerate the latter . . . maybe it was the threat of such public humiliation I couldn't stand.

"When I got to her room I half expected you to be there, and I felt jealous of that, too. She was practically raping you on the dance floor. But she was alone, and so drunk it took her forever to come to the door.

"That *body,* Walter. I suppose I'm pretty enough in a practical way, but I felt like an awkward girl standing next to Marta, her in that peignoir, and God, Walter, I could *smell* him on her.

"I just knew that I could never compete with her in the bedroom. I knew that Joe would always want her. Any man would want her. And I felt prim and chaste and *ridiculous* standing there in my little Sunday suit, my hat and gloves, and she practically nude and so, so seductive."

Hat and *gloves,* Walter thought.

"I said horrible things to her, Walter," Madeleine whispered, starting to cry now in controlled, small sobs. "Horrible, awful things. I called her a whore and a common tramp and said that she was nothing more than a public facility to Joe and that there were dozens of others. I used my *position,* Walter, as the wronged wife, as the proper young lady, who had so recently been, the ever so marriageable girl. I *said* that, Walter, I said that he would never marry a whore like her, that he had married me, and why didn't she just give him up. And she said, 'I have,' that was all, 'I have,' and she crawled back onto the bed and just curled up and stared at the wall."

Madeleine was quiet then, and Walter sat as still as a rock.

"I saw the bottle," Madeleine whispered, her tone flat and dead. Haunted. "I saw the pills. I knew what was going to happen."

Walter listened to an antique clock tick in the heavy silence. It seemed to go on forever.

Finally, Madeleine said, "I just stood there. I could have called a doctor. I could have called the desk. I just stood there thinking, 'She's going to die. She's going to overdose and die,' and after a few minutes I left. Left her there."

"Madeleine—"

She looked him in the eye, her own eyes red and streaming tears.

"I felt relieved, Walter," she said. "God forgive me, I felt relieved."

She started to cry hard. Great, silent sobs as her body heaved and she held herself tightly.

Walter let her cry, and when she finished he knelt beside her. He handed her a tissue, and while she was dabbing her eyes he said, "You had nothing to do with Marta's death. Nothing."

She looked at him curiously and asked, "How—"

He put his finger to her lips and said, "I just wanted you to know that."

He got up, kissed the top of her head, and left.

No, Walter thought as he studied the woman on the rumpled bed, Madeleine Keneally did not look like hell—Mary Dietz did. Her skin, which just a few days ago had been translucent, now looked yellow, except where it was gray under the sharp outlines of her cheekbones. Her lips were drawn tightly against her teeth, and as he wiped the spittle from her mouth he could smell the stench of illness, strong and smoky in this sweat-soured room.

"No more than an hour," Sarah said from the bedroom doorway. She was putting on her coat.

"An hour is fine," Walter said.

"Are you all right, Walter?" Sarah asked.

"Oh, yes. Fine," he answered.

Knowing, as did she, that no one was fine in this room. Knowing why Bill Dietz daily cruised the city for fresh sources of heroin to ease his wife's pain. Lining up with the junkies and the skin poppers, waiting for the pusher to show. And like the rest of them had been arrested, badge and all, but he was Bill Dietz, so they let him retire and beat up some hood as a cover story and now he peeped over transoms and listened for the sounds of bed springs and tried to do it quickly so he'd have time to cruise the city.

"Taking some time off?" Walter asked Jesus' picture after Sarah had left. "Rested up now, ready to roll? Bread and fishes, lepers, Lazarus, all that sort of thing? Because we could use you just now. Or are you just plain dead?"

Jesus mute on the cross. Sad, painted eyes cast down.

"I want an answer, God damn it!" Walter yelled. *"I demand a Goddamned answer!"*

He stood there out of breath, face red, arms raised in clenched fists and heard only his own labored breathing.

Shocking loss of control, he told himself. Anne would be so pleased.

He crouched on the floor and retrieved *One Lonely Night* from its hiding place under the bed. He sat down on the chair by Mary's head and said, "I might not be back tomorrow, gorgeous, but not to worry. Tomorrow's New Year's Eve, and I'm sure Bill has something special planned to kick in '59 . . ."

He read to her, not knowing whether she could hear or understand, and trying for some foolish reason of his own to finish the book this afternoon. It took more than an hour, and he heard Sarah come in, felt her presence in the doorway and heard the door shut and her walk back down the hallway. It wasn't long after that that he read, "No, nobody ever walked across the bridge, especially not on a night like this. Well, hardly nobody. The End."

He slid the book back under the bed, kissed her cheek, and said, "Happy New Year, Mary."

Sarah kept her good-bye to a wave as Walter headed out the door. He appreciated her discretion as it allowed them both to pretend that he wasn't crying.

As Walter came through the revolving door, he saw Mallon's eyes quicken. Then the doorman jerked his head quickly toward the opposite doors at two men in overcoats and fedoras. He nodded an okay to Mallon and walked to the bank of elevators. The two men nonchalantly rushed over to catch the same car.

One thing about the FBI, Walter thought. They were never very good at street work. And they all look alike, he thought as the two men came into the car and pointedly stared at the floor numbers. Strong-jawed, weak-chinned federal cops from the same cookie-cutter mold that the Director, as they called old Jedgar, liked.

Just to annoy them, Walter stood placidly and didn't punch a button. Instead he asked, "What floor?"

"Top," the older one said.

"The penthouse," said Walter. "That will be dresses, evening gowns, and lingerie."

A private joke, Walter thought, but a satisfying one.

He waited for one of them to push the stop button, which the older one did between the fifth and sixth floors.

"Are you Walter Withers?" he asked.

"My friends call me Zip."

"I'm not your friend," the older one said. "Neither is he."

"Then you can't call me Zip," Walter said. "Neither can you."

The senior one said, "I'm Special Agent Madsen, this is Special Agent Stone. We're with the Federal Bureau of Investigation."

"And here I thought you were with Otis."

"We have reason to believe that you're involved in the attempted perpetration of a crime against United States Senator Joseph Keneally," Madsen said.

"What crime?"

"Extortion," said Madsen.

"Blackmail," said Stone.

"Which?" asked Walter.

"You tell us."

"The only crime I'm aware of is feeding answers to that van Doren fellow on television, and, yes, you caught me," Walter said, holding out his hands to be cuffed. "Good work, G-men."

"If you're trying to blackmail Senator Keneally," Madsen said, "you'd be much better off just giving us the damaging material now."

"Right," Walter answered, "so Hoover can blackmail him."

"You can go to prison for one long goddamn time," Madsen said.

"Even for attempted blackmail," Stone added.

"Turn over the material, and we could probably be persuaded to forget about it."

"And you."

"A matter of national security."

"Oh, please," Walter said. "You boys haven't caught a spy since Benedict Arnold."

"I want those tapes, Withers."

"I beg your pardon? Tapes?" Walter asked. "Why do you think I have tapes?"

Because you have microphones in my apartment?

"If you have photos, we want them, too," said Stone.

"So does Joe Keneally," Walter answered.

"Well, he better not get them," Madsen said.

No, thought Walter. Hoover'll play them for him in good time.

"You didn't find it in my apartment, did you?" Walter asked.

"That doesn't mean you don't have it," Madsen said.

Stone crowded Walter and said, "Maybe you have it on you now."

He grabbed Walter's lapels and slammed him into the elevator wall. Walter drove the edge of his right shoe down along Stone's shin. When Stone screamed and bent over to grab his bleeding leg, Walter reached over his shoulders and pulled his overcoat up over his head, trapping the agent's arms. Then he swung Stone into Madsen and reached in and grabbed Stone's pistol from his holster, jammed it into Madsen's face, and cocked the hammer.

"I'm unskilled with guns," Walter said. "So please do as I say."

"Sure," Madsen said.

"Kindly press sixteen."

"You got it."

On the ride up Madsen said, "You're making a big mistake."

"I don't have anything that belongs to you."

Madsen smiled. "It isn't just you, it's your commie girlfriend. We can make life very hard on her. Bust her for dope, harass her friends, jerk her cabaret card and she'll never work again. By the way, did you know that she's a sex pervert? Hey, careful with that thing, it's loaded. It *is* loaded, isn't it, Special Agent Stone?"

Stone grunted an assent from under the overcoat.

"Leave Anne Blanchard alone," Walter said.

"That's up to you, Withers," Madsen said as the elevator came to a stop on sixteen.

Bill Dietz was standing in the lobby when the elevator doors opened and watched as Walter slipped the gun back into Stone's holster and stepped past the two FBI agents onto the floor. Dietz grinned as Stone struggled with his overcoat and the elevator doors shut.

"Everything hunky-dory, Walter?" Dietz asked.

"Just tickety-boo, William," Walter answered. He passed Dietz and headed for his office, cursing himself the whole way.

I should have known, he thought. I should have known that the Bureau would get in on this and that they would have a dossier on Anne's past. And even if they don't find out that she was a courier, if they trip over her errand for Marta . . .

Deliver the tapes to the Boat Basin at nine.

When he reached his office, the Howard file was back on his desk.

A curt memo from Intake and Assignment was paper-clipped to the cover: "Withers—Our I&A has the Michael Howard file as File#: AE576809. Your Investigation Report cites File#: AE578609. Please correct and resubmit along with attached Supplementary Correction Form (IA 141). DeWitt."

Walter glanced at his watch. It was 3:45, and so he'd missed the bats' afternoon run by a full forty-five minutes and the Howard file with attached supplementary correction form couldn't enter the system until ten the next morning. He sat down and retyped it, found a blank IA 141 buried in a desk drawer and filled it out, writing under the section entitled EXPLANATION OF ERROR: "Inadvertent inversion of third and fourth digits in file number."

He finished that task—a loose end that just keeps coming loose, he thought—and the phone rang.

"Mr. Withers," Mallon said. "You're a popular guy!"

"Is that a fact?"

"Oh, yes. You have friends waiting for you at every door."

If only that were the case, Walter thought as he hung up the phone. So who would it be downstairs? Certainly Madsen and Stone, perhaps with some little helpers, then there's Sam Zaif, and maybe Keneally's boys . . . and maybe the happy folks who are waiting for me at the Boat Basin don't really want to wait, and . . .

And whine, whine, whine, whine, whine, he thought. Get a grip, my boy. You have some cards to play. One, try to keep in mind, ego deflating as it might be, that it isn't *you* they want, it's the tapes. So two, none of the assembled mob is going to make a move on you until they're pretty damn sure that you have the tapes. And three, they can't very well take you in the middle of Manhattan in the middle of rush hour.

All of which leads me to four, Walter thought, which *is* a bit egotistic but the facts are the facts: This is *my* city.

I have the home-field advantage, and the crowd, and I'll take Manhattan—the Bronx and Staten Island too, if necessary—and if all I have to do is lose a desperate cop, two FBI agents, some hired thugs, and a couple professional killers and deliver the goods to the enemies of my country by nine o'clock, then that's all I have to do.

And if the strength-sapping question arises in my doubt-ridden psyche—How can you do what you have to do tonight?—well, the answer is inherent in the question, isn't it, my boy?

He stood up and raised the window blinds. Manhattan going to darkness was one of his favorite sights in the world. The city softening from its gray business suit to its pastel dusk to its black and sparkling evening clothes was a transformation that usually soothed his tired soul.

The sunset reflected a faint orange on the building across the way. He saw 16-C get up and approach the window, and this time Walter waved. There was no point in being antisocial.

16-C waved back, then reached down and put something in the window. A sign. With a phone number. Then 16-C pulled down his blinds, and the light went out.

Well, well, well, Walter thought. Well, well, well.

He picked up the phone and called downstairs again.

"Mallon," he asked casually. "How would you like to cause a small riot?"

Very much, as it turned out. When Walter stepped out of the elevator into the crowded lobby, Mallon, looming large behind his desk in his scarlet uniform, walked over to the newsstand and accosted Detective Sergeant Samuel Zaif, who was doing nothing at that moment but seemingly loitering.

Mallon locked a meaty hand on Zaif's wrist and hollered, "Stop, thief! I saw you take that wallet!"

While Walter thought Mallon's performance lacked the subtlety of say, Alec Guinness, it had the resonant theatricality of an Olivier, and most of the men in the lobby reached their hands into their jacket pockets to check on their wallets.

Not Walter. He kept moving, first swinging wide right to head for the Forty-Eighth Street exit, then cutting back, Gifford-esque, against the flow, down the stairs to the subway level. Not out, but down and out, and that got him the few seconds he needed to break into the open field.

Well, that and Mallon's diversion behind him. For as he was making his move Walter could hear Mallon yelling, "Police! Police!" and Zaif's irritated (to say the least) response of "You moron, I am the police!" Then Zaif tried to break away, which prompted Mallon to deliver a straight right to the side of Zaif's head, and then it turned into Finnegan's Wake as Stone and Madsen spotted Walter heading down the stairs and tried to push their way through the crowd to get to him.

As well they might have done, save for the timely intervention of the Mallonettes, who appeared seemingly from nowhere to join the fray. The eldest boy—was it Liam? Walter speculated—grabbed the unfortunate Stone by his lapels and lifted him off the polished floor with a touchingly filial cry of "I've got the other one, Daddy!" (For it was a well-known urban fact that the best pickpockets, the ones who live not in Ossining but in cozy East Side apartments, work not alone but in teams. One snatches the wallet, then hands it off to the other.)

This brouhaha brought Keneally's boys running in from

the Forty-Eighth Street doors, where they had been awaiting Walter on his usual route home. In they came—straight into the path of Billy, the youngest Mallon, the shortest Mallon, the Mallon who was actually insane, the Mallon whom the Marine Corps recruiting station on Times Square had rejected as too violent. On they came, three of them, burly lads with stocky legs and barrel chests, and Billy "Bad Seed" Mallon saw no other option but to lay down his body and *roll*-block them, which is what he did, knocking them off their stocky legs, turning the august foyer of this station of commerce and industry into a human bowling alley.

Thus Mallon and the Mallonettes gave Walter the precious few moments to get a head start on the variegated posse and make it into the subterranean level of Times Square.

Designed as a commuter's dream, the underground level runs beneath the various buildings, connecting each of them to the other and all of them to the subway system via the IRT and BMT trains. It was entirely possible, the denizens of Forbes and Forbes having proved it repeatedly, to go the entire working day without ever surfacing into the actual air of the city. (It was in fact rumored that "Dickless" Tracy had never been outside and arrived by subway and consumed all his meals at the coffee shop by the bottom of the escalator.) There were news shops and shoeshine stands, restaurants, clothing stores, and even florists shops to give the forgetful husband that last chance to buy flowers before hitting the train and thereby assuring himself a warmer welcome at home.

Walter had been ambivalent about the subterranean level, feeling that it had a troglodyte air that was a bit atavistic for his tastes, but now he tossed that reservation aside and joined the throng of commuters rushing down the long central corridor toward the subway. He didn't need to lose his pursuers—although he wouldn't mind a bit, either—as much as he needed a decent lead, and it was a good thing that his ambition was so modest, for, ignoring the advice of Satchel Paige, he looked over his shoulder and saw that Agent Madsen was catching up with him.

Ah, but it's too late, Agent Madsen, for my offensive line has sprung me into the open field and I am the Frank Gifford of the urban gridiron and will not be caught from behind.

So Walter knifed between two commuters, turned sideways, and edged along the wall, then crossed the corridor diagonally and picked up his speed again. He could feel Madsen struggling to keep up.

But there are too many blockers, Walter thought, blessing the usually accursed rush hour and the safety of numbers. He reached the subway turnstile well ahead of Madsen, dropped in his token, and moved forward on the platform just as the downtown train pulled in.

He made it to the second car from the front and hopped on board just before the doors slid shut. He had just squeezed in and found a strap to hang onto when the train jolted ahead. Then stopped. The doors opened again and shut again. When the train headed out, Walter figured that he had plenty of company.

He emerged two stops later into the sardine can that was Grand Central Station at rush hour. But even as he maneuvered through the chaos he could feel Madsen behind him, Madsen and maybe the others—for there were limits to what even the Mallonettes could do—but that was all right. All he had to do was maintain a lead, a lead of a few seconds.

Which he did, barely. No turkey trot now, no swiveling, this was a straight Titanic, a dash—if one could be said to dash through a Manhattan train station at five o'clock—to the storage lockers on the main floor. He fingered the key in his pocket and got it ready. There would be no time for fumbling. He reached the main level, sliced his way to the wall of lockers, and inserted the key that Dieter had slipped to him.

His hand shook a little as he opened the luggage locker and took out the manila envelope inside. He laughed when he saw the photographs—for they were truly grotesquely comical—laughed hard and then almost cried.

Sometimes, Walter thought, salvation comes with the trumpets of angels and the thunderous voice of God. And sometimes it comes as the last will and testament of a pedarest and pimp who, whatever else he was, was always a gentleman. So God bless Dieter. Bless him and take him.

On the street he gave himself the luxury of a swivel and saw that he was well ahead of a struggling parade. Madsen, Zaif, and Keneally's thugs all stretched out along Forty-Second Street trying to follow him and be subtle about it at the same time.

Walter turned up his pace. He was late for his dinner reservation.

Walter had decided to have what might be his last dinner in New York at the Palm, the old newspaper haunt on East Fifty-Third. He had opted for wit, simplicity, and good food, and The Palm fit the bill. Caricatures of newspaper cartoonists drawn by other newspaper cartoonists made up the scant but satisfying decorations on the dark wooden walls. The tables were also wooden, with plain, straight chairs, and the thick red wine was served in jelly glasses. Neither were the waiters overly impressed with the clientele. They served the reporters, artists, editors, and occasional ad man with cheeky benevolence, their general attitude being that the customers had come for good food and not to have their posteriors kissed.

Nor were the Palm waiters burdened with artistic descriptions of their entrees. The Palm served steaks—sirloin, tenderloin, T-bones, and New York cuts so big that they flopped over the edges of the oversize plates. Oh, you could get a pork chop, or a hamburger, or even chicken if you'd just wandered in and didn't know the little joint for what it was—the best steak house in New York City.

Probably the best steak house from the Atlantic to the rail yards in Omaha, Walter thought, and the service was as fast as you'd expect in a restaurant that catered to guys racing a deadline. Yes, the Palm's task was to fill their customers up with beef, booze, and maybe a potato and shove them back out to tell the tales of the city, and it was no accident that Walter had picked the spot for this potential farewell meal.

For one thing, it was on the East Side, and as he was eventually headed west it seemed like a good misdirection. For another, it was just chock full of newspaper reporters, which just might discourage Keneally's boys, the feds, Detective Sergeant Zaif, and whoever else was lingering outside to try anything outstandingly stupid while Walter was trying to enjoy his meal. And last there was the food itself, deliciously simple and simply delicious, Walter thought, although only the few ad men present might appreciate the delicate adverbial symmetry of the description.

But I do amuse myself, Walter thought as the headwaiter came over, and on a night like tonight that is not an unimportant thing.

"Got a single just opening up," the waiter said, letting Walter know that at this dinner hour he was going to damn well sit at that table and not a larger one capable of bringing in more money.

And that is fair, Walter thought, and just as it should be, and he stood patiently as Paulie Martino stood up from that single table, swallowed the last dregs of his grappa, wiped his mouth, and walked out the door without even a glance in Walter's direction.

But that was one thing you had to hand to the Mob guys, Walter thought. They might be vicious, sociopathic, parasitic lowlifes without a trace of style or taste, but they rarely if ever messed up an assignment. No, the Mob boys did exactly what they said they were going to do, efficiently and without excess drama, which was how he supposed they had pushed the Irish out of the crime business and made them junior partners in the police and judiciary.

Nor was Walter concerned that Mallon or Stone, doubtless outside now shivering on the street, would recognize Paulie as a wise guy. The feds just didn't see mobsters, in fact were institutionally blind to the Mafia and generally preferred to concentrate on small-time crackers with comic-book nicknames like "Machine Gun" and "Pretty Boy." Those bank-robbing years had been Hoover's salad days, and while he'd gone after Capone, he'd taken a pass on Luciano and Lansky. But by that time the fix was in and the G-men—speaking of comic-book sobriquets—had little to do until Mickey Spillane alerted them to the communist menace and Hoover started to do his Mitchell Palmer impersonation and saw Red spies everywhere.

An efficient busboy—he looked fifty and was clearly a career busboy—whisked off Paulie's dirty dishes, swept a clean checkered cloth on the table, and laid the plain dinnerware down in what seemed like seconds. Walter squeezed himself behind the table onto the bench against the wall and felt the briefcase at his feet. A brown leather attaché case, flush against the foot of the bench, just where it was supposed to be. You just had to hand it to those Mob guys.

The waiter came over *sans* pad or pencil and simply listened to Walter's order: a New York cut, rare, home fries, green beans, and a glass of red.

The steak was delicious, of course—steaming, juicy, and fragrant, and the home fries were a Palm specialty, with lots of paprika and bits of green and red pepper. Walter hadn't really wanted the drink, but he got such a kick out of drinking wine from a jelly glass that he couldn't help himself, and he was having such a good meal that he was only mildly annoyed to see Sam Zaif, red-faced and rubbing his ungloved hands, standing at his table.

"Jews don't do well in the cold," Zaif said.

"Well, you're a desert people," Walter answered. "One would have thought, however, with all those years of wandering the diaspora in such tropical climes as Poland and Russia . . ."

"We didn't do a lot of cross-breeding."

"That explains it, then."

"I told the headwaiter I was a friend of yours," Zaif said.

"Only a mild exaggeration," Walter answered, "and I wish I could invite you to sit down, but as you can see, there's only room for one."

"I could squeeze in beside you on the bench," Zaif offered.

"And I'm about to leave, anyway."

"With the briefcase?"

Walter said, "I hadn't thought to leave my work sitting in a restaurant."

"You didn't have it with you when you left the office."

"Hard to put anything past you, Detective Sergeant Zaif."

"I am a friend," Zaif said. "And I was right, wasn't I?

The chickens are all running around, Walter, and it's just a matter of which one sings first."

"I don't believe chickens actually sing," Walter said.

"You know, words to that effect," Zaif said. "There are guys out there, Walter, with the distinctly Neanderthal look of Keneally employees."

As well as some Cro-Magnon feds and probably a few homo sapiens as well, Walter thought, but you seemed to have missed them, Sam.

"Give me the briefcase," Zaif said.

"Sam," Walter said as he signaled for the check, "what you want is not *in* the briefcase, because the briefcase is a decoy. What you want is in an envelope in my coat pocket. Take it and leave. I, in turn, will lead this parade around Manhattan until such time as I figure that you have the goods safely stowed away. Call me with your best offer and make it a good one."

"You made the right choice, Walter."

"Thank you," Walter answered. "And please get going, Sam."

Walter didn't look as Zaif reached across the table and took the envelope. Rather, Walter watched Madsen and Stone as *they* watched Zaif take the envelope.

Zaif shoved it into his own coat pocket, and headed out the door.

Walter finished the last bite of steak and forkful of potato, left cash for the bill and tip, put on his coat and hat, picked up the attaché case, and walked out into the startling cold.

Warmed, however, by the splendid meal. Not to mention the sight of Agent Madsen putting a gun to Zaif's chest and relieving him of the envelope.

So Detective Sergeant Sam Zaif should spend the rest of

the night in federal custody, Walter thought, and when Madsen gets a load of what's in the envelope, well . . .

Walter ambled up the street, ignoring Stone, who fell unsubtly into lock step a half block behind him. Ignored too the limousine that started up the moment he stepped outside the restaurant and was now cruising obliquely behind him.

He knew that the sight of the briefcase would be sending adrenaline surges through the bloodstreams of his pursuers, along with the frustration that they had undoubtedly spotted not only him but each other. And were mutually thinking, discussing perhaps, what to do and when to do it.

At least I have that comfort, Walter thought, of knowing exactly what to do and when to do it. Have a drink at P.J. Clarke's. When? The moment I get there. And I will get there because neither the feds or Keneally or that other set of footsteps—gosh, who might that be—want to make their move just now. Which is just as well, because I really do want a drink at P.J.'s.

So up Third Avenue he strolled, whistling "My name is MacNamara, I'm the leader of the band," his breath visible in the icy night air.

As usual P.J.'s was packed with serious drinkers, among them writers, professional Irishmen, and husbands who were working late and taking a later train home. And cheery, for neither troublesome publishers nor Erin's sorrows nor potentially angry wives could dampen the whiskey-fueled vivacity of that most masculine of watering holes. As people went to the Palm to eat, people went to P.J.'s to *drink.* To drink and talk—not chatter, but *talk,* of philistine editors and British bastards and the bitch couldn't find the bedroom with a flashlight and a map, but the last royalty statement wouldn't support a blow job in a taxicab, never mind alimony.

Yes, packed P.J.'s was, with the practiced elbows as well

as a few part-timers getting warmed up for New Year's Eve, a holiday that the professional drinkers loathed because they too compete with the amateur horde for precious space at the bar. More than once Walter had heard grumbling in this place that dilettante celebrants should be banned, outright *banned,* from distinguished haunts such as P.J.'s, because they couldn't hold their booze, they dressed in funny hats and made annoying noises, and had the unforgivable habit of drunkenly saying such things as "Hey, don't I know you? Didn't you write blankety-blank? I didn't read it, but . . .", and maybe they should be shot, not merely banned, after all.

Walter was not a writer, a mick, or—more's the pity, he thought—a husband, but was nevertheless welcome among the crowd at P.J.'s, for Walter was a good drinker, a better listener, and could be great talker when the rare conversational silence occurred and called for a gap to be filled. His cheerful indifference to any modern writing outside of James Jones, predilection to pick up his share of the checks, and stock of good smutty jokes had earned him a spot around this metaphorical fire, in that ritual as old as human society, to wit, the men hunkered around the flames telling stories of the day's hunt.

On this evening Sean McGuire was holding forth to a little sub clan of his own on the periphery of the main tribe. He and his were dressed differently, to be sure, in checkered shirts and corduroy jackets instead of sports coats and loosened ties, but they were tolerated because of his pronounced Celticism and recent literary celebrity. He was something of a curiosity among the crowd at P.J.'s, was this purveyor of "prosetry," or "jazzetry," or "poese," or "typewriting," depending on who was describing it, and they all wanted to get a look at him, perhaps eavesdrop on his famed verbal style before he—as they believed he inevitable would—flashed in the pan.

So there were knowing smiles as well as welcoming nods when Walter walked in, ordered, and received a pedigree whiskey of a certain age, then meandered over to the edge of McGuire's sphere.

McGuire raised a mug of dark Guinness at Walter, lowered it to his lips, and took a long, sloppy draught before resuming for the benefit of listeners near and far, "It's New Year's Eve, a last chance for every Adam and every Eve to escape the smothering Garden and the paternalistic gaze of God! 'Cast out of the garden,' hell! We should run, run for our lives out into the dark and tangled forests of our souls to find for ourselves our true nature and what the hell, I'm drunk. Drunk with booze, with joy, with sorrow, with rage, with *life*. Have you ever seen the lightning flash behind a puffy cloud on a sunny day on an Indian reservation in South Dakota? I have, and that's the real god, man. That's real."

"Have you ever seen a copy of Strunk and White beside your typewriter on a cloudy day in New York?" Walter heard someone say behind him. Followed by laughter.

McGuire said a little louder, "The trace horses hate the mustangs! Hate 'em for what they might've been if they'd had the guts to run for the horizon."

Jimmy Keneally slipped through the crowd and sat down beside Walter.

"You have something for me, Withers?" Jimmy asked.

"My heartiest wishes for a wonderful new year," Walter answered.

"That's it?"

"A profound hope that Lyndon Johnson will be caught in the Menger Hotel with a young goat?" Walter asked.

"We can make life very hard for you."

Walter turned to look at him. Jimmy Keneally had his backroom face on him. A deadly serious, well . . . *deadly* look.

"Doubtless you can," Walter answered.

"I'm serious."

"I know you are," said Walter. "And you can probably sic Cerberus on me and take this briefcase. But you're not going to do it in the middle of P.J. Clarke's, so why don't you just settle in and have a drink? Did you have a chance to get dinner, by the way? The cheeseburgers are terrific here. My treat."

"You're a smart bastard, Withers."

"True."

"But I'm a smart bastard, too," Jimmy said. "And I have a lot more behind me than you do."

McGuire drained his mug and held it aloft in a signal that some admirer should see to a fresh one. It was not such an admirer but a fellow Walter recognized as an editor from *Time* who got up and fetched McGuire another ale to encourage yet more drunken ranting. It would be a story to tell, to have lunch on maybe, about the new literary lion puking verbally and otherwise all over P.J. Clarke's.

Madsen came in. Walter could see him in the big mirror behind the bar and made eye contact. Walter smiled, and Madsen smiled coldly back and then went to surveying the room.

Jimmy Keneally saw Madsen, too.

"This better not be what I think it is, Withers," he said.

"What do you think it is that it had better not be?" Walter asked.

"You giving the tapes to Hoover."

"Don't worry about Hoover."

"I do worry," Jimmy said. "I worry a lot."

"Ah, well . . ."

"How much do you want, Withers?" Jimmy asked. "What's the price?"

Walter turned to him and gave him his own backroom look.

"As I've told you, Keneally," he said, "I don't want your money."

In the bar mirror Walter could see Madsen staring at them. He's afraid I'm going to make the drop here, Walter thought. But the only thing I'm going to drop, my dear Agent Madsen, is you.

But where is your thick young assistant Stone? The one who would have made such a splendid brown shirt?

Brave talk, he thought, the whiskey talking, and the operations books said not to drink, but the operations books also said to do what you normally do, and what I normally do is to have a drink. So I will resolve this apparent conflict in my own favor and enjoy the whiskey. And settle the nerves.

McGuire started again, "I have seen the ocean sparkle phosphorescently at night to seduce the stars from the sky. I have seen the desert bloom motley with wildflowers. I have seen Chinese opium smokers dream themselves to death and lie crumpled and wrinkled in a Stockton Street sewer, and that is all the same god. I've heard saxophones slash through the night like razors. I've heard sailors grunt their climaxes through paper-thin flop-house walls. I've heard giant hemlocks crack in the cold and crash into the soft snow, and that is all god."

"I've heard about enough," one of the old tribe said, and laid some money on the table to cover his drink before he got up to leave.

"I've touched heaven and hell and a woman's moist heat," McGuire said. "And that is all god, and now I must take a piss."

Laughter and a smattering of sarcastic applause from the

old-timers, and McGuire curtsied toward them and weaved his way to the men's room. Walter gave him a second and got up, knowing that Madsen and Keneally would be waiting for him when he got back, but also knowing that neither the agent nor the fixer would ever for a moment dream that Walter would make the drop to a drunken beat poet.

The fixer, however, wasn't giving up.

"If I send them after you," Jimmy said, "it won't be pretty. They'll hurt you, Withers."

"I'm actually just going to relieve myself."

"And it'll never stop," Jimmy said. "I never forget and I never forgive. I'll hound you out of your job and out of this town. You *and* your girlfriend."

"You have a wonderful sense of symmetry," Walter said. "Is it instinctive or acquired?"

"You don't realize who you're dealing with."

"But I'm beginning to think I do," Walter said. "Now, if you'll excuse me, James, perhaps we can resume this charming conversation when I get back."

McGuire was splashing water on his head when Walter came in and locked the door behind him. The poet looked up, red-eyed and bleary, and said, "I brought you the tape. I did just what you said."

"Good man."

McGuire pulled the thin box from the back waistband of his jeans and handed it to Walter.

"We're even, man. Dig?"

"It is digged, dugged, duggeth, dug," Walter said as he put the tape into the briefcase.

McGuire examined his puffy face in the mirror.

"You know what hell is for a Taoist?"

"No."

"This is," McGuire said, jutting his chin at the mirror.

"Wants, attachments, ambitions, possessions, achievements . . . desire."

"Quite a list."

A knock on the door.

"New York," McGuire said, summing up. "It's not real."

"Come on!" Madsen yelled. "Open up!"

A trace of anxiety in his voice, Walter thought, not without some guilty pleasure.

"It's not real, man," McGuire repeated.

"Then there's nothing to worry about, is there?" Walter asked.

He slid open the men's room window and pulled himself up.

"God damn it! Open the goddamn door!"

"Hand me the briefcase, would you?" Walter asked.

McGuire gave him the case and said, "See you, Walter."

The door crashed into McGuire a few seconds later, but he didn't have anything interesting on him and Walter was already trotting down the alley.

Smack into a forearm shiver that sent him sprawling to the pavement.

He looked up into a pistol barrel and the long, smiling face of Special Agent Stone. Stone nudged the pistol into Walter's lips.

"You want to suck on it, faggot?" Stone asked. "You probably do, you're a fag, right? The cop told us all about you."

"Take it easy," Madsen said as he came up from behind.

"I owe him," Stone said.

"And I said to take it easy," Madsen repeated.

"Tell the Hitler youth here to let me up," Walter instructed.

"Let him up."

"But—"

"Let him up, asshole!" Madsen yelled.

Stone holstered the pistol and stepped back.

Walter got to his feet and brushed the dirt off his slacks and asked, "Did you enjoy the photographs?"

Madsen said, "Tell me what you want."

"What—" Stone started.

"Shut up," Madsen said. Then to Walter, "Tell us what you want us to do."

"What you're going to do," Walter said, "is take the next train back to Washington and tell the Director to keep his pudgy hands away from Senator and Mrs. Keneally."

"Okay."

"Okay," Walter said. "And rest assured that the negatives are in a safety-deposit box in Zurich or Berne."

"Okay."

"Okay," Walter said. "And you had better make sure that I stay safe and happy, or the whole world will get to see those pictures of the Director."

"Just take it easy, Withers."

"Oh, I'm taking it very easy."

"Anything else?"

"Yes," Walter said. "Tell him that black isn't his color."

Walter picked up the briefcase and left them standing in the alley.

To take a long walk.

There could be no taxis now, nothing that could later be traced. So he walked west to Fifth Avenue and then steadily uptown, keeping the same pace, safe again under the city lights.

Two down, he thought, Zaif and the feds. That still left Keneally's boys and . . . someone else. More of a feeling than anything, but there was someone else out there, waiting for the right shot.

Well, it won't come on Fifth Avenue, Walter thought, so enjoy the walk.

Up the avenue, Fifth Avenue, walking in the opposite direction of traffic so they couldn't pull up behind him, up past Saks and St. Patrick's, up past Tiffany's and Godiva and Abercrombie and Dunhills and Berghoff's, and then he was at the Plaza itself, and he turned west and walked along the downtown side of Central Park South. Against traffic again, make the bastards work for it, he thought. Past the St. Moritz and Rumpelmeyers and the swank apartment buildings with the doormen on the street. You're not going to take me out here, but where? Where, boys, because I'm going to have to lose you before the Boat Basin, so let's screw our courage to the sticking point and make a move here. And he had them figured now—they had two thugs on foot behind him and a car circling, around and around the gridiron looking for a spot to grab him.

But nothing. Not at Sixth, or Seventh, or Broadway, and as he turned uptown to Columbus Circle, he thought that he might have to *give* them a spot, a spot to make them commit and then shake them, but where could that be? Where, before the darkness of Riverside Park, much too close to the rendezvous for safety, could he give these Boston boys a shot and lose them?

Well, that would be Needle Park, wouldn't it? Walter thought. A place of darkness both spiritual and real, a place where no one will see or care about a kidnapping. And where I can make a move. A couple of five-dollar bills to a couple of junkies, and they would do anything. Charge into the guns themselves, and I am off into the chaos.

So up Broadway he walked toward Sherman Square, *with* the traffic this time. They must have let a couple of guys out of the car in front of him because they took him right on Broadway.

It was Callahan and Cahill, of course, and they each took an elbow, picked him up, and steered him effortlessly into the backseat of the limousine that pulled up and then parked on dark, quiet Sixty-Seventh Street off Amsterdam.

Walter cursed himself for being stupid and careless and underestimating these out-of-towners, but now they had him. Had him trapped in the backseat of a locked car.

Or "cah" as Callahan pronounced it when he said, "Get into the *cah*."

"Do you know the only thing I despite more than a *Baaastan* accent?" Walter asked.

"No, what?"

"The *Baaastan* Red Sox," Walter answered.

Callahan was going to hit him anyway, so Walter thought that he might as well get in a verbal shot before he did. Fortunately, the gorilla didn't have a lot of room to really cock his arm, but the punch hurt anyway, short and straight under Walter's left eye.

"Honestly," Walter groaned, "the whole city sounds like it's fornicating with sheep, which it probably—"

The shot to the ribs doubled him over and shut him up, and Walter sucked for air as he cursed himself again for being so stupid as to let Keneally's boys grab him so easily.

There wasn't going to be any rendezvous at the Boat Basin.

Cahill was already trying to open the attaché case.

"What's the combination, faggot?" Callahan asked.

When Walter didn't answer, the puncher grabbed his hand and bent his thumb backward.

"Nobody screws Joe Keneally," Callahan said.

On the contrary, Walter thought, everybody screws with Joe Keneally.

"Now tell me the combination and maybe I'll do one

322

thumb instead of both," Callahan said. "Or maybe you want a sample first."

Walter's thumb was bent back to the breaking point when a shotgun stock smashed through the window behind him and pebbles of glass scattered over the seat.

Dietz shoved the shotgun barrel ungently into Callahan's ear and said, "Do you have any brains or not? Shall we find out?"

"Jesus Christ."

"If you think that engine can start before I can pull this trigger," Dietz said to Brown, "try it. I haven't blown anyone's head off for weeks."

Brown took his hands off the keys, and Dietz reached down with one hand and opened the car door.

Walter looked at Bill Dietz's famous grin as the ex-cop said, "I hate Boston, too, Walter. I really do. It's a shitty little town with Harvard in it, not to mention it even got the wrong DiMaggio. And I get very angry when stiffs from Boston come to a real city and assault citizens on the street. You're going to have a hell of a shiner there, Walter. Do you want me to kill them?"

"I think I'd just like my person and property back," Walter said.

"Take it easy," Callahan said.

"Not so tough now, huh?" Dietz said, and in a move that was so fast Walter could hardly see it, Dietz swung the gun stock into Callahan's broad face, grabbed him by his red hair, and pulled him out of the car, then pointed the barrel at Cahill.

"The briefcase is yours, Walter?" Dietz asked.

Walter nodded, and Cahill quickly handed it back to him. Walter slid out of the car onto the sidewalk. Dietz nudged Callahan with his foot, and the big man crawled toward the limo door. Cahill helped pull him in, the door shut, and a second later the limousine pulled away.

A stunned pedestrian stood a few feet away on the sidewalk.

"Don't worry ma'am," Dietz said as he flashed his Forbes and Forbes badge in the faint streetlight. "New York's finest, just doing our best to keep the streets safe for nice people like you."

The woman looked at Dietz in horror and hustled away.

"Bill," Walter said, "a thank-you is hardly adequate . . ."

"Yeah, well I figured you was having some trouble," Dietz said. "Hey, Walter, maybe you'd forget to mention that you saw me here, okay?"

Buying dope for his dying wife.

"Actually, William, I was hoping the same of you."

"I'm assuming there's nothing you want to tell me . . ."

"A good assumption."

"You need some more backup?"

"Sort of a one-man job from here, thanks."

Dietz looked at him dubiously. "You sure? Because, no offense Walter, but you aren't exactly a tough guy."

"No offense taken," Walter said.

They looked at each other for a few moments, exchanging silly, embarrassed smiles.

"Geez, Walter," Dietz said. "Mickey Spillane?"

"What can I say?" Walter asked. "Your wife's literary tastes run to trash. And how did you find out?"

"Just because I have an enormous dick doesn't mean I'm a complete moron." Dietz arranged the shotgun underneath his coat to cover the awkward moment, then said, "Seriously, Walter, thank you."

"Seriously, William, thank *you*."

Deitz jutted his chin toward Needle Park and said, "I had to go out anyway."

"You should look up a musician acquaintance of mine," Walter said. "Name of Mickey Drury."

"Yeah?"

Walter nodded.

"Well, maybe I'll do that."

"Do."

A parting gift for William Dietz. Clean needles and heroin for his wife.

Walter shrugged and turned to go to the Boat Basin.

It shouldn't seem so out of place, Walter thought as he stood at the phone booth and looked down at the small marina dug into the banks of the Hudson. But the Boat Basin, with its small sailboats, seemed too quaint for this city with its giant docks for cruise liners and freighters. The Boat Basin seemed too tranquil, too small—just a few sailboats bobbing gently against their docks on this quiet, darkened section of the river, lit more by the warehouses on the Jersey side than by the Manhattan lights, blocked as they were by the thick woods of Riverside Park.

"The Boat Basin, nine o'clock," he said into the receiver, then hung up.

He watched as a light on one of the small, moored sailing boats blinked four times, the arranged signal. He took one more look around him to make sure that he hadn't been followed, then walked down to the dock and aboard the boat.

The Plodder greeted him with a pistol pointed at his chest and gestured him down into the cabin.

"You're a riot, Walter," Morrison said. He was sitting in a deck chair, his long legs spread out in front of him.

"Really cute stuff, swiping the tapes, leaving the message at the drop . . . I'm pretty pissed off at you for making me sail into territorial waters, though. Shit, of all the fucking security guards in the world, Keneally has to pick you. That's rotten goddamn luck. Martini? Real Russian vodka."

"No, thanks."

"Don't be a sorehead, Walter," Morrison said. He gestured to a second man in the cabin. The Sprinter. The man filled Morrison's glass with another drink.

The Plodder stepped behind Walter and started to pat him down.

"You're wasting your time, Igor," Morrison said. "Mr. Withers doesn't carry a weapon."

The Plodder ignored Morrison and finished frisking Walter.

"Told you," Morrison said. He gestured to a chair across from him and said, "Take a load off, Walt."

Walter sat down and laid the briefcase on his lap. The Plodder took a chair next to Morrison and laid his pistol hand on his lap with the barrel still pointing at Walter. The three men were so close in the cramped quarters that their knees almost touched.

"Is his name really Igor?" Walter asked.

Morrison shrugged. "The hell do I know? To tell you the truth, Walter, I wasn't so sure you'd make it tonight."

"I almost didn't."

"Yeah," Morrison said. "Igor and his little playmate were dead sure you wouldn't because you're not an operational guy, you know. But I made the point that you'd done pretty well against them so far. They weren't amused, but I'm kind of glad to see you. You're sure about that martini?"

"Does it have pentobarbitol in it?"

Morrison chuckled and said, "Now, don't be bitter."

"Did you kill her?"

"Personally?" Morrison asked. "No, I just got here. That was Igor, or whatever the hell his name is. I gave the order, though. Had to. You were on to us, and she was out of control. If you hadn't called me, Walter, I might never have known, and Marta would still be happily humping today. Instead she got a shot from Igor. He's an ugly mother, isn't he?"

He's a big mother, Walter thought, and yes, ugly. A big, bald bullet head with eyes set wide apart.

"And did he kill and rape poor Alicia?"

"I suppose," Morrison said. "Killed *and* raped? In that order? Igor, you nasty little Ivan, you."

There was no visible reaction from Igor except to harden his stare at Walter.

Morrison said, "I hope you brought the Joe Keneally sex tapes with you."

Walter patted the briefcase.

"Good decision, Walt," Morrison said. "The Russians said that you'd never betray your country, but I assured them that you were so pussy-whipped by the Blanchard broad that you'd do about anything to save her. True love and all that. Am I right?"

Walter nodded.

Morrison said, "So here's what you're going to do. One: You're going to hand over the tapes, of course. Two: you're going to go to Keneally and tell him the bad news that he was boffing a Russian spy and that he is *finished* unless he plays ball. And three: You're going to teach him how to play ball."

"You want me to run Keneally for you?"

"Sure," Morrison said. "Just get him to give you a little classified information, get him started down the slippery slope . . . Well, what am I telling you for? You of all people know how it's done. You turned half the comrades in Scandinavia."

"And most of them disappeared after a few months."

"How about that?" Morrison asked. His normal hang-dog expression was gone now, replaced with a cat-and-canary smirk that Walter found truly infuriating. "And I hear they all blamed you, Walter, in their interrogations. They'd have never betrayed the workers of the world if it hadn't been for the capitalist wiles of Walter Withers. Your name was a curse on their dying lips, I'm told."

Walter remembered. Mark after mark after mark—*his* marks, damn it—just disappearing off the radar screen. Or coming in with bad information, doubled back by the Soviets. And their own agents, Company men, walking into traps. And the old rumor of a mole resurfacing. Paranoia like a bottomless swamp threatening to engulf everyone in the Company. From paranoia to paralysis in a few months. And the nightmares of just that, the poor bastards dying with his name on their lips.

"I don't want to run Keneally," Walter said. "I just want to get out."

Morrison shook his head, "You know that's not how it works. We'll get you out when you're used up and not before. Then if you've been a good little worker, we'll whisk you and the little lady off for a vacation in Vienna, you keep going east, and you'll get a nice little apartment for two in Moscow and maybe even an icebox. By the way, those pictures of Anne and Marta . . . phew. Gave me quite the woodie, I can tell you that."

"I thought you had a problem in that area, Michael."

"Cover story, Walt," Morrison said. "Cover story. Every part of Michael Morrison is in fine working order, I can assure you."

"Glad to hear it," Walter said. "But as to your generous offer, I think I'll just go to the Company and turn myself in. Tell them about you."

Morrison looked taken aback briefly but covered it with his smirk.

"Walt," he said. "You're not in a position to bargain. I mean, please don't give me an incentive to shoot you right here and dump you in the river. And what *about* me? You were the one in the room with Marta, not me. You were the one who brought Keneally into the bugged room, not me. You were the old honey-trap artist, not me. Come to think of it, you have the tapes, not me.

"And then there's Anne. Jesus, Walter, you had a rendezvous with her in every city in Europe! She's been a courier for us since McCarthy! What's that going to look like? It's hysterical when you think about it: Withers falling into a honey trap. I love it!"

Morrison sat back in his deck chair, sipped his vodka martini with real Russian vodka, and laughed.

"Did Anne know?" Walter asked.

"Anne knows shit," Morrison said. "She doesn't know you were Company. Doesn't even know I'm the opposition. All she thought was that she was helping to blackmail Keneally so the Senate committee would lay off a couple of her friends. Of course, that won't help her when the Company boys turn the juice on in one of those cabins in Virginia, because they'll spend a lot of time and energy trying to make her tell things she doesn't know. They might believe her eventually, but by that time she'll be, you know, ga-ga."

He twirled his index finger around the side of his head.

"No," he said. "Poor Anne doesn't know anything. All she did was pick some tapes up from her old girlfriend Marta and deliver them to her new girlfriend Alicia. I'd play that dyke angle if I were you, Walter. It could really spice up the old sex life. But, Christ, it gives me shivers to think what the boys would do to Anne—and you, for that matter—if they get hold of her. I hear they have some new drugs that just make you crazy. Like, permanently."

Morrison shook his head and continued, "Years and years of that shit. Locked up. That's what I couldn't face when they turned me. They got me in the sack with one of those Czech honeys and I was a little indiscreet, and all of a sudden her handlers are threatening to tell the Company unless I do a little favor. And, Walter, I have to tell you that I just couldn't face the interrogation. I couldn't see the point. The CIA and the KGB? All the same animal, if you get my drift. The Russians have been all right to me, Walter. They'll do okay for you, too. So what's it going to be? Are you going to bow to reality here, or do you go down and take Annie with you?"

Walter smiled and said melodramatically, "Do I betray my country or the woman I love?"

"That's pretty much the issue."

"Well," Walter said, "I'm here with the tapes."

He dialed the combination and flipped open the lid of the briefcase.

"Don't feel so bad, Walter," Morrison said. "It could happen to anyone. It happened to me."

"That's cold comfort."

A shadow of real anger passed across Morrison's face.

"See, that's the thing with you, Walter," he said. "Deep inside you believe you're better than everybody else. You probably are. You're a true elite. But the days of the elite are over. This is the age of the common man. Anne knows that, so do I. And the common man has to win.

It's inevitable. There are a lot more of us than there are of you."

"Well," Walter said, "there's always hope that they'll make me a colonel."

"The Order of Lenin, at least," Morrison joked. "For turning a U.S. senator, maybe a president . . . ?"

He reached out for the tape. Walter handed him the box and started to get up.

"Sit down," Morrison said. He handed the Sprinter the tapes, and while he was threading them up on the player Morrison said, "We have a lot to discuss. Besides, you want to hear these, don't you? Marta was a very vocal lay."

There were a few scratchy moments of leader tape, then the full sound of a bass, then Anne's voice:

I'll take Manhattan/
The Bronx and Staten Island, too . . .

Morrison frowned and sighed, "You're trying my patience, Walter."

"I just wanted to see the look on your face," Walter explained.

He tore the silenced automatic from where Paulie had taped it on the inside lid of the attaché case and shot Igor twice in the face before the big man could lift his own pistol. Then he shot the Sprinter once in the chin and once in the forehead. The Sprinter crumbled to the deck. Walter pointed the gun at Morrison.

"Jesus, I wet my pants," Morrison croaked. "What is this supposed to accomplish?"

Walter found it hard to summon the breath to speak. His chest heaved and adrenaline coursed through his system. "I'm giving you to them."

Morrison turned white. "You just killed yourself," he said. "And Anne. Hers is the first name I'll give them."

"I'm afraid that's her problem," Walter said. "As for myself, I'll take my chances."

"Walter, I can't take it," Morrison said. "I can't handle it. The interrogations . . . being locked up . . . I can't . . . Christ, shoot me, Walter. Come on, we were friends. Just shoot me."

"I'd like to, Michael. Truly."

Truly, Michael. As the faces of the poor dead marks I seduced traipse across my memory. Along with Marta. And Alicia. And Anne. Oh, I'd like to, Michael.

Morrison was bent over now, crying softly.

"I turned all your marks, Walt," he said. "Every one of them. The ones who aren't dead will be."

"Don't tempt me."

"I *am* tempting you," Morrison said. "I used Anne to track you, Walter. I knew every city you were ever in and used her to track your marks. Pull the trigger, Walter."

"I expect that they'll keep you alive, Michael. Keep you talking for years," Walter said. "I can envision that little cabin somewhere, a little electroshock therapy from time to time to stimulate your memory . . . sort of a pre-hell hell."

Morrison looked up and spat. "Maybe I'll see Anne there."

Walter shrugged and gestured with the pistol for Morrison to get on his feet. He carefully walked him off the boat, onto the dock, and out to Riverside Drive. Two large men stepped out of the black sedan, grabbed Morrison, and handcuffed him behind his back.

"I'll say hello to Anne for you," Morrison said.

"Do that," Walter answered. Their eyes met for a second before the Company boys pulled a black hood over Morrison's head and shoved him into the backseat.

The front passenger window rolled down. 16-C poked his head out and said, "You rang?"

"It will need sweepers," Walter said to him.

16-C nodded. Walter knew that before the sun came up, there would be no bodies and no boat.

"The weapon," said 16-C.

"Sorry?"

"You probably want to give me the weapon."

"Oh, right. Here."

He handed 16-C the gun.

"Where is she?" 16-C asked.

"The Stanhope," Walter answered. "Will you . . ."

"We'll take care of it."

The window rolled up and the car rolled away.

Walter stood on the sidewalk for a couple of minutes, waiting for the adrenaline rush to subside. He was sorry when it did, because the back of his head started to throb again and his left eye felt swollen and sore. His ribs ached and his ankle hurt, and all he wanted was to go home, have a cigarette and a drink, and soak his abused body in a hot bath while some quiet jazz played on the hi-fi.

But for some reason he didn't move from the spot. He took out his cigarette case, lit a Gauloise, and stood in the freezing air thinking things over. Then he limped out to Seventy-second Street, caught a taxi, and went to the office.

He rang the outer bell and waited a few minutes before the youngest Mallon—Billy, was it?—the one who had been rejected by the Marine Corps recruiting station as being a little too short and much too violent, came to the door.

"Mr. Withers?"

"The same."

"You look like hell, Mr. Withers. You forget something?"

"Just some paperwork."

"Come on in out of the cold."

"By the way," Walter said. "Thank you for the little diversion today."

"Are you kidding, Mr. Withers?" Billy Mallon said. "It was fun."

Fun, Walter thought. I must be getting old.

"Well, thank your father for me."

"You bet."

Walter went up to his office and stood looking out the window for a while, enjoying his partial view of Saks and St. Patrick's, both quiet now in the late night, both softly illuminated by the streetlights.

Then he sat at his desk, took the Michael Howard report from the out tray, and tore it up. He carefully copied the file and report number onto a new sheet and typed:

The investigator observed the subject over the course of a period including 12/24/58–12/29/59. Neither a background check nor surveillance revealed any negative or suspicious information. Recommend the security classification of No Apparent Risk. (Pls. refer to Memorandum 328-F, 3/19/55, etc.) If we can be of any further assistance in this matter, please do not hesitate to contact our office.

Because, he thought, at the end of the day God expects at least an attempt at a little human decency.

He put the new report in the out tray, smoked one more cigarette, and phoned down to the desk to have them send for a cab.

When he got home he put on Miles Davis *Sketches of*

Spain, poured himself a bath and a drink, the former only marginally larger than the latter, then sank into the hot water. When he was done with his bath, he took three aspirin and fell into both bed and slumber.

His sleep that night was dreamless and he didn't wake up until almost one o'clock the following afternoon.

Isle of Joy

New Year's Eve

"Top of the afternoon, Mr. Withers," Mallon said. He handed Walter a coffee, two aspirin, and a Danish, explaining, "The office called down to say you'd be late."

"They're a wonderful office," Walter answered. "And good afternoon to you."

"You look like you attended Finnegan's Wake, sir."

"I feel more like Finnegan."

"Well, he came back from the dead, if you remember," Mallon said.

"Ah, yes."

Mallon leaned over with and whispered, "Me and the boys will be having a little of the good stuff throughout the day to say a proper good-bye to '58. Drop down and take a sip with us if you have a chance."

"I'll be sure to do that, Mallon," Walter said. "Thanks."

Mallon winked. "Big plans for tonight?" he asked.

"Nothing special. Yourself?"

"Quiet evening. Watch the ball drop on television."

All was quiet at Forbes and Forbes when Walter got up to the sixteenth floor. The place had all the industry of any office in the late afternoon of New Year's Eve. Most of the detectives had signed out on cases, and the secretaries sulked at their desks, polished their nails, and did what little they could to get ready for the evening's festivities.

Walter poured coffee into his mug and drank it standing up as he gazed out the window. He didn't feel as bad as he thought he would. He had a tolerable headache, a black eye that was certainly noticeable but not grotesque, and a couple of bruised ribs. His ankle gave him the most concern, still sore and prone to twist, but all in all his condition was preferable to the bullet or three in the head that he had expected.

If anything, it had been disturbingly easy to kill two human beings. *Just point the gun and fire twice, the Company instructors had taught. Shoot in bursts of two. The hand automatically corrects on the second shot.* And he had, and his hand had indeed corrected on the second shots. But still, at that range . . .

But he thought he would feel more. More than just the dunning fatigue he now felt. Remorse? Shame? God forgive me, pride? No, just tired.

16-C finally came to the window and raised his cup. Happy New Year to you, too, 16-C. I'll miss seeing you, I suppose. Walter lifted his own cup and then eased himself into his desk chair. He lit a cigarette and started in on the paperwork, chuckling as he remembered his father's irritation about holidays.

Holidays start when they start and not a moment before. That's what's wrong with this country: Everybody wants to stop working the day before the damn holiday and then rest the whole day after. Pretty soon we won't do any work at all, just have holidays.

So Walter completed his daily expense report and his activity log before checking his In-tray. Sure enough, the bats had dropped some guano on his desk in the form of five new files, but there was no point in starting in on them the afternoon of New Year's Eve. His Out-tray was empty, so the Howard report had entered the system and the system would crank away and Michael Howard would get his promotion.

And I have betrayed my company and my client, Walter thought. And subverted about a dozen rules.

But if the rules are wrong to begin with, he thought, perhaps we have a responsibility to subvert them. But much too tough an issue to grapple with in my delicate condition. Suffice to say, "Happy New Year, Michael Howard," and let it go at that.

He was relieved from further thought when the intercom buzzed and summoned him to Forbes' office.

Forbes took one look at Walter and asked, "What happened to you?"

"It's embarrassing, but I was mugged on the subway."

"No!"

Walter gave an abashed shrug.

"Are you all right?"

"My pride is hurt more than anything."

"Nice shiner."

"You should see the other guy."

Forbes struggled unsuccessfully with his pipe for a minute, gave up, and said, "I had a call from a Sergeant Zaif over at NYPD this morning."

"Oh?"

"He wanted to let me know that Marta Marlund's death has been officially ruled a suicide," Forbes said, "and assure me that you are completely in the clear."

"It was nice of him to take the time."

"Yes," Forbes agreed. Then he asked, "Howard report in?"

"Yesterday."

"And?"

"Oh," Walter said, "clean bill of health. No security risk at all."

Forbes frowned. "You took a rather long time to return a 'no risk,' don't you think, Withers?"

Walter pretended to think it over for a moment before answering, "Well, he was getting a little on the side."

"I didn't know they'd moved it," Forbes said.

Walter was stunned when he heard this old burlesque punch line. It represented Forbes Jr.'s first attempt at humor since Walter had joined the firm. He laughed in genuine delight, and Forbes joined in with helpless pleasure that his effort had succeeded.

"I didn't put it in the report," Walter said.

"No," Forbes agreed. Then he made himself get serious and said, "I've just read this book by this Englishman Parkinson. Do you know about it?"

"I'm afraid not."

"Parkinson has a theory that any piece of work expands to fit the time allowed. Let's not get mired down in Parkinson's law, shall we, Withers?"

"I get your point, Mr. Forbes."

Walter was about to leave when Forbes said, "Oh! Joe and Madeleine called. They're at a little do at the Waldorf this evening and would love it if you could drop in for a minute."

"On a social basis . . ."

"Strictly social," Forbes said. He lowered his voice and added, "Joe dodged the bullet on this Marlund thing, didn't he?"

"He walked through the rain without getting wet," Walter agreed. "Happy New Year, chief."

"Happy New Year, Withers."

Walter finished the day out at his desk, wished the secretaries a Happy New Year, then went downstairs to have a drink with Mallon and the Mallonettes.

As he left for the Waldorf, he bumped into Sam Zaif on the street outside. The detective stopped him and flashed a badge.

"Zaif, Canine Control."

"Oh, no, Sam."

"Well, not exactly," Zaif said. "Plainclothes, Brooklyn."

"It could have been worse."

"They killed the investigation," Zaif said. "National security interests."

"Oh, well."

"You tried to warn me."

Walter didn't answer. They stood beside the Christmas tree, which looked tired and droopy now. A few skaters made desultory circles around the rink.

"Listen," Zaif said, "I'll make it back to Manhattan."

"I'm sure you will," Walter said.

And he was. Zaif was too smart and too hardworking. And while the powers that be would never forgive those qualities, they couldn't do without them, either.

"Do you know," Zaif said, "that an unattended death file can always be reopened?"

"I wasn't aware of that."

"I'll be keeping an eye on you, Walter."

"I'd appreciate that, Sam."

And actually I would, Walter thought. I will almost miss Detective Sergeant Zaif.

"Good-bye, Sam," Walter said. "Or words to that effect."

"Walter Withers, you dear man! I am so glad you could come!" Madeleine Keneally enthused from across the Waldorf ballroom.

Walter thought she looked lovely in her white party

gown as she edged her way through the crowded room. Lovely and tall and what was the cliché? Regal? Well, regal did the trick, all right, but he thought that she had changed since the party a week ago. On Christmas Eve she had walked like a princess. On this eve of 1959 she held herself more like a queen. Perhaps because a queen, unlike a princess, knows about the sacrifices that go into maintaining the realm. She knows the sorrows and has learned to hide them.

"She's something, isn't she?" Jimmy Keneally said.

"You have a way of appearing at my side that I find disconcerting," Walter answered. "And yes, she's something."

"Do you think he deserves her?"

"I'm not convinced that love has anything to do with what we deserve," Walter answered. "At least in my case I'm quite sure that it doesn't."

"I got a strange message from Hoover."

"I imagine you did."

"Will you accept my apologies?"

"As long as you understand," Walter answered, "that anything I've done or have not done, it's been for her and not for you. And certainly not for him."

"It's a hard world, Walter," Jimmy said. "Even as the good guys we have to play a hard game if we expect to win."

"I always used to think so," Walter said. "I always used to think so."

Without taking his eyes off Madeleine he shook Jimmy's hand.

"In any case," Walter said, " 'auld acquaintance' *should* be forgot."

"Happy New Year, Walter."

"And to you."

Madeleine spotted him again, a dazzling smile spread

across her face, and she floated up and kissed him on the cheek.

"Come on," she said, guiding him by the elbow. "There are people you just *have* to meet."

He gently balked at her guiding hand, saying, "I'm afraid I can't stay. I just came to say hello-goodbye."

She formed her lips into a sociably seductive pout and said, "But it's early, Walter! Besides, I was so looking forward to giving you a kiss at midnight."

"Surely there must be some other frog . . ." he said, then spotted Joe Keneally in earnest conversation with a gaggle of older men who could only be potential contributors. "How about that one over there?"

"Do you think?" Madeleine asked. "Do you think if I kissed him he'd turn into a prince?"

"Darling, if *you* kissed him, he'd turn into a *king*."

"You *are* a dear man," she said, squeezing his hand.

He lifted her hand and kissed it.

"Good-bye, Maddy," he said.

"Good-bye, Walter."

He loitered on the edge of Keneally's crowd and caught the Senator's eye. Keneally smiled over the shoulder of a short, balding admirer and nodded his head toward the door.

They met a few minutes later in the washroom.

Without any preliminaries Keneally said, "I misjudged you, didn't I?"

"I think you did."

Walter had to admit that Keneally's smile was charming. A boyish, self-deprecating grin that made you feel like a stiff for not joining in the fun.

"For a while there I thought you were a blackmailer," Keneally added.

Walter shrugged. "For a while I thought you were a murderer."

Keneally extended a hand. "You want to call it even?"

"Not yet," Walter said as he launched a hard right uppercut into Keneally's stomach.

In the B movies of Walter's youth such a punch would have sent Keneally toppling to the tiled floor. But Joe Keneally was a heavy, solid man, and he caught his breath and straightened up again.

Walter saw the fighting look come into Keneally's eyes and thought for a moment that he was going to be on the losing end of an honest-to-God fistfight, but the look passed quickly and Keneally asked, "What was that about, Walter?"

"I don't allow people to manhandle me," Walter said. He felt a little silly and old-fashioned, but added, "Not even by proxy."

Keneally nodded. "The boys gave you a pretty good shiner, huh?"

"The punch was also for Marta."

"Okay."

"And Madeleine."

"Jesus, anyone else?"

"I think that will do it."

"Well, I guess I had it coming," Keneally said. He stepped over to the mirror and straightened his tie. He checked his image in the glass and said, "But you really should think about joining the twentieth century, Withers."

"It's not much of a century," Walter said as he walked out the door. "But I'll think about it."

He decided to start thinking about it downstairs in Peacock Alley, the dark little piano bar that perfectly suited his Old World tastes. He bought a whisky, sat down next to the old Steinway, and put a five-dollar bill into the glass.

"Happy New Year, Norman," he said to the pianist.

"Happy New Year, Walter," the pianist said. "Anything you'd like to hear?"

"Anything by Porter."

Then Walter sat and listened in what was close to rapture as Norman swung into a medley of the great songs on Cole Porter's very own piano.

Only in New York, Walter thought. Only in New York.

Cities change gender as the sun goes down.

Or so Walter thought as he stood on Forty-sixth and Broadway and looked downtown at Times Square. By day the city was masculine, a gray, gritty, harried man of business. But at night she was a lady with a black velvet dress and a necklace of sparkling lights. And the lights dazzled: The view never failed to quicken his pulse and stir his blood and leave in him the feeling that this was the center of the world.

So it made sense that this is where the throng would gather to see in the new year, to watch the ball drop, to cheer and kiss and believe that the only year better than 1958 would be 1959. And 1960 after that.

For there beneath the sparkling globes and flickering neon, every dream seemed a near reality, every carousel ring an easy grab, every fresh, bright moment a new beginning.

It was Times Square, New York City, alive in the dead of winter.

It was only ten o'clock, and Times Square was already filling up with people waiting for the big moment. They were a good-natured crowd, bundled up in their winter coats and doubtless fortified by some warming libations, and they jostled happily behind the police barricades for the best view of the giant ball that was perched for the final countdown.

Walter moved happily among them. He was happy to be away from the cloying atmosphere of the Waldorf, happy to bathe again in the warm lights of Times Square, happy to be alive to say farewell to the eventful year of 1958. From newspaper boxes the headlines shrieked of chaos in the Belgian Congo and of Castro's imminent victory in Cuba, and more happily trumpeted America's recovery of the Davis Cup from Australia. Which reminded Walter of his promise to start playing tennis again. And to cut down on the booze.

But not tonight, not on New Year's Eve in New York. So he took his flask from his coat, sipped some bourbon, and enjoyed the usually grating sound of the aptly named noise-makers, and the slow clopping of the hooves of the police horses, and the premature drunken choruses of "Auld Lang Syne."

McGuire was only a few minutes late. He arrived in his merchant marine garb—pea coat, watch cap, jeans, and a duffel bag.

"Buy you a drink?" Walter asked, yelling over the noise of the crowd, offering the flask.

McGuire took a healthy swig and said, "That's the real stuff!"

"It's been my experience," Walter said, "that while you can always eat cheap, it's a bad idea to drink cheap!"

"This is something!" McGuire said.

"You've never seen it?"

"Not on New Year's Eve! It's goofy, man!" McGuire said with an expression that led Walter to believe that it was high praise. The writer took the Joe Keneally tape from his duffel and handed it to Walter.

Walter tucked it into his overcoat.

"Where are you headed?" he asked.

McGuire shrugged and pointed west. "Out there!"

"The highway by night?" Walter asked.

McGuire laughed and said, "That's where I live!"

"There are worse places, I suppose!"

"Like this town!"

No, Walter thought, not like this town. This is the best place in the world.

"Well, good luck to you!" Walter said.

"I'm done with luck, man!" McGuire said. "I know when I'm beat!"

"That's good!" Walter yelled. "That's a good thing to know!"

McGuire grabbed Walter's shoulders and stared into his eyes.

"I've done a lot of thinking about you, Walter Withers!" he shouted. "I've decided that you're a Buddhist saint! One of those demon saints! A koan! An unsolvable riddle!"

"Well, maybe I'll solve myself some day!"

"That's the day you'll die!" McGuire yelled. "Give me another drink and I'll hit the road!"

He took another swig and hollered to the night sky, "A poem for Walter Withers: Under a million manufactured lights! Two saints limp! One a broken bard! One an errant knight! Both drunk! With sadness and ecstasy! Who knows where the road goes!"

Walter applauded and McGuire bowed. He backed his way into the crowd, turned, and was gone.

Walter watched the Times Square scene for a few minutes, then started to walk west on Forty-sixth Street. He crossed Broadway, then Eighth Avenue and kept walking west, away from the lights, against the crowd that was rushing to converge on Times Square. He was deep in Hell's

Kitchen, on the west side of Tenth Avenue, when he heard a limousine pull up beside him.

The passenger door opened and Walter slid in.

The Old One stuck out a withered claw and shook Walter's hand. His flesh felt as dry and brittle as old parchment.

"Hello, young Withers," he hissed.

Even in the dim light his thin face looked ghostly pale. His white hair contrasted sharply with his black dinner jacket, and Walter wondered what grim and grotesque assemblage he had come from.

"Hello, sir."

"Our Mr. Morrison is being very cooperative." The Old One smiled, showing long, yellow teeth.

"So you have your mole—" Walter began.

"One of them."

"—and now the Company owns a senator," said Walter.

"*Another* senator," the Old One corrected. "And probably a president."

Walter produced the tape from his coat and laid it on the seat beside the Old One. Sometime in the near future some functionary would play it for Joe Keneally, inform him that he'd had an affair with a Soviet agent, and explain to him that the Company always returns loyalty with loyalty. It would be a bad day for Joe Keneally, but on the other hand, Walter thought, it could have been a whole lot worse.

He pointed at the tape and said, "Your turn."

"You did a fine job," the Old One repeated. "Your father would have been—"

"Appalled," Walter said. "How long had you known about Anne Blanchard?"

"Since Hamburg, young Withers," the Old One said. "There was a signal, a brief flash from one of your marks before all the signals went silent, about an operation against a certain United States senator. A honey trap, young Withers,

347

and who better to unspring it, turn it around, in fact, than the Great Scandinavian Pimp and Deadly Recruiter himself?"

"Who was himself in a honey trap."

"All the more reason," the Old One laughed.

"And you put me in Keneally's way, didn't you?" Walter asked. "You knew."

"I knew," the Old One said. "I knew that you'd do fine work even if you didn't know you were on the job."

"Why didn't you just pick them up in Stockholm?"

"Too risky there," the Old answered. "They might have run. And then I wouldn't have Keneally. And I wanted Keneally, lest Hoover get him first."

"So that's what it's all been about."

"That's what it *is* all about. Are you sure you want to retire, young Withers?" the Old One asked. "Europe's out for you, but we could use a good man in Indochina."

"I'm sure."

"The war isn't over," the Old One said.

"It is for me," Walter answered.

"In that case," the Old One said, shaking his head sadly, "it's done. A deal is a deal."

He reached beside him and handed Walter the Company's thick file on Anne Blanchard.

Walter asked, "This is all of it? No copies anywhere?"

"Not with us. Your beloved's record is immaculate as far as the Company is concerned." The Old One's eyes widened in mock, hurt innocence, then he added, "Of course, I can't speak for the Bureau. . . ."

"No."

The Old One wheezed. "Of course, if you came back with us, perhaps we could work something out."

"I'll handle the Bureau," Walter said.

"Will you, young Withers?"

"Oh, yes," Walter said. The image of Dieter's gift—grainy

photos of the famous bulldog Director in a smashing black frock, hose, and tasteful string of pearls. Photos of him in this same outfit somewhat *dishabille,* shall we say? Red lipstick smeared . . . well, photos damaging enough to keep Walter and Anne safe from the Bureau for a long, long time.

"Yes, I believe you will," the Old On said, studying Walter's face. Then his tone sharpened as he demanded, "What are you laughing about, young Withers?"

"Nothing, sir."

The Old One leaned toward Walter. His breath smelled ancient and musty. "You're a clever young man," he rasped. "But see that you don't get *too* clever."

"I'll watch that, sir," Walter said as he opened the door and stepped back on the sidewalk.

A little later Walter stood on the landing of The Rainbow Room and looked down where Anne Blanchard stood singing, the silver light turning her blond hair to a shiny platinum and her white shoulders to a soft, warm gold. He couldn't see her face save in his mind but knew her precise expression as she sang:

"I'll take Manhattan / The Bronx and Staten Island, too."

As he stepped down the stairs, he saw the two Company watchers that 16-C had assigned to Anne. They saw him, too, and signaled their waitress for the check.

They were done now. Anne Blanchard was safe in the hands of the legendary Walter Withers.

The *maître d'* showed him to a small table in the back of the crowded room. The other revelers looked touchingly silly in their formal dress and funny coned New Year's hats. Bottles of champagne stood in tall ice buckets beside the tables. Some couples weaved on the dance floor, while others sat quietly at their tables listening to the tender bass chords and soft brushes on cymbals and Anne's delicate voice trilling.

"It's such fun going through / The zoo."

Walter could see her face now. Her translucent skin, her strong jaw, the gray sad and loving eyes that hadn't spotted him yet. This small woman, so brave.

"It's very fancy / On old Delancey / Street you know."

The waiter brought his martini. Walter sipped it, lit a cigarette, and sat back to watch her and listen to her. And, he noted with some amusement, with his aching body and aching heart he felt a little like Bogart for the first time in his life.

"As balmy breezes blow / To and fro."

And through the window he could see the city laid out beneath him like a lovely lady in a sparkling sequined dress.

"And tell me what street / Compares with Mott Street In July . . ."

Anne spotted him then. Saw him and turned to face him and smiled. And maybe those were tears he saw in her eyes, or maybe it was just the reflection of the lights as she sang to him.

"Sweet pushcarts gently gliding by."

And looking at her he remembered once in the full frustration of youthful pique asking his father, *But what does a*

man actually do? Actually do, son? Yes, what does he do?
His father had reflected for a few moments, then answered,
A man protects what he loves.

And that's all?

In this world, his father had said, *that's all there is to do.*

It's almost midnight, Walter thought, and the start of the
new year. A new year, Anne. For you, and me, and God
and the forgiveness of sins.

> *"The great big city's a wondrous toy*
> *Just made for a girl and boy."*

A man protects what he loves.
As she sang to him.

> *"We'll turn Manhattan*
> *Into an isle of joy. . . ."*

Brush of cymbals. Resolving chord.
An isle of joy, Walter thought.
Isle of joy.